Valiant

Laurann Dohner

ELLORA'S CAVE
ROMANTICA®
ELLORASCAVE.COM

An Ellora's Cave Publication

www.ellorascave.com

Valiant

ISBN 9781419967092
ALL RIGHTS RESERVED.
Valiant Copyright © 2011 Laurann Dohner
Edited by Pamela Campbell.
Design and Photography by Syneca.
Model: Nick.

Electronic book publication September 2011
Trade paperback publication 2012

Dedication

ℵ

Thank you to Mr. Laurann for always understanding those late nights I kept while writing. His love has taught me anything is possible. I'd also like to say thank you to Kele Moon. She's an amazing person, a wonderful friend and a fantastic critique partner. Also, last but not least, special thanks go to my lovely editor, Pamela Campbell, for teaching me so much and keeping up with this write-aholic. She's a saint!

Chapter One

ഇ

Tammy Shasta had experienced fear plenty of times in her twenty-eight years of life but this made all those other times pale in comparison. She'd known her job might be dangerous. Everything these days held a bit of risk. Driving on the highway could be perilous, someone crossing a street could be struck by a car, and even cleaning windows could be hazardous. After all, someone, somewhere, had accidentally broken a window, ended up badly cut, and had bled to death while on the job.

Shit happens. It had become her motto in life. She'd just never believed her job would really be treacherous. Not really. What really bad thing could happen, serving food and drinks? She had mentally gone over the list. She could slip and fall or get burned if she spilled hot food. The worst-case scenario she'd ever thought up was perhaps being shot at if she ever catered a party for the mob but the chances of them ending up living in a small town in Northern California were slim to none. Yet…here she faced the kind of terror she never thought she'd experience in real life. Not in a million years had she seen this kind of situation coming, even with her wild imagination working overtime.

She stood frozen, no matter how loudly she inwardly screamed at her body to turn and run for her life. *Nope. Not happening for me.* Her body refused to respond. All her best-laid plans of being tough, prepared for anything, had fled with her courage. She wasn't superhero tough. She mimicked a lawn statue instead or a mime locked in horror.

Her mouth hung open but the scream wasn't forthcoming. She couldn't even muster a whimper. Nothing. Her heart beat so rapidly she wondered if it could take flight right out of her chest and still no sound passed her lips. She couldn't even breathe and she really needed air. Maybe sucking some in would promote a scream but...no. *This sucks!*

She'd always heard that someone's life passed before their eyes when they knew they were about to die. She wasn't seeing images of her past flashing through her mind. *Nope.* Her wide-eyed gaze remained fixed on the huge man-beast who growled at her.

He *was* a man but not quite since no regular guy had sharp teeth or could scare her nearly to death with that horrible sound that rumbled from deep within his throat, mimicking a vicious animal. He appeared both beautiful and ferocious at the same time.

If a guy pumped up on steroids he'd resemble the massive man who terrified her. He had to be about six-and-a-half-feet tall. His arms were extremely muscular and his wide chest reminded her of a mountain. His skin had tanned to a golden tone but it was his hair that made him beautiful. It was the color of an autumn leaf—reddish-orange with thick strands of blond streaks running through it. It hung shoulder-length and parted slightly to the side of his face.

One really scary part about him had to be his face because he almost looked human but not quite. His eyes were the color of melted gold and they were shaped like a cat's, only with super-long eyelashes. His nose flared wide and flatter than anyone she'd ever seen. His cheekbones were prominent and dominated his face but they complemented his strong, square chin. That brought her attention to his really full, nearly pouty lips, and at the moment, they were parted, revealing some extremely white, pointed teeth. Again, not the kind of teeth normal people had.

"Back up, Tammy." It was her boss, Ted Armstrong, who yelled at her. "Don't make any sudden movements and come toward me. Do it now."

Back up? He expects me to move? She realized she had started breathing again when her lungs stopped hurting from lack of oxygen. She had the urge to turn her head and glance at Ted to give him an are-you-kidding-me look but she couldn't. She also couldn't force her terrified gaze away the huge man-beast slowly stalking closer, glaring at her with those large, oddly beautiful catlike eyes. His face was scary-angry and he growled at her again.

"Damn it, Tammy. Back up slowly right now. Just look down at the ground and come to me. You can do it."

She wished that were true but her body still refused to listen as she silently screamed at it to follow orders. Nothing moved but her chest as her heart hammered and air passed between her parted lips. She blinked, which was progress, but that was it.

"Valiant!" another man called out loudly. "Calm down and back away from the female. She isn't challenging you. She's just scared shitless." The new voice had a strong, deep pitch and he sounded angry.

The man-beast growled again when he took another step closer to Tammy. She wanted to run but her legs seemed rooted to the ground. She tried to tear her gaze from the golden eyes staring back at her but just couldn't break the connection.

Everyone had heard about the New Species. Anyone would have to never have read a newspaper or owned a television not to know they were humans who'd been secretly experimented on by Mercile Industries. The pharmaceutical company had funded secret testing facility for decades for some messed-up research supposedly done to find cures for diseases. The story had broken when countless numbers of survivors from those testing facilities had been freed.

Shit, she thought. *This is obviously a New Species.* She knew they'd titled themselves that, those surviving men and women who had been physically altered with animal DNA inside those places.

9

The man-beast stalking closer was obviously one and they'd really done a number on him since he sure didn't appear normal in any way. Tammy had never seen anything similar to him before and didn't want to ever see it again. He looked like a man...but not. That made her wonder just how much of his animalistic traits ruled him.

"Someone get a tranquilizer gun." It was a woman and she sounded scared. "Now. Move it."

"Valiant?" It was the man again with the deep voice. "Listen to me, man. She didn't mean to trespass into your territory. She got lost when someone screwed up the maps and it led her here. You know Justice is having a party and he hired caterers. She is just a terrified female who came here to serve food. It's not a challenge. She can't look away from you or leave because she's frozen with fear. Calm down and just back off. She can leave once you do."

Justice North was the appointed leader of the New Species Organization. He'd bought up the closed-down old resort and all the land around it for his people to live on and turned it into a New Species enclave called Reservation. He was also their spokesperson who did all the television interviews. He'd hired Ted's catering service to host their first party at Reservation and that's how Tammy had ended up in the wrong place.

She swallowed, grateful her mind still worked and knew all that information. She could at least follow the conversation that her life might depend on. It seemed to her that this would be her last job for Ted otherwise. *Hell, it might be my last day doing anything ever again.*

"Do you hear me, Valiant? Do you know how pissed Justice is going to be if you maul someone he hired? We're supposed to be throwing this dinner to make the people living in town feel comfortable with us being here. It's going to really set everyone off if you attack one of them." The man with the deep voice sighed. "Let me come get her. Is that all right, man? Can I come into your yard to take her away?"

"No," the man-beast snarled. He threw back his head and an earsplitting roar shattered the wooded area.

Tammy moved finally but it just wasn't in the direction she wanted to go, which would have been toward her work van and closer to the help that had arrived to try to save her on the other side of the gate she'd walked through. Her knees collapsed under her. She hit the grass but didn't totally fall flat. She remained kneeling.

He had to be a lion or tiger of some sort. She recognized the sound he'd made. He had a pretty distinctive roar. She studied his coloring, his wide nose, and finally those sharp teeth. *Shit. He's definitely some kind of big-cat mix.* She guessed lion. She stared up at him and wondered if her bladder would let loose from sheer terror. It wouldn't surprise her in the least. It wasn't as if her day could get any worse.

"Remain calm," the deep-voiced man demanded. "I won't come in. Talk to me, Valiant. Otherwise someone is going to tranquilize your ass and I know how upset that's going to make you."

Man-beast had a name. It wasn't human either, or normal, but Tammy let it sink in that it was his. *What kind of name is Valiant?* She knew it meant courageous, something she lacked at that moment. She wished furiously that she wasn't really there, wasn't staring up at her worst, never-thought-up nightmare.

Valiant jerked his focus off Tammy finally to glare at someone behind her and to the left. "Do not shoot at me." The threatening tone in his voice was loud and clear.

There was a deep sigh. "Let the female go. What's your deal anyway? Did she say something before she passed through the gate? She didn't know this is your house and not the clubhouse. She was given the wrong map. It looks to me as if all she did was get out of the van and walk toward your front door before you reached her. Did she piss you off?"

"She is here, Tiger. That is enough." Valiant growled.

"And it was an accident." Tiger tried to be logical. "Someone on our end screwed up and it was our mistake. We didn't realize what had happened until she showed up. She was the first one to arrive after the guy who runs the catering service. This is Ted Armstrong. He's been here a few times before and he realized the map was wrong when he glanced at it. We contacted the gate immediately but they informed me that her van had gone through already. Now here we all are. Come on, Valiant, you've terrified her enough. What did Justice say about trying to fit in? Remember that talk? God knows, I do. It's not polite to scare the living shit out of humans."

"He won't really maul her, will he?" Ted sounded a little high strung. That was saying a lot because her boss always remained cool under pressure. "I mean, Jesus! Was that a joke?"

Tiger softly cursed. "I'm sure I was kidding." His tone didn't sound convincing at all to Tammy. "So what do you say, Valiant? She can calm down a little and leave if you'll just back off. Would you reconsider allowing me to come get her? It would only take a second. I'll just rush in there, grab her, and leap right out."

Valiant growled again and his gaze returned to Tammy. She swallowed. She blinked. She breathed regularly again. She took note of all those functions that were under her control but her limbs were still unresponsive. The man-beast paused about six feet from her but she appreciated that he had stopped advancing to just stare at her. *That's progress, right? God, I hope so.*

She moved her mouth and it actually opened. She attempted to apologize for trespassing but nothing came out. *Damn it.* She had always thought she'd be different under stress. She'd always been a natural-born smartass who had a comeback for everything. She'd gained a reputation for being mouthy no matter how afraid she was, under any circumstances. *Obviously, I was wrong*, she conceded. When she'd dreamed up worst-case scenarios, none had covered man-beasts with sharp teeth or cat-eyes who roared.

"Stay back," Valiant threatened. He inhaled slowly, his gaze still locked on Tammy. He took another step toward her.

"Valiant!" Tiger, the man with the deep voice, shouted. "Stop now. Don't get any closer. Damn it, don't do this."

Valiant snapped his head sideways to glare at someone at whom he flashed sharp teeth and snarled menacingly. He sounded downright evil before he focused back on Tammy.

"Go get her," Ted demanded. "You're almost as big as him. Save her."

Tiger uttered a foul word. "I can't. He'd kill me in a heartbeat. He's one of the meanest sons of bitches we have on Reservation. It's why he's out here and why Justice bought this place. There are a few of our kind who aren't exactly people friendly. It will make things worse if I go inside there because he'll be able to kill two people instead of just one."

"Shoot him," a woman whispered softly, but her voice carried.

"Can't," a male explained. "They haven't gotten any tranquilizer guns to us yet."

"Use the guns in your holsters," the woman ordered, louder. "Don't allow him to kill her. My God! Can you imagine what this would do to public relations?"

"No one is shooting him," Tiger ground out. "Valiant?" He paused. "Tell me why you're so angry with the female. She's a little thing. Is that it? Are you fighting your instincts because you're seeing her as prey? Think hard, Valiant. This is an innocent human female. She didn't mean any insult to you or to invade your space. Talk to me, damn it. Just tell me what is going on inside your head."

Valiant turned his head, tearing his intense gaze away from Tammy once again. He closed his eyes and inhaled deeply. They snapped open. He glared at someone behind Tammy's left shoulder. "I'm not going to kill her."

"Thank God," Ted said and groaned.

"You just wanted to scare her?" The relief was evident in Tiger's voice. "Well, you did a good job. Can she go now?"

Valiant's exotic gaze fixed back on Tammy as he inhaled again. He made a low, rumbling sound. He looked away from her to glare at Tiger. "No. She stays. You go."

"You know we can't do that," Tiger explained calmly. "What is it, man? What's the problem?"

Valiant growled again. He moved another step and then another toward Tammy. She stopped breathing. Those cat-eyes of his were back on her. He suddenly crouched on all fours, sniffed at her again, and made a sound she hadn't heard before. It wasn't a growl exactly, more of a gruff purr, but scary. He settled on his hands and knees in front of her.

"Oh shit," Tiger cursed. "Valiant? Don't do it, man."

Valiant jerked his head up to shoot another threatening glare in Tiger's direction. He was close enough for her to notice that he smelled of the outdoors and something masculine that was really nice. She took a breath and kept breathing since he wasn't looking at her.

She lowered her gaze, taking him in, and decided he was big even crouched before her. He wore jeans and a T-shirt but no shoes. The guy had huge hands and feet. He inched closer to her until she could have touched him if she'd just moved her hand out toward him a few inches but she didn't, still frozen on her knees.

"What's he doing now?" Ted sounded panicked again.

"Don't ask," Tiger ground out. "Valiant, come on, man. What are you doing? You know better if you're thinking what I suspect you are. She's a little human thing and you don't want to attempt this."

Valiant blinked. "She's in heat."

"Oh fucking hell," Tiger cursed.

Valiant growled.

"Son of a bitch!" Tiger cursed louder. "Ted, I told you to make sure none of your women were ovulating. We went over this, damn it. No wonder he's acting crazy."

"How was I supposed to know?" Ted sputtered. "Do you know how many sexual harassment lawsuits I could be hit with if I asked women who worked for me if it's a certain time of the month? Come on. And how in the hell would anyone know anyway, Tiger? How?"

Tiger cursed again. "We'd know, Ted. I told you we can smell them half a mile away and I told you some of our men would react badly to it. I'm upwind from her but he's not. If he says she's ovulating—and trust me, she is—it's a problem. No wonder he's acting this way." The man paused. "Who was on duty when they let her in?"

"Smiley." A male voice spoke softly. "He's primate and his sense of smell isn't as keen. He obviously missed her scent."

"What does it mean if she is ovulating? Is that why he wants to kill her?" It was the woman speaking. "Is it like a shark going nuts if they smell blood?"

Tiger was silent for a few long seconds. "She's not bleeding. As a woman you should know the difference between menstruation and ovulation. She's ovulating. He doesn't want to kill her. He wants to breed with her."

"Thank God." The woman actually laughed. "I thought he would turn her into a chew toy and tear her to pieces."

"Marcy!" Ted yelled. "How can you laugh about this? It's not funny. We're all relieved he isn't planning on killing her but did you hear what Tiger implied? We have to get her out of there."

"Is she married?" Tiger asked.

"No." Ted hesitated. "Now wait a minute. Don't look relieved as if something is going to happen between them. Get her out of there."

Tammy stared at the New Species' profile. He didn't want to end her life. He wanted to breed with her. She was still in shock. She let her gaze take in the huge man-beast from head to knee and shivered. She'd been horrible with math in high school but she knew enough to do the mathematics of this one.

The guy seemed to be nearly two of her in sheer size and there was no way a physical relationship would be possible between them. *And besides that — What in the hell am I thinking?* She wanted to scream for help again but nothing came out of her mouth. *I'm screwed! NO! Don't say that. Find a new saying. I'm in deep shit. Yeah. That's better. Don't even think anything about screwed or screwing, considering.*

"I can't," Tiger explained. "He'll protect her if one of us tries to get close to them. Think of a really mean animal protecting his favorite toy. Well, that's about what we have here."

Tiger remained silent for a full minute. No one spoke. He finally must have decided on a new approach when he began to speak again.

"Valiant? I can find someone willing to take her place. You have to let her go. She's not Species, she's human, and you'd break her. Look how little she is. She's puny, a real runt of a female, and you know you don't want her. I realize she smells pretty good to you and hell, I noticed right off the bat that she's attractive, but again, she's human. We had some sodas together a few weeks back and discussed how frail they are. We don't do them, remember? Just back away from her and I'll call our females. One of them would be more than happy to come out here to take her place if you're in the mood to get frisky. Sound good, man? Work with me here."

"Mine," Valiant growled.

"Fuck." Tiger groaned. "Where is that tranquilizer gun? We're going to need it fast."

"I'm coming, Tammy," Ted shouted.

"Don't," Tiger yelled. "He'll tear you apart."

"Well, do something," Ted demanded. "I won't stand here just watching her be raped by that...that...person."

Valiant turned his head. His face was a foot from Tammy's. She stared into his eyes. At close range they were amazingly beautiful. She saw swirls of color inside them that resembled spun, melted gold. His eyelashes were very thick, reddish orange, and long. On his hands and knees, he stood face level with Tammy, kneeling on the grass. His mouth was closed, his sharp teeth hidden, as he inhaled again. A soft sound came from his throat, a deep purr. He blinked at her while inching closer.

Move, damn it. She ordered her body to fall back, do something, but it didn't listen. He reached up with one of his large hands and she saw his fingernails. They were thicker than normal, almost pointed, but with normal-sized, human-looking nail beds. He moved very slowly as his rough-feeling fingertips brushed her long hair back away from her cheek. His fingers caressed her face. The tips of his fingers were calloused. Goose bumps rose on her body and it was a weird but good kind of feeling. His hand cleared all her hair over her shoulder before it moved lower to cup her waist.

"Beautiful," he rumbled softly. "So beautiful."

She swallowed. "Tha—" Her voice broke. "Thank you," she got out in a whisper.

She wasn't sure what he thought was attractive about her. Was it her long hair or her face? She'd been told that she had beautiful blue eyes. Whatever it was that he found appealing, she was just grateful she'd finally found her voice. It wasn't much since she seemed to only be able to breathe out words but she hoped now that it worked, she might manage an ear-splitting scream if the need arose. She had a bad feeling it would be soon if this guy wanted to have sex with her.

He closed his eyes, inhaling deeply. "You smell so good. Strawberries and honey. I love those." He made another soft rumble deep within his throat. His eyes opened. "Don't be afraid. I wouldn't ever hurt you, Tammy." He shifted his big body closer.

Heart pounding, Tammy closed her eyes when his hair brushed her face and she stiffened as his cheek brushed against hers. His skin felt hot and his warm breath fanned over her neck, which he'd bared when he'd cleared the area of her hair.

What is he doing now? Some of her fear eased since he'd sworn he wasn't going to hurt her and he hadn't so far. *Scared the hell out of me, yes, but he hasn't done anything painful.* She jumped a little when he licked her where her neck and shoulder met.

"Uh," she got out but shut up. The feeling was unlike anything she'd ever experienced. His tongue had a slightly sandy texture but not gritty or abrasive. Shivers shook her body and somehow it seemed oddly erotic. His sharp teeth lightly brushed her skin next, creating another oddly seductive sensation.

"Shush," he breathed the word, as his tongue and teeth left her. "I'm not going to hurt you."

"What is he doing to her?" Ted's voice rose with alarm. "Make him stop."

"Where is that tranquilizer gun?" Marcy spoke.

"Everyone, shut up," Tiger demanded. "He isn't hurting her and we're going to anger him. He's got his hands on her so just be quiet."

The sound of a vehicle approaching broke the silence. A growl tore from the lips next to Tammy's neck. The sound made her eyes fly open and she whimpered, staring at his sharp teeth, which he bared as his head turned to glare at the source of noise. The hand cupping her waist tightened but it didn't hurt.

She gasped suddenly as his other arm curled around her back at her middle. In a blur of motion he stood, easily hauled

Tammy to her feet with him, and jerked her tight against the front of his body, keeping his arm around her.

Tammy stared up at the much taller man who held her against him with his strong arm. Her legs turned to rubber, collapsing, but his hold on her was enough to keep her locked against his big, solid body. The guy was terrifyingly powerful.

He glared at something over the top of her head. He had a really angry expression and suddenly another roar broke from his lips, loud enough to hurt her ears. She saw his sharp, white teeth flash again as he snarled, and he lifted her higher against his chest when he yanked her completely off her feet. He held her there, her body dangling above the ground, and he fled the yard.

Mine. The thought wouldn't leave Valiant's head. It repeated over and over. *Mine. Mine. Mine.* He moved faster, to take her somewhere private, away from the others, inside his home. They weren't going to take her away from him. He'd fight to the death to keep her and kill anyone who tried to tear her from his arms. The scent of her flooded his nose, made his body ache with need, and nothing else mattered.

She's a human. She's not what I had in mind or what I thought I wanted. Things change. It doesn't matter. She's all mine. He glanced at Tiger, the two Species males with him, and the two humans to make sure they didn't invade his territory.

The human male had a red face and gripped the fence, appearing ready to climb over it, and the human woman's mouth hung open as if she wanted to scream. He knew he horrified them but he didn't give a damn. They posed no threat to him. It was the Species he might have to fight if they attacked. He'd do it. He wasn't going to let the woman go.

Mine!

His arm tightened around the glorious woman he held, careful not to crush her, and grateful she didn't fight. She almost seemed docile in his hold, as if she knew as well as he did that she belonged to him. Hope soared that she'd want him as much as he did her.

You're not acting sane, he silently admitted but it didn't matter. She smelled wonderful, her delicate features were something he wanted to stare at forever, and holding her in his arms made the desire to keep her only stronger. The idea of spreading her out on his bed and stripping her bare to explore every inch of her skin had his dick aching painfully.

She'll be someone to talk to, someone to hold, and I'll convince her we will be happy together. I can do it. She'll want to stay. She has to. Mine. Mine. Mine. She belongs with me.

He had no real idea how to make it happen but he was a strong male, determined, and anything was possible now that he was free. He'd spent a lifetime locked in a dank cell, hurting most of the time, and always so lonely. The idea of having a mate, someone to get to know, to share life with, had become his ultimate dream.

He held her more tenderly, swearing to protect her with his life and not allow anyone to take her from him. It didn't have to make sense. She was in his arms, he'd claimed her, and he wasn't about to release her. Somehow, some way, he'd convince her he was the male for her.

He'd once dreamed of living outside the concrete walls and that had finally happened. Anything was possible. He inhaled her wonderful feminine scent, his arms secured her more firmly against his body, and one word repeated in his head.

Mine!

Chapter Two

ഌ

"Damn it, Valiant," Tiger yelled. "Bring that woman back this instant!"

"Tammy!" Ted screamed. "Put her down! He's going to kill her. Do something!"

"Leave," Valiant roared over his shoulder as he sprinted toward the house.

"Bring her back, man!" Tiger shouted. "Don't make me bring a hunting party in there to retrieve her. Justice is going to have your balls if you hurt her."

Tammy gripped his shirt when he slowed to a walk and clutched her against his body a little higher as he stomped up some steps. She couldn't see a thing but his tan T-shirt in her face.

The man-beast suddenly paused, they turned, and she heard a door slam closed. A second later the distinct sound of locks being turned registered before he moved again.

They climbed a lot of stairs. She closed her eyes and didn't fight. She could feel the strength of the arms that held her pressed tightly against his firm, hard body. She inhaled and admitted the guy smelled great, that whatever cologne he put on was a good one that wasn't too strong.

She bit back some self-loathing. She was losing her mind to be thinking about the guy's delectable-smelling cologne under the circumstances. She was being taken somewhere by Valiant, the man-beast, and was locked inside the house, which it turned out was his.

Another door slammed and Valiant stopped walking but his body twisted around and another lock being turned registered in her mind. He turned again, her legs swinging slightly from his sudden movements, and took about ten steps before he suddenly released her.

Tammy gasped as she fell but she didn't hit a hard floor, dropping onto a soft bed instead. She landed on her back with her legs over the edge of the massive mattress to stare up in mute shock at the man standing between her thighs. Valiant's exotic eyes were fixed on her.

Oh shit. She finally found the ability to move. She was on his bed and it smelled the way he did. She instinctively knew it was his bedroom. She glanced at the large room with the dark-wood bedroom furniture. She backed up, using her elbows and dug her feet into the bed to try to get away from him. The huge man watched her silently.

"Don't," he growled softly.

Tammy froze. "*You* don't."

His lips twitched and his eyes narrowed a little. "Don't what?"

"Don't..." She frowned at him. "Stop scaring me."

Full lips curved into a smile. "Are you afraid of me?"

She nodded. "Of course I am."

He suddenly moved, his hands flattened on the mattress as he bent toward her on the bed. Her body was under him instantly as he stretched his body over her, knocked her flat, and halted her plan to crawl backward away from him.

"Why? I won't hurt you. What I want to do to you will feel really good."

Is he kidding? She didn't believe he was, considering the intense look he directed her way. This situation was a lot of things but humorous wasn't one of the descriptions that came to mind.

"You're huge and you have sharp teeth and...you took me from outside. I want to leave."

"I don't want you to go. As you pointed out, I'm bigger."

Her mouth opened and closed as she stared up at him. "They will come in here to get me."

He nodded. "They will."

Huh? She frowned at him. "Why are we here if you knew that already?"

"Time." He actually grinned at her. "It's going to take them a lot of it to get enough of my people together to brave my home. Not many would be so foolish to attempt it. They fear me."

She started to feel nervous as she studied him. "Could you please stop hovering over me?"

He shook his head. "No."

"You're frightening me again."

The smile faded. "I don't want you to be afraid."

"What do you want?"

His gaze lowered down her body slowly before he met hers again. "I want you."

Her heart missed a beat. "That's not going to happen."

"Ummm." He didn't look convinced. He suddenly pushed up with his hands and straightened off the bed back onto his feet. He kept his sole focus on her. "Are you sure?"

"You promised you wouldn't hurt me."

Tammy watched as he gripped his T-shirt, his fingers hooked on the lower edges of it and he tore the material up his body. He threw it on to the floor behind him. She couldn't help but stare. The man's skin was a golden brown all over and he had a perfect chest. She imagined he'd be hairy but he wasn't. He was muscular and really cut with smooth, nearly hairless skin. She couldn't miss the six-pack abs clearly displayed over a flat belly.

His arms were massive, thickly defined with muscles, and he had a broad chest. The disks of his nipples were a light reddish color that nearly matched his eyelashes and his hair. Her gaze ran lower and saw that a thin line of reddish-blond hair lightly trailed from his bellybutton down to the top button of his jeans.

"I'm not going to hurt you." He reached for the snap of his pants. "Of all the things I want to do to you, pain isn't involved."

He opened the top button of his jeans, which revealed more of his flat stomach. Tammy's mouth fell open as he gripped the zipper. Her gaze jerked up to his face and couldn't miss how amused he appeared to be. His golden eyes shone with it.

"Don't you dare take those off."

The sound of the zipper going down was loud inside the bedroom. It had an icy-cold-water effect on Tammy, as if she'd been splashed with it. It startled her out of her dazed shock when it sank in that he really planned to have sex with her. She gasped in air, rolled over on the mattress, and frantically clawed at the bedding, trying to crawl away from him.

Big, strong hands gripped her hips and tossed her carefully onto her back and left her staring up at him again. Three things became instantly clear as her gaze jerked down to his waist. The man's jeans were open, she saw skin, and Valiant wasn't wearing underwear. She also couldn't miss that the guy didn't tuck upward judging by the large bulge she couldn't miss running down his inner thigh inside the jeans.

"Where are you going? You'd miss the really great parts if you run now."

"Stop it."

He grinned at her, showing fangs. "You have beautiful blue eyes."

She blinked. "You have beautiful eyes too. That doesn't mean you can..." She pointed at his waist. "That's not happening."

He chuckled. "Really?"

Tammy nodded. "Really. No way, no how. Do the math, huge guy."

"I'm glad you've gotten your voice back and my name is Valiant. You may use it."

"You stopped growling and roaring at me."

"So if I don't want you to talk or tell me 'no' anymore, I just need to roar and growl at you?" One of his eyebrows arched. "Thanks for sharing how to silence you. It's helpful information to know."

Tammy inched back on the bed, trying to reach the other side. "As I said, do the math. There's no way we're, uh, doing what people do inside bedrooms."

"Math has nothing to do with what I have in mind."

"Really?" Tammy was extremely grateful not to be mute anymore. She felt calmer now that she wasn't frozen with terror. She was adjusting to how the guy looked and since he'd brought her inside his house, he seemed more human than animal. He talked to her instead of just growling. "I disagree. You're huge and I'm small in comparison. The two don't add up."

He watched but didn't try to stop her as she climbed off the bed on the other side to keep the large piece of furniture between them. Tammy stood on shaky legs and faced him. She studied him as he watched her, only he smiled while she remained wary.

"I disagree. I think we could work. Do you think I'd hurt you? I wouldn't. I can be very gentle when I need to be." His gaze raked over her body. "I admit it's going to be tough to keep all my urges in check but I would."

"I'm not sleeping with you."

He laughed. "I'm glad. Sleeping is the last thing I want to do with you on my bed."

Tammy gritted her teeth, her anger flaring. "I'm not doing that either. I don't do strangers, and hell, I sure as hell won't be doing you."

His smile died and the amusement left as his gaze seemed to grow slightly cold, appearing a little scary. "Are you prejudiced? I'm not putting you down for being totally human."

She frowned. "That's, well, at least you know what I am." She focused on his mouth. "And I couldn't shred you with my teeth. I'm not scary, Mr. Lion. Is that what you partly are? Lion? Tiger? What?"

He just blinked but something in his expression hardened. "You could say that," he stated slowly.

She'd struck a nerve or something. She swallowed, deciding he looked a tad angry. "I'm sorry. I don't mean to insult you. I've never..." *Shut up*, she ordered her brain. She was digging a hole and knew it. "I didn't mean any disrespect or anything. You frighten me, okay? I've never met a New Species before today and you have to admit you're really intimidating. The one at the gate who allowed me into Reservation mostly looked human. You don't. If you were smaller it would help but you're huge, all muscular, and I know how badly you could hurt me if you set your mind to. I'm probably rambling but stop looking at me that way because you're scaring me again. I'm five-foot-four and I weigh a hundred and thirty pounds. You are what? Six-foot-four or five and..." Her gaze raked down him. "Two hundred pounds?"

"I'm six-foot-six and two hundred sixty pounds."

"Huge," she summed up. "Way bigger than me and you didn't exactly walk up to me politely to inform me that I was at the wrong place. You growled at me, glared, and terrified me more than I've ever been in my entire life. I never shut up. Never. Ask anyone. You had me so frightened I forgot how to breathe there a few times and I couldn't have spoken to save my life. I tried really hard too."

Valiant's lips twitched and the anger faded from his features. "You never shut up, huh?"

She shook her head. "Never. I've heard it since I was about four years old that I can blab anyone to death. My family kept telling me the worst mistake they ever made was teaching me how to talk and if they could go back in time, they'd have taught me sign language so they could close their eyes to shut me up."

The man crossed his arms over his broad chest. He grinned, showing those teeth. "You're really adorable and I enjoy the sound of you talking. You have a really nice voice. Come here."

Tammy glared at him. "No way. You stay over there and I'm happy right where I'm at."

"Come here," he ordered again.

She crossed her arms over her chest the exact way he had his and her eyebrow arched. "No. I want to leave now."

His arms dropped he sighed. "I'm not going to hurt you. Remember that."

Oh shit. Tammy tensed. She was certain she wasn't about to enjoy whatever he planned to do. He at least warned her before he moved, rounding the bed fast. She jumped on top of the mattress, hit it on her hands and knees, and started to scramble across it since she didn't have anywhere else to go.

A hand suddenly gripped her ankle, gave a hard enough jerk that knocked her flat to her belly, and he rolled her over onto her back. In the blink of an eye Valiant crouched over her until inches separated their bodies. He didn't put any of his weight on her but she was pinned between his arms and legs on the bed.

His gaze locked with hers. "Let's try an experiment."

"Let's not." Her heart pounded. She didn't try to touch him to push him away even though she wanted to shove at his chest. Fear gripped her. "Please?"

He smiled. "I insist."

She stared at his sharp teeth and swallowed the lump that formed in her throat. "Um, you look scary when you show your...uh...teeth. They look really sharp."

He didn't get angry. In fact, her words seemed to amuse him greatly. "The better to eat you with," he teased softly.

Tammy's heart flipped inside her chest. "That's a bad joke, right? Please tell me you're just kidding."

"I'm not a wolf."

"I'm not wearing red."

"I still want to eat you."

She was shocked by his candor, and realized that no man had ever spoken to her that way before. He didn't attack her but instead seemed happy to just peer into her eyes. She calmed a bit.

"I never thought I'd say this but you better be talking dirty to me."

He chuckled. "I am."

"Good." She blushed, realizing what she said. "I mean, not good. Bad. You know that's totally inappropriate to say to a stranger, right?"

His smile widened as he flashed more teeth. "Kiss me."

She studied his mouth warily. "That's not going to happen."

"I wouldn't hurt you."

She hesitated and bit her bottom lip for a few seconds. She was strangely attracted to the guy. He'd grabbed her, scared the crap out of her, but he wasn't doing anything more than pinning her down. He'd have torn her clothes off and raped her if he were a douche-bag loser. She actually appreciated his sense of humor.

They stared into each other's gaze. His eyes were probably the most beautiful ones she'd ever seen. Up close she could see his pupils were slightly oval shaped instead of round, reminding her of a cat she'd once owned. Definitely not human but oddly sexy. Her gaze dropped from them to his lips.

Full, masculine ones that she found appealing for some strange reason. *What would it be like to kiss him?* She was tempted to find out. *What are the chances of ever being in this situation again?* She really hoped the answer would be never. *Maybe. Think, damn it. You can't really be considering this! It's nuts.*

"I don't know you." She was proud she said that.

"This is a good way to."

"Most men buy women dinner and take us to a movie before they try to make it to first base."

"First base?" He arched an eyebrow.

"It's a saying that means kissing someone. It's a baseball analogy. First base is kissing."

"Is there a second base?"

"That's touching someone from the waist up."

"Third base?"

"That's doing a little more that includes touching sexual parts on the body from the waist down but usually through the clothes but there are exceptions such as light under-clothes groping."

She couldn't believe she was having this conversation with a New Species but he seemed genuinely curious and she was rambling, more than aware she should shut up, but nervousness always made her mouth go into overdrive.

"Fourth base?"

"Nope. Only three bases and then it's called a home run."

"What does that entail?"

"Everything. Going all the way."

He grinned. "In that case, I want a home run."

"No."

He chuckled. "Kiss me, Tammy. At least give me a chance to show you that I won't harm you in any way. I promise you'll enjoy what I want to do to you as much as I will."

"I don't kiss strangers." *But you're tempting me to break that rule.* She pushed that thought back, trying to focus on the reasons why she shouldn't. *He's New Species. Scary. Big. Yeah. Math, remember?* And she'd thought it would never come in handy in high school while suffering through those boring classes.

He blinked a few times and his smile faded. "We'll really get to know each other. Kiss me. I'm dying to taste you."

She was tempted, admitted being more than a little curious about what kind of kisser he'd be and if someone so intimidating could be just as passionate. She hadn't kissed a man in about a year, not since her last boyfriend had broken her heart by cheating on her. She debated if she should let Valiant kiss her or not when he lowered his face a few inches until their lips nearly touched. She took a shaky breath knowing that he wasn't going to give her a choice.

"Close your eyes and don't fear me," Valiant ordered in a deep, husky whisper. "Relax. I'm not going to hurt you."

Relax? Is he kidding? He was huge and had her pinned down on the bed even though he wasn't touching her. *Oops,* she thought as his lips brushed hers. *He's touching me now.* She tensed a little and reached up to flatten the palms of her hands on his chest. He was hot to the touch and his skin felt soft but so warm it was as though he were burning up with a fever.

His lips were gentle as he used his mouth to open hers. She didn't fight it but instead forced her body to relax. *I hope his teeth don't hurt my mouth.* That was the last thought she had as his tongue invaded. He didn't kiss her the way anyone else ever had and she was no lightweight in that department. She'd dated heavily in high school when kissing boys had been a nice pastime as long as they didn't turn into octopuses — all hands and grabbing. She wasn't that kind of girl in high school, drawing a very firm line between that and doing more with boys.

Valiant devoured her mouth. His tongue explored every inch, rubbed erotically against hers and even swiped the roof, which tickled slightly. His lips were firm over hers, opening her mouth wider to his dominance. When he growled softly she could feel vibrations against her palms and even against her tongue. It was a shocking turn-on and her body responded instantly when she kissed him back.

His hand fisted the bottom of her shirt, jerked it from of the waist of her slacks, and suddenly his hand brushed against her stomach. His calloused fingertips lightly explored her skin. The feeling was insanely good. She moaned into his mouth as his hand inched upward until he cupped her breast.

He wasn't gentle about that either. His hand was firm as he squeezed her sensitive breast and even through the thin material of her bra, she could feel the rough texture of his hand across her nipple. It reacted instantly, tightening, and the tip grew taut. Tammy heard someone moan loudly, only to realize the sound came from her again.

The mouth on hers tore away and left Tammy breathing hard. Her eyes flew open to watch Valiant stare down at her, an intense expression on his handsome but strange features. His hand still gripped her right breast and he rubbed his calloused thumb across her nipple. Her breast seemed to grow heavy and her nipple became so stiff she wondered if it could actually break. Tammy arched her chest against his hand, not meaning to, but she did. She could feel heat pooling between her thighs and her stomach quivered. She was turned on big-time and her body began to throb.

He inched his body lower over hers. "Just a taste," he growled.

It was a soft but deep tone that made his chest rumble again, vibrating against her hands. He jerked her shirt up higher until it was pushed over the top of her breasts to expose her bra completely. He stared at it before his hand released her breast. His finger slid under the center of her bra in a light caress until there was a tug.

She looked down to realize he'd somehow sliced open her bra in the front with one of his fingernails. The material was pushed away from her breasts, baring them to his view. Both nipples were hard peaks, her skin sensitive, and she didn't feel embarrassed. She knew she should try to cover them but she didn't.

"Beautiful and you have so much for someone so small," he softly growled right before his head lowered. "I bet if I lick them, they'll taste as good as they look."

Tammy closed her eyes when his breath fanned across her breast. He opened his mouth and swiped her nipple with his tongue. She made a surprised sound because the texture of it was soft but rough at the same time, the feeling unique, but it sent more heat flooding between her legs. Her arousal level shot up to nearly unbearable. She gasped when his mouth closed over her breast.

His raspy tongue moved, sliding quickly back and forth across her taut nipple. She moaned, arching her breast into his mouth. She could imagine instantly what that tongue could do if he used it on other places of her body. His teeth gently raked across her skin above and below her nipple and in response, her fingers dug into his skin where she clung to him.

She knew she should push him away but didn't. She curled her fingers around the tops of his shoulders instead, encouraging him. He growled again, vibrated against her, and another moan broke from her lips. The guy reminded her of a big vibrator on her breast and the way his tongue slid across her nipple was intensely pleasurable. She gasped when he swirled it around her nipple and then he was sucking on her. Her stomach clenched hard and the ache between her thighs started to scream with need.

His hand on her stomach slid down and there was a jerk at her waist. She couldn't really think about that though. Concentrating on anything other than what he was doing was too difficult as Valiant played her breast. She barely registered the fact that something pulled on her slacks until he released her breast. Her eyes flew open again.

"Lift your hips."

My hips? She stared at him, confused. "What?"

He smiled. His mouth lowered and captured her other breast. A moan tore from her throat. He didn't tease her breast, he sucked it into his mouth, using his tongue and teeth against her. The ability to think fled as he increased the suction and the sharp tugs on her breast made her clit throb as if they were connected. One of his hands slid under her back as she arched off the bed to press tighter against his mouth. His hand lowered, cupped her ass and squeezed.

That's when she realized his hand held bare skin. Her eyes flew open as she tried to shove him away. His mouth released her breast and their gazes met. She twisted, trying to see around his body and realized that he'd somehow gotten her pants open and down her thighs where they were bunched at her knees. Her panties were down there too, tangled up with her slacks. Tammy gaped at him.

"I didn't even realize. How did you get my pants down without me knowing?"

He chuckled. "That's all you have to say?"

Valiant tried hard to keep control of his desire. He wanted her so bad it had become a physical pain. She'd probably scream if he removed his pants, considering she seemed worried about the size of his cock. Their size difference could be an issue but women were designed to stretch for birthing. He could make it work if he were careful, gentle, and took it slow enough for her to adjust to him.

She's human. He clenched his teeth but finally relaxed. It didn't matter that he'd never believed he'd be attracted to a human or that he'd thought other males of his kind were idiots to want them, because it all boiled down to the truth. He wanted and needed this one.

He inhaled her wonderful, sexy scent, and fought back a snarl. She had admitted the sound frightened her. Species women would know he did it because he was aroused but

Tammy wasn't one of his kind. She wouldn't be turned on if he didn't restrain his animal instincts. It had been tough to do, but for her, he'd fought hard to remain in control.

He had to take some deep breaths to calm. He resisted the urge to just tear her clothes from her body, shove her legs apart, and bury his face between those soft, sensual, pale thighs of hers. The scent of her arousal made him long to bury his tongue deep into the source. He fought to think but it was difficult as an image of how it would feel to taste her desire, to know the warm depths of her sweet pussy, and how she would make more of those soft moans if he fucked her with his mouth.

His dick hardened until he wondered if the material of his jeans would actually split apart and it would break free of the confinement. His shaft had swollen to a painful size from just thinking about where his tongue wanted to go—inside her. Fear cooled his blood though. She wasn't Species. He couldn't just make her climax, flip her over, lift her ass up into the air and pound into her until he came. He'd hurt her.

Valiant stared into her beautiful eyes. The blue of them reminded him of the ocean. He'd never seen it personally but he'd watched plenty of DVDs featuring Hawaii. It was just one of the places he'd seen on his television that he'd never be allowed to visit.

First he'd been sealed inside concrete prisons, then later in the hot, miserable desert in a horrible motel with nothing around but flat miles of emptiness. Reservation had been bought to provide a better, permanent location for Species and now he had trees, blue sky, and a home. His. Something that belonged to him.

She blinked and took a deep breath, her breasts lifted as she inhaled, and he realized there was something else he wanted to belong to him—her. He could happily stare into those eyes every day. To have her spread out naked on his bed would be a joy. The scent of her was something he could easily grow addicted to. Everything about her drew him, mesmerized him, and he wasn't about to allow it or her to slip through his fingers.

He would just need to get her addicted to him and convince her she belonged in his life. He'd wanted a mate but he'd imagined she'd be Species. He mentally shrugged that fantasy away. None of them had affected him the way the small human under him did. He'd been denied a lot in his lifetime but he would have her.

Mine! All mine. I'm not giving her up. Never.

Chapter Three

ॐ

"Get off me."

Valiant shook his head. "Kick the pants away and open your thighs for me. I want to touch you."

Panic gripped Tammy. The guy had practically managed to strip her and she hadn't even realized what he'd done. She'd wanted to kiss him, she'd admit that, but now her pants and panties were around her knees, her body mostly exposed and she had to call a halt. She couldn't have sex with a stranger and especially not one as scary as Valiant.

"Go to hell. Get off me and pull my pants back up."

He shook his head again before he lifted away from her and sprang backward from the bed. He landed on his feet gracefully with his thighs spread apart enough to make room for her legs between them. He smiled at her while raking his gaze down her body. Desire showed clearly as he examined every exposed inch.

She gasped, trying to shove her shirt down over her bare breasts with one hand as she also reached frantically for her pants to pull them back up with her other. *Holy shit! How did that happen?* She was completely exposed to the guy.

He gripped her slacks with both hands and jerked them out of her frantic hold, tore them down her legs, and tossed them to the floor. Shocked and miffed, Tammy stared up at him but then he dropped down on her again. He braced his arms, pushup style, legs still spread, and his body hovered over hers. He didn't touch her. Inches separated their bodies as they stared into each other's eyes.

"Spread your legs for me, sexy. I'm going to touch you." His voice came out gruff, raspy and deep.

She locked her thighs tightly together and reached up to push against his chest again. He had a sexy voice when turned on, but she couldn't allow him to have sex with her. She needed to remember that she didn't do strangers, no matter how much she wanted to, or how bad she ached for his touch. *New Species. Part animal. So wrong. Yeah. Remember that.* She pushed again.

He wouldn't budge and looked really amused that she even attempted to move him. She tried to ignore how sexy he looked with those exotic eyes and those bulging muscles, from holding his weight off her. She had the urge to stroke about every inch of his amazing body that her fingers could reach.

"This is so not happening, Valiant." Saying his name sounded strange coming from her lips but she got it out. "You stated I'm ovulating, right? You can really smell that? For real?"

He chuckled and gave a sharp nod. "I can scent it. That's why I'm so aroused. Do you know how hot and wet you're going to be for me with your body in heat? Haven't you been feeling your sexual desire rise while you're in this state?"

She swallowed. "Nope. My fingers were a little swollen this morning but that's about it. I wouldn't have known that was the reason without you telling me." She cleared her throat. "I'm not having sex with you. I don't know you and I don't do that with strangers."

"Spread your thighs and I'll change your mind."

She stared up into those beautiful eyes of his. She knew how he kissed and how he could make her feel when he touched her. No one had ever tempted her that much and her body had reacted to him in ways it never had before to any other man. She still ached between her thighs and her breasts were tender.

"Spread your thighs," he softly growled. "I want to taste you so bad I'm trying not to drool from the need."

He drools? That's totally NOT sexy. Yeah. Focus on that. She frowned and pushed against his hot-skinned chest once more but he didn't budge an inch. He shifted his weight, lowering down her body and his legs slid a little off the bed so, instead of hovering over her face, he hesitated over her stomach. His gaze left hers to stare at her thighs. Another soft growl came from deep in his throat.

"Open up for me. I need that at least. Your scent calls to me so strongly I hurt. Let me lick you until you come, screaming for me. Let me enjoy your cream." He purred suddenly, his head lifted until those catlike eyes of his locked with her shocked gaze. "I love cream." He licked his lips slowly.

Her body throbbed. *Damn, he doesn't fight fair.* Her traitorous body responded full force to his words when mental images shot through her brain of him settling between her thighs. She bit her lip hard before softly cursing, losing the battle with desire and knowing she shouldn't.

"I can't believe this. This never happened, okay? I've lost my mind but I'm hurting for you."

She unlocked her knees and felt her cheeks heat with embarrassment. She had let few men go down on her and while it wasn't bad, it wasn't that great either. She'd sworn off doing it again unless she was drunk or with someone she really, really cared about. She didn't do strangers but she'd never seen this situation coming.

She spread her legs a little and watched Valiant's head snap down. Another growl rumbled from his throat, this one deep and a little scary. She grabbed for his thick hair, holding his head up until he met her gaze.

"Don't bite me. You're not going to do that, right? I want to be sure we're on the same page and you need to be careful with those vampire teeth of yours. You're not into blood, are you?"

He suddenly flashed a grin. "I know what I'm doing and there will be no pain. I'm not going to bite you."

She released his mane of hair, embarrassed as she spread her legs a little more, and tried not to tense up. She glanced down once when the bed moved to see that Valiant had totally slid off the bed and knelt next to it.

Big, strong hands gripped her hips, pulled her ass to the edge of the mattress and gripped her knees, gently nudging her into the position he wanted, which was her heels on the edge of the bed, legs spread wide apart. His gaze fixed on her totally exposed pussy, a purr came from him and she looked away to stare up at his ceiling as her fingers clutched at his comforter. She wasn't sure about this at all.

"You have no hair anywhere." He sounded surprised.

She wondered if she could actually die of awkwardness. "I shave it off. Either get on with it or let me go. I can't even believe I'm agreeing to this because it's totally insa—"

She gasped instead of finishing her sentence when Valiant pushed against her knees to widen them even more. The guy had broad shoulders and his hair fell over her stomach as he leaned in closer to her until she couldn't miss feeling his hot breath fanning over her exposed sex. His hands were gentle as he spread her labia to expose even more of her to his view. Another loud purr came from him and his hot tongue swiped her clit.

Her fingers clawed the bedding as he started to lick her in rapid, long strokes. Pleasure was instant and intense. Valiant's tongue was raspy and he could move it in ways she'd never thought possible while he teased and zeroed in on the exact spot that sent raw ecstasy cascading through her body.

She tensed hard, her back arched, and she would have slammed her legs closed to stop the too-powerful feeling but his shoulders held her pinned open and his hands held her labia spread to expose her clit to him. He held her down when her hips started to rise from the mattress.

The climax tore through Tammy brutally and she cried out. She was shocked at how fast and hard she'd come. Her eyes were closed when she floated down from the euphoria and tried to calm her ragged breathing. She heard Valiant panting harder than her and gasped when his tongue suddenly lowered to the opening of her pussy.

He growled, vibrated against her, and his thick tongue breached her body as he parted her vaginal walls. Her muscles were still twitching and contracting with her release and his hands slid under her ass, lifting her from the bed a few inches to give him deeper penetration.

"Oh God," she moaned.

He growled deep in response and his tongue moved inside her, in and out, before it withdrew completely. She forced her eyes open and stared in stunned shock as he lifted up until he bent over her. He had a wild look in his amazing eyes and he nearly lunged for her breast, drew it into his mouth hard and frantically suckled on her. It made her cry out again at the new, wonderful sensation. Something thick and hard nudged her pussy. She gasped as his cock started to press into her where his tongue had just been.

He was thick and incredibly hard. He lowered over her, her body pinned flat under him with just enough weight on her to keep her where he wanted her. Her muscles stretched to accommodate his size. He entered her slowly, allowing her body to adjust to his cock, and her fingers grabbed at his head, sliding into his thick tresses for something to hold on to. Pleasure and near pain gripped her as he sank into her. She experienced a wave of panic when he drove in even deeper.

"Stop!"

He froze and his mouth left her breast. He had a definitely wild look in those exotic eyes, the sheer need of his desire marked clearly by the harsh tension of his features.

"Don't make me stop." His voice was so deep and gruff that he didn't sound human. "I need you."

"You're too big." She was afraid.

"I'm turning us, all right? You're going to be on top and take as much of me as you can. I don't want to hurt you."

He rolled, displaying his immense strength. One second Tammy had been under him and the next she straddled his lap. He made sure he didn't enter her any deeper by holding her slightly away from him and waited until she braced her knees on either side of his hips before he released her. One of his hands wrapped around her waist, holding her in place, while his other hand slid under her to position his fingers to massage her clit. She threw back her head and sank down on him a little more.

His cock felt really thick. It had been a long time since she'd had sex. She lifted up and the pleasure of him inside her forced a moan from her lips. He was merciless with his fingers as he played with her sensitive bundle of nerves, making her pant. She moved up and down, only taking as much of him as her body desired.

The feeling of being stretched, filled, the sheer bliss of those sensations, shocked her because it was the best thing she'd ever experienced. She could feel every extremely rigid inch of him inside her and, combined with what his fingers were doing, she needed to come again.

She rode him frantically, taking his cock a little deeper each time she ground her hips down. Moans tore from her throat as her body seemed to ignite into flames. The man under her growled and snarled, making noises she'd usually find terrifying but instead it just heightened her passion. Her body tensed, shook, and she cried out when she climaxed hard again, her muscles clamping around his thick shaft as she jerked violently from the force of it.

Valiant roared as he climaxed and she wasn't even startled at the sound. His steel-hard cock was buried deep inside her and his hips shook under her and warm heat spread into her pussy as he kept coming. She collapsed onto his broad chest.

They were both winded. One of his hands gripped her hip and his other hand moved to her back to caress his fingertips up her spine until he fisted her hair in his hold at the base of her skull. He didn't hurt her but he forced her head up until she had no choice but to meet his gaze. His golden eyes appeared absolutely gorgeous in the aftermath of sex. He smiled at her, showed sharp teeth, and his hand slid from her hip to cup her ass gently.

"I'm keeping you forever."

She stared at him in shock. "What?"

"I decided I'm keeping you forever. You're mine."

He was good at making her speechless. Tammy stared at him and was absolutely mute. *He wants to keep me? Forever? For real? Does he think I'm a pet?* She wasn't even sure how to take his words or exactly what they meant. *I'm his? He decided?* She didn't even know where to start or what she thought of him making those wild statements.

The smile died on his lips as he suddenly tensed under her, his big body seeming to turn to stone. Tammy gasped when he rolled them over and slowly withdrew his still-hard shaft from her body. He gave her one last passionate look before rolling away to leave the bed.

"They are coming for you but I won't allow anyone take you from me."

Who is coming for me? Tammy sat up on the bed. She realized her shirt remained on, bunched up over her breasts, and her sliced-apart bra cups were under her arms. She watched him quickly yank up his pants, growling and cursing under his breath the entire time.

She removed her damaged bra and pulled down her shirt while she scooted off the bed to stand next to it. She watched Valiant carefully. His expression was scary when he turned to face her. She hadn't known him long but she could identify rage when she saw it.

"Stay inside this room while I handle them. No one is taking you away. You're mine now."

Mouth open, she watched him put on his shirt and fasten his jeans as he paced the room. Like a caged animal. Lion. That's what he looked like. Only there weren't any bars between them. *What did I do? Oh yeah. Had sex with lion guy. Hot, screaming, came-so-hard-I-think-I-hurt-myself sex.* And he was going to hurt someone or be hurt to keep her.

Tammy backed away, stepped on something and glanced down. Her pants lay on the floor by her feet. Her shoes were there too. She didn't even remember them coming off but they were just slip-ons so he'd just brushed them off her feet when he'd yanked her pants off.

Valiant walked to the window, glared out and snarled viciously.

"Six of them are approaching." He snorted. "They think only six Species males could do it. It's insulting. I won't be gone long, sexy. Why don't you climb back into bed and wait for me? I'll grab some food before I return. You're little and I want to feed you. I'm going to take very good care of you and you'll want to stay with me."

Tammy glanced at the lamp nearby, her mind working frantically to stop what she feared might happen. Valiant was a big guy, ferocious, and she didn't want him to be killed or seriously hurt by the New Species coming to save her. He would fight them to keep her in his bedroom. She saw the outlet next to the bedside table where the lamp was plugged in. She turned her attention on him, noted that his back remained to her while he watched out the window, and another growl tore from his lips.

"I'll beat them until they go whimpering away before they take you away from me. I'll try to scare them off first but there's no way they are taking you, Tammy. I'll do whatever it takes."

She wouldn't be able to live with it they killed him. Tammy bent and yanked on the cord. Her gaze stayed trained on Valiant to make sure he didn't turn around and notice her movements. She gripped the lamp with a shaky hand, hesitated, and realized it would hurt him less than a bullet. She couldn't allow that to happen. She inched forward but he didn't turn, too focused on whatever he saw out the window.

"Idiots." He growled, bent forward a little, and his hands gripped the windowsill with enough strength to make the wood groan. "I want you to stay inside this room. It shouldn't take more than five minutes. If they won't leave, I'll—"

Tammy brought the lamp down hard on the back of his head. The glass base shattered and rained down Valiant's back to the floor. He grunted and spun around to face her. *Oh, I'm so screwed. I didn't hit him hard enough.* She could have hit him with more force but had been afraid of hurting him too severely. He appeared utterly taken aback as he stared down at her when he straightened to his full height but then his eyes rolled back and he swayed before collapsing onto the carpet. Tammy stared down at him with the broken lamp still clutched in her hands.

She instantly tossed it aside and dropped to her knees beside his body. She checked Valiant's pulse, found it strong and steady, and her fingers brushed through his hair where she'd hit him. She could feel a slight bump forming but there wasn't any blood. His chest rose and fell easily as she climbed to her feet, sure that he wouldn't be out long. She needed to leave before he woke. She was pretty sure he'd be super pissed at her for knocking him out.

"Son of a bitch." Her hands shook as she quickly finished dressing and shoved her feet into her shoes. She shoved her destroyed bra down the front of her pants, not wishing to leave it behind but wanting to keep it hidden after she left. A glance at Valiant showed he remained sprawled on his side on the floor. She took a step closer, hesitated at leaving him, and a twinge of regret flooded her. *Maybe I should stay and— No!*

What am I thinking? He wants to keep me forever and we're strangers. That would be nuts! She fled.

He'd locked the bedroom door and she had to unbolt it to leave. She glanced down the hallway at a few closed doors but the stairs were within sight. She ran for them. When Valiant came to she knew he would be really upset. She'd hit him with his own lamp and knocked him out cold. It was very doubtful he'd understand she'd done it to make sure he wasn't hurt and she didn't want to stick around to find out if she could reason with him.

She ran down the stairs to the large entryway. She unlocked the double doors, tossed them open and stumbled from his house.

She slammed the door behind her and walked quickly down the path. Her arms crossed over her chest to hide the fact that her bra was missing. She hoped no one would notice since she didn't want to have to explain. She spotted her work van, four Jeeps, and the other catering truck parked on the other side of the fence. Men had already entered the yard through the gate.

They were New Species. All wore black fatigues with NSO emblems in stark white on their chests and they carried real guns along with what she assumed were tranquilizer guns. She'd seen a few of the New Species officers from a distance at the front gate when she'd entered Reservation. A thirty-foot wall protected the boundary of it and men dressed in those same uniforms had patrolled the top of the wall. The ones in Valiant's yard stopped.

"Hi." Tammy didn't look at their faces, keeping her gaze averted instead. "I'm fine." She walked faster toward the gate and around the men who stood blocking her way.

"Tammy!" Ted rushed forward. "Are you all right?"

She kept moving and nearly plowed into one of the NSO officers, but he jumped back.

"I'm fine, Ted. I'm going home. I've had a stressful day but I'm really fine. We talked and he let me go. Problem solved," she flat-out lied.

A man moved into her path when she walked through the open gate to where the vehicles were parked. "Are you all right?"

She recognized the deep voice immediately as being Tiger's. She stopped and lifted her chin to peer into his strange features, not shocked that he appeared to be part feline. Not only did his name give it away but he had some features that were similar to Valiant's.

This guy stood a few inches shorter though and was not as broad chested as Valiant but he was still huge. Tiger's catlike eyes were an amazing blue and he had the same distinctive cheekbones and the same flatter nose as Valiant. He had sandy brown hair with red and blond streaks throughout. The red color wasn't nearly as bright or beautiful as Valiant's.

"I'm fine. I think I'll just go home now and relax. It's been a weird day."

He inhaled and his gaze widened slightly. "I'll take you to our medical facility."

Tammy tensed, alarmed that he'd say something she didn't want him to reveal in front of her boss and guessed he could smell Valiant all over her. They did seem to have a really freaky-strong sense of smell. She shot him a warning look, silently hoping he'd understand.

"I'm not hurt. Nothing happened."

"What did that bastard do to you?" Ted gripped her arm, spinning her to face him. Ted stood about five-foot-nine, only five inches taller than Tammy, and he looked unusually pale. "Did he touch you? Did he hurt you?"

She met her boss's worried gaze and hoped she appeared calm. "I'm fine. Nothing happened. We just talked, he saw reason, and he said I could go home. It's that simple," she lied.

Ted's features relaxed. "Thank God. They were going to go in and get you. The tranquilizer guns finally arrived and more of their men showed up to storm his house. I imagined the worst and I heard you scream once and a roar."

"He was scary." She jerked her arm out of his hold. "I just want to go home. It's been an ordeal and I have a pounding migraine," she lied again.

Ted nodded. "Of course. I'll pay you for today. I'm so sorry about the mix-up with the directions and I'm just glad you're not hurt."

"I'm absolutely fine," she muttered, silently wondering if she should keep track of how many lies she told, but quickly dismissed the idea. The truth would be much more of a hassle and she didn't want to go there.

Ted stepped back with an uncertain smile. "It's been an exciting day, huh?"

"Yeah." She forced a smile. "I'm out of here. Do you mind if I take the van?"

Her boss hesitated. "I need it. You're carrying most of the food for the party. It hasn't been canceled."

"I'll drive her home," Tiger offered softly. "Come this way, Miss Shasta. My Jeep is right here."

She walked to the van to retrieve her purse, silently praying that she got away before Valiant woke. She followed Tiger to one of the Jeeps and climbed inside. He didn't immediately start the engine. He studied her intently. She decided to be somewhat honest because the minutes were ticking by and she didn't know how long it would be before "Trouble" rose from the floor of his bedroom.

"We need to go right now. Please start the engine and get me out of here."

Tiger started the engine and yelled over his shoulder. "Clear this area out now."

The Jeep moved and the stress inside Tammy eased. She remembered to put on her seat belt. "I live about five miles from here. Thank you for driving me home."

He hesitated. "I'm taking you to our medical center first."

"No. I just want to go home."

He frowned grimly at her. "You need medical attention and we will call in a counselor. You need to make a report about what Valiant has done to you. We handle all justice at Reservation but he's going to be punished severely for this attack on you."

Shocked, Tammy gaped at him. "He didn't hurt me and I don't want him punished. I don't need a doctor and I sure don't need a shrink."

He hit the brakes and turned to face Tammy. His blue gaze locked with hers. "You can lie to Ted and Marcy. They are human and will believe what you said back there. I'm not them and you smell strongly of Valiant. I can also smell sex. He obviously hurt you and forced you to breed with him. You need to allow our doctors to take a look at you, you should talk to someone about what happened and you need to file a report to make sure he's punished for what he's done."

Her mouth had fallen open so she closed it as she stared at Tiger, feeling the heat of a blush warming her cheeks. She swallowed the lump that formed so she could speak.

"I know he hurt you."

"I'm fine. He didn't force me. I want to go home."

His frown deepened. "What happened?"

She hesitated. "He didn't hurt me but he also didn't want to let me go. He wanted to keep me as if I was a pet or something. He was about to attack anyone coming after me. I nailed him with a lamp and knocked him out cold. You might want to have someone check on him but I think he'll be fine. I tried not to hurt him but I figured it was better than someone shooting him. You need to get me away from here though because I think he's going to be upset that I got away when he wakes. I just want to go home."

"Son of a bitch," he cursed as he released the brake and stomped down on the gas. The Jeep lurched forward and picked up speed. "Let me take you to the medical facility."

She gritted her teeth. "He didn't rape me, didn't force me, and the sex was consensual, okay? Just get me home. Please? I just want to forget this day ever happened."

Tiger jerked his head in an angry nod. "Fine." He reached for the radio clipped to the top of his vest. "This is Tiger. Everyone clear a wide path from around Valiant's. I want tranquilizer guns with everyone patrolling that area. Put his ass down and secure him if he tries to leave his territory. Clear?"

Tammy glanced at the guy on the seat next to her. He had an ear clip-on comm device. Whatever was said made him look more relaxed. "Good. Tiger out." He hooked the radio back to his vest.

"I'm very sorry for all of this. You need to contact us if there's anything we can do for you. Our legal department will be getting hold of you."

"For what?"

"They just will. When you agreed to work here you had to sign forms. You know anything that happens here stays confidential or you could face huge lawsuits so please don't go to the press. Our legal department will make sure anything you need is taken care of so whatever issues you face, they will make sure you're well compensated. That's all I can do if you refuse to press charges against him."

She had signed a ridiculously long confidentiality contract. She wasn't allowed to talk about anything she saw or heard at New Species Reservation. She wasn't permitted to sue them for it if she suffered any injures while being a guest. It was a come-at-your-own-risk kind of deal but they had put in the clause that they'd pay for any medical bills if she were injured. Now she knew why.

"I would never talk to reporters."

Five minutes later Tiger parked the Jeep in front of her small house and two other vehicles parked behind them. She'd been escorted home with a full security detail. She knew New Species were targeted by hate groups and hadn't needed to ask why the extra vehicles had followed them to her home.

She glanced at her home and tried to hide her embarrassment. The house had been left to her by her grandmother. It had been in bad shape to begin with and Tammy had never had the extra money to fix it up. The porch sagged in spots, making it appear uneven, paint had chipped off in large sections, and one of the front windows had duct tape over it where the glass had broken. It was a small two-bedroom, one-bath house, but it was all hers. She wondered what the New Species thought as he stared at her home with a confused look on his features.

"Are you sure you don't want to see a medical doctor or a shrink? We will make him pay if you file a complaint. We're harsher than your justice system."

She shook her head as she undid her seat belt. "He didn't hurt me, I don't want him punished and I don't need a doctor. I'm not sure about the shrink part yet but I'm tough." She paused. "I just want to forget this ever happened. Okay?"

He met her gaze, watched her silently, but nodded slowly.

Tammy climbed out of the Jeep and walked to her front door, unlocked it, and stepped into the small room. She turned and noticed that Tiger watched her silently from the black unmarked vehicle. She firmly closed the door and twisted the deadbolt.

"Son of a bitch." She sighed. She headed for the bathroom and the shower. "I never saw today coming." So much for always trying to be prepared. Ha! Man-beasts with killer kissing skills and the ability to seduce women. She shook her head. My life just gets weirder and weirder. Why can't it ever be normal?

* * * * *

Valiant groaned. His head throbbed and he couldn't remember why. His eyes opened to stare at the carpet. He lay sprawled on his side. He blinked before someone shoved a big plastic bag of ice in front of his face. It hovered there. He inhaled and softly growled. It made his head hurt worse.

Tiger crouched down, still holding out the bag of ice. "Put that on the back of your head." He spoke softly.

Valiant grabbed it. His hand trembled a little and he found the spot where it hurt the most. He winced and snarled as the bag made contact. His attention fixed on Tiger.

"Are you all right?"

"What happened?"

Tiger took a deep breath. "It will come to you. Just stay down when it does."

The ice helped reduce the haze of pain and he took a deep breath, allowing the scents inside the room to fill his nose. *Tammy!* He tried to sit up but the room spun. He groaned again, sank back to the floor and bared his teeth at Tiger.

"Which one of your men crept up on me?"

"Tammy did it. She hit you with a lamp." Tiger stood and backed away, putting a safe distance between them. "She's safe and off Reservation."

Rage surged through Valiant and he snarled. "Bring her back. She's mine."

In response, the other Species leaned against the wall, crossed his arms over his chest, and sighed. "She hit you to get away, asked to be taken home, but refused to press charges. You're lucky, man. She could have had you locked inside a tiny damn cell and Justice would have had to decide if you needed to be put down for good. If you're too dangerous to live— Fuck, don't get me started. That's a nightmare concept we never want to have to face."

The pain receded more and Valiant sat up without the room spinning. He glared at Tiger. "She's mine."

"I got that." He sniffed the air. "You had her all right." His gaze flickered to the bed and back. "But you can't keep her. She's human. You wouldn't even pull that stunt on our women. You know you can't just claim them and force them to live with you."

"She's little. I could easily keep her here and change her mind about leaving. I planned to feed her and care for her."

"She mentioned you seemed to think she was a pet. I thought she had read the situation wrong. Humans tend to see us in a messed-up light but after hearing you talk, she was dead on. She's not a pet."

"I know this." Valiant frowned, worried that he might have given her the wrong impression. Regret gripped him. "Is that why she left? Why she hit me? I'll tell her she's my mate, not my pet."

"She's not yours, man." Tiger pushed away from the wall. "She wanted to leave. Deal with it. You and I, we're not for humans. We talked about this, remember? They are too fragile, they scare too easily, and you wanted a Species mate. A feline one."

"Not anymore. I want Tammy."

"Too bad. You can't have her. You talk about our kind growing soft and how you hate it. You're the one who sounds soft right now. Toughen up and face facts. A human would never get past how we are. At least not for guys like us. We're too in tune with our animal sides. I just look more human than you do."

Sadness was an emotion Valiant loathed but it filtered through him all the same. "She's not coming back to me, is she?"

"No," Tiger's gaze softened, "she's not."

"Leave."

"I'd rather stay a while to make sure you recover fully. I'll make us dinner. We'll have some sodas and talk. I heard a few felines you haven't met yet are being transferred here. Maybe one of them will be the one for you."

Images of Tammy flashed through Valiant's mind. "Leave me. I need to be alone."

"The new felines arrive tomorrow. I'll pick you up and take you to the hotel for you to sniff them out."

Valiant struggled to his feet and his gaze drifted to the bed where Tammy had been. Her scent still remained strong inside the room. He moved toward it and tossed the bag of ice away. He'd rather feel the pain than return to the numbing state in which he'd existed before he'd felt all those wonderful things with Tammy. He crawled onto the bed and lay where she had been, inhaling her scent.

"Valiant? I'll pick you up at two o'clock."

"Don't bother. Just go. Lock the door when you leave. I don't want to meet any felines."

He breathed in Tammy's scent, wanted to memorize it before it faded, and listened to his friend go away. His eyes closed as his hand gently brushed the comforter. He couldn't remember the last time tears had wet his eyes but they did at that moment. He'd lost her and she would never return. He'd known peace with her. *Happiness. Hope.* And now it was gone. She was…lost to him forever.

Chapter Four

∞

Why can't I just forget Valiant? Tammy felt totally disgusted with her lack of control over her thoughts as she lined up the pool cue and the white ball. She glanced at the red ball and the pocket. Loud music played in the background. Someone had been in a mood for old-time rock. A sigh sounded near her.

"Take the shot already, Tam. You know you're going to kick my ass anyway."

She turned her head to grin at her longtime best friend Tim. The two of them had known each other since grade school and they were really close. He'd wanted more than friendship during high school but Tammy hadn't returned his romantic feelings. Now years later they'd settled into a comfortable but strictly platonic friendship that both of them were happy with.

"I can't help it if I'm better at this than you are."

A smile twisted his lips. He appeared to be kind of awkward but he had a sweet smile and soft brown eyes. Tim resembled the average computer geek because he was one. He wore a logo T-shirt and sweatpants and worked from home as a computer programmer who made game software. His glasses glinted from the bar lights.

"I can kick your ass at video games any day."

"Yes, you can." She took the shot and sank the red ball into the corner pocket. "That's why I'm smarter than you are and the reason we're at the bar instead of your house in front of a game system. I wanted to win."

He scoffed. "You're not smarter. I'm just a gentleman."

She sank another ball. "Too bad you never bet money on our games."

"I make good money but not that good." He laughed. "You'd wipe me out of my life savings within an hour with the way you play pool."

Tammy winked at him. "You know I need a new roof."

Tim's smile faded as he stared at her. "You do? Why don't you let me pay for it?"

Major goof. She'd made a slip. She should have known better but her mind still remained distracted by the memory of a pair of cat-eyes the color of melted gold attached to a body that still made hers heat up at the very recollection of Valiant. She'd thought about him a hundred times a day since they'd met nearly five weeks before. She shook her head.

"I was kidding."

Tim wasn't buying it. "You were not. Is it leaking again? Come on, Tam. Let me help you. We're friends. Hell, we're practically family. I know what you make and its shit. You couldn't go to college the way I did. You had your grandma to take care of and I know you're still paying off her debts. That house she left you is a death trap. Let me buy you a new roof. Do you need any other repairs? I have the money and it's just sitting inside a bank account. It's not as though I have a girlfriend to blow my money on."

Tammy sank the black ball. Game over. She frowned at her best friend. "We've had this argument before and I won't take your money. Thank you from the bottom of my heart but I'm not a leech."

"That's bullshit and you know it. I'd never accuse you of that. You always had to do everything for everyone so let me help you this once. It's what friends and family do for each other."

"I don't want to fight."

She walked away from the pool table and moved to their table. She gripped her beer, peered at the lime stuck inside it, and took a sip. She rarely drank alcohol but sometimes she had the urge. She finished off her first and last beer of the night as she drained the bottle. She'd felt the need to feel a slight buzz more often since she'd met Valiant.

"We're not fighting. I'm trying to reason with you. I live with my parents and I don't pay a mortgage. The house is paid off. I just pay the taxes, which are chickenfeed. I make really good money and I have all the toys I want. Let me help you out. Do you remember when my dad had his stroke last year and they sent out that shitty home nurse from the hospital for him? You came and took care of him. You found the wonderful woman who takes care of him now. You changed his diapers for weeks and wouldn't take a penny. Now let me help you."

"Tell you what," Tammy sighed, turning to face him, "you can come change my diapers if or when I ever have a stroke. Until then, don't shove money at me. It's different."

Tim laughed. "Finally! You're giving me a green light to take your pants off."

Tammy laughed and shook her head. "You're disgusting."

He wiggled his eyebrows. "Hey, that's the closest thing to an invite to see you naked that I've ever gotten."

"That's not true." She disposed of her beer bottle inside a trash can and gripped her purse. A glance at her watch showed it was just after eleven. "Don't forget the time I wanted to go skinny dipping when we were ten. You chickened out. You thought a snapping turtle would latch onto you in a bad place if you took off your underwear and waded into the pond. You could have seen me naked."

"That doesn't count. I thought all girls were yucky at that age and besides, you hadn't grown up enough yet to see anything good."

She laughed and waved. "Neither had you. I have to go. We have to cater a luncheon tomorrow at the church and I have to be at work at seven to help prepare. Ashley Bless met some guy and is getting married. Tomorrow is their engagement luncheon."

Tim shuddered. "Someone is marrying her? Did she have a personality transplant? She's the most annoying person I've ever met. Poor sucker." He took a deep drink of his beer.

Tammy snorted. "No. She's still a bitch but she's convinced this idiot it's somehow cute to listen to her rant about everything. That or she uses that big mouth of hers to give him amazing head."

She walked toward the door, waved, and blew him a kiss. She heard Tim choke on his beer over her parting comment and laughed as she left the bar.

Summers in northern California could be weird. It had been hot during the day but the sun had gone down, bringing a chilly breeze that stirred around Tammy as she headed for her car. She glanced around, enjoying the quiet night. Growing up in a small town had always been great. She knew almost everyone and she'd had a lot of freedom since her grandmother had been half senile. Tammy had moved in with her just after her eighth birthday but she still remembered living in a big city before that. She loved the rural area more.

"Hey," a man called out. "Are you Tammy Shasta?"

She'd already withdrawn her keys for her car. She turned to stare at the tall stranger who wore jeans with a green, long-sleeve, cotton, button-down shirt. He had finished his outfit with a pair of faded brown cowboy boots. He was definitely not someone who lived in her small town. He had short brown hair and appeared to be in his midthirties. She instantly became more alert. She had been taught to never trust strangers, especially men.

"Who wants to know?"

The man paused and hooked his thumbs through the loops of his jeans. "I'm Terry Briggs. I heard there was an incident with you at that New Species place they just opened up near here."

Her heart began to race. *What has he heard? Who is this guy?* "I don't know what you're talking about," she lied. "You have a nice night." She unlocked her car door but kept her gaze on him. Scary scenarios began to play inside her head and she wanted to groan. A shrink would have a field day with her love of overthinking everything.

"Don't be that way," he demanded as he took a step closer. "We heard you had a run-in with one of those animal experiments out there and he put his paws on you."

Tammy tensed and fear inched down her spine. He had moved within a few feet of her now. He stood tall at about six feet but that wasn't saying much. Everyone was usually taller than her but he was a stranger and she felt threatened. She glared up at him and didn't like that he invaded her personal space. She couldn't open her car door unless she inched closer to him, which she wasn't about to do.

"Look," she glanced down at his boots and then back up to his face, "cowboy. I don't know what you're talking about. Whatever you heard, that rumor was wrong. Now you need to back up because I want to leave."

A look of disgust crossed his face. It made his features ugly and harsh. "They brainwashed you, didn't they? Those animal things do that to some people. It's all right, lady. They've done it before and you aren't alone. You need to come with us and we'll help you think straight again. We want you to hold a news conference to tell everyone what those sick animal bastards did to you. That will show the world they aren't something us decent folks should be living with. They all need to be put down."

She heard everything he said. His blatant hatred for New Species stunned her a little but the most alarming part of his little speech had been the "us" part. She turned her head and sure enough, spotted three more men edging toward her from the shadows of the building where they'd hidden. *Not good.*

Shit. She peered at the taller man as her heart accelerated from fear. *Think. Don't panic.*

"Fine. You got it. Why don't you follow me to my house and we'll discuss it there?" She could drive to the sheriff's station if she could just get inside her car or get her hands on her cell phone to dial for help. She had no intention of allowing them to follow her home.

He blinked and appeared a little surprised but his mouth tightened. "We'll take my truck."

She nodded, quickly assessing she needed to keep him off guard. It would be easier to surprise him if he thought she was a complete idiot. "Okay. What about my car? I can't just leave it here. Sam, the owner, will have it towed first thing in the morning if it's left in the parking lot. I'll drive and you can follow me."

A hand shot out and gripped Tammy's arm. "Your car is the least of our concerns. You're going to help us turn everyone against those animals."

Tammy fisted her keys to force a few of them to slip between her fingers. Four men against her weren't good odds. She silently prayed someone would walk out of the bar to help her but it didn't happen. Her other hand grabbed the handle of her car door.

"I can't just leave my car here. I'm willing to listen to what you have to say but I can't afford to pay the tow yard to get it back."

The jerk suddenly tried to yank her away from her vehicle. She clung to the car handle, he pulled on her hard enough to open the door slightly, and the interior lights inside her car came on. He yanked harder and the metal she gripped slipped from her fingers. She spun and knew she needed to attack to break free.

She punched the guy hard in the gut with the pointed keys sticking out between her fisted fingers as her foot came down on his. Her hand hurt from the keys when she struck him and her other hand clawed at his face. Her fingernails dug into his flesh just under his eye. He bellowed and released her just as Tammy let out a piercing scream to try to draw attention to her predicament.

Tammy shoved him and started to run for the bar but only got a few feet before someone grabbed her hair. She screamed again from the pain that shot from the back of her head. The stranger jerked her in his brutal grasp and slammed her into someone's parked truck. Their side mirror struck her cheek and pain shot through that side of her face near her ear.

He released her hair so his strong arms could wrap around her waist and they kept her from hitting the ground when her knees threatened to collapse under her. She screamed again and kicked at the jerk who hefted her off her feet. The back of her head made contact with a face behind her when she threw it back in a frantic attempt to force him to drop her. He cursed loudly and released her.

She hit the ground and nearly fell to her knees but managed to stagger away a few steps instead. Two of her attackers had put themselves between her and the bar. She fought back a wave of dizziness from the pain in her face and the back of her head where she'd head-butted the jerk. She bumped the truck again, used it to push against, and sprinted for the road instead. She made it out of the parking lot to the sidewalk, even to the pavement of the street, and spotted headlights coming at her.

Tammy ran at them, sure that those jerks would run in the opposite direction. Traffic was normally light at that time of night but whoever drove the car approaching her had to be better than those she fled. She waved her arms, yelling to get the driver's attention, and realized the vehicle started to slow.

She recognized the vehicle as it drew closer. Pastor Thomas' beat-up old car was a welcome sight when he hit the brakes completely, stopping just feet from where she stood. She couldn't miss the shock on his features as he peered at her through his windshield. Relief flooded her until his gaze shifted from hers, his lips parted, and his eyes widened in alarm at something he saw to the side of her.

Tammy twisted her head to stare over her shoulder and saw the four men rush at her. The one in cowboy boots who'd lifted her off her feet had blood running down his chin from his busted lip she'd caused and that's all she saw before they reached her.

Tammy screamed, kicked, and tried to punch but the men grabbed her arms and one of them grabbed her legs. They yanked her off her feet and ran with her body carried between them toward the parking lot of the bar. A loud horn blared while Pastor Thomas screamed her name.

They hoisted her into the air and tossed her over the rim of the bed of the truck as if she were a sack of potatoes. The force of the impact when she landed knocked the air from her lungs and pain exploded inside the back of her head where it slammed into the metal truck bed hard. She gasped in air, ordered her body to move, but the second she tried to sit up, two bodies crushed down on top of her.

She struggled and clawed at both men but they easily kept her pinned under them. The truck engine roared to life and doors slammed a second before the transmission was thrown in reverse. Wheels spun and everything moved rapidly.

The sudden and abrupt movement of the truck rolled two of the men away from her as they slammed into the side of the truck bed. It rolled Tammy onto her side. She glimpsed the night sky. The truck brakes locked up and rolled her in a new direction a second before the driver changed gears again. The transmission protested loudly when it made a grinding noise.

Tammy reached for the edge of the truck in hopes of climbing out but the driver punched the gas before her fingers could make purchase. The momentum of truck's forward motion made Tammy slide toward the lifted tailgate. Hands grabbed her and two bodies came back down on top of her, pinning her under them. She managed to scream.

The truck speed at a fast rate but over the stressed engine and the heavy breathing from her captors, she heard a horn honk repeatedly behind them. Pastor Thomas followed the truck and refused to stop trying to draw attention to what had happened.

Bless him! Unfortunately it made the driver of the truck more reckless. The truck hit some potholes and Tammy groaned in agony as the men on top of her slammed and crushed her tighter against the painful metal under her back.

Her ribs and head hurt. She also fought to breathe with their combined weight compressing her lungs. The horn kept honking behind them and it seemed to go on forever. The men holding her down were swearing when the ride turned really rough after the driver seemed to leave the road, driving over what Tammy guessed was grass from the way she could feel the ass end of the vehicle sliding and how bumpy and violently it moved. The sound of a horn grew fainter. She realized her attackers were smart enough to go off-road since the pastor's car wouldn't be able to.

Tammy nearly passed out from the pain when a loud grinding noise came from the truck and it slowed until it came to a stop. A man yelled curses from the cab. The men holding her down eased their hold. Tammy kneed one of them in the stomach hard. He made a horrible retching noise and she clawed her hand across the arm of the other man who tried to grip her thigh. Her nails dug into soft flesh until he screamed, jerking away.

Tammy fought with her fists and legs to get away from her captors. She managed to do enough damage that they winced away. She sat up and lunged in the other direction. Her fingers gripped the side of the truck. Desperation and terror made her find the strength to drag her body up until she fell out of the back of the truck and hit the dirt on her side. She lay there for a second, in pain, but stumbled to her feet when the cab door near her squeaked open.

She was able to make out the heavily wooded area that surrounded her with the help of the moon. She ran for the dark, dense tree line, hoped she could hide there, and knew it would be her only chance to lose the bastards. She barely made it to the trees when she heard them shout at her. It encouraged her to run faster and fear motivated her to press on while ignoring the pain in her side.

Someone panted heavily behind her, closing the distance, and the urge to scream gripped her hard. They were gaining on her. She dodged a dark shape and hoped they'd hit what she'd avoided. Instead something slammed into her back. It sent her sprawling hard into the leafy dirt and a heavy, painful weight pinned her down. Pain ripped through her with an intensity that made everything go black.

* * * * *

"Valiant?" Tiger yelled again.

Valiant walked out of his house, approached the gate and stopped. He glared at his friend. "Is there a reason you're bellowing at me at two in the morning? I was sleeping."

Tiger looked grim. "We got a call a few minutes ago from the local sheriff. They need our help."

Valiant narrowed his eyes in anger. "You know humans aren't my favorite. Go help them if you wish to do so. Why are you bothering me?"

Tiger bit his lip. "You need to remain calm, all right?"

Valiant's gut tightened. Tiger would only warn him if whatever he had to say would make him angry. "Why? Are more humans planning to attack us? Do you need me to patrol the Wild Zone? Have they breached the walls? I'm not patrolling outside with the human security. I'll just kill the intruders if they come here."

Tiger hesitated. "A human woman has been kidnapped from the town and there is a witness. The guy who saw her taken followed the truck but lost it when her kidnappers drove into the woods where the witness's car couldn't follow. He used a cell phone to call for help but it's a small town. It took the cops a few minutes to get to where he'd lost them. They found the truck but not the woman. Four men took her and fled into the woods. The local law enforcement doesn't have immediate access to tracking animals. They'd have to wait for daylight and it may be too late for her by that time. The sheriff thought of us. A few of our officers are heading there with me to help and I thought you would want to go with us."

Valiant hated the idea of any woman at the mercy of human males. They were unstable and mean. "I'm sorry for that female but I still don't understand why you came here. You're wasting time by talking to me if you plan to search for her. You should go after her instead."

"To make matters worse, when the sheriff and his deputies found the truck, they searched it, looking to identify the owner. They realized these guys are members of one of those anti-New Species extremist groups. They had some flyers inside the truck that pointed to that conclusion." Tiger hesitated. "They took Tammy."

Shock tore through Valiant. "My Tammy?"

Tiger nodded grimly. "Yeah. Your Tammy. I thought you'd want to help find her." He paused. "I figured you'd still remember her scent well enough to be able to track her faster."

A roar erupted from Valiant. Rage gripped him at the thought of males attacking his Tammy. Hate groups killed humans who associated with Species. Her beautiful face surfaced in his mind instantly. He panted, going insane a little at the thought of what they'd do to her and he struggled to think.

Tiger flinched. "I take it you're coming?"

Valiant spun around and sprinted for his home. "Let me get a few things," he snarled loudly. "Do not leave without me. I'm going to tear them apart with my bare hands if they have harmed her in any way."

"I figured!" Tiger yelled.

Valiant stormed back outside a few minutes later. Tiger noticed the shoes Valiant had donned and glanced at his thigh. He didn't say a word about the wicked-looking knife strapped to it, but instead just climbed into the Jeep. Valiant jumped into the passenger seat. Tiger waved an arm in the air to signal the two other vehicles behind them to follow.

"I'm going to kill them if they hurt her," Valiant swore.

Tiger bit his lip. "Remember, we're not going to be on Reservation. Their law might have a problem with that but they did kidnap a woman. Keep in mind that their law is going to come down harshly on them when we capture them. I want to make sure you realize that. Couldn't you just maim them a little and let them live? It would be bad press to return these humans in pieces to their law enforcement."

Valiant growled. "It depends on if they hurt her or not."

"That sounds fair enough to me." Tiger punched the gas.

* * * * *

White-haired Sheriff Cooper, who appeared to be in his midfifties, gaped openly as at the four New Species who climbed out of three Jeeps. Tiger had told Valiant the human's name on the way there and warned him to try to be polite. Valiant had snarled.

He just wanted to find Tammy. He didn't give a damn about impressions they made or if Justice wanted them to be nice. Tiger seemed to think it was a big deal that humans would ask them for help, a first step to acceptance by the town, but Valiant figured they were just desperate enough to ask anyone for aid.

His gaze darted to the other three Species. Tiger, Brass and Rider wore their uniforms. The sheriff seemed to fixate on Valiant the most and fear widened the human's eyes. It could be because he didn't wear a uniform, instead sporting jeans and a gray sweater he'd tossed on when Tiger's presence had awoken him. He met the sheriff's direct gaze and realized the human seemed unable to look away from his face. He resisted baring his teeth to really put on a show. Obviously it wasn't the jeans that put the guy off as much as his facial features.

The human seemed to get a grip on his fear and stepped closer to them as they approached. He cleared his throat and held his hand out to Tiger, who had taken the lead to meet with the group of humans waiting at the side of the road. "I'm Sheriff Greg Cooper and these are my deputies. Thank you for coming. You got here very quickly and we deeply appreciate it."

Tiger stopped near the human and shook his hand. "I'm Tiger. These are my men." He released the guy's hand to point. "That's Brass, Rider and Valiant. We're glad to be of service, Sheriff Cooper. Has anything changed since you called us?"

Sheriff Cooper shook his head. "No. I don't know how this could happen. I've known Tammy Shasta since she moved here when she was just eight years old and I don't know anyone who'd want to hurt her. She's a nice little gal. Our pastor is the one who witnessed those men snatch her and he followed them out this way. The truck they used to abduct her broke down about a mile from this road. They tore out the oil pan and the engine seized up. Those men are strangers to this area because Pastor Thomas knows everyone who lives out this way and they aren't anyone he recognized."

Tiger nodded. "We'll take it from here. You're more than welcome to come with us if you want. We can track anything between us two cats and the two canines."

"I insist on it," the sheriff stated as he gave them all a nervous glance, seeming unsure about not being there to watch whatever they did. "I've seen a lot of things in my life and when we find Tammy, I have a bad feeling that if she's still alive, she might want to see a familiar face. I can't think of why four men would grab a pretty woman unless it's for the worst. I have an ambulance on standby if they didn't just rape and kill her flat out." He paused, frowning. "Two cats and two canines?"

Valiant snarled and startled all the humans around him as they backed away fearfully, their gazes locked on him. If any of the humans had put their hands on Tammy sexually he'd tear their fingers off. He'd rip their arms from the sockets while they screamed and then proceed to beat them with the their own limbs. He'd —

Tiger spoke, ending his violent plotting. He flashed a warning look Valiant's way, silently conveying that he needed to keep a leash on his rage. "Valiant and I are feline species while Brass and Rider are canines."

"Oh." The sheriff seemed at a loss for words.

Valiant's irritation couldn't be contained. Tiger wanted to play polite with the humans but he just wanted to hear what the sheriff knew to help him track Tammy. He hated wasting time. He lifted his lip to flash fangs at Tiger, conveying a silent message of his own. He wasn't patient and the bullshit needed to stop. A gasp from the humans made him glare at Sheriff Cooper, who stumbled backward, his gaze horrified, and stared at his mouth.

"Are those…"

"Teeth," Tiger acknowledged. "Don't worry about Valiant. He's just very angry that the woman was taken and wants to go after her right now."

The sheriff finally glanced at Tiger. "I sent somebody to her car at the bar where she was grabbed to see if he could find something of hers that would have her scent. I know when we use hounds they need something from the victim. My deputy should return with it at any time. He radioed in that he has her jacket."

Tiger pointed to Valiant. "That won't be necessary. We've both met her. She did a catering job at Reservation and they've become friends. That's why he's here. He spent more time around her than I did. He's very familiar with her scent. He'll have an easier time tracking her."

The sheriff shot a horrified glance Valiant's way. "Well, I guess that's good. That means you fellas know what a nice gal she is and that we've got to find her before the kidnappers have time to really hurt her."

"I'm going after her," Valiant snarled, done listening to them waste time when Tammy needed him. "You stand here bullshitting. I'm getting her back." He took off toward the woods at a run.

"Damn, he can move fast." The sheriff sounded amazed. "I won't be able to keep up. Just go. Find Tammy. They have an hour lead."

Tiger snarled. "Wait up, Valiant. I'm right behind you."

Valiant's eyes adjusted to the darkness and followed the clear and deep impressions the truck tires had left in the long grass. He knew Rider and Brass followed him closely. They probably were under orders to make sure he didn't slaughter the human males when he found them. Two Species males wouldn't be enough to prevent that from happening if they'd done anything bad to Tammy. Tiger should have brought a dozen males with them if that was his intention.

Valiant located the truck and smelled Tammy right away inside the back of it. He leapt into the truck bed and discovered blood. He crouched down, sniffed, and only calmed slightly when he realized it wasn't hers. He closed his eyes as he took a few breaths to memorize the stench of the males. Pure rage coursed through him because he could smell Tammy's fearful scent along with those who had taken her. He stood and jumped out of the truck. Tiger and the two security officers watched Valiant, waiting for his assessment.

"Two of them had her in the back of the truck. There's blood but not hers."

Tiger nodded. Valiant walked to the open driver's door. He stopped and sniffed, moving around it to the busted side mirror. He growled as his entire body tensed.

"What is it?" Tiger moved forward but the answer was there as he inhaled. "Blood."

"Hers." Valiant threw back his head and roared. "Her blood is on that broken mirror so they hurt her. I'll kill them for this."

Brass cleared his throat. "She fell here and ran away but they followed." He stood about ten feet from the truck near the tree line of the woods.

Valiant lunged forward. The four of them sniffed the area and studied the tracks on the ground. The small impressions were harder to detect at night. "It's not old."

"That's what the sheriff stated." Tiger confirmed. "They took her about an hour ago. Do you think she got away from them?" He stared at the smallest tracks—a female running. He glanced at Valiant. "How physically fit is she? Do you think she could outrun her attackers?"

"No," Valiant snarled. "She's small and no match for four males."

"We better find them fast," Brass growled.

The four men ran. They stopped where Tammy had been tackled and the signs of where clear to each of them that she'd impacted the ground. Valiant roared again when he discovered more of Tammy's blood.

"Easy," Tiger snarled low. "We're all allowing our animal sides to rule but we're dealing with humans. Control your instincts while we hunt. They aren't deer. Keep that in mind."

Rider growled where he crouched, examining the disturbed leaves. "One man is carrying her. His track impressions show the added weight."

"He's dead when I reach him," Valiant promised. "Let's go."

* * * * *

Tammy woke and softly cursed. Her shoulder, arm, back, and head hurt. She stopped listing what ached and tried to concentrate instead on what didn't. Her feet and her ass were fine but that was about it. She forced her eyes open to stare at a blazing campfire. She rested on her side facing it, a few feet away from the flames. She turned her head, only to instantly regret it.

Four men sat on a fallen log glaring at her. One of them, Terry, had his cowboy boots off. Dried blood stained his chin and shirt. She'd head-butted that one. Another one had strips of his torn shirt stuffed up his nose that seemed to be actively bleeding, while another one had his hand clamped over his arm where bloody claw marks from her fingernails assured her he'd been one of the jerks in the back of the truck with her. The fourth man appeared unhurt.

She looked away from them and glanced at the trees surrounding them. She had been placed on grass but as she tried to lift up, she couldn't move her arms. She tugged and realized they were bound behind her. She glared at the men.

"My leather belt is wrapped around your wrists, you little hellion. You just stay down." It was the unhurt man who spoke in an angry tone. "I still say we should just kill her. Look at all the shit we're in because of her. She broke Ned's nose when she kicked him in the face on her way out of the truck."

Surprise registered to Tammy. She didn't remember doing that but hid a smile, happy it had happened. She vaguely remembered using her feet to help kick off to shove her upper body from the bed of the truck. She'd thought she'd used the floor to do it. The fact that it had actually been his face made it better.

"I think two of my teeth are loose. She slammed her head into my mouth," Terry said and grunted while he glared at her. "I say I take my belt and blister her ass with it."

"Stop all of that whining," the guy with the scratched arm ordered. "We need her help. You heard what our informant on the inside of that animal land told us. One of those animals grabbed and carried her off. We need to convince her to go public and tell everyone what he did to her to gain support for our cause."

"Like that bitch is going to do that." Ned paused. "Right. She broke my nose. She's as much of an animal as they are. Did she come with us peacefully the way a real lady would? Hell no. She fought as though she were an animal. Now here we are stuck in the woods without a truck. That car followed us and I'm pretty sure that guy went for help. He probably got the license plate. We probably have half of the state searching for us because she wouldn't just be reasonable."

"We should have waited, Paul." Terry frowned at the guy with the scratched arm. "He ordered us to wait to take her when he arrived. You're the dick who thought she'd be easy enough to grab. You said it would be as simple as eating pie. The boss is going to be here in a few days and he's going to tear you a new asshole and us along with you since we were dumb enough to listen to your screwed-up plan. You know the boss wants her bad, he told you he has big plans for her. He said he could talk her into doing whatever we needed her to do but now it's all turned to shit."

Chapter Five

❧

Paul cursed. "I can fix this. We can convince her to tell the press what we want but it just might take a bit more time."

"We don't have that," Terry ground out. "Our boss is going to have all of our asses for this mess. We screwed it up bad."

Paul glared at Tammy. "All you had to do was come peacefully. We're human, damn it. We're your kind. What did that animal do to you when he carried you off? Did he rape you? Did he take a bite out of you? Did he try to turn you into one of them? Tell us the truth right now!"

Tammy glared at him. "He was a gentleman and brought me tea. After that, he asked me how my day was," she lied. "He didn't toss me into the back of a truck and crush me into near suffocation, nor did he drag me out into the woods and use a belt to tie my hands behind my back. He was actually intelligent and polite."

She hoped she wouldn't go to hell over stretching the truth because while Valiant was intelligent, the polite part would be considered a little shady.

"They are animals." Terry glared at her. "You're sticking up for them?"

"You're calling *them* that? That's priceless coming from four thugs who kidnapped me." She snorted loudly and rolled her eyes.

"Bitch!" Ned yelled as he lurched to his feet. "You broke my nose. I'll show you what kind of animal I can be."

Paul gripped his arm. "Sit down."

"She's asking for it," Ned whined but he sat.

Terry sighed. "She's never going to do what we want. We should just get rid of her and tell our boss she accidently died when we grabbed her."

"You don't go against the doctor's orders ever. I told him I'd make this happen and that, in the end, he'd get her alive when we were done with her." Paul shot a frightened look at his men, seeming to be in charge of them. "Trust me. That's one man you never want to disappoint. He is allowing us to get a taped statement from her but after that, he plans to use her for one of his experiments. Our informant believes something sexual happened between her and the animal who took her. He overheard a conversation between Justice North and one of the security animals. They said she could be hurt and they wanted a doctor to check her out but she refused to press charges against the animal for rape. They didn't say attempted rape. He was clear about that."

Tammy knew the color drained from her face. Someone had leaked information to a hate group, someone close to Justice North. She'd never met him but she'd seen him in interviews on television since he was the most well-known New Species. His people had voted him into leadership as though he were some kind of president. He made most of the decisions for them. Someone obviously was spying on him and telling these men what was being said. Worse, they knew about her and Valiant. Not good.

Four pairs of eyes studied her. Tammy glared back. She guessed the only way out of the mess would be to convince them they had the wrong information. She could only hope they wouldn't kill her.

"I don't know who you've been talking to but it's bullshit. That never happened," she bluffed. "I'd find someone more reliable if you're paying that person to feed you information. Maybe you should hire them to write fiction since they seem to be good at making up stuff. Is your informant some reporter for one of those gossip rags? Did an alien attack me too?"

"She fucked one of those animals?" Terry sounded stunned as he stared at her as if she were something he'd never seen before, something disgusting. "You screwed an animal?"

She closed her eyes, counted to five, and opened them. "Listen, cowboy. Did you just hear me? Whoever told you this crap is full of it."

"That's what we were told," Paul confirmed. "He hauled her up off the ground and carried her away. Our informant heard the conversation between the head animal and his security dog."

"I think his head of security is a cat." Ned shrugged.

"Does it matter? Dog? Cat? What's the difference?" Terry snorted. "They are animals that walk around on two legs thinking they are as good as us but they aren't. They are nothing more than test rats that grew brains. I'm so sick of them breathing and seeing idiots on the news praising those abominations for what they are doing by setting up their own living environment. It's like patting a bird on the back for making a nest in their cage with newspaper bits. They are tainting our country and now they are putting their dirty paws our women. We've got to stop them."

Ned stared at Tammy. "Maybe he brainwashed her. We know it's possible." He leaned over, staring at her. "Is that why you're protecting your animal lover? Did he torture you into submission? Maybe he bit her and infected her with some disease that makes her one of them. Is that it? Are you infected? Have you started to grow a tail or fur?"

Tammy couldn't believe she'd been kidnapped by such morons. It made her almost feel ashamed that they'd succeeded. "Why don't you come over here and take a look?" She wanted to kick the son of a bitch since her legs weren't tied down.

He stood and walked toward her. Tammy tensed. When he was close enough she twisted and kicked him as hard as she could in his shin. He screamed, jumped back and fell on his ass.

"You bitch!" he yelled.

"You moron!" Tammy shouted back.

"Enough," Paul demanded. "Stay away from her. She's obviously sick in her head if she let one of them touch her. We'll have the doctor take care of her. He's a vicious son of a bitch."

"It's a good thing those animals are shooting blanks or she could have a litter of puppies if she got pregnant by that thing." It was the unhurt man who spoke while he studied her. "Do you think, if it was possible, that she'd have as many as a dog bitch would have? My pit bull had six puppies last time."

"Shut up, Mark." Paul shot him a glare. "Everyone knows they are sterile so don't even go there. It makes me sick. That's a blessing they can't have kids. They probably would breed like animals, with litters. Let's just get some sleep, rest up, and in the morning we'll hike out of here and take her to the house. Our reinforcements will hit town the day after tomorrow with the doctor. We just need to keep her alive until he arrives. That should give us plenty of time to make her tape a statement that we can send out to the press to show everyone that those things are dangerous."

Ned stumbled to his feet and glared at Tammy. "Two days waiting around with her is a long time. She loves animals, obviously. I think I know how to pass the hours." He reached for the front of his pants and started to unfasten them.

"Don't," Paul ordered. "The doctor wouldn't be happy. I know what kind of experiments he's into. He'll castrate you if you injure her in any way that might screw up his plans."

"She's already done an animal. Who really gives a fuck what we do to her as long as we don't kill her?" Ned opened his pants, shoving them down his hips.

Terror gripped Tammy as she realized he planned to rape her. Mark, the unhurt guy, stood quickly. "We don't screw with the doctor. Pull your pants back up, damn it. I don't ever want to see your dick again."

"Mark is right." Paul stood too and moved between Ned and where Tammy lay bound on the ground. "The doctor would go ballistic if you raped her. You're the new guy on the team and don't know much about what he does but he'd kill you if you jeopardize his work. He's the one who signs our paychecks. Find a whore if you want to get your rocks off or take a walk out into the woods and jerk off."

"But she's the bitch who broke my nose. I'm not just going to take that shit without some payback."

"I understand." Paul's voice lowered. "I'm angry too." He held up his arm. "I have to explain how the hell this happened to my wife when I get home. She's not stupid and this looks just like what it is. Fingernail marks. She'll be convinced I cheated on her. That pisses me off but the doctor scares the hell out of me. You can't rape her."

Mark turned his head to glare down at Tammy, his dark eyes narrowed, and he smiled in a way that turned her blood to ice. Pure glee transformed his features as he turned to face her. Whatever plan he'd hatched wouldn't be good for her.

"We won't rape her or do anything the doctor would get mad about but we need to get that statement from her." He turned his head to grin at Paul. "Do you have the video camera with you? I don't know about you guys but I'm not tired and we're stuck here until morning. I say we use the time well."

"I've got video camera function on my phone." Paul had a confused look as he dug it out of his back pocket. "But she isn't going to agree to say anything bad against them. You heard her. She's somehow been brainwashed by those animals."

Ned jerked up his pants and zipped them. "The animal infected her. I'm telling you they carry diseases. The doctor probably wants her because he knows that. I bet he's going to document it when she becomes one of them. That would definitely turn the public against them and help our cause. Everybody will panic, they'll want them dead before it spreads past their gates, and we'll finally get to watch them die."

"What are you thinking, Mark?" Paul stepped closer to study Tammy before he glanced at the other guy. "We can't do any damage. The doctor wants her healthy. He calls her a money-making opportunity. You know he's in a financial jam now. All of them are."

Mark's grin widened as he peered down at Tammy too. "There's a lot you can do to a woman without doing permanent harm or causing internal damage. We'll get her to say whatever the hell we want and make our boss happy at the same time."

Tammy whimpered at his vicious glare, knowing whatever he planned had to be horrific. She struggled against the belt that held her wrists together but they didn't allow her to wiggle out of them. When Mark dropped to his knees next to her and his hands grabbed her shirt, she cried out in fear as he shoved her onto her back and pinned her arms under her. He leaned over until his face hovered inches above her own and she could make out his hazel eyes clearly from the firelight.

"Not her face," Paul ordered. "I can video her up close but if you beat on her, do it from the neck down."

"Don't do this," Tammy begged. "I won't press charges. I'll swear it was some prank from friends who grabbed me or something. Just let me go."

Material tore as he gripped her shirt and ripped it wide open. Shock made her gasp as air hit her skin. His hands didn't stop at just parting it. He totally destroyed the thing, tossing it away once he'd yanked it out from under her.

"I still say we should rape her," Ned grumbled, stepping closer to watch. "She's got nice tits."

"Shut up," Mark ground out. "I like silence while I work." He reached down and came up holding a pocket knife. He flicked it open, hooked his finger between her breasts and sawed at her bra.

Tears blinded Tammy and she took a deep breath. A scream tore from her throat as brutal hands continued to strip her. He sliced the straps, jerked her bra completely away and tossed it into the fire. When she tried to turn away, he dropped down on her waist, straddled her, and grabbed her throat with one hand to hold her flat. She stared up at him in horror when she realized she couldn't breathe.

"I hate screaming," he hissed at her. "Shut up. You're going to tell Paul that the animal who grabbed you brutally raped you, bit you repeatedly, and whatever else you can think up to horrify the public."

She nodded, unable to speak, and just wanted air.

"She agreed." Paul chuckled." Move back and I'll film her."

The hand eased enough for her to suck in air. "I don't believe her." Mark suddenly pinched one of her nipples hard, twisting it while his finger and thumb squeezed together. Pain forced another scream from her throat. The agony subsided when he eased his vicious hold. He laughed. "This is fun." His hand slid over her rib cage to her stomach. He patted her once before he lifted his hand away.

Tammy began to sob. Her nipple throbbed, hurt badly, and she wasn't sure it was still attached. She questioned that because of the pain radiating from it. The monster sitting on her suddenly dropped his palm down hard over her belly, the sound of the slap louder than her crying, and she groaned.

"Are you having fun?" Ned stepped closer. "Let me hurt her a bit. She broke my damn nose."

The guy on top of her lifted his weight higher onto her stomach and pressed down until it hurt. His hands reached behind him and she stared into his eyes while he glared at her.

He made sure she couldn't get away as he fumbled with her jeans.

"Pull them down. Wait until I remove that underwear if you think her tits are sensitive. We won't rape her but a little bruising in that area won't make the doctor upset. It's her insides he'll be interested in."

Tammy tried to scream as her shoes and jeans were torn down her legs but Mark just leaned forward, glared at her, and clamped his hand over her nose and mouth. She couldn't breathe, her eyes widened, and it seemed to please the monster watching her struggle for breath.

"There. Got them off." Ned chuckled. "She's wearing a blue thong. She's a whore. I knew it. That's why she won't tell us she was raped by the animal. She probably wanted it and begged him to fuck her." His amusement left. "Think the doctor would care if I fucked her in the ass? That doesn't really count, right?"

"Shut up, you moron. No rape. Get over that concept already. She'll be in hysterics by the time I'm done and it's going to really look good for the video. They'll think she's really been traumatized by those animal bastards when we send it to the news stations for broadcast." Mark released her mouth so she could gasp in air and he scooted down her body to sit over her hips again. He reached up and pinched her other nipple hard, squeezed, and twisted.

The sound that tore from Tammy actually hurt her throat. She couldn't get away from the pain and worse, she heard them laughing when she ran out of air, making it clear her pain amused them greatly.

* * * * *

Frustration gripped Valiant as he dropped to his knees, pressed his nose closer to the ground and tried to pick up the stench of his enemy. The men had reached a rocky area and the wind had picked it. He refused to give up even though he'd lost the scent. His eyes narrowed as he scanned the area for any recent signs of disturbance.

"Spread out," he ordered the other Species. "Find it."

"Easy, Valiant," Tiger crooned. "You're sounding a little wild with the way you're snarling."

Valiant snapped his head around to glare at Tiger. "They have my Tammy."

"Understood." Tiger backed away, heading to the left to try to find the trail.

Valiant doubted anyone understood what he was feeling. He'd missed her and she'd occupied all his free thoughts. Her scent had faded from his bed and he'd mourned the loss. Not finding her would be unacceptable.

"Here," Rider called out softly. "I found a trace."

Valiant was on his feet with a leap, sniffed the area, and picked up the faint stench of sweaty human. One of them had rubbed against the trunk of a tree. He moved forward and scanned the darkness, searching for the easiest way to walk if he'd been a weaker human carrying a woman over his shoulder.

"Follow him," Tiger urged. "Don't let him out of your sight."

"I'm going to kill them," Valiant swore.

"That's why we're sticking close. You're so agitated that you might get her and us killed." Tiger closed the distance between them, keeping close behind him. "Think before you act."

"I'm going to do whatever it takes to save her."

"That's what we're afraid of," Rider sighed. "We want to rescue the female too but be smart about it."

"Leave him alone," Brass growled. "I understand wanting to protect a female. I am very close to Trisha. They aren't as strong as our females and this Tammy won't be able to defend herself. That's why I wanted to come along. Harley and Moon wished to come as well but knew you didn't want to overwhelm the humans with too many of us. If these males have harmed Val's female he should get to kill them. They are assholes who need killing."

Valiant snarled in agreement.

"Great. Really helpful, Brass." Tiger shot him a glare.

Brass shrugged. "It's the truth."

A high-pitched scream rent the air, coming from the east, and Valiant responded at the pained call of his woman. He threw back his head as he darted forward to find her.

* * * * *

"She's going to say whatever the hell you want her to, Paul. See?" Mark laughed. "It's all just a matter of convinc—"

A loud roar suddenly shattered the night. Tammy's ears rang from the sound. She'd heard that roar before. Valiant was out there and close.

Tammy glared at the jerk who pinned her down. He frantically swiveled his head toward the woods around them, searching for the source.

"What in the fuck was that?" Ned inched closer to the fire, peering around the woods.

"I don't know," Terry whispered. "It was close."

"Was that a lion?" Ned whispered. "Are those common in this part of northern California?"

"I don't know," Mark whispered back. "I know they have cougars and bobcats in mountainous areas." His hand eased away from her breast and he fumbled behind his back at his waist. "It's close though. Prepare for an attack. Her screams probably drew it, thinking there's food to be had." He withdrew a handgun he'd had tucked in his waistband under his shirt.

"That didn't sound like either one." Terry reached down, tugged up the leg of his jeans and revealed a gun holster. He yanked the weapon out as he straightened. "Whatever it is, it's nearby."

Tammy sucked air into her lungs and screamed again, despite her sore throat. She wanted Valiant to find her and figured it would make it easier if she helped.

"Shut her up." Ned sounded panicked.

Mark gripped her jaw to force her mouth closed. He glared down at her. "Do it again and I'll smother you until you pass out."

Ned and Terry moved away from Tammy. Her relief was instant that their focus wasn't on her anymore. They took positions around the fire to watch the woods. Her heart hammered with hope that Valiant would save her. *How does he know I'm in trouble? Why did he come for me? Does it matter? Hell no. He's here.*

It had to be Valiant unless there were other New Species who could roar the way he could. That was possible. Either way, she knew nothing lived in the area before the New Species arrived that could make that kind of roar. It had to be one of them and she'd never been so grateful in her life to have them as neighbors.

A howl broke the silence, startling Mark. Ned cursed softly, spun to face another section of woods, and his gun lifted. "Shit."

Mark looked terrified as he jerked his head around. "Was that a wolf?"

"A wolf and a lion?" Terry hissed a curse. "Shit. It's not real animals out there. It's them. Those damn two-legged animals."

Another howl broke the night and another one joined in. Tammy tried to twist away from the asshole who still held her mouth but he grabbed her throat suddenly and clamped down tight. He glared at her.

"You move an inch and I'll strangle you. Don't scream either."

She believed him. He appeared terrified and she could see sweat breaking out over his upper lip and forehead. He released her throat and lifted his hips off her enough that she was no longer pinned. He gave her a warning glare.

"Don't move or I'll kill you. Got it?"

She nodded very carefully, keeping her lips sealed. She had heard them say that whoever they worked for wanted her alive but judging by their terror, they weren't thinking clearly anymore. Her gaze shifted to the guns the men held. Even Ned and Paul had guns now. Fear for Valiant's safety worried her. Or, if it wasn't him, for the other New Species who were out in the woods coming after her.

"If any of you are out there and can hear me," Mark screamed. "I'll kill the bitch if you attack at us."

Ned inched close to the fire. "What do we do?"

Terry held his gun, watching the dark woods. "We wait until morning when we can see good, because they have the advantage in the dark. As long as we keep a gun on her, they won't dare attack. They obviously want her. Keep the fire burning bright to keep them back."

"Maybe we should put her clothes back on her so they don't know we messed with her any," Ned whispered.

"I'm not moving." Mark shook his head. "I don't give a damn if they are pissed that we stripped her down to her underwear. I'm close enough to blow her brains out if they come at us."

"We could make them rush us and take them out." Terry held a gun in one hand and a knife in another, slowly turning circles to keep a close watch on the woods outside the circle of firelight. "One of us could hurt her to force them to come in and we'll have the advantage. There are only three of them and we can handle that many of those upright animals."

"How do you know there are only three?" Ned whispered. "There could be dozens of them watching us right now. They could have us surrounded."

"I heard two wolf howls and one roar." Paul stated. "I agree with Terry. There are only three of them and if there were more they would have sounded out to go for ultimate intimidation. My guess is they are closing in on us and are doing it to give positions. It's basic hunting tactics when using animals. It's to sound out to know where the prey is so you don't shoot each other when you have a few teams closing in on the same target."

"They carry guns?" Ned whined. "Nobody told me that."

"Fuck yeah," Terry nodded. "I saw them when I joined that rally a few months back at their Homeland. They were lined up along the top of a wall with sharpshooters defending the gates in case any of us decided to try to break in again."

Tammy knew with certainty the jackasses who'd kidnapped her would shoot the New Species. Did her rescuers know the jerks were armed? Her gaze darted to the nervous assholes again and she slowly drew a deep breath in. She was willing to bet her life that they wouldn't kill her outright. She knew she'd become the only leverage they had to keep the New Species from coming at them.

* * * * *

Valiant lunged toward the camp when the smell of Tammy's fear filled his nostrils. The urge to protect her, to help her, became so overpowering he couldn't even form coherent thoughts anymore.

An unexpected, heavy weight landed on his back and his knees collapsed. Two strong arms wrapped around him, one around his throat to cut off his oxygen and another hooked around his chest under his arms. He grabbed at the male body but the words hissed in his ear prevented him from fighting.

"She'll be dead before you can reach her. Calm now," Tiger demanded. "Think, my friend." The arm around his throat eased. "Take a few deep breaths, fight your instincts, and trust me."

Valiant sucked in air through his mouth, bit back a roar and knew Tiger made sense. "The humans would kill her. I need to get to her." He kept his voice low to keep it from carrying to the camp.

"We need to get to her without them killing her first. I understand and I can feel your rage. I smell it. You want to save her and so do I. We have to do it right. Look. See the fire? Do you notice the male with the gun sitting on top of her? He's there to shoot her if we rush them."

Valiant noticed more than the human pinning his Tammy down. They'd stripped her, her pale skin exposed to the chilly night air and to the view of the males who had stolen her. Murderous rage gripped him until his entire body shook from the emotion.

"I know," Tiger crooned softly. "I can smell how strongly you want to rip their hearts out and tear their heads from their bodies. It will get her killed. Are you in control?"

He shook his head before he nodded. "Yes," he rasped.

Tiger's hold around his chest eased and his weight left his back as he stood. A howl from Rider sounded on the other side of camp. He was in place. It made thinking a little easier for Valiant to know the humans were surrounded. The Species males would attack from the other direction to draw attention. He just needed to wait a few moments before he'd reach Tammy. He'd protect her and murder the males who had stolen her.

Tiger eased down to a crouch next to him. "I'll allow you to take out the male on her. Use your knife. We'll open fire when you strike. She's safer on the ground, Valiant. Leave her there and don't go into the open. They will fire at you. You won't be able to help her if you're dead. You're a big son of a bitch but half a dozen holes torn through you would take you down. Do you understand me?"

"Yes." He didn't want to though.

"Prepare, but wait until you have a perfect opportunity."

85

Valiant stood, his hand going for the knife strapped to his thigh and tested the weight of it in his palm. His focus fixed on the male straddling Tammy's hips, rage boiled, and he knew he wouldn't miss.

"Go for her when we're clear. Take her away and we'll clean them up."

"I want them all dead. I want to do it."

"Her, Valiant. Focus on her. Take her away the second you get a chance to grab her when we pin the males down with gunfire but not before. You can't help her if you're dead. Remember that, damn it."

"I'll remember." His gaze narrowed, he fought back another roar and couldn't wait to kill the bastard who sat on his Tammy.

"They have guns," Tammy screamed out, making sure the New Species were warned about what they were facing from her attackers if they entered the camp.

Mark clamped his hand around her throat but it had come too late. She'd been able to call out to the New Species. They had to have heard her, she hoped at least, as she glared up at the asshole on top of her. If looks could have killed, she knew her life would end with those hazel eyes glaring at her.

"It's a sad day when someone picks an animal over their own kind," Paul grunted. "Back to back, men. Shoot anything that moves."

Tammy frantically struggled with the belt holding her wrists. It didn't help that they were pinned under her ass, making it tougher to wiggle free. She was careful not to brush against Mark's spread thighs where they straddled her hips. She became aware that his hold didn't ease and she couldn't breathe. As seconds ticked by she realized he didn't plan to let go.

Panic gripped her and she jerked both knees up. He cursed when they hit his back, had to release her to use his palm to catch his weight before he pitched forward, choosing to let go of her throat instead of his gun. Tammy gasped in air and let her legs drop.

"Don't do that, bitch," he hissed at her.

"I couldn't breathe," she gasped.

He glared at her. "Fucking bit—"

Tammy stared at Mark as his words were cut off and his eyes widened. His mouth stretched open, almost if he were going to scream, but only a very soft hiss came out. His gaze lowered slowly to the knife handle that protruded from his chest. Red suddenly flowed from his mouth and splattered on Tammy. The warm, wet, bright blood spread over her bare skin.

Tammy reacted after a split second of utter horror. She twisted hard and lifted her hips, bucking her body toward the fire. Mark's weight shifted, crumpled, and Tammy rolled hard in the opposite direction to get out from under him completely. Once free, she used her shoulder to brace her upper body on the grass since her hands were bound behind her back.

She crouched on her shoulder and knees, ignoring the debris from the ground that dug into her skin. She heard someone fire a gun, the sound really loud, and all hell broke loose as more gunfire erupted a heartbeat later. She didn't know if they shot at her or not. She struggled to her feet in frenzied desperation and bolted for the darkness of the woods.

Tammy kept moving even though some bullets tore up tree trunks around her but she didn't stop. She left the campfire behind without feeling anything strike her body and managed to avoid running into any trees. Once the firelight faded it left her totally blind.

She ran until her shoulder slammed into a low branch and the impact sent her sprawling to her knees. She fought her way to her feet and painfully leaned against the rough bark, trying to catch the breath that had been knocked from her lungs and ignored the roughness against her skin.

A male screamed behind her — a horrible, painful sound, but it motivated her to keep moving. She jerked her wrists but the leather still refused to give. Frustration and fear battled as she stumbled forward. She wanted to put distance between the bullets and her.

She walked and prayed her vision would adjust to the darkness. It sounded as though a war was being waged behind her with guns going off and all the yelling that shattered the night. Tammy could finally make out dim shapes and her pace increased to a fast walk. She didn't make it far until something suddenly shifted into her path. The shape moved in from the side — something big, whatever it was, and it came right at her.

She opened her mouth to scream as she attempted to twist away to run in a new direction but it moved faster. Large hands grabbed her waist.

"Tammy," Valiant rasped.

She froze. The hands pulled her against a cloth-covered chest. She inhaled the masculine scent she hadn't forgotten. In that moment she admitted she'd missed it and him. His big body felt warm and large with his arms secured around her waist in a hug. Her knees gave out but she didn't fall. He kept her firmly against him.

"I've got you."

Tammy's fingers itched to grab hold of him but she couldn't. She sniffed and fought her tears of relief that he'd found and saved her. She'd been terrified. Those men had hurt her but she knew safety in Valiant's arms. Her nightmare had ended. He'd make sure they didn't get a chance to take her again. She had absolute faith in that.

"I'm going to sit you down and give you my shirt," he softly rasped. "Your skin is cold. Do you understand me?"

She nodded against his chest and Valiant softly growled as helped her down to a patch of chilly grass. She stared up at his dark shape when he crouched in front of her. He wasn't more than a big, comforting shadow in the darkness with a raspy voice. Cloth brushed her leg.

"Raise your arms for me."

"I can't. My hands are bound behind my back."

He cursed. "I forgot. I'm so enraged it's hard for me to think straight."

Valiant wrapped his arms around her once again. Tammy appreciated and felt comforted by his warmth and the security of being inside his arms. He worked the leather belt with gentle fingers and yanked it open to free her wrists. She moved her arms forward and whimpered at the pain that shot up both of them. Even her shoulders ached from being secured in the same position for too long.

"I'm going to kill them," he growled. "Every one." He leaned back until some space opened between their bodies and he gripped her wrists gently to brush his thumbs over her injured skin. "I smell blood on you."

Valiant lifted her hands to his face and inhaled. He did the last thing she expected. She jumped but didn't yank away as his tongue gently licked the painful, burning area of her wrist. It actually made the excruciating sensation fade. He turned to her other wrist and used his tongue on it.

"What are you doing, Valiant?"

"Does it hurt less?"

She nodded but remembered he probably couldn't see well in the dark either. "Yes."

She noticed when it suddenly grew unusually quiet. The sounds of the forest completely died along with the gunshots. Only the soft breeze in the tree branches above sounded in the eerie moment.

"They will come soon and I need to get you clothed," Valiant urged softly. "I'm going to put my sweater on you." He released her hands.

"Who's coming?" Fear gripped her, hoping he didn't mean the men who'd kidnapped her.

"My people will search for us and it won't take them long. Don't worry. Those men who stole you are taken care of one way or another. Lift your arms for me."

Between the two of them they managed to put his sweater over her head and damaged wrists. The thick, soft material was still warm from his body and it smelled of Valiant. He helped her to her feet and she realized his sweater hung down to her mid thighs, more of a minidress on her shorter frame. He rolled the sleeves to her elbows.

"I don't want the material to rub your injured wrists," he explained.

"Thank you." It touched her that he'd be so thoughtful.

Tammy saw his form shift in the darkness as Valiant stepped back and his arms rose. The little moonlight straining through the treetops reflected something white. Material ripped. "Hold still for me, Tammy. I'm going to carry you and I'm using my tank top to protect your modesty. I'll use it to fashion you some shorts."

He dropped down to his knees in front of her. His head was level with her chest even on his knees. *He is freakishly tall,* she remembered. He pushed his sweater up to just under her breasts. She wasn't even embarrassed to be naked with him. He softly urged her to hold it in place.

From the feel, he slid part of his shirt between her legs and tied each side at her hips to cover her panties. It reminded her of what a Sumo Wrestler would wear. He stood and she let the sweater drop. Valiant stepped closer.

"I'm going to lift you. You're barefoot and injured. You're safe now and no one will hurt you."

"I know," she said softly. "Thank you."

He remained silent for a long moment. "You never thank me for protecting you, Tammy. You're mine. It's my duty and my honor."

His words stunned her into silence. She'd never had a man say that to her before, never expected one to either, but everything about Valiant was special. She couldn't see any of her past boyfriends charging into the woods at night to try to save her life. Tears filled her eyes and she rapidly blinked them back. She feared he'd get more upset if she totally lost it and crumpled into sobs at his big feet.

He leaned in and very gently wrapped one arm behind her back and hooked his other arm behind her knees to cradle her in his arms. He did it easily, as though she didn't weigh a thing. Without hesitation, Tammy wrapped her arms around his neck and hugged him tightly.

His bare skin comforted her. She rested her head on his hot skin near the curve of his shoulder when Valiant walked with her. Exhaustion and pain had drained her both physically and mentally. The sway of Valiant's careful stride soothed her.

Chapter Six

✂

Noise roused Tammy. She realized she'd either passed out or fallen asleep. Valiant still carried her. She inhaled his wonderful scent and his warmth surrounded her as firmly as his arms did. He softly growled.

"Humans are ahead of us. We'll walk out of the woods soon but I'll warn you now, I go where you do. They will want their doctor to examine you and I would insist on that, Tammy. Just tell them to allow me to stay at your side. I'll fight anyone who tries to take you from my sight."

"Just don't roar or growl at anyone, please." She lifted her head. "You're scary enough without that."

He stopped walking for a moment. She could barely make out his face in the dim moonlight but he nodded. "Just don't think I'm going to let you go. I did that before and look what happened. You might have been killed tonight. Those men wouldn't have been able to take you if you'd stayed with me. No one would have gotten that close to you without dying first."

Guilt ate at her. "About that lamp…"

His face snapped in her direction and he growled low, his chest vibrated and he sucked in air. "I don't want to speak of it."

"I didn't want you to get hurt." She said the words quickly.

He turned his head away, sniffed the air, and proceeded to walk. "We'll speak later. You're safer with me. I will protect you, and don't try to flee me again. It would be foolish."

She couldn't argue with his statements. She didn't want to admit it but she didn't want Valiant to go far from her either. She'd spent the last five weeks missing and thinking about him. It could be the trauma she'd survived and the fact that he'd saved her life, had come for her even though he had to be angry at her for hitting him with the lamp, but being in his arms felt right.

"I'm sorry."

Valiant stared into her pretty eyes. The day she'd fled from his home she'd gotten the drop on him, sneaked right up behind him, and he'd never sensed her coming. He'd underestimated her and it had been a costly mistake that had allowed her to leave him. Regret was an easy emotion to read on her face and he liked that he could identify her emotions.

"I was distracted by the males coming for you."

"I know. I totally used that to my advantage. Did I hurt you?"

His head wound had quickly healed but inside he hadn't. He'd wanted to keep her but she'd abandoned him. He remembered the rare times females had been brought to his cell when he'd been a prisoner. A lifetime of rejection filtered through his memories.

Most of the Species females had been too terrified of him to allow his touch. A primate female had shrieked and cried until one of the techs had returned to take her away. He'd known none of them had wanted him to breed with them but some had taken pity on the lonely male he'd been.

Seeing his kind had been rare and engaging in sex with them had been even rarer. Tammy had rejected him at first but she'd responded to his touch as no other female ever had. He didn't have the breeding skills that most of the males had learned but he hadn't felt inadequate with Tammy in his arms and on his bed. He'd been very motivated to use every sexual bit of advice the females had given him during those rare times they had allowed him to mount them.

Tammy mattered to him and it worried him deeply that she'd want to leave him again. He'd known confinement and didn't want to do that to her. Making her a prisoner inside his home might make her hate him. To threaten was one thing but in reality, he never wanted to hurt her in any way. He'd have to convince her to stay of her own free will.

He wasn't sure how to do that and needed to figure it out quickly. The humans would want to take her away from him. Many of them feared Species, believed they would harm humans, and he knew his appearance didn't help. He looked less human than the other males of his kind. Not that they would fit in with a group of humans but they weren't as intimidating. There wasn't anything he could do about his looks but he could try very hard to act more civilized.

He held back a growl. Playing nice with humans and acting docile wasn't something he would ever have believed he'd do for anyone. Staring into Tammy's eyes changed everything though. It was all a matter of what he wanted to keep most. Her or his pride. It was a difficult thing to swallow but he made a decision.

"I'll try to speak nice to the humans for you, Tammy. I wish to stop this talk. It isn't a good discussion."

Point made and taken. Valiant didn't want to talk about the day she'd escaped his house. "Just let me do the talking, okay?"

He shrugged. "Fine, but just remember, I go where you do. I'm going to become very scary if someone tries to take you away from me, sexy."

"Deal." She relaxed in his arms.

She got a warm feeling when he called her sexy. *Yeah, right. I need a shower in the worst way.* She'd been pinned on a ground and didn't have to touch her hair to know it had become a ratted mess with dirt and God only knew what else stuck inside it. She'd been crying, her body was bruised, and she knew she had dried blood on her face. She was the anti-sexy if there ever was one but it was sweet that he'd lie that boldly to make her feel good.

Cars were parked along both sides of the road when they walked out of the woods. The sheriff, some deputy cars, and an ambulance were among them. More cars were parked on the grass next to the pavement, including a large white van with lettering on the side. The voices suddenly stopped in the area lit by car headlights. Tammy knew they'd been spotted as a hush settled.

Sheriff Cooper ran toward them with one of his deputies, Carl Bell, right on his heels. "Tammy!"

She forced a brave smile. "I'm fine. Valiant and his friends saved me."

The sheriff hesitated a few feet from the much taller and bigger New Species holding her. He glanced nervously between Tammy and Valiant. "You can hand her to me, son." Greg Cooper held out his arms.

Valiant shook his head. "I'll take her to the ambulance. She's been hurt."

"Where are the men who took her?" The sheriff's gaze searched the dark woods behind them.

Valiant shrugged. "It isn't my problem. The only thing I care about is Tammy. I'm sure my people will bring her attackers to you if there's anything left of them." He stepped around the stunned sheriff and deputy to take Tammy to get medical attention.

Tammy wanted to flinch when she peered over Valiant's shoulder as he strode away from the duo. Sheriff Cooper stared at the woods for a few seconds more before he turned. She didn't miss the curious glance that passed between him and his deputy, who shrugged. Both men quickly jogged to catch up to them.

Tammy knew both people waiting by the ambulance. She'd gone to high school with Bart Homer and he grimly watched as Valiant gently eased Tammy down onto a gurney he'd yanked out as they approached. Debra Molmes, the other paramedic, was a woman a few years younger than Tammy but she'd gone to school with her older brother.

"Shit." Debra gawked at Valiant and swallowed hard, a look of wariness crossing her features. She tore her gaze from him and visually examined Tammy. Debra flinched. "Jesus. You're a mess, Tam."

"It's been a rough night for me and I'm sure I'm not looking my best."

"Uh, excuse me, sir," Bart said softly to Valiant. "I, uh, need in there to help examine Tam."

Valiant hesitated a second before stepping out of the way. A bare-chested, huge, buff Valiant was something to behold. He appeared massively masculine in a sexy way when he wasn't growling and showing off his sharp teeth in a silent snarl. Tammy met his gaze with a forced smile. He crossed his arms over his chest, which only showcased his bulky, muscular arms. He returned her regard with a grim look. Tammy turned her head and caught Debra nearly mooning over Valiant. She seemed to have gotten past her initial uncertainty about how to react to him.

"Tammy?" Sheriff Cooper stepped closer. "You need to tell us exactly what happened. Have you ever met those men before? Did they tell you why they kidnapped you?"

Tammy tried not to wince as Bart and Debra checked her over and cleaned her wounds. Her face hurt when they washed away the blood and treated the area near her ear where her cheek had slammed into the side mirror of the truck. Her wrists hadn't hurt much after Valiant tended to them.

As the paramedics worked, she slowly told the sheriff what had happened when she'd left the bar and how the men had grabbed her but she skipped some parts. She chose not to mention anything related to the New Species except to say they'd made comments that made it clear they hated them. She flat-out lied.

"They said they knew I'd gone to New Species Reservation." She tried to stick to some of the truth to keep her story straight. "They targeted me because I had worked there and they accused me of being a traitor to humanity for liking New Species."

Sheriff Cooper sputtered with anger. "Those assholes took you because you worked on Reservation one time? Damn. The entire town is going to be targeted by those assholes next if that's all it takes to set them off. Where in hell are your pants and why are you wearing his sweater?"

"They…" She dropped her gaze, unable to look at the sheriff while she spoke, afraid she'd burst into tears if she did. "They stripped me, held me down and tortured me," she got out. She couldn't look at the man she'd known most of her life as heat flamed her cheeks. "That's why I'm wearing Valiant's sweater. He and the other New Species got to me before they seriously injured me but they stripped me down to my panties."

"Son of a bitch," Sheriff Cooper cursed. "Did they rape you, Tammy?"

She shook her head. "No. One of them wanted to but the others were happy to settle for just hurting me. They wanted me to make some video stating I hated New Species too. They were nuts."

Sheriff Cooper turned to Valiant and offered his hand, to shake. "Thank you, Mr. Valiant. The entire town owes you and your friends a great debt of gratitude for stopping those bastards from killing her."

Valiant frowned but he took the sheriff's hand. "Don't thank me. She's mine and I will always protect her."

Tammy winced as she shot Valiant a warning look and shook her head at him. "Remember our agreement about how I do all the talking?"

He released the sheriff's hand and shrugged. "It's true."

Sheriff Cooper looked confused as he spun to face Tammy. "What does that mean? You're his?"

She hesitated. "We're involved." She left it at that.

"Oh." The sheriff's eyes widened as he jerked his attention to Valiant first and then back to Tammy, his gaze ping-ponged back and forth. "I never would have guessed you two would date. Nope."

"Miss Shasta!" a woman yelled. "Can you give an interview?"

Stunned, Tammy turned her head to watch a woman and a cameraman attempt to shove past one of the deputies to reach the back of the ambulance.

Sheriff Cooper took a few steps away to yell at his men. "Shove those reporters back. No comment, you ambulance chasers. Get them back, Byron and Vince. I mean it."

"Why are reporters here?" Tammy wasn't happy about the situation at all.

The sheriff uttered another curse word under his breath. "Some idiot let it get out that a woman had been kidnapped and that we contacted New Species Reservation for help. Those nasty newshounds showed up by the vanloads and our phones at the station are being bombarded with calls from press from everywhere in the world."

"You need to get her out of here," Tiger informed the sheriff, walking from the front of the ambulance. "It will quickly escalate into a media frenzy otherwise. We also have to leave the scene immediately."

"Did you catch those men?" Sheriff Cooper faced Tiger.

Tiger hesitated. "We captured three of them and transported them by helicopter to Reservation. Didn't you hear it? The fourth one is dead but it couldn't be avoided." His pretty catlike gaze met Valiant's for a few seconds before he focused back on the sheriff. "They had weapons and refused to surrender. One of my men has been shot too but he'll live. It was just a flesh wound. We'll put the dead man on ice until you can arrange to have him picked up at our medical facility. I gave one of your deputies a detailed description of where they were camped out, holding Miss Shasta. It should be easy for you to find the crime scene."

"You had a helicopter out there?" The sheriff seemed surprised. "Where are my prisoners?"

"We will transport them to your station when they are medically cleared by our doctors, who are treating them at this moment." Tiger studied Tammy before he returned his attention to the sheriff. "They are receiving medical attention at our facility but you may send deputies to pick them up if you wish to transfer them that way. One of the prisoners is in critical condition and as I stated, one of my men was shot. The helicopter transport was faster than trying to carry them through the woods to here. We keep one on standby at Reservation at all times." Tiger glanced at Tammy again. "We have excellent medical facilities if you'd allow me to call the helicopter back to transport Miss Shasta and allow our doctors to treat her."

"They need a real hospital," Sheriff Cooper replied.

"It's fine," Bart the paramedic interrupted softly. "They have a top-rate facility. As a matter of fact, we have used them twice so far in severe, trauma situations. They have better equipment and skilled trauma doctors, something our local hospital doesn't boast. We just don't have those kinds of machines. The prisoners are better off if they were sent there." Bart gawked at Tiger, looking intimidated. "We can handle Tammy's medical needs but thank you, sir."

Tiger nodded and addressed the sheriff. "Do you want to pick up the prisoners when the doctors are done treating them or do you want us to transport them to you? We will write full reports and give you a detailed account of everything that transpired when we reached their camp. My men and I will be fully at your disposal to answer any questions you have."

"I'll come there," Sheriff Cooper decided. "Thank you so much for everything you've done tonight and I appreciate you getting right to the scene when I called."

Tiger shook his hand. "We're neighbors and that's what neighbors do. We at New Species Reservation extend our help at any time, Sheriff Cooper. We're just glad that we were able to locate Miss Shasta before they'd seriously harmed or killed her." He released his hand and stared at Valiant. "Let's move it. Rider has been shot but it's minor and Justice is expecting us to brief him by phone immediately when we return."

Valiant's expression turned scary and his voice came out a deep growl. "I will not return unless Tammy comes with me."

An irritated expression twisted Tiger's features. "You can't go with her. Her attackers were members of an organized hate group. You can bet there will be more arriving soon if four of them are in this vicinity. More of their group may already be here. I can't have you running around this small town. You're a target and if you're alone it will make you easier prey for them. There's the innocent factor too, Valiant. They could hurt anyone around you if they attempt to kill you and that includes Miss Shasta. We are under orders from Justice to return home now."

Valiant flashed sharp teeth and Tammy saw trouble brewing instantly. She knew Valiant wasn't going to leave her side. "I'll go with him," she offered loudly. "I'll go to New Species Reservation." She shoved at Debra's hands to halt her from bandaging her wrist and tried to climb off the gurney.

"Now wait a minute," Sheriff Cooper sputtered. "I need to interview you."

"You can do it at Reservation." Tammy gave a pleading look to the sheriff. "I'm scared and I'm staying with Valiant.

Please don't make a big deal out of this because I've been through enough tonight. Please? You can interview me all you want but just let me go with him."

The sheriff studied Valiant, his gaze roaming the big New Species before he sighed. "I'd think twice before trying to tangle with them. I see where you'd feel safer with him. I've seen the setup they have over there and you'd be better protected behind those patrolled walls than you'd be inside town. It's actually a good idea. I don't have the manpower to guard you from more threats or even those damn reporters. I need a statement soon if you go to Reservation."

Relief hit her. "Of course."

Valiant moved before Tammy could stand and lifted her into the cradle of his arms. Debra grabbed one of the sheets and moved forward to wrap Tammy's lap and bare legs, winking at her.

"Lucky bitch," Debra whispered.

Tammy's mouth almost dropped open. Debra winked again before turning away, muttering something under her breath that Tammy didn't catch as she climbed into the ambulance. Tammy's arms wrapped around Valiant's neck and she noticed his smile.

"What did she say? Did you hear?"

His amused gaze met hers. "I have excellent hearing." He moved his lips to her ear. "She said she'd enjoy my arms wrapped around her body and she mentioned she'd want her thighs wrapped around me too."

"Oh." Tammy blushed before the anger set in as a bit of jealousy struck. She glared at him, not enjoying his obvious amusement at what the paramedic had said.

Joy surged through Valiant when he watched anger flash in Tammy's gaze. She cared that another female found him attractive and was interested in breeding with him. Her mouth was clamped into a firm, tense line. She kept silent though.

101

He resisted grinning but he wanted to. Tammy didn't want other females to offer him their bodies. That had to mean she felt possessive of him. He'd take that as a good sign that he might be able to convince her to stay with him. He had a new weapon in his arsenal if he needed to fight to keep her at his side. He wouldn't ever use it, she was the only female he wanted, but he *was* tempted to allow her to believe he might be interested in another.

As he stared into her eyes though he didn't enjoy the sudden uncertainty he saw lurking there. Fear of rejection wasn't something good or kind. It would be mean to her allow to think he wasn't fully committed to her when there wasn't a chance he'd ever choose another female. Of course that didn't mean he couldn't enjoy the warmth that her anger made him feel.

"Do you think my attraction is so easily swayed?"

She hesitated. "I don't know."

Her honesty wasn't welcomed at that moment. "You insult me. I've made my desire for you very clear. I have no interest in any other female."

"I'm not looking my best right now and I feel a lot worse."

"You've been through a lot and you're very brave."

"Right. Sure. I wasn't feeling it. I was terrified."

"Did you stop talking?"

"No. You're the only one who has that effect on me."

A smile curved his lips.

"You find that amusing?"

"A little. I affect you in ways no other does. It pleases me to hear that."

She rolled her eyes. "Great."

"Tammy?"

She met his gaze and he resisted the urge to kiss her. Her mouth tempted him. It would be as easy as lowering his head and capturing her lips. He didn't give a damn if the humans surrounding them stared. He'd happily stake his claim on her in front of anyone, Species or human. He hesitated too long.

"What?"

Valiant enjoyed when she smiled and hoped a little teasing would do the trick. He chuckled. "I only want your thighs wrapped around me so do not get angry."

Tammy glanced away and calmed. It was nice to hear Valiant say that. She didn't know if she believed him since she believed most men were not monogamous. But again, Valiant wasn't similar to any other man she'd ever met before. *That's the understatement of the year.*

Tiger led the way and Valiant followed him to one of the Jeeps. There were a few more New Species with Tiger.

"Miss Shasta!" The male reporter yelled to get her attention. "What happened? Where are you going with them? Who is the New Species holding you?"

Tiger softly cursed. "Ignore them."

Valiant dropped into the passenger seat, keeping Tammy firmly on his lap. Tiger glanced at them and started the engine. "You know about seat belt laws, right? We're not on Reservation."

Valiant growled in response.

"Fine. I don't think we're going to be pulled over or anything but I thought I'd mention it."

"I heard and we're fine." Valiant cuddled her closer to his body. Tammy twisted her head to peer at Tiger. She shrugged and wrapped her arms tighter around Valiant. She turned back and rested her cheek against his warm chest. She felt safe. Tiger took the lead position of the five black vehicles as they drove to New Species Reservation.

"There is something you should know," Tammy said loudly so both men could hear her.

Valiant looked down at her until their gazes met and held. "What is it?"

"Can you hear me, Tiger?"

"I can. I've got good hearing."

"I didn't tell the sheriff everything about those men. They knew that Valiant had carried me into his house the day I met him. They said they have an informant who overheard a conversation between Justice North and maybe you, Tiger. They talked about their boss and how he wanted me because of what happened."

She focused on Valiant and continued, "They knew I'd slept with you. They never said the name of the man they work for but they referred to him as a doctor. They also said they wanted me to videotape statements saying horrible things to make people hate you. They said that doctor, their boss, wanted to experiment on me inside some testing facility. One of them thought I'd been infected and would turn New Species but I lied and told them nothing happened between Valiant and me. They mentioned having an informant a few times, someone close to Justice North."

"Son of a bitch," Tiger growled. "You're sure?"

"Positive." Tammy hesitated. "Does any of this make sense to you? I didn't want to tell Sheriff Cooper any of that because he'd want to know about what happened between us too."

"Did you tell anyone what happened at Valiant's home?" Tiger sounded alarmed.

"No." Tammy turned her head to peer at him. "I didn't tell anyone but I asked Ted not to mention it either. He swore he wouldn't tell a soul. He totally believed me and thinks Valiant and I, well, he thinks I told him the absolute truth. Those men tonight were certain that I had been with Valiant sexually and they said their informant had overheard a conversation between Justice North and his head of security speaking about whether I'd press charges for rape or not. They also said their boss and more men in their group were coming here the day after tomorrow."

"Not good," Tiger growled. "Justice and I had that conversation."

Valiant's arms tightened around her. Tammy looked at him. His eyes were narrowed as he glared at her with a hurt expression on his handsome, albeit scary face.

"Don't look at me that way. I never said the word rape. I said you didn't do that to me."

"She never accused you of forcing her," Tiger agreed. "She made it clear there was nothing for you to be punished over but I just wasn't sure I believed her words or not. You carried her off, Valiant. You weren't yourself that day and you were being aggressive. I considered she might be lying. Some women who are raped deny it. Justice and I had a conversation but obviously someone overheard it and fed information to those terrorist groups."

Valiant still looked angry but his hold on her relaxed while he snuggled her deeper into his arms. He sighed. Tammy closed her eyes and rested her cheek on his chest again. She was tired but managed not to doze off.

The Jeep stopped when they reached the main gates of New Species Reservation. She lifted her head and stared at the high walls that protected the property from intruders. She knew everyone in her town and the towns around theirs had been thrilled because they had hired a massive workforce to build them. Guards were lined up on top of the walls with weapons. A guard shack stood next to the gate and two heavily armed men walked out to openly study Tammy.

"Is everything all right, Tiger?"

"Yes. Miss Shasta is going to be our guest for a while."

The officer nodded. "I'll call guest housing and have them prepare her a room and get a security detail lined up."

"She's going home with me," Valiant stated firmly.

Tiger shook his head. "You can't take her to your place."

"She is going home with me," Valiant growled.

Tiger hesitated. "Valiant, you can't take her out there. You can move into the hotel if you want to stay with her. Those assholes specifically targeted her and as head of security, I'm telling you that she's safer at the hotel with all of our security nearby than she would be at your remote home. The sheriff wants to get a statement from her too and I'm sure Justice might want to talk to her. She also needs medical attention. Once things cool down, and if she wants to go home with you, we'll discuss the matter. Right now I'm pulling rank. She stays at the hotel and that's not up for debate. You can shut up and stay with her or you can go home alone."

"Fine," Valiant growled. "We stay at the hotel."

Tiger turned his attention to the waiting gate officers. "I don't want her around the other humans. She's to stay inside one of the suites with Valiant. She'll need clothes and medical attention."

"The doctors are pretty busy." The officer still studied Tammy. "Can she wait? One of those assholes is in critical condition and the docs are all operating on him."

"She will not wait second to one of the men who harmed her," Valiant snarled. "Let him die."

Tiger lifted his hands to make a gesture for Valiant to calm. "I'll call Slade and ask him to bring Trisha to care for her. All right, Valiant?"

He nodded. "I would prefer Trisha look at her anyway. I trust her with my woman."

His woman? Tammy arched an eyebrow.

Valiant scowled at her. "You are mine."

"We're a possessive lot," Tiger informed her softly.

"Really?" Tammy rolled her eyes. "I never would have guessed."

The gate officer snorted. "Valiant's got himself a human woman. I thought they were too fragile, Val."

Valiant growled at him and the gate officer to took a step back. "Just kidding." He glanced at Tiger. "You know the rules. All incoming humans are to be searched. I need her out of the vehicle."

Valiant snarled again. "You won't touch her."

Tiger intervened. "She doesn't need to be searched. All she has on is Valiant's sweater and..." his attention lowered to Tammy's waist. "And a sheet with Valiant's undershirt covering her panties. I'm vouching for her. I'm pretty sure Valiant already did a thorough search of her to make sure she wasn't too injured. Is she carrying any weapons, Valiant?"

"No."

The gate officer sighed. "Understood, fine, go on in, Tiger. I'll make those calls to the hotel and the supply building to order her some clothing."

Tiger drove through the gates when they opened. He reached for his cell and dialed. "Hi, Slade. Valiant is requesting that Trisha come look at his girlfriend. I'm driving them to the hotel. She's been injured." He paused. "Human." He paused again. "It's a long story." He listened for a few seconds. "Thanks." He hung up.

"Slade is bringing Trisha. He said he usually wouldn't bring her out this late but there's no way he's missing out on seeing this."

Valiant flashed sharp teeth to show his displeasure. Tammy frowned at the unusual comment but decided to just let it go. She wasn't sure she wanted the answers to the questions floating around in her head. She hadn't been to this part of Reservation so she carefully studied her surroundings. She saw a small two-story building.

"That's the guest housing," Tiger said. "It's where visiting humans stay. There are six two-bedroom apartments inside. It used to be the staff housing when this place was a resort but we had it remodeled. Up ahead is the hotel where most of our people live when they are here. It was remodeled as well. It's mostly one-bedroom units but there are a few two- and three-bedroom suites. We're putting you up in one of them and you should be comfortable there. All meals are served by the cafeteria but yours will be brought to your rooms. You won't be permitted to leave your suite without an escort. Do you have any questions?"

More than a few, actually. "Why don't you want me near other humans and why are we referred to in that manner? You are human too but you just have extra stuff that I don't."

Tiger chuckled. "Extra stuff as in boy parts or extra stuff as in my changed DNA?"

"Your DNA."

"We refer to your kind as human because we want to be called New Species. We've been set apart all our lives. It's difficult for everyone, including us, to consider us just plain ole human. It wouldn't be true anyway. We aren't plain ole anything."

"Thanks. Why can't I leave the suite without an escort?"

"You're going to be living inside a building that is totally New Species and you'll make some of them nervous. Most of us have a hard time trusting your kind. It will make them feel better if they see less of you and you'll be safer. Some Species aren't real keen on humans."

Valiant growled. "It might have had something to do with being locked up by them for most of our lives and dealing with the kind of men who took you tonight."

Tammy met his angry gaze "You sound as though you hate humans." She bit her lip. "Does part of you hate me too because I'm not New Species?"

He frowned at her. "I don't hate you."

"But—"

"I can only think of two humans that I don't hate and you are one of them."

"Because you're attracted to me?"

"Because you are mine."

She blinked at him. "Why am I yours?"

"Just go with it," Tiger sighed and said. "Trust me. It's going to make about that much sense. He's attracted to you, he likes you, and hell, I'd be happy enough not to question it. Remember the day you met him when he didn't seem to like you? Compare the differences in your mind and I think I've made my point."

She nodded, staring at Valiant. "I definitely prefer you liking me."

He winked at her and the gesture made her gawk at him. She'd never expected him to do that and with his catlike eyes it was just startling. He frowned.

"Did I do that wrong? I tried to put you at ease. You jumped and you have this expression on your face that I've never seen before. I can't say it is attractive."

"Don't ever wink at me again." She smiled. "Please?"

"What did I do wrong?"

Tiger parked in front of the hotel. About fifteen New Species men and women walked outside, staring openly at them, and some faces were outright hostile. Tammy instantly felt ill at ease and clung to Valiant a little tighter. The women were tough-looking, tall, and muscular. She could totally see every one of them, both male and female, playing extras in a film where they portrayed vicious villains. Worst of all, they appeared downright furious to see her.

"Tammy? What did I do wrong by winking at you?"

She forced her attention away from the large, mean-looking people glaring at her and turned her head to stare up at Valiant. "Wink at Tiger."

Valiant turned his head and winked again. Tiger laughed.

"I'm with her. Don't do that again. It just looks too weird on feline species. It looks good on humans but not so much on us."

Valiant sighed. "Fine. I won't wink at you anymore." He shifted his large body and stepped out of the Jeep with Tammy in his arms. He shifted her body easily, holding her tighter against his chest.

Fear inched up Tammy's spine. She'd only met a few New Species but now she was surrounded by at least fifteen of them that she'd never seen and they appeared to be really irritated at her arrival. They blocked the double doors into the hotel and her fright increased along with her heart rate. She hated being afraid but couldn't help it.

Tiger moved in front of Valiant and Tammy. "There's nothing to see here. This is Tammy and she's with Valiant. They are going to be staying at the hotel in one of the third-floor suites. She was attacked tonight by one of those hate groups that target us."

No one moved. Tammy shifted in Valiant's arms, gripping him tighter. She would have made him put her down, if she were able, and stood behind him. He was definitely big enough to hide behind. Valiant's arms tensed around her. She looked at him and saw he'd bared his teeth again. He glanced down at her.

"Cover your ears right now."

She released his neck and lifted her hands to do as ordered as he took a deep breath. He glared at the men and women standing in their path and roared. Tammy turned her head to watch Tiger jump about two feet after being startled by the sound.

"Move!" Valiant roared. "Now!"

Tammy watched New Species scatter as Tiger laughed. Tammy wrapped her arms back around Valiant's neck. Not even one person remained in the lobby when they walked inside as Tiger held open the doors.

"Remind me to get you the next time I need to clear a room." Tiger appeared highly amused. "I'll grab the key to the suite and meet you at the elevator."

"Thank you." Valiant turned and stormed across the lobby.

No one was anywhere to be seen. Tammy wondered how fifteen people could just disappear that way, guessing they had to have run to get away from Valiant so fast.

Her gaze returned to the man cradling her inside his arms and studied his angry features, understanding how his people could be afraid of him. She'd never forget the day she'd met him and he'd left her utterly mute with terror. That wasn't something anyone had ever been able to do in her entire life.

Chapter Seven

ಬ

"I'm taking a shower." Tammy put her hands on her hips. "Move it."

Valiant growled softly at her. "Allow Trisha to take a look at you first. She should be here soon."

"I want to get clean first. *I* can even smell me and I stink. I have," she released her hip and touched her head, "things inside my hair, maybe even some live stuff, and I can't stand it. I could be all nice and clean before the doctor gets here if you would get out of my way. I bet she would appreciate it. Now move."

"You are hurt and limping. I will go inside the stall with you if you insist on showering." He reached for the waistband of his jeans.

"No!" She glared at him. "No way. Keep the pants on. Now, behave and stop ordering me around. I know you think I'm yours but let me tell you something. I don't take orders well. I'm going to go shower alone and you are going to stay here. Now let me get past you."

He growled again but he stepped out of her path to the bathroom. "I don't take orders well either."

"I won't order you around if you don't order me around. That's fair." She stopped at the bathroom door. "Could you pretty please see if you can get me some clothes?"

"I will make a call and see if they can bring them now."

"Thank you." Tammy walked into the bathroom, flipped on the light, and closed the door. It had a lock so she pushed it.

"Unlock that!" Valiant roared.

She clenched her teeth as she turned the knob, unlocking it, and yanked open the door. "Do you know how loud you are? It's the middle of the night and I'm betting some people are probably trying to sleep. Could you please keep it down?"

"Don't ever lock a door between us or I will break it down."

Her eyebrows lifted as she stared into his golden, exotic eyes, reminding her that he wasn't completely human. She'd probably tell him off if he were a regular guy and said that to her. She'd have fled as quickly as possible thinking he was a fruitcake. Valiant didn't think the way most guys did though.

"You could get hurt if you fall and it would slow me from getting to you."

She took a calming breath at hearing his words. He'd just saved her life, she knew he had risked his life for hers, and he hadn't had to come after her in the first place. Maybe he feared she'd faint or something. She could deal with his orders if they stemmed from worry. She wasn't so sure that was the real reason but she was willing to go with it.

"Fine. I won't lock the door if you don't come in." She closed the door before he could say anything but she didn't lock it again. She walked to a mirror and flinched.

"Oh man," she sighed. "I look horrible. Look what the cat dragged in."

She instantly winced as soon as the last words passed her lips, realizing the bad pun. She glanced at the door, bit her lip, and hoped he hadn't heard what she said. Her gaze returned to the mirror when he didn't make any angry sounds she could hear. *Thank goodness. He missed that slip. There's another saying I have to forget. Cross off saying screwed and now all cat references.*

Her hair was mangled, with dirt and dried leaves sticking out of it. She had dirt on her face and since she'd cried, cleaner lines tracked down her cheeks from her tears. The only truly clean spot was the cut, purple area where she'd hit the truck's side mirror. The paramedics had cleaned it. She turned her head and saw the scratch wasn't bad but the purple area was definitely going to turn some ugly colors over the next few days.

She eased the really large sweater off her body and dropped it onto the counter to study the rest of her body, nearly crying again. She had bruises forming on her hips, on one side of her ribs and on her shoulders where one of those dickheads had shoved her down. She lifted her chin and uttered a nasty word. She could almost see a handprint under her chin in a forming bruise. Her gaze lowered to her tender breasts and she clenched her teeth when she noticed the swollen appearance of her nipples from them being nearly pinched off. Scratches marred her too from running and hitting things.

"Are you all right?" Valiant spoke right against the door.

"I'm just taking in the damage to my body and bitching to myself about it. I'm fine but mad." She removed the bandages on her wrists so they wouldn't get wet.

"Can I come in?"

"No. I'll hurry." She spun away from the mirror and attempted to untie the diaper-like thing Valiant had made for her with his undershirt. She tried next to tug it down her body but softly cursed. He'd tied knots with the ripped material and she couldn't get them undone.

"Valiant? I do need some help."

She cupped her hands over her breasts as the door suddenly opened before she could even finish speaking and he stepped inside the bathroom. His gaze locked immediately to her hands, filled with cleavage. Tammy bit her lip. *Well, he might not resemble a regular man but he sure acts as if he's one.*

"I can't get this thing you fashioned for me off. The ties are too tight."

His gaze remained locked on to her cupped breasts. She turned, presented him with her back, but stared over her shoulder to watch him. He frowned immediately, obviously not pleased she hid that view from him.

"I need help with the diaper thing. I don't need you staring holes into my boobs."

He grunted as he walked up behind her. *Wow, he's big,* she once again noted, sure she'd never get used to staring up at a six-foot-six man. His focus lowered to her covered ass and his fingertips brushed her skin right at her waist when he slipped his fingers between the material and it.

"I tried pushing it down but you tied it too tight and it won't go down over my hipbones."

She heard the material tear as he sliced through the knots he'd made. It hit the floor to pool at her feet. She twisted a little, looking at his fingers and at the ruined T-shirt on the floor. She released her breast with one hand and grabbed at his finger. She was careful to grab him by his knuckle and avoided the sharp tip. She lifted his hand up to stare in shock at his thick fingernails. They weren't really long but they were slightly pointed and obviously sharp enough to cut cloth.

"You really should cut your nails down."

He grunted again.

She released his hand looked up at him. "Thank you."

His gaze drifted slowly down her body and he growled again. "I want you."

She stepped away fast toward the shower stall. "Thank you, but get out. I am going to get clean and isn't that doctor coming?"

She stepped over the tub rim and firmly closed the nearly clear shower doors between them. He made a purring noise when she bent over to turn on the water faucets. She adjusted the temperature, deciding to ignore him if he was determined to watch her through the door.

"I need clothes, Valiant. Please?"

"Fine," he agreed loudly but he sounded irritated since his voice came out deeper than usual, something she noticed he did when he became angry or aroused.

He quit the bathroom and Tammy relaxed. It amazed her that he wanted her in the messed-up condition she was in. She turned on the shower spray and was surprised when she glanced at the fully stocked shower shelves. She turned to stare.

She'd stayed at enough hotels to expect samples. The New Species gave the real deal. She examined the two kinds of shampoo, two kinds of conditioner and they even stocked full-sized body-soap dispensers. There were two razors—one pink, one blue—shaving cream and a pumice stone with a handle on it. She smiled over it. *They really go all out for their guests.*

She showered quickly and unfortunately found a cut on the back of her head when the shampoo made it burn. She shaved her legs with the pink razor, stalling a little on time so she wasn't alone with Valiant too long before the doctor arrived. She knew he wanted her and she wasn't certain how to handle that.

She dried off and wrapped a towel around her head and another around her body. She stood there a second and sighed. She was clean and she couldn't hide inside the bathroom forever. She opened the bathroom door and gripped the towel tightly as she stepped into the bedroom.

"Did someone find me any clothes yet?"

Tammy froze instantly upon seeing that Valiant wasn't alone inside the room anymore. She stared at the large New Species male and the smaller female with long blonde hair. The woman was human and obviously pregnant. Three pairs of eyes met her surprised ones.

The blonde smiled, moving forward. "Hi. I'm Trisha—"

"A doctor," the man standing next to her said quickly. "I'm her security officer. She's a visiting human who's applied to be a doctor here and she's a friend of Justice North's."

The woman frowned while shooting him a dirty look before she turned her attention back to Tammy. "I heard you had a rough night. I'm sorry it took so long for me to get here but Slade had to wake me and I had to get dressed."

"I woke her from two rooms away," the tall man with really blue eyes growled. "I protect her while she's visiting."

The woman flashed him another frown. "This is Slade and he's very protective of me." The woman looked highly amused. "He's my security guard."

He tensed. "Security officer."

The doctor laughed. "Whatever."

Tammy glanced at the blue-eyed man. She stood in nothing but a towel and it wasn't a big one. He got points for not staring at her though. She turned her full attention back to Trisha. "Thank you for agreeing to look at me so late or I should say so early in the morning, since that's more accurate."

"It's my pleasure. The men will leave us alone while I take a look at your injuries."

Valiant growled. "I don't have to leave. I've seen her bare. Make Slade go. He can't see her that way."

Tammy shot a glare at Valiant. "Please leave. Don't make me argue with you in front of the nice pregnant doctor and the guy protecting her. She got out of bed to come all the way over here to examine me and the last thing she needs is to listen to us go another round."

Valiant growled at her again.

"Stop that," she snapped. "Stop growling at me. I've had a long night, I'm tired, and I'm in pain. Can't you just do one thing without making me argue with you? Please?"

He stormed out of the room. The New Species man laughed and a look of joy passed over his features. "This was so worth getting dressed to see." He grinned a second before he spun on his heel and left the room too. The door closed behind him.

"Thank you," Tammy called out. "I appreciate it." She looked at the doctor, knowing her cheeks blushed slightly with embarrassment. "I'm sorry about that."

Trisha grinned. "Don't be sorry at all. I would have paid to see someone stand up to Valiant." She had a bag with her that she set on the edge of the bed. "Why don't you tell me where you hurt and we'll see what I can do? What happened to you specifically?"

Tammy walked closer to the bed, hesitated, and dropped the towel. "I guess looking is telling. Four men grabbed me, kind of beat me up a bit in the back of a truck, and dragged me through the woods. They tortured me too but Valiant and his friends came to my rescue." She slowly turned a full circle to show all her injuries. "My shoulder hurts the worst and I'm limping. My hip took a few big bumps inside the back of the truck bed when two of those assholes were making a dog pile out of me. I was stuck on the bottom so their weight slammed me into the truck bed." She stuck her wrists out. "This is from a belt they used to tie my hands behind my back."

The woman wasn't smiling anymore. She had Tammy stand while she sat on the bed and opened her bag. "Let me treat some of these scratches and bandage them." The woman touched Tammy's hip, feeling it. "Sorry if this hurts. I just want to make sure nothing is broken."

"It's not broken but it sure hurts."

Tammy stood there while the doctor put some kind of cream on her cuts and bandaged the worst ones. The doctor gave her a few ice packs and told Tammy to shake them to make them cold. Trisha stood and asked Tammy to turn so she could rotate her shoulder. Tammy winced.

"That hurts the most."

"You have some bad bruising. Does your throat hurt?"

"It's uncomfortable but I don't think any real damage was done. The soreness feels about the same as when I have a slight cold."

"I'm going to give you some pain medication that I brought just in case you needed it. I want you to take two as needed for the pain and if you run out, have Valiant give me a call. I want you to visit the medical center in a few days if the pain in your hip or shoulder worsens or doesn't subside. We'll get some X-rays."

Tammy nodded. "Thanks." She retrieved the towel and wrapped it around her. "I really appreciate it."

Trisha sat on the bed. "So, have you seen Valiant since the incident at his house?"

Tammy wanted to wince but didn't. "You heard about that?"

Trisha nodded. "Yeah. Slade, Tiger, Justice, and I know you had sex with him but that's everyone who knows."

"No. Tonight was the first time I've seen him since that day. I can't believe he forgave me for knocking him out with the lamp and was great enough to come looking for me tonight."

Trisha's voice dropped in volume drastically. "You knocked him out with a lamp? I was under the impression he let you go. Tiger didn't tell us that."

"I coldcocked him."

A grin split the woman's lips. "Thank you," she whispered. "I'm going to have a great laugh about that when it's safe. Their hearing is amazing so always keep that in mind."

"Thanks for the warning," Tammy whispered back. Her gaze lowered to Trisha's stomach. "I bet you and your husband are really happy. Is this your first baby?"

The woman touched her stomach with a grin and her voice rose loudly when she spoke. "I'm not married. The guy knocked me up and just took off on me."

A growl sounded from the hallway and someone knocked on the door. "Is she decent? I'm coming in."

Trisha winked at Tammy. "Come on in, Slade."

Slade looked furious as he shot a glare at Trisha. Valiant followed at his heels. Trisha chuckled.

"I was just telling Tammy about my baby." She tapped her stomach.

"When are you going to have the baby?" Tammy gripped her towel tightly around her body, trying not to feel too weird that Slade was inside the room.

The woman hesitated. "I'm not really sure. I'll find out whenever he decides to be born."

Tammy let that sink in. "I meant when is your due date?"

The woman hesitated again. "I'm five months pregnant."

Tammy's gaze dropped to the doctor's protruding stomach again. "Wow. Are you sure you aren't carrying twins? One of my friends is eight months pregnant and she…" Tammy closed her mouth and blushed. "I'm sorry. You aren't big or anything. I just realized how that must sound. It's just that you are so small and your tummy looks as if you're more pregnant. I—"

Trisha burst into laughter. "Stop! I'm not insulted or offended. I know I'm huge and look as though I'm ready to pop. The father is a big guy and the baby is too."

Tammy was happy she hadn't offended her. "Do you even speak to the father? You really should force him to pay child support. Kids are really expensive these days."

Slade growled again. Trisha laughed. "We worked things out and he realized he was a bonehead for leaving me. I'm going to make him marry me. I love the jerk a hell of a lot but he's kind of thick-headed, you know? I brought up marriage just a few weeks ago and he said it wasn't necessary since we were already a family."

"Men." Tammy shook her head. "They just don't get it."

Trisha grinned. "All too true. I'm thinking of going on a sex strike."

Tammy smiled at her. "That might work. You could also tell him that, if he won't marry you, someone else will. You're beautiful. I'm sure another man would be happy to if he's not smart enough to seal the deal."

Slade growled again. Tammy glanced at him with concern. Her gaze flashed to Trisha. "Is he all right?"

Trisha handed Tammy a bottle of pills. "He gets cranky when he gets woken up but he'll be fine. I'll send him to the guestroom when we get back to where I'm staying and he can take a nap. It was nice meeting you, Tammy. Have Valiant call me if you need anything. Maybe one day this week I can bring lunch. It will be nice to talk to another woman."

Tammy grinned. "I'd enjoy that if I'm still here. Thank you again, Trisha. It was really nice meeting you."

Trisha turned to study Tammy. "By the way, Tiger interfered with you making a statement tonight. The sheriff is going to come back in the morning. I hope that's all right but I told him you would need rest. I asked him to tell the sheriff that you'd been given pain medication already and he will be back at nine in the morning to interview you."

"That's great. Thank you. I am kind of done in."

Trisha stopped next to Valiant. "She's got some bad bruising. Be nice to her and make sure she gets plenty of rest. She needs two pain pills every four to six hours, depending on how much pain she is in. Have her eat before taking them."

"Thank you." Valiant hesitated before he opened his arms.

Trisha laughed as she hugged him. "You're learning."

He stepped back. "It's not so bad. You still smell nice."

These people are just weird. Tammy watched as the woman left the bedroom. Her security officer suddenly slapped the woman on her ass when he stepped into the hallway with her. Trisha jumped, turned her head, and laughed up at the large man following her before they moved out of sight. Tammy gawked after them. Valiant moved suddenly, blocking her line of vision.

"Did her security guy just slap her butt?"

Valiant smiled. "Yes."

Tammy shook her head. "Her boyfriend might not like him doing that."

Valiant shrugged, grinning. "I don't think he'd object. He and Slade are very close." He laughed.

Tammy let that one slide, not wanting to ask questions that were too nosy. "Did I get clothes yet?"

"They are in the other room."

"Could you bring them in to me, please?"

"You don't need them." Valiant moved to the bed and threw back the blankets. "Drop the towel and get into bed. It's late and you need sleep. I will get you a glass of water to take your pills. Have you eaten tonight or should I have some food brought to you?"

"I ate." She hesitated. "Could you at least turn around?"

He turned. Tammy dropped the towel and climbed into the bed. She pulled up the covers to her shoulders. "All in."

Valiant walked toward the bathroom. He returned with a glass of water. Tammy still held the pill bottle. She took out two pain pills and swallowed them down with the drink. Valiant set the glass down on the nightstand by the bed.

"Are you tired?"

"Yeah. I'm wiped."

He blinked. "Does wiped mean tired?"

She nodded. "Slang isn't your thing, is it?"

"I'm learning. I was raised around doctors, techs, and security guards. I'm afraid my vocabulary is limited to what they taught me. I didn't get as much exposure to them as some of the other Species did. I was different."

She frowned. "Do you know how to read?"

"Yes. I learned after I was freed in the months we spent in hiding waiting for our home to be established." He sat on the edge of the mattress. "Most of my kind were taught before then but I wasn't slated for any interaction with humans. It was a waste of time according to them. They just wanted to keep me alive because I was so strong and closer to animal than most."

Tammy stared at him mutely. She was too shocked to even reply. Valiant looked a little sad as he gazed into her eyes.

"How much do you know about New Species?"

"Just what I hear on TV and read sometimes in the newspapers. I know that some pharmaceutical company did illegal research on you guys and they finally got popped. I know they made you part human and part animal. That's really about it except for how you guys have your own Homeland down south near Los Angeles and how you opened up this place recently." She shrugged.

Valiant sighed. "We were altered with different animal DNA. Some more than others, such as myself. They made mistakes and I am one." Anger tightened his expression as he regarded her, seeming to be waiting for a reaction.

Tammy stared into his exotic eyes. "A mistake? I don't understand."

"I'm different—my animal traits are more dominant than my human ones."

She stared at his face, taking in his eyes, nose, mouth, and cheekbones. "You appear more New Species than most."

"It's not just how I appear. My instincts are stronger than most of my kind."

"What does that mean?" She was glad she was sitting down, almost afraid to hear whatever he wanted to share with her.

"I'm more animal than man. It's the only way I can explain it. The testing facility 'mistakes' such as myself were trained to be aggressive, to fight and to take a lot of pain. We were regarded as expendable and therefore heavily abused by their drug research trials. They tested the most dangerous ones they make on us. We were useless for any other purpose."

She had one of those rare moments where she couldn't form words. Valiant had a talent for making her speechless.

"They performed a lot of drug research on most New Species. They expected huge profits from enhancement drugs to that would make soldiers and athletes stronger, faster and better. They trained them to show off what their drugs could do. They were valuable. The failures were not. They tried breeding experiments with me but decided after a few unsuccessful attempts that they didn't wish to produce more of us."

"Breeding experiments?" She got the question out but wasn't sure she really wanted to hear the answer.

"They brought some females to my cell to breed with me to see if I could impregnate them. The other males hadn't produced results. Their testing failed with me as well."

Tammy tried hard to hide her horror. She knew she hadn't done a good job of it when Valiant's gaze dropped and his shoulders sagged. The sadness on his face tore at her heart. He hadn't had a choice, had been horribly abused, had been a victim.

Valiant refused to look into Tammy's pretty eyes any longer. The revulsion he saw hurt him deeply. He'd wanted to be honest with her by telling her everything about his life. His mate would need to know. It wouldn't be fair to ask her to spend her life with him if he kept secrets. He stared at the blanket covering her lap.

"We have heightened senses of smell, hearing, and our eyesight is better than most Species. We are stronger, faster, and even our intelligence was heightened in some cases. We are experimental prototypes that failed and in order to recoup their losses they even tried to turn us into perfect killing machines. They wanted to stamp out our humanity so we could be trained as pure animals that would follow their commands. It didn't work out for them so well when we wouldn't break. We fought them instead, killed them when given the chance and refused to do their bidding. They were still working on us when we were discovered and freed."

"They tried to turn you into a killer?" She whispered the words.

He glanced up and stared at her. "Please don't get that look in your eyes. I know how to fight and kill. It doesn't mean that I'm some mindless slayer. They tried to salvage the failures by making us fighters mostly and since we were so impressive looking they believed we might turn a profit. They wanted me to be their…" He paused. "'Display' New Species for the failures they wished to sell. I would not comply."

"Display?"

"To sell us." Valiant's voice tightened. "Third-world countries, private armies for rich fanatics, or whoever was willing to pay a fortune for an animal that could talk and kill efficiently on command. Luckily for us, we never heeded orders well. We had too many flaws for them to actually put us up for sale." He shrugged. "At least most of us. We now have found out that some of our women were sold."

Tammy stared at him in horror. "So some of your women are out there being forced to kill people?"

He shook his head. "I do not know exactly what DNA I was changed with. It might have been multiple large feline species from my looks and abilities but we guess the lion is most obvious. Their records having to do with how we were created were destroyed. Mostly our experimental prototypes were changed with species known for tracking, hunting, strength and fighting. Canine. Feline. Primate. We discovered that some of our females were mixed with weaker animal DNA strains to make them smaller and less aggressive. They were sold to provide funding to continue the research."

"Sold to whom and for what?"

Valiant looked furious. "Sold to whoever wanted to make large donations to Mercile Industries. They called them Gift Females and in exchange for large sums of money and for helping them cover up what they were doing and to avoid being caught, they handed them over to humans. They were giving our women to those bastards as sexual slaves. We have recovered some bodies and some living females."

Tammy swallowed and tears filled her eyes. "I never heard any of that on the news. My God. That's terrible. Those poor women."

"You won't hear it on the news. Justice thinks, if the press takes it public, that the men holding our women will kill them immediately to destroy any evidence that they ever had them. Justice and your government are tracing financial records and serving warrants to search for our missing ones. We don't know the numbers with the records being destroyed but we find another one every few weeks lately."

She reached out and her fingers traced the back of his hand. "That's horrible. It just is sickening, isn't it? Those poor women." She paused. "I hope that all of them are found."

He nodded grimly. "We do as well. We're free and it bothers us that some of our people are still being tormented and imprisoned."

"There's no way to recover all the information to find them?"

"When the testing facilities were breached by your government law enforcement it triggered alarms where we were hidden. The staff started fires in the record rooms and destroyed the computers holding the information. They started killing our people too. Some died but most of us lived. Very few records were salvaged."

"I hate to say this but it's probably a good thing. You know how information goes. Someone could get hold of it and use it start all over again. You guys are pretty impressive. I'm betting that company would be tempted to start new testing facilities with new people to experiment on."

He shivered. "We were told by a doctor who was arrested that the leading researcher who created us destroyed that information. She didn't agree with what Mercile planned to do with us after she succeded in creating us and she disappeared, taking that knowledge with her. That's why they began to try to breed some Species to create more. I hope no one could ever replicate what was done to us. It's enough to give us nightmares. We're trying to financially destroy Mercile Industries. We've won in your courts often on financial matters and your government has put a lot of them in your prisons."

"It is your government too. You're Americans, aren't you?"

He nodded. "We have always been separate. It's hard to try to think any other way. It's why Justice and our council fought so hard for our independence by acquiring Homeland and used some of the money from the lawsuits to buy Reservation."

"I heard you guys kind of have something close to diplomatic immunity on your own Homeland and here too. A news guy said it was similar to a consulate and you have your own laws and justice system."

"I assume so. Your government can't breach us or force us to comply with your laws. Not on our lands."

"So I'm kind of in another country right now, huh?" She suddenly grinned. "And I don't even have a passport. How cool is that?"

He fought a smile. She was adorable when she smiled and he resisted the urge to reach up and cup her face. He studied the bruise on her cheek and fought back anger at what had been done to her by humans. "Is it cool?"

"Kind of."

His gaze held hers. "I want to kiss and touch you. Let me, Tammy."

Her grin faded as she stared at him, chewing on her bottom lip. "I don't know."

"What don't you know? Did I hurt you last time? Did you not enjoy my touch? I know you did." Hope flared inside him that she'd be tempted. He longed to touch her again.

Tammy couldn't deny it. The time she'd spent in Valiant's bedroom had haunted her for five weeks. He had turned her inside out. When he touched her, she lost the ability to think. He seemed to take her silence for agreement when he slowly leaned closer. His hand reached out and caressed the uninjured side of her face.

"I would never hurt you."

She believed him. He'd terrified her when they had first met but after what he'd just told her about New Species, she understood he hadn't meant to. He had instincts and urges that most people didn't. He'd wanted her and he'd taken her. It was kind of sexy.

Valiant's hand eased away and he stood to kick off his shoes. He reached for the front of his jeans next. Tammy didn't protest as she watched him strip out of them. No underwear again. She stared at a naked Valiant with a little fear. The guy was so big. Her eyes lowered. *All over.* She forced her gaze to his face.

Valiant bent, gripped the blanket covering her, and yanked it to the foot of the bed. Tammy tensed but didn't try to use the pillow to hide her body. Valiant's gaze raked down every inch of her exposed skin, which was all of it that she wasn't lying on. He suddenly growled viciously. It made her eyes widen and her heart race.

"I want to kill all of your attackers. Look at what they did to your beautiful body. It infuriates me. I want to take them apart with my bare hands and watch them die a painful death."

"I'm fine."

"I still want to kill them. I would have bathed in their blood if they had raped you."

She stared at him. *Gross. But the meaning is sweet.* She believed him. *Well, the part about wanting to kill them.* Valiant put his knees on the bed and slowly crouched over Tammy. She stared up at him. He held her gaze but didn't touch her.

"You will stay with me forever and no one will ever hurt you again."

She didn't correct him. She couldn't really stay with him indefinitely. She'd have to get back to her life soon. She licked her lips. Valiant watched her tongue and groaned. He moved, backing down the bed toward her feet. She wondered if he'd changed his mind about wanting to have sex with her until he stopped when his face hovered over her lower stomach.

"Open your thighs for me."

She spread them wide apart. Valiant gripped her ankles, lifted them out of his way and scooted over until he sat on his legs where hers had just been. He eased her legs down until the backs of her thighs rested over the top of his parted ones. A foot of space separated his lap from hers while his gaze studied her from head to pussy.

"You are so small compared to me. I'm always afraid I'll accidentally hurt you."

Yeah, she silently agreed, *I understand that fear.* He weighed twice what she did and was a foot taller. His chest was massively wide and as she glanced at his buff arms, she knew if she measured them against her thighs, he would come out the winner for more inches around.

"Trust me not to hurt you."

She decided to use humor. "I'd be screaming right now if I thought you would."

He smiled. "I want you screaming but not in terror of me."

Tammy suddenly pushed up off the bed and used her elbows to prop her upper body to get a better view of all of him. She appreciated the sexy sight of his tan skin and beautifully sculptured body. He growled again before a soft purr came from his throat.

"Are those good or bad sounds?"

He flashed a grin. "I'm deciding on what I want to do to you first."

"What options are available?"

His smile widened, revealing more of his sharp teeth. "I growled when I thought about flipping you over and mounting you from behind. Riding you hard and fast makes my blood boil. I purred because I want to feast on you. I'd enjoy lapping at your pussy with my tongue to taste you again."

Her heart pounded and her body heated up. "We could do both."

He nodded. "Good plan."

Tammy stared at him as he lifted up and shifted his position to flatten on his belly until his legs dangled off the end of the bed. He adjusted her feet to rest on his broad shoulders, her knees bent. His tongue came out and his eyes locked with hers. He licked the hollow of her hip.

She took a shaky breath. The guy's tongue wasn't human feeling. It was soft but kind of rough. The sensation was strange but in a really good way that made her hot. He opened his mouth and raked his sharp teeth gently over the curve of her hip. Tammy took another shaky breath as desire began to burn inside her. She really wanted him to inch lower, the memory of his mouth something she'd never forget.

Valiant suddenly reached under her and his hands cupped her ass to tilt her the way he wanted. He leaned forward. His shoulders were wide and pushed her thighs farther apart to make room for his mouth.

"I grow impatient. Patience is not my strong suit," he growled. "I know you deserve more foreplay but I want you too much."

"Okay. I'm not complaining and I wish you'd go for it." She knew she blushed over being so bold but she really wanted him to touch her throbbing clit, which seemed to have grown a pulse.

He lifted her ass a little off the bed. She fell back and her head hit the pillow. He spread her wider open and his wonderful tongue started to lick her. Tammy squeezed her eyes closed and moaned in pleasure. Valiant wasn't a tease. He aimed right for the good spot. No side ventures. No taunting by licking her anywhere but her sensitive bundle of nerves. This tongue pressed tight against it and began to move, rubbing with enough force to assure her she wouldn't last long. He seemed to know the exact spot that sent sheer ecstasy straight to her brain.

Tammy dug her fingernails into the sheets, her nipples hardened and moans tore from her throat. Valiant growled and she moaned louder. *Good God! He's a licking vibrator.* His lips closed over her clit and he began sucking on her along with the vibrating and rubbing of his tongue. Her body tensed until she wondered if her back would snap. A scream tore from her as she climaxed so hard she almost passed out.

Valiant lifted his mouth from her. Tammy panted. She couldn't even open her eyes. Her body had that floating, limp-as-a-noodle, couldn't-move-if-the-bed-caught-fire feeling as spasms from her climax still twitched her vaginal muscles. His hands gripped her and then she gasped when he easily flipped her over onto her stomach.

Tammy forced her eyes open as Valiant gripped her hips and lifted them. He pulled her to up onto her knees. His strength probably should have frightened her but she wasn't alarmed when the bed dipped from the weight of his knees when he moved behind her, spread his legs on the outside of hers and trapped them to keep her pinned.

She tried to rise into position on her hands and knees but she didn't have the energy. Valiant snarled, a wild, animalistic sound, as the bulky crown of his cock pressed against the entrance to her pussy. One of his hands kept hold of her hip to keep her in place while she assumed his other one gripped his shaft to make sure he didn't slide away because of how wet she'd become from the climax he'd given her.

Her body shook as Valiant slowly eased inside her, pushing forward, forcing her vaginal walls to stretch to admit him. She moaned at the wonderful sensation of being filled. She wasn't sure she could stand the intensity of it with her climax still vibrating through her body but he didn't give her a choice as he sank deeper into her. A thrill of arousal surprised her. She hadn't realized how much it turned her on to feel helpless while he remained totally in control.

Her clit was a little oversensitive after what he'd done to her but he didn't give her time to recover. His hand on her hip slid on her skin to wrap around her waist. His other hand grabbed her breast and squeezed. She cried out in surprise at how sensitive her nipples were from their earlier abuse. He didn't pinch though, instead his fingers massaged the mound he gripped.

"Sensitive," she panted.

He released it instantly and gripped her hips with both hands. He withdrew almost totally from her pussy but slowly slid back inside, deep. She moaned, encouraging him as he worked his cock in and out of her, made her take him a little deeper each time. He suddenly released her hip with one hand and dropped it onto the mattress to brace his upper body as he curled around her. His hips slammed against her ass as he seemed to lose control. He pounded into her fast, hard and deep. Snarls tore from his throat to match her panted cries of pleasure.

Tammy lost the ability to think. The feeling of him inside her had to be the best sensation in the world, even superior to his tongue licking her until she came. She enjoyed every rock-hard inch of him hammering in and out of her pussy while she made sounds she'd never made before.

Valiant's grip around her waist changed and he slid his thumb between her vaginal lips, pressed the side of it against her clit and fucked her harder. The rubbing sensation against her already oversensitive, swollen clit became too much.

Another orgasm built, her inner muscles tightened around his driving cock and it blew her mind when pleasure tore through her again. She screamed his name, climaxing hard, and Valiant roared from his own release. His hips ground against her ass, he buried his cock into her deep and heat spread inside her as he kept coming. Valiant groaned softly with each jerk his body experienced as his semen shot into her, until he fell over on the bed with her still locked in his arms.

Tammy panted, her eyes closed, and a smile curved her lips while her inner muscles gripped Valiant still, clenching around his shaft. He snuggled closer, kissed the curve of her shoulder and that was last thing she remembered.

Valiant held Tammy close, wrapped his body tighter around hers to spoon her in front of him, and ran his fingers along her skin to make sure she wasn't chilled. Her breathing had slowed, he knew she'd fallen asleep, and he tried not to feel guilty. She'd been through a lot but he couldn't regret taking her.

She's mine and I'm never allowing her to leave me. I couldn't survive without her. That realization slammed home. The woman in his arms meant that much to him. She did the one thing that some of the meanest, cruelest humans he'd ever dealt with hadn't been able to do. He suddenly knew terror at the thought of losing something that mattered so much to him.

His arms tightened around her and he swore he'd show her she belonged with him.

He'd make her happy, feed her, fill her every need and she'd have to see how much she meant to him. He nuzzled her wet hair, enjoying having her so close.

He'd show her that he was the right male for her. A good protector, a lover who would see to her pleasure, and he wanted to make her smile all the time. He loved it when she laughed, the way her blue eyes sparkled, and the sound was infectious. It made him happy. *She* made him happy.

I can't lose her. I just can't.

Chapter Eight

හ

That feels so good, was Tammy's first thought. She smiled, having the best dream ever, where she lay on her side with a big, hot body pressed along her back. Someone nipped her shoulder and a hot, wonderful tongue teased the spot. She shivered, warm breath tickling her skin as teeth gently raked across it, creating an erotic jolt through her body. She moaned.

A hand slid from her hip to the inside of her thigh, gripped it, and spread her legs when it was lifted. She groaned from pleasure as a hard, thick cock teased her clit, then lowered enough to enter her pussy in one slow, fluid thrust. She grabbed at the arm connected to the hand that held her leg, just for something to cling to.

Valiant slid into her deeper and a sexy purr rumbled from his mouth next to her ear. He started to fuck her slowly and she moaned louder. The hand gripping her leg adjusted it higher and she hooked her foot behind his thigh. He released his grip to trail his hand along her inner thigh to her clit where his fingertips drew circles over the swelling bud. She threw her head back against Valiant's chest and bucked her hips to meet his thrusts.

I'm not dreaming. It feels too good not to be real. Tammy opened her eyes. She moaned and her nails dug into the sheets and his skin where she gripped his upper arm. Valiant shifted his leg between hers to drive into her pussy a little deeper and kept up the slow, steady rhythm that began to drive her mindless. Her breathing grew choppy and her nipples hardened. Her body tensed and bucked against him more frantically, seeking release.

"Faster," she begged.

"Not yet," he growled.

Tammy gripped the bed hard to get a good hold on the sheet and moved her hips, shoving back at Valiant. He groaned as he slid into her harder and faster. His finger matched his hips, sliding over her bundle of nerves rapidly, applying more pressure. He knew exactly what she needed while his cock pounded inside her and he manipulated her clit to make her come.

Tammy's muscles tightened, the ecstasy became so intense it was nearly too much, and she screamed, jerking violently against Valiant with him deeply buried inside her pussy as the climax tore through her.

Valiant roared. His hand left her clit and he gripped her hip. His hips jerked, his body tensed and he seemed to turn to stone behind her as every muscle in his body tightened. He suddenly relaxed as his climax ended.

She smiled as warmth spread through her from his release, amazed she could feel him jetting into her body when she'd never experienced that sensation with other men. Each time, he shivered a little and pulled her tighter into his embrace. It was soothing when his heat poured into her after making love to him. She smiled. Valiant bit her shoulder.

Tammy yelped. "Hey. Watch the teeth."

Valiant licked where his teeth had just marked her skin without breaking it. "Sorry."

She turned her head to stare at the man who always gave her such intense sex and decided that he looked sexy in the morning. His hair was messed up, his wild mane fuller, and he had a lazy, happy glint in his beautiful eyes. They really did remind her of melted gold and it was absolutely stunning. There were swirls of different shades of shiny yellows when she studied his irises up close. He had a gaze she could happily stare into forever.

"What did you bite me for?" She wasn't upset but curious.

"It was for passing out on me last night. I wanted to..." He paused. "Make love to you again but you were dead to the world."

"I was tired. You blew me away, sexy."

His eyebrows arched and he frowned. "I don't understand. Isn't that a human term for shooting someone? I thought you enjoyed the sex. You seemed to. I made certain to please you."

She laughed. "I didn't quite mean it that way. I meant it in the 'you blew my mind' way."

He smiled. "I see. I enjoy waking to take you first thing. I think we should do this every morning."

"I could live with that." She grinned at him. "And I wouldn't mind going to bed every night, the way we did last night, on a regular basis either."

"I can do it. We are known for our strength and endurance. Stamina. I have a lot of that. My sex drive is very active. I'm always ready to mount you."

She stared at him, realizing he meant it. "How active?"

He studied her face. "I crave sex every day, seven days a week, every day of the year. I could do it more. We could go to bed after meals and stay in bed until the next time we eat. Do you want to do it again?"

She gaped at him. "I wouldn't survive that. You'd have to bury me if we stayed in bed every day of the year and only stopped having sex for sleeping and meals. I'm only human, Valiant. You'd kill me."

His hand slid to her breast, cupping it. "I could revive you."

She tensed but realized her nipple no longer hurt. His caress was very gentle and it actually felt good. "Okay. I'd never walk again."

He chuckled and eased his big body away from her, slowly withdrawing his still-stiff shaft from her pussy. "You are fragile. I have to remember that. I don't want to break you." He completely released her and climbed off the bed. "I already made you pass out. I should feed you."

"I am starving." She sat up and glanced at the clock by the bed. "Wow. It's already eight o'clock."

Valiant glanced at her. "Is that relevant?"

"I'm supposed to talk to the sheriff at nine, remember? That barely leaves me time to shower and get ready before I have to give him a statement."

"You will eat. You can shower while I order the food. He can interview you while you eat or he can wait until you are done." Valiant's eyes narrowed. "You need lots of food. You are small and need more of it until you grow bigger and sturdier."

She stared at him. "As in fattening me up? Is that what you want? To make me plump?"

He grinned. "I don't make deals with witches if any exist. I have no plans to fatten you up so I can toss you into an oven to eat you."

"What is it with you and fairy tales? You know them. I thought I was the only weird one who did that." She laughed.

He hesitated. "I was told the stories a lot when I was young. My caretaker said I could learn many things from them. I memorized them all."

Part of her heart broke for Valiant. She climbed out of bed without hesitation and walked right up to him. She threw her arms around him, hugging him hard. Valiant hesitated before his strong arms came around her to clutch her tightly to him. They stood by the bedroom door, naked, holding each other.

"Why are we hugging? Are you thanking me for great sex?"

"No," she laughed. "I'm hugging you because..." She didn't want to admit she'd felt sorry for his sad childhood. "Because I wanted to hold you. I enjoy being in your arms."

His hold tightened. "You can hold me any time you want, Tammy."

She hugged him for a long minute before she eased back to smile up at him. "I'm going to jump in the shower. I need clothes to wear."

"I was on my way to get them. I'll be right back."

She walked into the bathroom and turned on the water in the shower and stepped in. A contented sigh broke from her lips as the heated water ran over her body. She reached for the shampoo. Seconds later a naked Valiant opened the shower door and stepped into the stall with her. Tammy laughed, backing up to make room for him.

"Did anyone ever tell you that you take up a lot of space?"

He grinned. "All the time. Turn and I will wash your hair."

She shook her head but grinned. "I have to eat then talk to the sheriff. I'll wash my own hair and you wash yours. Hands to yourself, Valiant. You touch me and I stop thinking."

"But—"

She grinned. "Behave."

His smile died and he nodded grimly. "Fine."

They rubbed against each other when they switched places to allow Tammy to rinse her hair. Valiant's body responded. She grinned at the sight of his cock growing, hardening, until it pointed at her.

"Is that your idea of behaving? You could hurt someone with that thing."

He laughed. "You could let me pick you up and I could fuck you against the wall right here. It would make me behave really well."

Tammy shook her head. "I'm already limping and not just from my bruised hip. You're trying to kill me, aren't you?"

Laurann Dohner

"No." He frowned, all traces of humor fading from his features.

"I was kidding. It was a joke." She reached for the bottle of body wash. "Lean against the wall."

He frowned but backed up. Tammy spread the soap onto her hands and set the bottle down. She started at his shoulders and her hands scrubbed down his body. He growled at her when she reached his nipples, a very sexy sound coming from him now that she had started to learn the difference between arousal and anger when he made those noises. His nipples pebbled under her fingers and palms while she massaged them.

"You are trying to kill me," he groaned.

She laughed. "Not yet."

Her hands traced down his stomach to his hips and curled around the girth of his shaft. Valiant growled deeper, closing his eyes. Tammy leaned closer until her body brushed against his. She used her hands, rubbing and massaging his cock, increasing the pace as Valiant started to breathe heavily. Growls and purrs tore from his throat.

Tammy stepped even closer, until the tip of his cock rubbed against her belly while she stroked him faster, her hands tightening enough to make him react by growing even stiffer inside her hold. He suddenly tensed, threw his head back, and a loud, unusual sound tore from his throat. Not quite a roar but close. Tammy leaned her body in closer, making sure his heated semen spread across her stomach as she trapped his shaft between her skin and hands. Valiant shook slightly in the aftermath.

"Feel better?"

He opened his eyes and his lips twitched into a near smile. "Your turn."

Tammy laughed, releasing him. "Not yet. I have to finish my shower and get dressed. I need to eat and have that

140

conversation with Sheriff Cooper. You can return the favor after he leaves."

"You are aroused. I can smell you." He reached for her hips.

"No!" She laughed. "I mean, yes, I am. You turn me on but we don't have time right now."

He sighed. "Does this sheriff mean more to you than I do?"

Tammy had turned into the spray to wash the front of her body. She looked at Valiant over her shoulder. The hurt look on his face was an easy one to read. "No. Why would you even ask that?"

"Because you could have me touching you but you prefer talking to a human instead."

She faced Valiant. Her hands flattened over his chest until she pushed him back against the wall. He allowed it. Her gaze met his and she refused to look away, wanted him to see the sincerity of her words.

"It's because I want to make sure those men stay locked up. He's the sheriff and locking those bastards away in prison for a really long time is important. I need to help him accomplish that. Without my statement, and if charges aren't filed, they could go free. Do you understand? No witness, no victim, no crime. That's how the law works in my world."

"I understand." His body relaxed and he nodded.

"The sheriff is also a friend. He and my grandmother were close. He's almost an uncle to me. He's not more important to me than you are, don't ever think that, but I told him I'd do this. He needs my help and I need his to make sure those assholes pay for kidnapping me."

He nodded. "I could carry you to our bed and lick you until you scream my name if I had just killed them instead of allowing my people turn them over to yours."

The guy had a point. Tammy grinned. "Yes, but it would have been wrong."

"Licking you until you scream my name is not wrong."

"I meant about the killing part." She laughed. "I love the licking part a hell of a lot. That's definitely not wrong."

He growled. "Let the sheriff wait."

She backed up and her hands dropped away from him. "I'll talk to him and he'll leave. Once he does, we can go back to bed. Okay?"

He nodded. "Fine." He turned, grabbed the pumice stone, and studied his free hand, palm up.

"What is that for anyway?"

He made certain she could watch as he used the stone on his fingernails. "It cleans them." He opened his hand palm out to her. "It also helps keep the rougher spots on our skin smoother."

Tammy reached out and ran her fingertips over his fingers. She could feel calluses on the tips of his fingers and at the top of his palm where his fingers began.

"What causes that?"

"Being Species. Some of my kind have this. Some don't. I do. It helps me climb trees without tearing up my skin." His eyes narrowed warily. "Does that make me less appealing to you?"

She shook her head. "I kind of find the rough texture of your hands a turn-on. They make me shiver and goose bumps break out. I like it."

"Good. I worried my differences from a human male might make me less able to attract your sexual interest."

She fought a smile. "Don't worry, Valiant. I am learning to appreciate all your differences."

He stared into her eyes, seemed to gauge her honestly, and smiled. "I am glad."

Tammy quickly finished her shower while Valiant attended to his nails and his calluses. She quickly dried off, wrapped a towel around her body, and walked into the bedroom. Four shopping bags waited on the bed. She dumped them out to see what she had to work with. Two bags contained clothing for Valiant but the other bags were for her. She chose a pair of cotton knee-length pants and a black, oversized T-shirt. They had bought her bikini-cut underwear and two exercise bras that were stretch-to-fit.

Valiant entered the bedroom behind her. His wet hair had been brushed back. He looked different with it combed away from his face. He kind of looked more frightening to her. His mane-like hair softened his features a little and made him look more cuddly and attractive. Tammy smiled but didn't say a word while Valiant dug through the pile she'd made for him of the large-sized men's clothing.

Tammy nearly stepped on a shoebox peeking out from the bottom of the bed. She retrieved it and opened it, guessing they were for her since the box wasn't big enough to contain anything for Valiant's big feet. Inside was a pair of white flip-flops. She hated them but she at least had shoes. She left them in the box. She wasn't planning on leaving the suite. She heard a doorbell chime and her startled gaze flew to Valiant.

Valiant smiled. "There are doorbells in the suites. It's our food." He had pulled on a pair of black boxer briefs. "I'll go get it."

"I'll go. I'm dressed." She smiled at him. "You're showing way too much skin. It could be a woman delivering our breakfast."

He laughed. "Would you feel jealous if a female looked at me?"

She hesitated. "Yes," she answered honestly.

His humor faded. "You are mine and I am yours. You don't need to feel jealous. I would not allow another to touch me."

"I'm glad to hear that," Tammy called out as she quickly left the bedroom. She liked that he'd said that. She walked through the living room and opened the door. "Hi," she said instantly.

The woman who stood there had to be just over six feet tall. She had long brown hair and dark eyes. Tan skin and strong features made the woman appear intense but beautiful. It was the first time Tammy had been that close to one of the females. The woman had wide cheekbones, the flatter nose, and she looked down at Tammy with a smile that showed off some sharp, pointed teeth. Her expression wasn't threatening.

"Hello back, small human. I have brought you food."

Tammy couldn't help but laugh. "Thank you very much. I'm Tammy."

"My name is Breeze."

Tammy moved out of the way to allow her to push a cart from the hallway into the living room. Tammy almost winced as she saw food containers nearly slide off the tray. The tall woman didn't seem to notice or care when she turned, her gaze studying Tammy from head to foot. She chuckled.

"So you are Valiant's mate." The woman didn't hide her amusement. "You're so small. I believed he would pick Sunshine. She's as tall as I am."

"Sunshine?"

"One of us. He has been looking for a mate. I had to see for myself the human woman I heard about from last night. They said you were small the way Ellie and Trisha are. They were right. Are all of your woman about your size? I don't get to be around many of your females."

"I met Trisha last night, right? The pregnant doctor? Who is Ellie?"

"She's a human mate to Fury. He is canine but they are not here. They live at Homeland. She is my good friend. I came here with some of our women months ago to help with the opening of Reservation. I miss my friend and I wanted to meet you. I enjoy being around human females." She grinned.

Tammy smiled back at her. She saw the woman's grin swiftly turn into a tense line when her gaze fixed on something behind Tammy. She guessed Valiant had entered the room. The growl that rumbled a second later dispelled any doubt. The New Species woman backed toward the door, her gaze dropping to the floor. Fear showed on her face.

Tammy spun and put her hands on her hips. "Don't growl at her."

Valiant's angry glare shifted to Tammy. "I don't want anyone near you."

"Deal with it. I'm making a friend." She turned back around and smiled at Breeze. The woman looked surprised as her gaze lifted to meet Tammy's. "Don't mind him. He's," she shrugged, "protective."

Breeze nodded. "He has reason to be. Some of our people don't tolerate humans."

"Well, you aren't one of them. You said so yourself that you are friends with women like me. It was really nice meeting you. I hope I get to see you again soon."

The woman flashed Tammy a smile. "I will be delivering all your food. No one else wanted to."

"Because they don't want to see me?"

The woman's gaze flashed to Valiant as she shook her head. She glanced at Tammy. Her attention returned to Valiant. "I'll see you again at lunch." The woman fled, closing the door behind her.

"They are avoiding me." Valiant walked to the cart to remove the lids on the plates.

Tammy frowned. "Why would they do that?"

"I frighten them. I'm not," he shrugged, "social."

"You mean because you roared at them last night when they stared at me?"

"Yes. Exactly." He nodded. "Let's eat."

Tammy and Valiant moved the food to the coffee table. Someone had sent a few different drinks. Tammy lunged for the chocolate milk. Valiant made an unpleasant face.

"What's that look for?"

"That stuff is disgusting."

"Chocolate milk?"

He nodded. "It makes me sick."

She hesitated. "Oh. I see."

"What do you see?"

"Well, I had a dog once. He ate a candy bar and threw up. It's probably that animal DNA of yours. I love chocolate."

"I'm not a dog."

She managed not to laugh at his horrified expression at the mere thought of being accused of something he obviously thought was insulting. She found it cute. "You're a lion. I bet chocolate makes lions sick too. It probably doesn't agree with your stomach."

He set the plate of meat in front of him. Tammy noticed for the first time what had been brought to him for breakfast. She couldn't help but stare. Four thick, partially cooked steaks dominated the plate, nothing else, and they were really rare. Blood pooled under them as though it were gravy.

"That's what you eat? Is that even cooked inside?" She managed not to shiver with dread.

He took a bite. Tammy verified the meat was almost raw after he bit into it. She forced her eyes away. Valiant ate barely seared meat. She studied her food, grateful she'd ended up with a typical breakfast of bacon, hash browns, scrambled eggs and toast. She wouldn't have touched them if they'd brought her mostly raw steaks.

"Do you want some? It's good."

She shook her head. "It's all yours. I only eat my steaks cooked all the way through and with some steak sauce. A nice baked potato to go with it too." She hesitated and glanced at

146

his plate. "How many pounds of meat do you eat in one sitting?"

He shrugged. "A few."

"Is that all you eat?"

"No. I eat deer too. Cows are good. I enjoy chicken and pork but I want them cooked more. Fish raw is excellent. I catch them with my hands from the river. I will catch you some when we move to my house. You probably want them cooked though."

She just nodded. *Man, I'm so totally not going to watch him eat.* She forced her attention to her plate and kept it there while she finished her meal. She tried not to glance at Valiant.

The doorbell chimed again about fifteen minutes later. Valiant opened the door. Tammy set her empty plate on the tray and smiled as Sheriff Greg Cooper walked inside the suite. Two New Species officers flanked him, obviously escorts. The sheriff smiled back at Tammy.

"You're looking much better, Tam." He peered around the suite with a whistle. "And they are sure taking good care of you. Nice place. Fancy."

"Thank you. Would you like to sit down?" Tammy smiled at the security officers. "All of you?"

The two New Species shook their heads and remained standing by the door they had closed. Sheriff Cooper walked to one of the chairs to drop into it. Tammy sat on the couch. Valiant took a seat next to her.

"You need me to make a statement, right?"

Sheriff Cooper reached into his pocket. "Actually, that was kind of taken care of already. They," he glanced at Valiant, "are very efficient. I just need you to read it and sign this if it's accurate."

"Oh." Tammy accepted the papers and unfolded them. She started to read. Someone had typed out an account of what had happened, most of it anyway, minus the stuff about the doctor who ordered the men to take her or any mention of an informant. Some of it wasn't quite precise but it was all damning for the four men.

Valiant stood and walked away. He returned quickly and handed Tammy a pen. "Here. Sign it with that." His features were grim.

Tammy nodded and signed the last page. She handed the statement back to the sheriff. "Here you go."

"It's all correct? I take it they interviewed you already?"

She nodded. New Species had written it up and she trusted them. "Yes. It's perfect."

"How are you feeling today? You look good. The bruising on your face isn't as bad as I thought it would be."

"I'm feeling a hundred percent better. One of their doctors came by last night to give me pain medication and examined me."

Valiant rose to his feet. "I'll get you the pills. You ate." He walked out of the room.

Sheriff Cooper leaned forward and whispered, "Are you good here? You can leave with me if you want to."

"I'm great." Tammy smiled at him. "I have to call Ted though to tell him I won't be to work for a few days."

Sheriff Cooper leaned back with a grimace. "What happened is all over town. You know how it is. Ted called me first thing this morning wanting to know if the rumors were true. I told him what happened and where you were. I wasn't sure how long you'd be out here." He paused. "Your friends would appreciate it if you would call them. Tim was especially worried about you. He tried to call you here but they told him you weren't accepting phone calls."

She blinked. "I was sleeping until just a little while ago. I'll call Tim first chance I get."

Sheriff Cooper stood. "Well, I better get going. I have four of my deputies with me. We're here to collect two of your attackers. The third had to be moved to a hospital in Sherver. He survived surgery."

Tammy stood and hugged Sheriff Cooper. "Thank you for everything. Especially for thinking to call the New Species to help find me."

"I'm glad I did the right thing. It was all I could think to do. Once a person goes missing, the longer they are gone, the less chances of finding them alive. I promised your grandma on her deathbed that I'd look out for you like my own family."

Tammy walked the sheriff to the door where his escort waited. Valiant walked up behind her. The second the door closed, Valiant held out a glass of water and two pain pills. She swallowed them and handed the glass back to him. He slammed it onto the nearest table, spun, grabbed her and lifted her off her feet. Tammy gasped, staring at him as he curled her against his chest. He headed for the bedroom.

"Put me down."

He ignored her request. "You spoke to that man, you ate, took your pills, and now I get to take you to bed. That was the deal."

"It was." She laughed as he tossed her onto the bed.

Valiant gripped her cotton pants and pulled them down her legs. Her panties were quickly removed. He crouched over her on the bed, grinning. "I get to lick you now."

The doorbell chimed. Valiant's humor instantly vanished, anger tightened his features and he snarled. "Ignore it."

Tammy hesitated. "But…"

His hands gripped her thighs, spread them wider, and he lowered his head. Tammy fell back against the mattress, digging her fingernails into the sheets, no longer caring who was at the door as his mouth fastened over her clit. He nuzzled his face tighter between her thighs, rapidly tonguing her clit in strong flicks that instantly made all thought leave her head. He growled against her.

"I love when you vibrate," she moaned.

Valiant purred, vibrating more. The sensation became so good she could barely stand it, her thighs tightened around his head and his strong hands forced them apart again. He held her immobile until all she could do was arch her back and cry out her pleasure. In minutes Tammy screamed his name, twitching under his mouth, as she came hard.

He lifted his head away and dragged her limp body toward him at the edge of the bed. Her eyes opened and she peered at him where he knelt on the carpet. Valiant's eyes were narrowed, his beautiful gaze intense and filled with passion. He released her when her butt nearly slid off the edge of the mattress and gently placed her feet on the carpet to keep her from slumping to the floor.

He didn't look away from her gaze as he tore open the front of his pants, shoved them down his legs, bent to completely remove them, and kicked them away. He leaned down, grabbed her hips, and rolled her over onto her stomach.

Valiant bent her over the mattress. He used his feet to gently urge her thighs apart. She spaced her knees and he crowded in behind her. She moaned as his cock nudged her pussy and slowly pressed inside, parting her vaginal walls.

"Mine," he growled as his big body curled around her and his arms braced his upper body from crushing hers under him.

"Yes," she moaned, gripping his hands on the bed next to her. "God yes."

Valiant tensed for a second but began to rock his hips against her ass to drive his cock into her harder and deeper. He moved his legs to the outside of hers, lowering his hips to fuck her at a new angle and Tammy urged him on with soft moans and pleas to move faster.

He felt incredible to her, every hard inch awakening and stroking wonderful nerve endings that drove her pleasure higher and higher until she knew she was about to come again.

Her vaginal muscles clamped around him and she screamed his name as it happened.

A roar tore from his throat. Tammy clung to his hands as he drove into her the last time, still climaxing around him, and loving the warm heat spreading from his release. He collapsed over her to pin her tighter under his body but he made sure she could still breathe.

"We should do this after every breakfast," he said and chuckled next her ear.

She smiled, turned her head, and met his gaze. "I could take a nap."

He hesitated. "I would take one with you but I have to see what our company wants first. They are waiting in the other room."

Her mouth fell open. "What?" She tried to push him up but he was too heavy over her back and didn't budge. He grinned at her.

"We have company in the other room. They are probably waiting for both of us."

Tammy twisted her head the other way. The bedroom door stood wide open. She frantically shoved at Valiant. "Get off. Damn it, why didn't you tell me? They could have walked in here and seen us!"

Valiant shrugged, seemed unconcerned, and separated their bodies. He rose to his feet and strode to the bedroom door. "We'll be out in a minute." He slammed it closed and turned to face her.

Tammy shot him a glare as she grabbed her discarded pants and underwear, trying to put them on quickly as she sat on the edge of the bed. "You knew someone came into our rooms and you just ignored it? What if they walked in here? What if they'd seen— Hell, anything we've been doing?"

His arms crossed over his chest, and he appeared highly amused. "I would have killed them for disturbing us."

She yanked her shirt down her body from where it had ridden up when Valiant had been riding her. She smirked at that thought. "You go out there. I'm hiding in here. They had to have heard everything."

"They probably heard us two floors away or more and definitely on this entire floor."

Her mouth dropped open. "Seriously?"

"Yes. We have good hearing." He looked really happy about it too.

"Damn it, Valiant. That's not funny. You mean to tell me every time we have sex, everyone probably on two or three floors knows what we're doing?"

"You scream my name and I can't stop from voicing how good you make me feel."

Tammy remained sitting on the bed, not sure her knees would hold her weight at that moment as shock rolled through her. She put her hands over her face. "I can never face anyone again. That's so embarrassing."

Hands suddenly grabbed her as he yanked her to her feet. Tammy's head jerked up. She stared in shock at Valiant's enraged expression. His hands weren't hurting her but he had a firm hold on her.

"Do I embarrass you?" He snarled the words.

"No!" It horrified her that he'd come to that conclusion.

"Does it embarrass you that others know you enjoy being touched by me and having me inside you?"

"No! Don't think that way. How can you even say that? I wanted to come here with you. I'm from a small town, Valiant. Fifteen minutes after I demanded to stay with you, agreed to allow you to carry me off in one of your Jeeps, my entire town knew about us. I'm not ashamed to be with you one bit. I'm embarrassed because it's just uncomfortable to think that everyone can hear us having sex. That's kind of private and personal."

His expression relaxed and his hold on her arms gentled until he barely touched her. "Yes. I'm sorry I got the wrong impression."

"What you got was pissed. You were livid with me. You do not embarrass me, Valiant. I'm not ashamed to be with you. I am really attracted to you. I…" she softly cursed. "I really am drawn to you deeply and I don't give a rat's ass what someone else thinks about that if they aren't happy with it. Are we clear?"

"Yes." He swallowed hard, his expression softening. "I was so angry because it hurt me very deeply to believe you didn't want anyone to know about me and you. I know humans hate us and the idea of you thinking less of me for not being human hurt."

Something inside her chest broke a little for him. It tore her up that she'd mistakenly hurt his feelings and made him unsure of where he stood with her. She pulled out of his arms, glanced at the bed, and gripped his arm to balance her weight when she stepped up onto the mattress. She turned, released his arm, and met his surprised look at her new position of being slightly taller than him.

"You're just so tall. It's hard to do this otherwise. Step closer to me."

He didn't hesitate. He moved to stand before her. Tammy gripped his cheeks and bent enough to go nose to nose with him. She stared into his exotic eyes, loving them and probably loving him too. She pushed that concept back, not wanting to go there at that moment. Falling in love with him as deeply as she suspected she was would complicate her life beyond imagination.

"I am not ashamed of you. You are better than any human man I've ever met, Valiant. A thousand times over. You're incredibly sweet to me, you always seem to want to take care of me, even though I'm not sure about fattening me up." She grinned. "And the sex is amazing. You're smart, caring, and while some things about you drive me nuts, such as how aggressive you can be, I kind of like it. I actually really like it when you get all possessive. I don't care who knows we're seeing each other. I just don't want anyone seeing me naked besides you. Okay?"

His arms wrapped around her waist to pull her flat against his body. "I'd beat them senseless if they did. They fear me, but you never should. I will never hurt you, Tammy."

"I believe that." She did. "We probably should go see who is waiting in the other room."

"Let them wait. I want to hold you right now."

She nodded and released his face to wrap her arms around his neck, her face buried in the curve of his shoulder, and he wrapped his arms around her to cling tighter to her. Tammy wrapped her legs around his waist. He held her entire weight easily — the guy was a breathing tank on legs. She grinned.

Valiant slid his arm lower to hook Tammy under her ass to make sure she didn't release him any time soon. He breathed in her scent, his eyes closed now, and nuzzled her hair. She hadn't said she loved him but he could find patience for her.

He refrained from stating they were doing more than seeing each other. She was his mate, his other half, and now a part of his soul. He loved her. It was a new emotion but he wasn't afraid to admit it. She warmed him inside, made him happy, and having her against his body was just right. Perfect. They fit despite their size difference. She was wonderful to him in every way.

Except she's too small. I need to feed her more. He smiled.

He remembered when he'd entered her wondrous body and told her she was his. He'd told her "mine" and she'd said yes. His grin widened. She'd actually said "God yes". She'd brought her religious faith into it. That had to mean she had been completely honest and sincere. Hope turned into joy. Tammy was his. His hugged her a little tighter.

"Mine."

She didn't protest and he knew then he'd be able to keep her forever.

Chapter Nine

ဆ

"Okay. Now let's go face whoever is in the other room." Tammy smiled at Valiant after he lowered her back to her feet.

"It's Slade and Trisha. They brought Brass with them."

Valiant smiled when he stepped back from her. He held out his hand that Tammy accepted, opened the door, and they walked together down the hallway. Trisha, Slade, and a New Species man waited inside the living room, sitting on the couch and on a chair. The men looked amused. Trisha just smiled.

"What do you want?" Valiant glared at Slade. "We had to get dressed. We would be taking a nap right now if it weren't for you being here."

A grin spread across Slade's face and his blue eyes sparkled. "Trisha wanted to talk to both of you. She was tired last night and says she didn't think about it. She demanded we come over here right now."

Valiant glanced at the other man. "Hello, Brass. What are you doing here?"

"I'm with them." He studied Tammy and winked.

A growl tore from Valiant as he instantly moved, released her hand and took a threatening step toward the other New Species. He'd put his body in front of Tammy's, blocking Brass from seeing her.

"Do not look at her and do not flirt." Valiant snarled louder. "Mine!"

"Wow, and I thought you were possessive," Trisha muttered. She stood. "Calm down, Valiant. Brass didn't mean anything by that facial twitch. He winks at everyone. Even

156

men. I need to have a private discussion with you two." She paused. "Inside the bedroom."

"But—" Slade protested.

Trisha spun to face him. "Enough. I know you guys wouldn't give a damn what is discussed in front of you about any topic under the sun but she's a woman. I wouldn't want to have this conversation in front of two men I don't know. Now please sit back down and work more on that patience—or lack of—issue you have." She turned back around to meet Tammy's shocked stare. "You, me, and Valiant need to have a talk."

"Just tell us whatever you need to say." Valiant crossed his arms over his chest. "The faster its out, the faster you leave, and I can take Tammy to bed for a nap."

Tammy sighed, stepping from behind him. "He does that arm-crossing thing a lot. Valiant has spoken. Subject over." She glanced up at his face and grinned at his threatening expression, which he seemed to use to intimidate others. "Do what he says or get glared at."

Trisha laughed. "They all do that. It's a New Species thing. It's adorable, isn't it?"

Tammy wasn't sure she'd go that far but as she glanced up at the scowl on Valiant's face as he regarded the doctor, she refrained from laughing. Her focus returned to Trisha.

Trisha edged around Valiant and took Tammy's arm. "Trust me. This is a talk we should have in private."

"Let's go into the bedroom. He'll follow." Tammy led the way.

Trisha took a seat on a chair and her hands gently massaged her extended belly. Tammy grabbed the comforter off the floor and tossed it over the messed-up sheets. She tried not to feel embarrassed about the state of the bed. It was obvious that they'd had sex on it recently. Valiant stood by the door doing his New Species thing. She smiled as she looked away from him, sitting on the edge of the bed near Trisha.

"I don't want to embarrass anyone," Trisha explained softly. "But I now know for sure that you two are having sexual intercourse." She kept eye contact with Tammy. "Are you on the Pill?"

Tammy shook her head. "No."

Trisha glanced at Valiant. "Have you been using condoms?"

He snorted. "Never."

Tammy winced. "I see where you're going with this. Okay. Last year I dated this asshole and he cheated on me." She refused to glance at Valiant. "I found out and flipped out. I immediately got in to see my gynecologist. I was terrified he might have given me something. We used condoms but not for everything. I had my doctor run every test, it all came back clean, and six months ago she retested me. I'm venereal disease free. I'd be happy to allow you to examine me and run tests if you're worried I might give Valiant something."

Trisha's mouth opened and closed. "That's good to know but they don't catch venereal diseases easily. They are different enough that most of the common ones won't transfer to them. They have a really tough immune system that would attack most of them anyway."

"That's good to know." Tammy smiled. "I figured it was fine. I mean, I kind of got that Valiant hadn't slept around much by things he's said."

Trisha blinked a few times. "He could get you pregnant."

Tammy let the words sink in and shook her head. "That can't be right. I mean, I watch the news. They are always discussing how New Species are sterile. They can't have children. The testing facilities purposely made them that way. It's a well-known fact."

"Do you believe everything you hear on the news?" Trisha sighed. "Forget that question. It's not general knowledge. It's actually classified information that only New Species, or in this case, women who are having unprotected sex with them need to know. You fall under that category since you're not on the Pill or taking other preventative measures. You needed to be told of the risk of pregnancy."

Valiant growled. "I am not sterile."

Trisha glanced at him and then back at her. "I am a New Species doctor, Tammy. Mercile Industries did breeding experiments on New Species trying to make them reproduce but it never worked. They never sterilized them since they encouraged them to procreate. It was just recently that we discovered that it is possible that a human and a New Species can have a child together under the right circumstances."

Tammy gaped at the doctor, mute.

Trisha paused. "We have been doing a lot of testing. I just wanted you both to be aware of that risk." Her gaze shifted to Valiant. "You're more..." She paused again. "Of a more pronounced New Species and unless I test your sperm, I'm not sure you could get her pregnant. Your DNA could be too altered for it to work but I wanted both of you to be aware of the possibility." Her attention returned to Tammy. "I could put you on something right away if you want to make sure you're protected."

Tammy blinked. "But we've already been having sex. That means I could already be pregnant, right?"

Trisha nodded. "Yes. I can order you a pregnancy test in a few weeks."

Tammy softly cursed and didn't miss when Valiant's focus jerked to her. He looked pissed off again.

"Is it such a bad thing?" His gaze dropped to her stomach. "To carry a child of mine?"

Tammy just stared at him. Valiant growled, his eyes narrowed and he tensed. He growled again, deeper.

"Stop," Tammy whispered. "Don't get angry. I'm in shock since I didn't think it was possible, okay? Give me a few minutes to stop freaking out. I never even considered I could get pregnant."

"It doesn't change anything. You are mine and I am yours. It will be a good thing if we make a child. I am strong and will provide well for you both. I will protect you and I would welcome a baby. You said I do not embarrass you. Would having my child embarrass you?"

"No." She frowned. "I just don't know you well enough to be thinking about starting a family, okay? People should be together for years before they make that decision. Trust me, I know. My parents were married because my mother got knocked up and by the time I was two years old, they hated each other. They fought all the time until my father finally walked out on us when I was four. My mother started drinking and finally met a man who hated having me around. She just dumped me on my grandma without a backward glance. I never saw her again."

He took a step toward her. "You are mine. I would never hate you nor would you ever hate me. I would never leave you. Never. You are mine."

Tammy looked to the doctor for help. "What exactly does that mean to them?"

Trisha hesitated. ""Valiant, could we please talk alone?"

"No." He crossed his arms over his chest again. "You can speak to her in front of me."

"I don't want to offend you."

He shook his head at Trisha. "You won't."

She didn't appear so sure about that, but Trisha began to speak. "They were never allowed to have anything of their own. As in possessions. They couldn't even become attached to any of the other New Species they were exposed to. That was a rare occurrence for the most part since they kept them locked in separate cells. If they did, if the staff figured out they cared what happened to another New Species, it was used against them to punish or make them do what they were told while they were imprisoned. Now when they think something is theirs they will not give it up. They want to keep it forever."

Stunned, Tammy just stared at the doctor. "Forever?"

"Until one of you dies."

"So I can't leave him no matter what he does? He won't leave me?"

Trisha bit her lip. "What do you think he would or could do that would make you want to leave him? I know he's kind of pushy but it's just their way. He really would kill or die to protect you and you can't say that about many men. Yes, they are controlling but they do it trying to keep the person safe. That actually counts for something once you adjust to their ways."

"What if he cheats?" Tammy refused to look at Valiant.

A smile curved the doctor's mouth. "They are very loyal. There are only a few couples so far but from what we have learned, the males will kind of scent imprint you. The more time you spend with him, the more he'll kind of get addicted to you. After a while he won't be able to stand the smell of another woman if he gets close to one. As an example, we had a couple where another woman hit on the male by trying to kiss him. He grew very agitated at being touched by her. He almost crushed his wife when he rubbed up against her body to remove the scent of the other woman. He couldn't stand it. It enraged him and he said he felt sick to his stomach when I later asked him about it."

"Was it that married couple, Ellie and Fury? The ones on the news?"

"Yes."

"Fury was mixed with some breed of dog, right? That's what I read. Valiant is a lion. Won't that mean something different? Dogs and lions are nothing alike."

"I can't say I know for sure but you could ask Valiant. If there's one thing you can count on, trust me, they are brutally honest."

Tammy finally looked at Valiant. He sighed as he watched her back. "I would hurt another female if she tried to have sexual contact with me. I want you and only you. I would not allow another female to touch me."

"See?" Trisha drew her attention. "You don't have to worry about him cheating."

"I will bathe in his blood if another man touches you." Valiant growled deeply. "I'll tear off his limbs. I'll rip off his head." He paused, took a deep breath. "He'll die horribly. I will never hurt you though."

Trisha managed to keep the smile in place. "Did I mention they are very possessive and graphic too?" Trisha shot him a dirty look and shook her head. "Can you cut back on the gory details a bit? Humans aren't keen on hearing that stuff. It isn't a great selling point. Work with me here."

He growled. "I always tell Tammy the truth."

"I'm learning that. I'm not ready to have a baby though." Tammy met Valiant's angry glare. "I want to get to know you better first before we even discuss having one together, if that's even possible. Please understand that and don't get mad or hurt. I'm not saying no forever, I'm just saying that right now I want to spend more time with you before I consider that option." Tammy faced the doctor. "Could you put me on something?"

Trisha nodded. "Of course. I'll have to call it in and have it delivered since we don't carry birth control on Reservation. In a few weeks you will need a pregnancy test to make sure you didn't already conceive and we'll put you on the Pill." Trisha paused. "I don't want to start them right now in case you've already conceived. Let me know immediately if you start your period. I—"

"No sex?" Valiant interrupted.

Tammy frowned. "Quiet and allow her to talk."

Trisha glanced between them, settling her focus on Tammy. "I would also appreciate it if you didn't tell anyone about this discussion. There are a lot of hate groups out there who would be very unhappy if they learned it was even possible for us to have children with them."

"That's an understatement if I ever heard one." Tammy grimaced. "They'd go ballistic. I saw a show a few weeks ago about some idiots who started a business taking bets on how long each known New Species will live."

Horrified at what she'd said, her gaze darted to Valiant, hoping it hadn't hurt his feelings. He met her stare calmly, not appearing shocked at hearing that someone wanted to make a profit of their deaths.

"Yeah. We heard about that." Trisha got a sad look on her face. "And they'd probably do anything to kill the woman carrying that unborn baby and the baby if it had already been born. A lot of them are looking forward to the thought of New Species dying out in time. It would send some of those assholes into a rampage if they discovered that generations more of them were possible."

"See? That's another reason why I don't want to have a baby right now. I've already been targeted once. I may as well buy a bull's-eye T-shirt and live in it. I'm not ready to take that chance just yet. I want the pills as soon as you're able to prescribe them to me."

Tammy turned her head to see how Valiant reacted to her decision. He was gone, had left the room, and she softly cursed. He'd walked out without saying a word. Obviously he didn't agree with what she wanted. *Damn.*

"Give him time." Trisha reached out and touched Tammy's arm. "I think he might feel a little rejected."

"I didn't mean for him to take it that way. You understand, don't you? I met him five weeks ago, he scared the hell out of me, we had incredible sex, and I hit him over the head with a lamp. Last night he came back into my life when he saved me. I'm very attracted to him but we need to spend a lot more time together before we purposely take risks of that kind. Hell, I think I'm falling—" She closed her mouth.

"In all, I've spent so little time with him and certainly not long enough to make a lifelong commitment of having a child together."

"I do understand."

Tammy saw compassion on the other woman's face. "There's the whole we're-different factor. I was kidnapped last night because someone heard I had slept with him. Just slept with him. What if I got pregnant? Those stupid bastards and every stupid asshole like them would want to get their hands on me. And that's not even touching the subject of what the press would do. I watched what they did to that married couple. Those two can't do anything without having reporters all over them. They don't even leave Homeland anymore, do they? I heard the press stalked them as though they were movie or rock stars. Hell, I think those two groups of celebrities have it easier than that couple does."

Trisha sighed. "Yeah, I know. Luckily they don't mind since they both work at Homeland and their lives are inside the secure walls there."

"I don't know if I could live that way. Right now I am not supposed to even leave this suite. Is that how it is with Ellie? Is she locked down inside their home?"

"No. She has a job at Homeland and it's more settled there. Reservation just opened and that's why you've been kept inside the suite. The New Species are used to humans but not the ones who live here. It's just for your safety. I can't walk around either without an escort. I don't have that issue at Homeland. I have a house there."

Tammy desperately wanted to change the subject. "How did it go with the father of your baby? Does he live around here? I might know him since it's a small town."

Trisha shook her head. "He usually works and lives in Southern California."

"Oh." Tammy nodded.

"He's working somewhere else right now on assignment. In a few months he'll be back in Southern California where his home is and so will I. We did talk this morning and he's reconsidering marriage."

Tammy did a thumbs-up sign. "Good for you."

Trisha nodded. "Yes. I want to marry him and I love him more than anything."

Tammy sighed, her mind refusing to budge from the worry that rose inside. "Valiant is really angry with me."

"I think he's hurt because you mean a lot to him. I don't think you realize how attached he is to you. We have New Species who have engaged in sex with humans but they didn't stake claims to them. I think for whatever reason, he imprinted you already."

"What if he meets someone else and changes his mind?"

"As I said, they are very loyal. They aren't the kind of men we're used to. They had hellish lives and they really value something they care about. He obviously cares about you or he wouldn't have claimed you."

Tammy nodded. "I'm really confused."

Trisha nodded too. "I understand. Trust me, I really do."

"Thank you for telling me everything. Once I start taking the pills how long until they work?"

"A month. I'll send a large supply of condoms. I can get them to you today." She hesitated. "You will probably have to show him how to use them since I doubt he's ever had to. Mercile Industries only permitted them to have sex with females when they were doing breeding experiments. It was the only time they were ever allowed any kind of physical closeness with another of their kind. I don't think he's ever had any physical contact with anyone human except you. You'll have to ask him. I don't know much about where he was kept before they opened Reservation but from what I understand, it was in a remote desert location. They tended to assign women, human ones, to guard them since New Species won't attack females. Who knows if any of them were attracted to him." She cleared her throat. "I'd bet not. He's pretty intimidating."

Tammy couldn't imagine many woman approaching Valiant without being super brave. "It's horrible what was done to them."

"I know. As I said, they had rough lives." Trisha made ready to leave. "I'll bring a picnic lunch in a few days so we can talk again. I make a mean fried chicken. Talk to Valiant and try not to lose your temper if you get frustrated with him. Sometimes they don't understand things but they learn quickly and if you explain it clearly, they usually get the gist of what you're trying to say. Their feelings do get hurt and they tend to react by appearing angry. It's one of those his-bark-is-far-worse-than-his-bite kind of sayings that fit."

"Thank you."

Trisha left the bedroom and Tammy sighed loudly. Valiant was probably hurt that she wasn't jumping for joy at the concept that she might be pregnant. She barely knew the guy and they were just so different. It wasn't anything bad against him, not a form of rejection, just a smart decision to take things slower.

She glanced at the bed and snorted. She was having hot sex with the guy, often, and nothing about their relationship so far seemed to have any brakes to it. She couldn't resist him once he started growling and purring at her. His mouth needed to come with a warning label. She smiled and finally stood. She needed to talk to him and clear the air. The idea of him feeling rejected didn't sit well with her.

Tammy walked out of the bedroom. After a quick search of the other bedroom, bathroom and the living area, she came to the conclusion that Valiant had left. She hugged her chest and walked toward the suite door. She hesitated before opening it.

A New Species man stood on the other side. He had black hair and gray eyes. He turned to peer at her curiously. She wasn't really surprised that someone had been posted. She knew she wasn't allowed to leave the suite.

"Do you know where Valiant is?"

He shook his head. "He looked really angry when he stormed out and I wasn't going to ask him anything. I didn't want him to roar at me."

"Thank you." Tammy softly closed the door.

She finally settled on watching television but then remembered what she'd said to Sheriff Cooper. She wondered if she was allowed to make phone calls. She returned to the suite door and opened it. The New Species turned, studying her again.

"Am I allowed to use the phone?"

He hesitated. "No one said you couldn't. Go ahead."

"Thank you." She closed the door and decided to use the phone inside the bedroom. She sat on the bed, got comfortable, and dialed her best friend's number. Tim answered on the second ring.

"Hello?"

"Hi, it's me."

"Tam! How are you? Are you home? I'll grab some pizza and be right over. I've been so worried about you."

"I'm not home but I'm fine. I'm still at New Species Reservation and I'm going to be here for a while." She paused. "I'm kind of seeing one of them."

"Have you lost your mind?" Tim yelled. "Do you know what has happened since you were attacked? We have everything from news crews to protesters who hate those New Species people swamping the town. The support groups for those people showed up to counter protest early this morning. It's a madhouse and on top of it, there are all kinds of rumors flying about how you are dating one of them but I thought it was bullshit. I'm your best friend and you would have told me. I yelled at the reporters who knocked on my door that it was absolute bullshit that you were hooked up with one of them. They showed a video of you and him on the news this morning with footage of him carrying you to a Jeep and sitting with you on his lap."

Tammy tried not to flinch over how upset Tim seemed to be. She wanted to try to calm him down. "Great. I was on the news and missed it? Did you happen to tape it for me? How cool."

"That's not funny."

"Did my hair at least look good?" She winced, remembering how dirt and leaves had been stuck in it.

"Damn it, Tam. I'm not kidding. I drove by your place this morning to feed that feral cat you toss scraps to since the sheriff said you were hurt and had been taken out to Reservation to be seen by their doctor. He said you would be out there for a day or so while you recovered. There were protesters picketing in your yard and you should have read the signs they carried, Tam. That bitchy old woman next door is threatening to put a petition together to force you to sell your grandma's house. She came outside to scream at me that she wanted you gone because she wasn't going to live next door to that kind of crap."

"What did the signs say?" Tammy could feel a headache coming on. She remembered her pain pills but couldn't reach the bathroom with the corded phone.

"Nothing you'd want to read, let me assure you. It was reported that you were dating the guy and that he was your lover. You can guess. It was brutal."

"So Mrs. Haller is pissed, huh?"

"She yelled that she was putting a petition together to try to force you to sell. Did you hear that part?"

"Well, she is a bitch and I'm sure she'll give it her best shot." Tammy suddenly chuckled. "Are there a lot of protesters? Are they really loud? Do you think they'll stay out there all night and drive her insane? She complains at me constantly if my TV is even at a normal level. There's a bright side, right? Maybe she'll get so upset she keels over. That woman has hated me since I was a kid and moved in with Grandma."

"Tam, damn it, that's not funny. I'm going to come out there and get you. You can hole up inside our guestroom to hide out from everyone. My parents are worried sick about you too. They don't think you are safe out there and neither do I. You don't know much about those people."

"Don't be an ass, Tim. I know more about them than you do. I'm extremely safe."

"Since when?"

"Since I've gotten to know them."

"That old bitch is really going to get a petition going, Tam. She's really going to try to make you sell your house. What will you do if she succeeds?"

"Well, remember a few years ago when I went through my heavy-metal stage? She put a petition together then too and asked all the neighbors to sign it by saying I worshipped the devil by trying to call demons into the backyard every time I lit the fire pit. They just laughed at her."

"This isn't her hating your taste in music. This is super serious. There are at least twenty protesters on your yard carrying signs that are accusing you of liking to screw anything on a leash with four legs."

"That bad, huh?" Tammy winced again. "Well, even if I came to your house it wouldn't make them go away, would it? They would only start picketing at your place if they learned I'd gone there. I'm staying here."

"You need to come back to town and tell everyone the news had it wrong. You need to denounce that guy until it stops."

"What do they have wrong? I am seeing one of them."

Tim remained silent for a long minute. "Why?"

"Why do you think? He's wonderful, sweet, and I just want to stay with him."

"You could have told me if you were that lonely. You don't need to date one of them. Let *me* take you out."

"Oh, stop it. Don't even go there, Tim. I swear, just don't. You and I are best friends. I get asked out often, if you must know. I'm not desperate for any guy. I really, really am attracted to him."

"But he's—"

"Don't say anything bad," Tammy warned, cutting him off.

"Fine. I hope you realize it's going to ruin your life. When you stop seeing this…him…no guy in town is going to want to touch you. I have to go. You obviously have your mind made up and I just can't even talk to you right now." Tim hung up.

Tammy held the receiver in her hand for long seconds before returning it to the cradle. She wiped at tears that momentarily blinded her. Tim had never hung up on her before. She scooted off the bed, walked into the bathroom and filled a glass with water. On her way back to the bed she stopped in her tracks when her gaze met Valiant's. He leaned against the wall inside the bedroom right next to the door, his expression grim.

"You're back."

His golden eyes regarded her and a frown marred his full lips. His arms were crossed over his chest and he took a deep breath.

"You are going to lose your house?"

"You were listening."

He shrugged. "I have good hearing. I took a walk downstairs to get some fresh air and came back when you were talking on the phone. I stood outside the door so you could talk to your friend without interruption. You said he was your best friend." He shifted his weight, pushing away from the wall. "He made you cry. Answer me. Are you going to lose your house?"

She shrugged. "It was a shitty one with a leaking roof anyway, but I doubt it. Most of the neighbors have been there forever and have known me for most of my life. My next-door neighbor is the Antichrist. She's making waves but she always does that kind of bullshit. I have protesters picketing at my house."

"You don't need your house anymore, sexy. You have my home and you have me."

Tammy stared at him. "But for how long?"

He moved. "You won't ever get rid of me." He stalked toward her. "Not even if you try. You belong to me and I belong to you."

Tammy stared up at Valiant when he stopped inches from her. He reached for the glass and set it down. They stared at each other for a long moment before Valiant suddenly grabbed her, taking her flat to the bed. His hands tore at her clothes as his lips kissed her throat. Tammy moaned.

Valiant pinned Tammy under him tighter, inhaling her wonderful scent, wanting to get her totally naked to be skin to skin. She'd stood up to her best friend for him, refused to leave him, and he wanted to make sure she didn't change her mind.

She might lose her home because of her association with Species. Guilt ate at him as his hands caressed her bare breasts. He stared into her passion-filled eyes and swore he'd make her forget everything but him. He'd make sure she knew being with him was worth any sacrifices she made.

He growled at her, working at getting her pants off as he slid off the bed to the carpet, onto his knees. The scent of her growing arousal drove him nearly insane to taste her, to claim her, but she suddenly wiggled up the bed. He snarled at her and gripped the bed, intent on going after her. Her hand lifted, palm out, in a gesture to stop him and he froze.

"Condoms."

He wanted to roar. She was his. He knew what the things were but he wanted nothing between them when he took her. He wanted to mark her with his scent, fill her with his seed, and if life took hold—so be it!

"Please? I'm not ready to have a baby."

He stared into her eyes while he fought his anger and hurt.

"Valiant?" Her gaze softened. "You could totally seduce me, I want you, but I'm just asking for more time before we risk that. Can you please do this for me? Please?"

He closed his eyes, snarled, and jerked to his feet. "Get naked. I'll be right back." He stormed out of the bedroom, down the hall, and to the suite door. He jerked it open and glared at Flame. They'd just changed guards.

Flame watched him warily as he backed away. "What'd I do?"

"I need condoms." He spat the last word.

Flame did a poor job of hiding his amusement. "Um, all right. No glove, no love, huh?"

Valiant snarled at him.

Flame backed up a few feet more, reaching behind him. Valiant tensed, believing the officer reached for his weapon. Instead he pulled out a wallet, opened it, and removed something that crinkled in a long wrapper.

"Here." He stepped forward. "The no-glove-no-love thing was mentioned in a class we held at Homeland about human women. It means some of them don't want sex without a condom." He braved another step. "We carry these in our wallets at Homeland if we interact with human women just in case we decide to share sex. I'll make sure more are brought to you but that's all I've got for now." He held them out. "Do you know how to use them?"

"No." Valiant hated to admit it. He accepted the weird package that had four round things sealed in weird-looking plastic on one side and shiny stuff on the other.

Flame swallowed. "We really need to hold classes here at Reservation. You carefully open one of the packages containing a round rubber thing. You put it over the tip of your dick and it rolls down to the base of it." He glanced at Valiant's hands. "Let her do it. You've got the sharp-nail issue. You'll tear them. Just look cute and helpless while you tell her you need help. Human women dig that."

"Thank you." He met Flame's eyes. "I appreciate the advice."

Valiant backed up, slammed the door closed and locked it. He clenched his teeth, gripped the condoms, and stormed back toward the bedroom. *The things I will do for my Tammy.*

Chapter Ten

ഇ

Tammy knew Valiant was angry when he returned to the bedroom and slammed their door closed. She had stripped, climbed under the covers, and watched him face her. He held up a roll of four condoms.

"I don't know anything about these."

She was extremely touched that he'd gotten them somehow. She threw back the bedding and rose to her feet. "It will be fun."

His eyebrows arched and he didn't appear convinced.

"Will you trust me?" She slowly approached him and took the roll from his open palm.

"I want you to be happy," he grudgingly admitted. "But I am not."

She backed up. "Remove your clothes. I can remedy that."

"Will it hurt?" His gaze fell to the condoms.

"No."

"It's not natural." He began to strip though.

This coming from a guy who is part lion. She kept that observation silent. The sight of his bare body always did wonderful things to her. He followed her to the bed and glared down at her, showing his displeasure, but she gave him credit for getting condoms. An idea struck and she grinned.

"Will you stretch out over the bed on your back for me?"

His gaze narrowed. "Why?"

"Because I asked?" She grinned at him. "Pretty please?"

He blew out a deep breath. "This better not be painful."

He turned and just threw his big body across the mattress. She held back a laugh as he rolled onto his back, locked his arms behind his head to use his hands for a pillow and glared at her. She climbed on the bed and straddled his thighs. The shock on his features was instantly apparent.

"What are you doing?"

She dropped the condoms on the bed next to his hip. "Just lie back and I'll show you that condoms can be fun."

He softly growled at her. "You're acting strange."

"I like seeing you this way." Her gaze lingered over his taut, muscular belly, his broad chest, before lowering to his partially erect cock. He'd been circumcised. She hadn't noticed that before since he'd never given her time to really examine that part of him. He also had no pubic hair although he did have a thin trail of hair from his bellybutton down to his lower belly. She leaned forward, kept eye contact with him, and braced her arms as she hovered over him. A smile curved her lips.

"Can you hold real still for me?"

"Why? What are you planning to do?"

"Getting you so turned on that you don't mind wearing a condom."

"I always want you."

"Just hold still, okay? Don't sit up. Don't grab me either or roll me onto my back. Am I clear? Freeze just the way you are."

He seemed to ponder her request. "You're my Tammy and you may do as you wish to me."

He wasn't happy about it but still agreed. It amused her but she refrained from laughing. She leaned up, studied his rib cage, and her mouth lowered to his body. The muscles tensed along his abdomen when she licked his skin and her hair fell forward to brush against his side. She kissed him, allowed her teeth to lightly nip him and began to explore down over his six-pack abs with her lips.

A growl tore from Valiant. "What are you doing?"

"Relax." She felt his cock stiffen against her ribs where it lifted and poked against her as he became more aroused. "Enjoy this." Her mouth returned to his skin.

The muscles of his legs tensed against her thighs as she inched lower until her face hovered above his cock. He was big, thick and impressive. She glanced up at his face to see his eyes were closed, his sharp teeth dented his bottom lip and he had an edgy expression on his face. She wondered if anyone had ever done any of this to him before. He'd admitted to having limited sexual experience.

She licked her lips to wet them, lifted one hand and wrapped her fingers around his rigid shaft. A snarl tore from Valiant and his eyes opened, his head lifted, and he stared at her with obvious surprise.

"You are putting one on me now?"

"No. Not yet."

He swallowed and breathed a little faster. "You wish to study me?"

"Nope." Her gaze lowered and she tilted her head a little as her tongue dipped out to drag over the crown of his cock.

Valiant jerked, a strange sound coming from him, and his ass pressed tighter against the mattress, enough to pull him away from her mouth. She glanced up at him.

"What are you doing?" He gaped at her in absolute shock.

That answers that question. "You've never had a woman do this before?"

"Lick me? Not there. Males do it to females to prepare them for sex and to enjoy their taste but I'm ready to take you."

"Shut up and enjoy this, baby."

She gave her full attention to his erection and opened her mouth wide. She was afraid he'd protest so she decided to show him how good it would feel instead of teasing him a little first. Her mouth wrapped around his cock as she took a few inches inside and began to lick and suck on him as she tightened the seal.

He didn't fight, didn't tear her off, but his body did stiffen. She took more of him, working him deeper inside, to the back of her mouth, and began a slow and steady rhythm of going up and down in steady stokes, her tongue rubbing him.

Loud, raspy purrs came from Valiant and she knew he enjoyed it a lot. A sweet taste began to tease her and she moaned, realizing his pre-cum had to be the source.

Every time she nearly slid him out of her mouth more of it spilled onto her tongue and then a loud noise made her jerk her mouth completely away and lift her head to discover the source.

Valiant's hands were digging into the bedspread near his head and she saw where the material had torn. His head was thrown back, his mouth open to allow those deep purrs to come from his throat. His head lifted until their gazes locked. He had a wild look in his sexy eyes, which were so filled with desire she was amazed he'd kept so still.

"I'm going to come if you do that again. Is that how it feels when I lick your pussy to enjoy your cream? It's wonderful. It's so good." His voice came out sounding inhuman, more of a growl than an actual tone.

Her gaze darted to the poor bedspread, happy it had felt the bite of his nails instead of her skin. "I think you're ready for a condom."

He nodded. "Anything."

She leaned up, still straddling his thighs, and reached for them. She made sure he could see what she did as she tore one free from the roll, used her teeth to rip open the top edge of the packet, and showed him the round disk. She was happy to note the brand was designed for bigger men. She doubted she could have gotten a regular size on him. Valiant definitely wasn't a one-size-fits-all type of guy.

"Watch."

She placed it over the crown of his cock and slowly rolled it down to the base of his shaft. He groaned and more of the bedding took the brunt of his fingernails. He didn't look away though as she demonstrated how the condom worked. Her body ached too and she wanted him inside her. As tempted as she was to finish him with her mouth, she felt selfish at that moment, hurting to fuck him.

She released his sheathed cock and crawled up him until her thighs gripped his hips. One hand reached back to wrap around his incredibly hard shaft and she guided him to her pussy as she wiggled her hips until they aligned perfectly.

Her gaze locked with his. He appeared stunned as she sank down on him, her wet and welcoming body already prepared for him. She moaned as her vaginal walls were parted by Valiant's thick cock.

Valiant snarled and she gasped when he suddenly grabbed her and rolled them over. She ended up under him, pinned, his cock buried deep inside her pussy. He grabbed her wrists, jerked them above her head, and used his upper arms to brace his weight. Their gazes locked.

"Wrap around me." It wasn't a request but more of a snarled demand.

The wild look in his eyes had grown downright feral. She didn't feel fear though as she spread her thighs more, bent them higher, and wrapped them around his waist until her calves squeezed over his firm ass.

He spread his knees, dug them into the mattress to find traction and withdrew a little, only to slam back into her deep. She cried out from the pleasure. He snarled, his mouth lowered and he nipped her shoulder, nudging her head out of the way.

The sharp bite of his teeth did amazing things to her. It didn't hurt so much as send a jolt of desire through her. Valiant's strength turned her on more as he paused, completely in control, and then started to rock his hips to fuck her slowly.

"I'm fighting my instincts," he groaned against her skin.

"Don't fight," she moaned, locking her legs tighter around him.

His head lifted and he stared into her eyes. "I just hurt you."

"That didn't hurt. It felt good."

"Tell me if I cause you pain. I'm always afraid I'll be too rough." He stared into her eyes while his hips started to move, the muscles of his ass tensing against her calves, and he began to drive into her in deep, steady thrusts.

Tammy threw her head back, her eyes closed, and could feel each powerful plow of his cock as he rode her frantically, creating a delicious tight friction between their joined bodies that quickly turned into a powerful climax. Valiant roared as her vaginal muscles clenched around him and she cried out his name.

They panted and Tammy smiled. Valiant smiled back.

"That wasn't so bad, was it? I told you condoms wouldn't hurt."

"I prefer not to use them but it didn't hurt." He hesitated. "Do I just leave it on? I want to flip you over, put you on your knees, and mount you from behind."

"Give me a minute to catch my breath first and um, no. That one has to be tossed into the trash and I'll put a new one on you."

His lips curved. "I understand." He slowly withdrew his cock and rolled off her body to stretch out on his back. "Go ahead. I enjoy your mouth."

Tammy turned on her side and grinned. "I think I've created a monster."

His smile slipped. "What does that mean?"

She laughed in response. "Nothing. I was teasing."

She sat up and glanced around for a trash can. If teasing him with her mouth got him to wear condoms, she could totally get on board with that plan. He tasted good.

* * * * *

Tammy smiled when Trisha sat on the couch. "I'm so glad you came. Valiant left about two hours ago and I've been bored. He wanted to get some of his own clothes from his house and he needed to feed a few of his friends." She paused. "I was too afraid to ask what that meant."

Trisha grinned. "He likes the squirrels around his house. He's forbidden anyone from killing them. He puts nuts and berries out for them to lure them closer to his house. He's trying to teach them that he won't eat them or something like that."

"Is that an issue?" Tammy took a seat next to the doctor and glanced at the cooler the woman had placed on the table. "And what's that?"

"The Wild Zone is a heavily wooded area on Reservation and that's where Valiant lives. There's a few dozen New Species who live as his neighbors. They're not as human as most of the others are. Their facial traits are more animal than human, to be blunt, and some of them are gruff the way Valiant is. They hunt rabbits and deer in the woods but the squirrels are off the menu now. Valiant enjoys watching them for some reason and has deemed them non-food." She grinned. "I just nod when I hear stuff like that. Some things are, well, I just accept it. I promised you fried chicken. I thought you'd want to talk again today instead of waiting. How are you feeling?"

"A lot better. Thanks."

"Good." All humor faded. "How goes things with Valiant? Did the condoms arrive?"

"Yes. One of the guards brought them before he left to go home. Thank you."

"They prefer to be called officers." She shrugged. "It's a New Species thing. Have you talked him into using them yet?"

"We worked it out."

Tammy studied her and smiled. "I take it that he didn't fight it too hard?"

"I showed him the plus sides."

The doctor chuckled. "Good. I was worried. That's why I really came today. I figured you might have more questions or just needed someone to help you talk him into using protection. Is he still feeling rejected?"

"I don't know. He seems okay with it. I just need more time before we even consider having a baby." She paused. "And to be honest, it's a lot to take in."

"Yes, it is. Being with one of them will change your life."

"One of my friends told me that I've got protesters on my yard at home."

"Damn. I'm sorry."

Tammy shrugged. "I'm not there. I kind of really hate one of my neighbors so I'm hoping it's really annoying her." She smiled. "She's spent years harassing me. That's a bright side."

Trisha grinned. "Good. Keep your sense of humor. It helps." She stood. "I'm going to grab some plates from your kitchenette. I swear I'm always hungry." She stepped around the coffee table.

Tammy rose to follow, staring at the corner area. "These suites are nice."

"And they come fully stocked." Trisha opened a cupboard, pulled out two plates, and turned. Her face suddenly paled and she gasped. The dishes nearly slipped from her fingers that seemed to go lax.

Tammy saved them before they hit the floor, set them on the counter, and spun to face the doctor. "What's wrong?" She had to grab the other woman when her knees collapsed, to help her sink to the carpet without getting hurt.

Trisha groaned, wrapped her arms around her stomach, and her blue eyes widened. "Get Slade."

Tammy released her, spun, and sprinted for the door. The New Species posted in the hallway seemed startled when she flung open the door. "Get Slade now. Trisha is in pain and grabbing her stomach. Call him and get in here. I don't know what to do or what is wrong with her."

She left the door open when she bolted back to Trisha. The doctor still held her stomach protectively as she sat on her bent legs. She had begun to pant, and Tammy dropped to her knees next to the woman. She gripped her upper arms to make sure she didn't fall over.

"What is it? What can I do?"

"Contractions."

"But it can't be. You're only what? Five months along?" Terror tore through Tammy. "I'll call an ambulance."

"No," Trisha frantically shook her head. "No outsiders. Slade will come and he'll take me to see Harris. He's another doctor who works here."

The New Species officer from the hallway rushed inside the room with a fearful expression. Tammy jerked her head up. "What is your name?"

"Flame."

"Flame, please very carefully pick her up and lay her on the couch. She's having contractions but it's too early. We need Dr. Harris right now. She doesn't want me to call an ambulance."

Flame bent down and carefully touched Trisha's shoulder. "Slade is coming. Can I lift you? Will I hurt you more? Should you even be moved?"

Trisha's face scrunched up in pain as another contraction hit. She pointed toward the couch with a shaky finger. Flame hesitated before gently lifting the woman into his arms and carrying her to the couch, where he tenderly placed her on her back. Trisha groaned and kept panting.

Tammy ran for the spare bedroom to yank the blanket off the bed and ran back into the living room, not sure what else to do. She covered Trisha's legs since her skirt had ridden up her thighs and knelt next to the couch. Flame had moved to the open doorway to speak on his radio. Tammy took Trisha's hand.

"Help is coming. Flame is calling Dr. Harris and your bodyguard. I'm right here, Trisha."

"Can I do anything?" Flame hovered behind them, now done calling for more help.

"I don't know." Tammy panicked. "She's only five months along. It's too early. I got her a blanket in case she's going into shock."

He cursed viciously. "I'll wait at the door to direct the doctor inside. Tell me if you need something." He paused. "Hang in there, Trisha. Slade is coming fast. He was downstairs at the cafeteria."

Trisha finally stopped panting. Her face had turned a little red and the hold on Tammy's hand eased. The doctor opened her eyes. "That was a strong contraction. Do you have a watch or can you see a clock? I need to time them."

Tammy glanced at the DVD player. "I'm watching the clock. What else can I do?"

"Nothing. I just want Slade."

"Flame said he's coming. Did you hear him? Slade is just downstairs."

"He always stays pretty close to me."

"TRISHA!" A man roared and then Slade launched through the doorway. "I'm here."

Tammy had to scamper out of the large man's way as he almost landed on top of her to get closer to Trisha. He gripped the doctor's hand and cupped her face with his free hand. He had a frightened expression on his face. Tammy backed up and stood, putting some room between them.

"Talk to me, sweet thing. Is the baby coming?" Slade inched closer.

Trisha nodded. "We need to get to the trauma bay."

"All right. I'll carry you. Just hold on. I'm going to move you very carefully."

"Not yet. I feel another one coming." Trisha's face contorted as she threw back her head and moaned loudly as she started to pant again.

Tammy glanced at the clock. "Uh-oh. She said to time the contractions but a minute hasn't even passed since her last one."

Slade's head jerked in Tammy's direction. "What does that mean?"

"It means the contractions are really close together. The closer they get, the faster the baby comes. Under a minute apart is usually birth time from what I know." Tammy shrugged. "At least that's what I've been told."

"Damn it," Slade growled. "Trisha? Sweet thing? I'm right here." He rubbed her face with his fingers to comfort her while he kept hold of her hand too. "I'm right here and I'm with you."

"Hurry," Flame shouted from the hallway. "This way. She's inside here."

A man wearing a doctor's coat rushed into the room with two men wearing scrubs on his heels. The two male nurses each carried a large duffle bag. There was a boxlike machine with a small oxygen tank that the doctor set down. The guy in the white coat, who had to be Dr. Harris, yanked gloves from his pocket and put them on.

He bent over the back of the couch to reach Trisha, pulled back the bedspread that covered her lap, and paused. He met Slade's gaze, who nodded, and the doctor reached under Trisha's skirt. He removed her panties with her help. The doctor gently nudged his elbow against her knee to push her thighs apart.

"I'm examining you, Trisha. I need to see if you're dilated."

Trisha nodded, still panting. She looked as if she were in a lot of pain. The contraction lasted for a long time. Dr. Harris withdrew his bloody glove.

"Slade, we need to lay her flat. She's having this baby right now." The doctor gave orders to the two nurses. "Open up everything and prepare for anything. Move!"

"I won't allow her to have the baby on the floor," Slade growled.

Tammy glanced at Flame, who still hovered by the door. "Go grab the top mattress from the bed in the first bedroom and bring it in here." Tammy tried not to panic as she grabbed the coffee table and dragged it to the corner of the room.

Flame carried the queen-size mattress into the room as easily as if it weighed nothing. Slade moved a second before he dropped it on the floor by the couch. Tammy moved back to stay out of the way. Slade lifted Trisha into his arms. She moaned, but wrapped her arms around his neck. He gently turned and laid her flat on the mattress. Slade moved until he sat on his bent legs above Trisha's head. He gently reached under her arms and pulled her up until his thighs acted as a pillow for her.

"I'm right here, sweet thing. I've got you," he crooned to her.

Trisha started to relax. She reached up to grip Slade's thigh with one hand and clutched his hand with her other. "Don't leave me."

"Someone would have to kill me to take me from your side."

A smile curved Trisha's lips. "You always make me laugh." Her focus fixed on Dr. Harris. "Well?"

"The only thing stopping you from having the baby is your water hasn't broken. When did the contractions start?"

Trisha glanced at Tammy expectantly. Tammy darted a look at the clock. "About six minutes ago."

The doctor didn't appear happy with that news. "This is happening way too fast."

"We knew it would probably happen early," Trisha said softly. "The baby is ready to come. I guess he can't even wait on a regular labor timetable to be born."

The two nurses spread open the emergency medical supplies. The duffle bags had long zippers down them that opened similar to suitcases with everything neatly stored inside two sealed halves of plastic pockets. Tammy stepped back farther, now trapped in the corner, to give them more room. She'd have to step around medical supplies to leave. She stayed put.

"There's more blood than I expected," Slade growled.

"Not much," Dr. Harris sighed. "It's a normal amount. She's lost her plug. Once I break her water, if it doesn't break on its own, this baby will come." He glanced at his two nurses. "Are we ready? We aren't sure if the lungs are fully developed. They looked great on the ultrasounds but we need to be prepared in case there are complications."

"His lungs will be fine," Trisha groaned. "Here comes another one."

"We're ready," one of the nurses said, grabbing the box thing with oxygen the doctor had brought, and set it near the supplies within their reach.

"As ready as we can be in a hotel room," the other one agreed.

"We don't have time to move her to the trauma bay." Dr. Harris bent on his knees between Trisha's thighs. "I'll leave the skirt on since it's loose."

Slade nodded. He turned to stare at the door. Flame stood there and a few more New Species had arrived to hover inside the open door. "Clear out."

They retreated and the door closed firmly behind them. Slade's gaze locked with Tammy's but then he ignored her. Tammy assumed that meant she could stay since he hadn't told her to leave as well. She didn't really have a choice since she was trapped. Trisha panted before she gripped Slade's hand tightly again. Slade lifted her hand to kiss the one he held and the fingers of his other hand ran through her hair to caress her.

"Her water just broke with the contraction." Dr. Harris cleared his throat. "I'm going to examine you again." Dr. Harris put on a new glove. He examined Trisha and nodded. "I'd say a few pushes and your son is going to be here. You're ready."

Trisha nodded, peering up at Slade. "Don't look so scared. I'm being brave so you have to be too. He's going to be fine and healthy. I've run every test there is and we've found nothing wrong."

Slade nodded. "I know, Trisha. I can't help being scared for you and him."

"Don't be. We'll be— Shit! Another one is coming."

"Go ahead and push if you get the urge," Dr. Harris encouraged. "Only if you get the urge."

"I know," Trisha panted. "I'm a doctor too, remember?" She groaned, sucked in air, and her face turned a splotchy red. Her body tensed when she began to push.

The nurses began to remove things from their plastic holders. Tammy hugged her chest tightly, worried she was about to see a tragedy happen. Babies born at five months usually didn't make it and her heart was breaking for Trisha.

"I see the head." Dr. Harris sounded excited. "He's coming, Trisha. He's got a full head of hair."

Slade reached over, yanking at Trisha's skirt until it bunched near her ribs to totally expose her rounded stomach. His focus centered between her bare, parted thighs to watch the baby being born. Trisha gasped in air and pushed harder.

out. Stop pushing," the excited doctor

... t help but stare over Slade's shoulder. Dr.
_ grabbed a suction bulb to clear the baby's mouth. Trisha
had stopped pushing and panted hard. Tammy couldn't look
away from what was taking place. A nurse handed over a
small towel next that the doctor took, shoving it out of sight,
maybe under the baby or Trisha.

"Push, Trisha. I know you're tired but I need one strong
push from you to clear his shoulders."

Trisha gasped in air and tensed as she pushed. A scream
tore from her as the baby slid out of her body to land in Dr.
Harris' waiting hands. The doctor lifted the baby up. Tammy
stared at what should have been a tiny preemie but instead
seemed to be a full-term baby.

Dr. Harris cradled the baby's upper body against his arm
and chest, his palm holding the baby's bottom and used the
towel to gently rub the baby's torso and face. A newborn
scream rent the air. Tammy nearly collapsed from relief at the
wonderful sound. One of the nurses leaned in to clamp the
umbilical cord and cut it. He assisted in delivering the
afterbirth and cleaning Trisha up after the delivery.

The baby wailed and wiggled inside the doctor's hold. He
actually appeared healthy and normal-sized, if not a little
bigger, than a full term baby. The doctor accepted another
towel from one of the nurses to rub the baby dry. The baby
stopped crying but he continued to wiggle and kick his chubby
legs. Dr. Harris grinned as he wrapped the baby in a blanket,
securing him papoose style.

"He looks great, guys." Dr. Harris laughed, grinning
widely. "Absolutely healthy. His color is perfect, he's
breathing like a champ, ten fingers and toes, and he's strong."

Trisha grinned while Slade absolutely beamed with
happiness. He hesitated and then held out his hands. Dr.
Harris leaned up and transferred the wiggling baby to Slade.

Slade's large hands cupped the baby gently and he lowered it into Trisha's waiting arms. They both held the baby together, smiling and staring in wonder at the newborn.

Dr. Harris tore off his gloves, grinned, and high-fived the nurse closest to him. "YES!"

Laughter erupted from all three. Dr. Harris climbed off the mattress and stood. Tammy watched in shock as the doctor bear-hugged both of the nurses who had assisted him. They turned then, watching Trisha and Slade with the baby. All three of them seemed over-the-top happy.

"We have our first healthy New Species baby!" Dr. Harris laughed. "Congratulations, Trisha and Slade. He's beautiful."

Slade smiled, grinning at the doctor. "Thank you, Harris."

The doctor nodded. Trisha suddenly reached up with her free hand, gripped Slade's hair at the base of his neck, and dragged his face down to hers. She kissed him soundly on the mouth.

"I love you so much, lollypop."

He laughed as he kissed her again. "I love you too, sweet thing. Our son is a miracle. A gift. Thank you."

Tammy let their words and actions sink in until it hit her as if she'd been slapped. She gaped at Trisha and Slade, the big New Species man with the sandy-brown, blond-streaked hair. Trisha had just given birth to Slade's baby.

Tammy's gaze flew to the baby, realizing he was the first New Species baby. *That's what Dr. Harris said.* Trisha had been only five months pregnant. The baby was huge and obviously had been born healthy. Her gaze locked on the tiny features of the baby that she could see from her position in the corner. She realized his little scrunched-up face wasn't totally human. His nose looked too flat, too wide, and she'd never seen a baby with cheekbones that prominent before. Babies had pudgy, rounded cheeks but this baby different.

Trisha didn't have a boyfriend somewhere else. Slade was her boyfriend. He always remained with her. Always. They kissed again, laughing. That's how Trisha knew it was possible for human women to get pregnant by New Species. Tammy pieced it together quickly. Trisha knew because Slade had gotten her pregnant. Not only that, but a baby fathered by a New Species could be born at five months into a pregnancy.

Tammy leaned against the wall, needed the support to stay on her feet, and watched the couple bond as a family. The love between Trisha and Slade, their joy at having a healthy son, made her ache a little. They were incredibly happy and it showed. She bit her lip as her full focus fixed on the baby. She'd always loved holding them when her friends had them and had always wanted to one day become a mother.

I could have that with Valiant if I got pregnant by him. That could be us one day. The thought shocked her.

* * * * *

Valiant couldn't help but grin when he walked into his bedroom. Tammy sat on the bed with pillows stacked behind her back, watching television, but her gaze met his as he closed the door softly. He'd just returned home to find his new living quarters a mass of activity.

He dropped his bag of clothes on the floor by the door he'd closed. Trisha had given birth to Slade's child, it had gone well, and security was about to remove them from the suite to relocate the new family to the medical center. He'd seen the baby and it had brought pure joy to his heart.

"He's perfect. Did you see him?"

She nodded.

She seemed pale to him and he frowned, some of his happiness fleeing. "They said you know the truth. Are you angry with me for not telling you that Slade was the father of Trisha's child? I wasn't allowed to share that information. I'm sorry. It wasn't my secret to tell."

"It's not that."

He paused, needed a shower after running around in the woods, but he wanted to know what was wrong. He approached the bed and stood at the end of it. "You are angry with me for not telling you that Slade was the father."

"I'm not. Really. I've been sitting here doing a lot of thinking. I get why I wasn't told. I still wouldn't know who the father of her baby is if she hadn't gone into labor in our living room, right?"

"I won't lie to you. No. Probably not."

"I saw him."

"Slade? He never leaves Trisha side or if he has to, he doesn't go far."

"The baby." She licked her lips. "He looks just like his father. I mean, it's hard to tell when they are newborns but he's got the features."

"Slade is his father. He's the first New Species baby born."

"There's a lot of people in the world who aren't going to be happy when they find out about that baby."

Valiant's entire body tensed. "Are you going to tell them?" The pain of possible betrayal tore through him.

"No!" She frowned and glared at him. "I just meant I understand why I wasn't told. I get it. Trisha and her baby are going to be in danger if those hate groups and fruitcakes find out. Men like the ones who kidnapped me would come after her and the baby. Or worse. They'd just want to kill them outright."

He could breathe again now that he knew she'd keep the baby a secret. "Yes. It's our worst fear and why very few know about Forest."

"Forest?"

He smiled. "It's what they have named the baby. Forest Slade North."

"I like it." She smiled.

"He was conceived in the forest."

Tammy laughed. "Seriously?"

"Yes. Trisha insisted on the name and Slade agreed. He liked it."

"They really love each other. I saw them together. They are so happy about the baby."

"They are." He tilted his head, watching her, trying to guess what bothered her. "What is wrong with that?"

She suddenly moved and crawled toward him over the mattress. Valiant's heart raced and his gaze traveled over her body. His cock instantly hardened as he watched the sexy way she stalked closer to him. She stopped inches from the end of the bed, her gaze held his, and she smiled.

"It made me feel a little jealous."

He tried to understand what she meant but he wasn't sure.

"The way they looked at each other and the love between them. Even the baby. I swear he's the cutest one I've ever seen. Please sit down."

He sucked in air as he sat next to her. His heart rate increased and suddenly Tammy rose and threw her leg over his lap to sit on top of his thighs. Her arms wound around his neck and her fingers brushed through his hair. She smiled at him.

"I think any baby by you would be absolutely adorable."

He couldn't speak. His mind blanked. He didn't want to take her words wrong but it almost seemed as if she were offering to try to have his baby.

"I'm not ready to have one yet but now I'm considering it."

He smiled. "Really?"

"We need to get to know each other better but I want to give us a chance. Do you think I could get a job here at Reservation? Maybe stay a while? I'm in no hurry to return to

192

my life. I would like to stay with you and see where you and I go."

"We'll go to my house." His arms wrapped around her. "You don't need a job. You're mine. I'll care for you."

"It's not that simple."

"Yes, it is." He pulled her tightly against him. "You belong with me."

She curled into his chest and his heart swelled with warmth.

"I want to stay with you."

Her admission made his heart swell with more love for her. "I'll never let you leave. You're mine and I'm yours."

She chuckled. "You make it sound so easy."

He nuzzled her head with his cheek. "It is. You just stay with me."

Chapter Eleven

ॐ

"I'm not selling my grandmother's house." Tammy frowned at Valiant and then at the attorney who sat in their living room. "Do I have to sell it? I have some money saved to pay the taxes on it this year. It was the house I was mainly raised in. It's all I have."

Valiant growled softly. "You do not need that house anymore. You are going to live in our house here. My home is yours now. There is no reason to keep it."

Charlie Artzola cleared his throat. "She owns a lot of things that she would like to keep. It is normal. It was the place where she grew up and it's filled with her belongings and memories."

Valiant hesitated. "Fine but you no longer live there. You can keep it but you are to never live there again. You live with me at our home here. It's not safe for you to leave Reservation. You were already attacked once."

The attorney blew out a relieved breath and flashed Tammy a grin. "Now, can we get on with the paperwork? You need to sign this so I can obtain a marriage license."

Tammy hesitated. Valiant wanted to marry her and had the attorney arrive with the paperwork to start the process. It seemed he wanted to push her into a fast marriage. She hadn't expected him to want to seal the deal immediately when she'd said yes to his proposal earlier that morning.

Tammy turned to stare at Valiant. "What if I want to go back to work? I like working sometimes."

He growled and his golden eyes narrowed. "You will be too busy to want to work. I will keep you very occupied." He closed his mouth. "I want you to be at home with me. I will care for you."

She closed her eyes and counted to ten. Valiant tended to be super pushy. It wasn't always an attractive trait with him. It was the one thing that drove her crazy. She opened her eyes to find Valiant watching her with his sexy gaze that always got to her.

"I love you."

The words made her heart melt. "You do?"

"You're everything to me." Valiant suddenly slid off the couch and walked on his knees to face her. His hands cupped her face. "I'm happy for the first time in my life and you are the reason. I want to spend the rest of my life with you, Tammy. I know you're surprised that I want to marry you right now but I know what I want. That is you."

"Um," the attorney cleared his throat. "Should I come back later?"

"No," Valiant growled. His expression softened. "I love you. You are mine and I am yours. We will work these things out. We want to be together. We are happy and we're mates."

Tammy stared into his eyes, unable to look away. He meant every word. She could see that as clearly as the golden flecks in his exotic eyes. The past few days together had been the best ones of her life.

They had a lot to work out but didn't all couples have issues? She figured they did. The idea of life without him seemed bleak. She wanted to go to bed, be held in his arms every night and wake to him nibbling on her and making love. She knew how she felt about him. He was impossible not to fall head over heels in love with.

"Okay. I love you too." Tammy smiled at Valiant "I'm all in. Move out the way and let me sign the papers."

The attorney looked relieved when Valiant sat back down and Tammy bent forward to put her signature on the forms where he pointed. She might be making a mistake but as she glanced at Valiant, she figured he was more than worth the risk. *Sometimes you have to say what the hell.* She grinned. *Shit happens. Sometimes it's good shit.*

"Well, I'm on this." The attorney quickly shoved papers into his briefcase and stood. "It was very nice meeting you both." He nearly ran for the door and fled their suite.

Tammy laughed. "That was a big lie. He wanted away from us so bad I could almost taste it."

"I frighten him. I could smell his fear."

"Really? I just thought he was annoyed because I didn't just sign on the dotted line right off the bat. He really didn't seem happy to be here."

Valiant smiled. "I frightened him. Fear has a smell, sexy." He leaned closer to her. "I smelled your fear when I met you. You smell sweet when you are afraid and it turned me on."

"Well, in that case, I bet you're sorry you don't frighten me anymore."

"You get frightened when I get mad at someone else. You think I will harm them." He moved closer. "I always wonder if your fear is for them or for me."

"Them. Definitely. I know you'd kick ass and take names."

"I don't care what their names are if I want to kick their asses."

"It's just a saying," she laughed. She pressed against Valiant and rubbed her palms over his chest, wishing he wasn't wearing a shirt. She loved touching his bare skin. "I'm trying to say that I know you would win a fight but I don't want you to actually kill anyone."

"Why not?"

"Well, there's that whole life-behind-bars reason."

He shrugged. "Our laws here are not the same as the ones you are accustomed to. I would never kill someone without a good reason. I wouldn't be punished for that."

The doorbell rang, startling Tammy. Valiant frowned before he rose from the couch, stalked toward the door and yanked it open.

Tammy stared at the New Species man who stood there. It was someone she had never met before but he seemed familiar somehow. She just couldn't place him. He was tall, stood about six-foot-four, had long, flowing, black hair, and the darkest catlike eyes she'd ever seen.

He smiled widely at Valiant, showed off some sharp teeth, and smoothed his hands down his sides. He wore an expensive tailored black suit but it didn't camouflage the dangerous vibe he put out. Tammy tensed.

Valiant didn't smile back. "It is an honor that you are here."

The stranger nodded. "Thank you for saying so. I heard the news and wanted to personally congratulate you on finding a mate. I know how excited you must be. It's wonderful news."

Valiant smiled. "Yes. Thank you." He moved to allow the stranger to step inside. "Justice North, I'd like to introduce you to my Tammy."

Justice North? That's why he looked familiar to her. Tammy forced a smile, tried not to gawk at him, but he was a celebrity. He was the leader and figurehead of the New Species Organization and the most well-known of them. On television and in print his eyes and hair didn't seem so dark. Tammy wasn't sure if she should just keep smiling at him or if she should try to shake his hand.

"It's nice to meet you," she rose to her feet but stayed in place.

He smiled at her but she noticed he carefully made sure his sharp teeth weren't noticeable when he faced her. She almost smacked her forehead as she realized why she hadn't recognized him. That was why she hadn't gotten it was him. It wasn't just the hair and eyes but he smiled without showing his sharp teeth every time she'd ever seen him on TV or in pictures.

"It is good to meet you as well, Tammy."

"Did you see the baby?" Valiant closed the door.

Justice chuckled. "I did. He's perfect. Slade and Trisha are very proud and happy. We all are overjoyed with his healthy birth."

"And the boy is Species."

Justice seemed to beam with joy. "He is definitely Species."

"I had wondered if the human traits would be stronger than Slade's." Valiant spoke softly. "I hope, if my mate and I have a child together, that it will resemble me. Tammy believes our baby would be adorable."

"We all hoped Species traits would carry on when the baby was born. It is a good thing to no longer be alone and know we will live on in our children with future generations." Justice paused. "But to have a child who would appear fully human would be a blessing too. To just be given the gift of them is enough."

Tammy kept silent, not sure what to say, as she watched the two men talk. She wondered if she should give them some time alone but then Justice looked at her. He chuckled as he glanced at Valiant.

"You are so small." Justice studied her. "Forgive me for my amusement but Valiant was adamant in some discussions we held that we should never be with humans and if any of us were going to mate with one, they needed to be strapping, large females. I find it humorous that he would claim you. I mean no offense but it is," he grinned, still hiding his teeth, "amusing."

"I understand." Tammy smiled. "I'm not offended. He's huge and I'm not. Would you like to have a seat?"

"I unfortunately can't stay. My life is filled with schedules that always keep me on the move. I will be here for the day to meet with security and I have an appointment with the person who does my hair." He reached up to touch it. He sighed heavily. "Our public relations team demands that I lighten it before I go before any cameras." He met her gaze. "Do I appear more frightening with dark hair, to you?"

"I didn't recognize you at first. I thought you looked familiar but I didn't know why until I heard your name. Your eyes seem darker right now too."

"I am forced to wear contacts too. Again, they seem to think humans will accept me easier if I appear softer. They also change my looks when I'm traveling in public to try to hide my real identity since I'm so well-known."

"You look fine to me," she admitted. "But different."

"Thank you."

Valiant studied the other man. "Are you staying in the hotel tonight? We'd enjoy sharing a meal with you."

"I wish I could but I have to hold a press conference tonight at Homeland for the evening news. A helicopter will fly me home after my last meeting this afternoon. I'll probably eat dinner on the ride home. One day I wish to take a few days off. Unfortunately, I don't see that happening any time soon. I will be back the day after tomorrow. I have to fly in for a meeting with the mayor of the town before I go back to Homeland for an interview with a local newspaper. It's endless."

"You should find someone to claim." Valiant gave him a sympathetic look. "A mate would make you happy."

Justice chuckled. "I don't have the time, Valiant. Every day is usually this hectic. There are always meetings and conferences or places I need to go to for more meetings. No female would wish to share my burdens."

"You have a hard life." Valiant inched closer and grasped his shoulder to give it a squeeze before his arm dropped. "You have sacrificed much for us, Justice. We all owe you and appreciate it."

Justice shrugged. "Someone had to do it, Valiant. I was the best at adapting to humans and had the best ability to blend in. It was just natural that I took the job."

"If there is ever anything…" Valiant left the rest of that sentence unsaid but his meaning was clear.

"Thank you and I already know that." Justice smiled at Tammy. "It was very nice to meet you and welcome to the family."

Valiant closed the door after the departing New Species leader and walked to Tammy. He had a sad expression on his face. "I do not envy him his life."

"He's a busy man, that's for sure."

Valiant nodded and suddenly pulled Tammy into his arms. "I am glad that my only responsibility is to make you happy. He carries the weight of all New Species on his shoulders."

"Are we going to take the last name of North too when we marry?"

Valiant nodded. "Yes. It is an honor to carry the name he chose. I support him and everything he has done for our kind."

"What did that mean when he said welcome to the family?"

"You are one of us now. You are family. We do not have parents or uncles or cousins the way humans do. We only have each other. Family is very important to us and all New Species is considered such. Together we stand strong."

Sadness filled Tammy. "Do any of you know who your birth parents are? I mean, you had to have parents once, right? At least a mother who carried you."

Valiant growled. "We are all orphans. Our parents abandoned us to hell. They allowed Mercile to create us, we were nothing more than donated material to them, and the females who birthed us were done as soon as they cut our umbilical cords. We learned that from some of the doctors who were arrested."

"I'm so sorry, Valiant." She hugged him, heartbroken over his past. "I always said love is all you need to form a family. My mother abandoned me. I will never understand how she could do that but I'm grateful she gave me life. I wouldn't be here without her."

He stared into her eyes. "Where is she? Does she live?"

Tammy shrugged. "I have no idea. She dumped me with Grandma and we never heard from her again. My grandma thought she probably died. She said my mom would have at least contacted her for money otherwise. I used to pray that she'd show up one day to tell me she loved me and how sorry she was over leaving me. You know?" The pain still made her chest ache a little. "That she'd tell me she made a horrible mistake. After a few years I realized it wasn't going to happen. I began to hate her a little and that turned into outright anger. I don't want to see her now if she is alive."

Valiant smiled. "You have me now and I will never leave you, Tammy. You belong to a large family. He or she will always know love and how it feels to be a part of a large group who will love them greatly if we ever have a child. Our child would never suffer loneliness or pain. Or ever experience a loveless life."

Her heart broke a little more for him. She heard the pain in his voice. Had anyone ever loved him as a child? She'd at least had her grandmother to love her. Tammy tightened her hold on him.

"I love you, Valiant. I love you so much."

"I love you too and you make me happy that you love me."

The doorbell chimed. Valiant growled. "I was going to take you to our bed."

"I would have let you."

The doorbell chimed again. Valiant released Tammy when she stepped away from him. He stormed to the door, looking irritated. Tammy had to fight a grin. He had no patience whatsoever. Valiant flung it open.

"We have a problem." Tiger stood there looking grim. "Sheriff Cooper called us. Two more women have been taken from the town. They need our help to track them. I need your help, Valiant. I know it is not Tammy this time but these women work for us. You are one of our best trackers with your stronger sense of smell and though other males from the Wild Zone have keen senses like yours, I can't trust any of them around humans. The humans lost the tracks in the woods. Will you help?"

Valiant studied Tiger. Long seconds passed.

"Valiant?" Tammy waited until he glanced at her over his shoulder. "Please help them."

He blinked at Tammy before he nodded. "I will do this for you." He moved toward the bedroom. "Let me change my clothes. I will be with you in a minute."

"Thanks," Tiger whispered when they were left alone.

Tammy nodded. "Do you think this is related to the men who took me? Their boss should be in town by now unless you figured out who he is. Did you?"

"The survivors haven't broken and given up the name of their boss yet. We have no idea who hired them to kidnap you. I don't know many details but the sheriff said the women are roommates and they work here at Reservation. They are both cooks who decided to live in town instead of accepting human housing inside the gates. Someone broke into their home and took them. The neighbors heard screams and witnessed at least six men removing the women by force. It happened half an hour ago. They found the van they were taken away in at the location where you were found."

"I hope you find them."

"Me too." Tiger sighed. "The sheriff thinks they were targeted because they worked for us. This means that all of our human employees need to be warned and we will offer them protection here again. I don't know where we will put them but we look after our own. There aren't that many of them at least. Slade is notifying them and will handle those arrangements."

Valiant returned wearing jeans, a black T-shirt, and running shoes. He walked to Tammy, looked down at her, and said, "I will be back soon. I will miss you."

"I'll miss you too and thank you for doing this. Be careful."

"Always."

Tammy watched the two men leave. She sat on the couch and began to worry. She wondered if she knew the two women, if they were locals she might have grown up with, and wished she'd asked Tiger their names. She stood suddenly and walked to the phone to dial her boss, Ted, at home. The phone rang six times but his answering machine picked up. She left him a message to warn him that he might be in danger just in case New Species hadn't thought to contact subcontractors who dealt with them.

She was worried about Ted and all the people she worked with. They'd done more than a few catering jobs for Reservation since that first one when she'd met Valiant. She proceeded to call her other coworkers but got their machines as well. She left them messages and included the phone number printed on the phone so they could call her back. She wondered where they all were, hoped they were out on a job, and not also kidnapped.

Seconds later the phone rang. She grabbed it up. "Hello?"

"Hello, Miss Shasta. This is Charlie Artzola. We just met, remember? I am at my office down the block and there seems to be a problem."

She sighed. "Did I forget to sign something?"

"No. It's just that I can't find you in the system. It's as if you don't exist."

"Excuse me?" She was shocked. "What system? I don't have a criminal record."

He laughed. "No. I mean I ran your driver's license number but you don't exist according to the database. I need to fax a copy of it to get your marriage license since there's some kind of computer glitch. I'm sure it's just a misunderstanding but we need to clear this up. I called the hotel and asked if someone from security could escort you to my office. I'm sure we can sort this out if you could bring me your identification. They'll accept a faxed copy of it as proof that you do exist." He laughed. "So, do you mind coming down here? It shouldn't take more than maybe ten to twenty minutes. Just bring your wallet with you and your license."

She sighed. "Sure. Let me get my shoes and find my purse. It's a good thing the sheriff returned it to me. It's around here somewhere. Did security say it was all right for me to leave? I'm supposed to stay inside the suite."

"I obtained permission from Tiger before he left. Someone will be there to escort you when you are ready to leave. Thank you, Miss Shasta. This is a big help. I know Valiant wanted this done quickly and I can't get the marriage license without submitting proof of who you are."

"I'll hurry."

She hung up and walked into the bedroom. At least it would distract her from worrying about Valiant for a little while. Her purse still sat on the closet floor where Valiant had placed it after the sheriff had brought it with him to interview her. The New Species had to check it first and it had been delivered later that day. She'd also learned that the sheriff had her car safely towed to her house when he'd retrieved her purse from the crime scene.

She brushed her teeth and hair again. She didn't bother with makeup. The quicker she could get back, the better, her mind was still on her coworkers. She didn't want to miss their calls when they got her messages. Flame stood outside in the hallway when she opened the door. She smiled at him.

"That attorney called and said he needed me and my purse." She lifted it to show him. "And here we both are."

Flame smiled. "He called. Are you ready to go? His office isn't far. I'll call for a Jeep and I'll drive you there."

"Thanks." They left the suite.

Flame used his radio to ask for the vehicle to be pulled up in front of the hotel while they waited for the elevator and by the time they walked out of the lobby, it had arrived. Flame helped her climb inside and rounded the vehicle. He drove from the hotel to where a two-story office had been constructed. He parked and helped her out.

The reception area was empty and silence filled the air. It seemed the building wasn't currently in use. Flame hesitated. "I'm not sure where his office is. I haven't been in here before. Only a few human employees work at Reservation and I haven't been assigned this post. Did he tell you where it was?"

"No."

Flame sighed. "Let's find him. I'd make some calls but we're on high alert right now and I don't want to bother anyone when I can sniff him out." He drew in air a few times through his nose and pointed to a hallway to the left. "This way. Male, human, and recent. His aftershave stinks and not in a good way."

She grinned. "Most guys are clueless and wear stuff that reeks."

"We tend to be sensitive to smells. Most of our people use natural-scented products. Humans don't."

Tammy followed him through a maze of hallways. "Are you on high alert because the two women were taken in town?"

He nodded. "Yes. We have tightened all incoming security and put our snipers on top of the walls in case someone decides they want to try to breach Reservation. We will never forget the attack that happened at Homeland."

She'd heard about that on the news. A hate group had attacked the New Species Homeland right after it had opened. They'd rammed the front gate and a bunch of men with guns had invaded with trucks.

Deaths had resulted from that attack. Luckily those killed had been mostly the hate-group members. Tragically, a few human security guards who worked for Homeland had also died. It had been shocking that something like that could happen. Obviously the New Species were afraid of another attack and she didn't blame them.

They found Charlie Artzola on the second floor in one of the offices. He sat behind his desk digging inside a drawer. He glanced at them both when they entered and he smiled.

"That was quick."

"I told you I'd escort her immediately." Flame leaned against the wall right inside the office.

"Have a seat, Miss Shasta." The attorney jerked his chin at a chair. "You and your men can come inside and have a seat too. There's four chairs and they may as well get used."

"It's just us. I'm fine standing." Flame relaxed his stance.

The attorney nodded. "I'm looking for the notes I made. I'm very sorry about this. I was nervous and think I wrote the information down wrong. I might have just put in a wrong license number and the computer system will find you so we don't have to fax it to them." He leaned over farther behind his desk as Tammy took a seat closest to him. "Aha! I found it. I'm sure this is just an error. I probably just have it off by one or two digits." He closed the desk drawer.

Tammy leaned back against her seat and set her purse on her lap. The attorney straightened. She barely had time to react before seeing it wasn't a paper he lifted from behind his drawer. It was a weird-looking weapon he pointed at Flame and fired. Tammy gasped. Flame grunted behind her and crashed to the floor.

Tammy jerked around in horror to stare at Flame sprawled on the carpet. The gun hadn't made a loud sound. Flame had fallen on his side by the door. She gawked at him, too stunned to do anything else for long seconds. She didn't see any blood as she sat motionless. She finally regained the ability to move. Her head turned toward the attorney to discover he'd pointed the strange gun at her.

"You will do exactly what I tell you to if you don't want to die, Miss Shasta. I have no qualms about killing a woman."

Her mouth opened but no sound came out. The gun was no more than three feet away, pointed right at her face. She knew he wouldn't miss at that close range. The attorney slowly rose from his chair with a frown twisting his lips. The wide muzzle never wavered.

"Stand up slowly. I will shoot you in the back if you try to run."

After a long moment of trying to get her body to move, she managed to rise to her feet. Her purse slid to the floor since her fingers refused to hold onto it. The attorney motioned toward the door with the weapon.

"We're going to walk outside to my car and you are going to get inside the trunk. I'm going to kill you if you don't. Do you understand me?"

She swallowed. "Why are you doing this? What do you want?"

He glared at her. "Someone I know wants to talk to you. He's deeply worried that you've been compelled into marrying a New Species."

Her brain began to function. The attorney wouldn't be threatening to kill her if someone just wanted to talk to her. He was lying about that. She bit her lip and took a tentative step. She didn't see any way to get away from him without being shot. He couldn't miss her if he fired the weapon.

Her gaze dropped to the fallen New Species. He wasn't moving at all but she still didn't see blood. As she took slow steps toward Flame and the door, she realized two things. Flame's eyes were closed but his chest rose and fell, proof that he was still breathing. She had to step over his arm and then his leg to exit the office.

She glanced back at Charlie Artzola. He stayed close and still pointed the gun at her. She walked, following his orders as he directed her where to go. Tammy's heart pounded with fear but Tiger's earlier words surfaced in her memory.

The New Species were on high alert. The attorney would never be able to get her off Reservation without them finding her. When she'd brought her catering van to the gates they'd searched every inch of it. She had to trust that they'd check the trunk of the attorney's car and find her. They exited the building from a back door where a nice four-door sedan had been parked.

He made Tammy wait as he unlocked the trunk. He moved back, aiming the gun at her chest. "Climb inside and be very quiet. The trunk is too small for me to miss you if I fire through the backseat. Do you understand me? You better not scream when we go through the checkpoint. I'll kill whatever New Species you tip off. Your life is only in danger if you make me shoot you. My friend really does want to talk to you, Miss Shasta. He'll be angry if I have to kill you so do us both a favor. Get in and keep quiet."

"Who told you to do this to me?"

"It doesn't matter. All that matters is you'll walk away from this in the end if you don't give me any problems."

Tammy wanted to scream and launch her body at the guy and attack him. Of course she didn't believe that she wasn't in danger if she complied. The attorney was a big liar. She felt torn. Fight or do what she was told?

He softly cursed, seeming to sense her dilemma. "This is a special dart gun filled with strong drugs designed to take down and kill New Species. You wouldn't stand a chance of survival if I shot you. Get inside the trunk and be quiet."

As long as she was alive there was hope that she'd be saved when they reached the gate. "I'll do it. Just don't shoot me," she managed to say. "I'm going."

The trunk was small. Tammy had to lie curled in a ball on her side, her knees pressed to her chest. He looked down at her grimly as he reached inside his pocket to fish for something. He pulled out a syringe and gripped the cap with his teeth to jerk it open.

"What is that?" Terror pulsed through her.

"Something to make sure you stay quiet. You'll be fine. I just can't risk you screaming when we get to the checkpoint." The attorney jabbed the needle into her outer thigh through her pants.

Tammy groaned from the sharp sting of pain. She stared up at him with terror and hatred. "Valiant is going to rip out your guts and feed them to you. That's his favorite thing to do."

He clenched his teeth. "You're a sick animal whore." He slammed the trunk closed.

She fought when the darkness surrounded her and she wasn't under direct threat from the gun any longer. After a few ineffective hits to the roof of the trunk, horror spread through her mind when her limbs began to grow heavy. Her hands refused to fist anymore, her arms drooped at the elbow, and finally fell limply to the floor of the trunk.

Panic came next. Whatever drug he'd injected her with seemed to paralyze her. She could breathe fine and blink, stare into darkness, but the rest of her body refused to function. She tried to scream but her throat had even been affected. She could barely swallow and couldn't even push her tongue against her teeth. She screamed inside her mind but the sound didn't pass her lips.

The car started. Tammy tried to calm down, realizing how dire her situation had become. *Think!* The New Species checked trunks. She'd seen them do it to a car in front of her the first day she'd visited Reservation. Two of the security officers had checked Tammy's van next.

They'd done a very thorough job. They'd even opened the mini refrigerators inside the back of the van and opened sealed trays to make sure they carried food and not weapons. They'd used handheld devices over the food to make certain nothing had been stashed inside.

She'd be found. Charlie Artzola wouldn't get her off Reservation. She knew large, thick walls enclosed the entire place with only two entry gates. He wouldn't be able to get her out except to go through those checkpoints. Tears of frustration slipped down her cheeks and she couldn't even wipe them away. *They'll find me.*

The car slowed at one point but didn't stop before it picked up a lot of speed. A long time passed. The car finally stopped. Hope soared inside Tammy. At any second one of the security officers would make the attorney open the trunk. They'd discover her, she'd be rescued and returned to Valiant.

Instead the car moved again, picking up speed. More time passed. The car stopped again, the engine died, and Tammy fixed her gaze toward the top of her prison. It was dark inside, pitch black, she couldn't see a thing, but she knew where the trunk lid opened. Any second she'd be saved. She heard keys. Hope soared.

Light blinded Tammy when the trunk was jerked open. Tammy looked up but she didn't see a New Species face. Charlie Artzola glared at her instead before he turned his head to look at someone else.

"I told you they'd just wave me through. They trust me." The jerk snickered. "Here's the bitch I told you about. They wanted a marriage license. She wanted to marry one of those animals. She's living with and screwing him. He looks worse than the rest of them do. He doesn't even appear kind of human. He is a tiger or something. He is about as freakish as I've ever seen."

Tammy screamed inside her head. *NO!* The officers at the gate couldn't have just waved him past. Another man walked closer until Tammy stared at the face of a man in his sixties. He wore glasses and was bald. He looked as if he could be someone's nice grandfather. That was until he turned a pair of ice-cold green eyes on her that froze her. He frowned.

"So," the older man said softly. "We finally have a test subject. She survived breeding with one of them. Something about her attracted one and, if my theory holds, that chemistry should attract 927 to her as well. You said the one she was breeding with was a tiger? Well, let's see how she fairs with a dog." He laughed. "I hope he likes her as much as the tiger did."

Two scary thugs in their twenties suddenly stood over Tammy. They reached for her and lifted her out. One of them gripped her legs and the other one grabbed her under her armpits. They hauled her out of the car. She saw a flash of trees while they carried her between them as though she were a large bag.

She glimpsed a house—a white one badly in need of paint. It was a single story and she didn't recognize it. That meant she wasn't close to town. As they entered the structure she stared up at a cracked, plaster ceiling. They dumped her on a soft mattress.

The twin bed had been set up inside a living room. One of them grinned at her and pulled out something from his back pocket. He yanked her hands up and handcuffed her to something above her head. She couldn't turn her head to see what he'd locked her to but then her legs were jerked down flat and straight. Metal enclosed each ankle. The scary one by her head leaned over to stare into her eyes.

"Wait until you meet 927. He's going to love you." He laughed, his gaze lifting to the other man. "For about ten seconds until he snaps her neck and kills her."

Tammy heard the other man laugh.

The jerk still leaning over Tammy looked down. "I almost feel sorry for you. 927 is the meanest beast ever made but since you like to do their kind, I guess you might enjoy the rough treatment you're going to get when he mounts you. *If* he'll mount you. The doc thinks he might since one of his kind liked you."

"Get away from her," the older man demanded loudly. Tammy recognized his voice. "We don't want your smell on her because he'll just kill her outright since he hates the two of you so much. We need her to smell like the tiger."

Valiant. She silently screamed his name. Would he be able to find her again? Save her? Would he even know by now that she'd been taken? That someone had kidnapped her?

Tears streamed down her face. She screamed again in her head. *Valiant!*

* * * * *

"This doesn't make sense." Tiger frowned at Valiant. "Why would they take those two women, walk them a few miles from their home and just leave them tied up alone? It was too easy to find them."

Valiant shrugged. "I do not know but they are fine. That is what matters, right?"

Tiger nodded. He glanced at the three other men that he'd brought along on his team. They watched him back. Tiger sighed. "Something just isn't right. I can't put my finger on what it is but this just makes no sense. What was the point of taking two women to just tie them up and abandon them?"

One of the men shrugged. "They are human. They sometimes don't make sense."

Sheriff Cooper approached Tiger and his group with a wide grin on his lined face. "Thank you so much. Again, we owe you. The women are fine. They were scared but they only have a few bruises. They wanted to give you their thanks.

They said the men didn't talk to them at all. The only thing they heard was one of the men asking if they thought they had moved them far enough for them to be hard to track. It doesn't make sense to me but that's all they heard. The women said the men carried them through the woods, took turns tossing them over their shoulders to get them this far, and just dumped them at the base of that tree. They tied them up good and just took off."

"Perhaps they were planning to come back later." It was one of the deputies who worked with the sheriff who had joined them. "Maybe they wanted more women and are searching for other victims. We should keep a few deputies out here just in case they return."

Tiger's cell phone rang. "Excuse me. It's Reservation." He turned and stepped away to answer it. He listened and spun around. Tiger locked his grim gaze on Valiant and he hesitated.

"I think I know why the women were taken." Tiger kept his focus trained on Valiant but then he glanced at the sheriff.

"You specifically asked me to bring Valiant. Why?"

The sheriff frowned. "Well, he's your best tracker. That's why I asked for him."

"Who told you that?" Tiger clenched his teeth.

"It was one of the news reporters who've been hanging around town since Tammy was taken. They practically camp outside our station. He said he covers stories all the time for you folks and that Valiant was the best tracker you had. He said if more women were ever kidnapped to be sure to ask for him because he'd be the best chance at finding them fast."

"What is going on?" Valiant frowned. "How would any reporter know my name? It was never released, was it?" He glanced at Tiger for an answer.

"No, it wasn't." Tiger appeared killing mad. He glared at the sheriff. "Do you remember the reporter's name?"

The sheriff hesitated. "No, but I know his face. Why?"

Tiger growled. He turned his head to Valiant. "Tammy has been taken from Reservation by force. She's gone, Valiant. Flame was asked by our attorney to escort her to his office. When they didn't return to the hotel within twenty minutes and Flame didn't respond to the radio, a team immediately went in search of them."

Shock jolted through Valiant. "No."

"They found Flame on the floor unconscious inside the attorney's office. He's been drugged with an unknown substance. The attorney and Tammy are missing. Her purse was found but she was not. Our people picked up only the attorney's scent and Tammy's. That led them to the parking lot, which makes it apparent he took her. We are sure she didn't go willingly because her scent of fear lingered. He drove right out the gate. We trusted him. We check incoming cars but not outgoing ones when they are driven by trusted employees.

"He took her, Valiant. The kidnapping of these two human women was obviously a ploy to lead you away from Tammy." Tiger growled and glared at the Sheriff. "The man who spoke of Valiant used you to lure him away."

Valiant threw back his head and roared in rage.

"We'll find her," Tiger swore. "Everyone is on this."

Chapter Twelve

∞

Tammy had fallen asleep at some point but awoke when the thugs released her from the bed. They'd dragged her on barely working legs, her entire body sluggish, to push her into a bathroom. To her humiliation, they'd refused to give her any privacy, leering as she used the facilities. She'd had no choice. One of them had threatened to hit her if she didn't comply.

They'd gripped her arms at that point and dragged her back outside to a white van. The sun had gone down, assuring her she'd been unconscious for hours, and she wasn't given the opportunity to escape. Both men kept a tight hold on her wrists. They threatened to beat her if she put up any resistance. One glance at their faces made her a believer. They had cold eyes and cruel demeanors.

They'd put a metal collar around her throat and locked her inside a large cage at the back of the van. The collar was chunky and had a two-foot chain they connected to the bars of her tiny cell. She'd peered at that large cage with terror. Even the fact that they contained her in one was terrifying. Why would they need a cage like that and what did they usually transport inside it? She touched the wide metal bars, guessing, whatever its purpose, it would hold almost anything.

One of the men climbed out while one remained inside the back of the van with her. He turned on an overhead light to watch her with a smirk. The departing guy slid the side door closed and then opened the driver's door, got in and started the engine. Tears filled her eyes from fear and not feeling well from whatever drug they'd given her. She had a headache, her tongue was a little swollen-feeling, and her limbs still moved sluggishly.

"Don't bother putting on the waterworks," the man in the back snickered. "Nobody gives a shit if you cry."

"Why are you doing this?" Tammy hated the way her voice shook. "Who are you people?"

"Why? Because you like to fuck them. Because one of them fucked you and didn't kill you. That's why. The doctor we work for is really interested to see if 927 will breed with you. You better hope he likes you. It will be fun to watch, either way."

The man in the front laughed. "I doubt she'll think it's fun."

The man in back laughed. "Yeah. True." His eyes sparkled with glee. "Do you want to know what happens if that beast doesn't tear you apart with his claws and toss your body parts outside the cage? The doctor is going to strap you down to a table and flood your system with hormones and drugs to try to get you to conceive with that beast. Afterward, we get to toss you back inside with him so he can fuck you again. The doctor has all kinds of formulas he's thought up to try to get you pregnant by the beast. It could take months before he figures out how to get the results he wants."

The driver laughed again. "That will be a lot of fun to watch if he accepts her. I'm not getting my hopes up though. He killed the other two women we locked up with him. That last one was the one who got to me. She was one fine piece of ass. I almost cried when he snapped her neck and threw her at the door. Maybe we should toss in men to the beast."

"She was hot." The man in the back scowled at Tammy. "This one is cute but nothing even close to the other one. She's definitely not playmate-of-the-month material. I think the doctor is excited for nothing. I think the beast will kill this one just as fast as the last one."

"Who knows?" The driver sighed. "Maybe the doctor's theory is right and he'll accept her because she's doing one of them and she'll smell like him. They never killed their own women. He's also sure it's got something to do with their sense of smell and body chemistry. Whatever drew that one, might draw another. We'll find out soon."

"Please," Tammy begged. "Let me go. I have a lot of it if this is about money." She didn't have a single qualm about lying. "My grandmother died and left me two million dollars. You can have it all if you just take me to a bank."

The guy in the back studied her. Tammy nodded, giving him her I'm-totally-serious-trust-me look. She'd gotten that expression down pat as a teenager dealing with her grandmother.

"I'll give you every penny of it, sign it all over to the both of you, if you let me go. I know that you can't be getting paid that much money. It's enough for you both to retire."

"Don't even think about it, Mike," the driver warned. "You know you can't spend money if you're dead. The doctor would put a bounty on your head and there isn't a corner on Earth you would be safe."

Mike sighed, his gaze leaving hers. "Shut the fuck up, bitch. Don't say another word. You can't bribe us because Pete is right. We can't spend money from a coffin. If you want to beg and cry then forget that too. We didn't get this job because of our warm fuzzy hearts." He snorted. "Right, Pete?"

"Right." Pete, the driver, laughed. "Warm and fuzzies. You're too funny."

"How long until we get there?"

"About ten minutes. I wish we were still in Colorado. It's too hot here. I don't know why the doctor had us move 927. We should have just brought her there instead."

"He wanted to move here. Don't ask me why. Maybe he gets his jollies knowing how close they are and how oblivious they are to him being so near them." Mike shrugged. "Maybe he wants to be closer to spy on them while he works and doesn't want to fly back and forth. It may be because he's afraid her scent would change if we had to take her that far.

We sure can't load her on a plane. We'd have to drive there. I am just going to hate it next month when we have to transfer ten more of them down here."

"Fuck. Don't remind me. Transporting 927 was bad enough. That son of a bitch fought the drugs the entire drive. He bent one of the corners of the cage before you were able to shoot him again. I about shit my pants when I heard him moving. I hit him with enough dope to knock him out for a full day but he woke in less than five hours. I thought we were going to run out of drugs."

Tammy turned her head and examined the cage she'd been tethered to. Sure enough she saw one of the top corners of the cage had been bent a little. The cage could have easily house a large bear. The vehicle was a full-sized commercial van. She knew that because she drove one for work. The cage took up half the back of the van. She guessed the cage was at least six feet long by five feet high and wide. The bars were fist thick and she guessed 927 was a New Species who'd been strong enough to damage them.

Confusion clouded her mind, the drug still in her system didn't help, but the picture forming made her horrified and scared. New Species had been given names when they were freed. Only one still imprisoned would have a number. *That would mean – Oh my God!*

"927 was never freed, was he? He's still property of Mercile? You work for them, don't you?"

The thug grinned at her but said nothing.

She had a sick feeling her suspicions were correct. A testing facility had been missed. She had read the papers not too far back about how more New Species had been discovered. The doctor they worked for had to be a Mercile employee and that meant these men worked for that horrible company too. They'd mercilessly experimented on human beings for decades, had done horrible things to them, and now they'd kidnapped her.

"You won't get away with this." Her voice shook.

"Hear that, Pete?" Mike grinned coldly. "Bitch, we've never been caught because we're the best."

Pete turned his head to glance back. "Instead of making threats, you should be saying your prayers. You better hope 927 likes you. He's killed two other women we gave him to fuck."

They planned to toss her to the mercy of the New Species who'd bent those bars. The doctor believed she wouldn't be killed because she carried Valiant's scent. The horrific clues just kept coming together inside her mind. The doctor thought that since Valiant was attracted to her that another New Species would be too. She didn't buy into that theory one bit. Valiant had only been drawn to her at first because she'd been ovulating. It wasn't until after he'd spent time with her that he'd said he wanted to keep her. They'd fallen in love but, then again, he'd been freed from Mercile, had learned that not all humans were vicious jerks who thought New Species were nothing but animals to use and hurt. The one they were taking her to had probably never known kindness from a human being. It made her close her eyes to fight tears.

She needed to remember facts if she was to survive. They'd said they wanted to transport ten more New Species and they'd come from Colorado, where the hidden testing facility had to be. She calmed slightly, forcing her mind to concentrate on that information.

Valiant would try to find her, he wouldn't give up, and they'd have to figure out that jerk of an attorney had taken her. She hadn't seen him so maybe he'd try to flee the state. Maybe the police would catch him and make him tell where she'd been taken. She clung to that bit of hope.

"Don't fall asleep," Mike ordered her. "We're almost there."

She opened her eyes and glared at him. "I hope you roast in hell."

He sat forward and made a fist. "You want to know what a little hell feels like?"

"Don't," Pete ordered from front. "You heard what the doctor told us before he left. We aren't to hurt or touch her unless we absolutely have to. I bet she's scared shitless and is baiting you to kill her. Can you blame her?" He laughed. "I'd want someone to kill me."

Mike dropped his fist and leaned back. "Yeah. I'd want to die before one of them got their hands on me too. Fucking beasts. Want to bet on if he kills her or not? Twenty bucks says she's toast."

The driver hesitated. "Sure. I'll take that bet. The doctor is pretty smart and he's sure the beast will want to fuck her once he gets a load of how she smells. We're here."

"Great." Mike smirked at Tammy. "We're under instructions to take you right to 927. The doctor is already here, waiting."

The van stopped a few minutes later. Pete climbed out and opened the side door. Mike crawled over to a side cabinet and opened it. He pulled out a pair of shackles with a length of chain that was about six feet long. He glared at Tammy as he unlocked the cage and jerked the door open.

"Stick your hands out now."

"Go to hell." She hugged her waist, refusing to give him her wrists.

Mike glared at her. "Do it or I swear, you're going to suffer."

She hesitated, knew he'd get in trouble if he hit her, but held out her wrists in the end. She could fight but she'd lose. Either way, they were going to take her wherever they wanted so she could go on her own steam or be bleeding when she arrived.

Mike shackled her wrists and tossed the chain toward Pete, who grabbed it and wrapped it around his fist. Mike didn't touch Tammy, careful not to, as he unlocked the chain securing her collar to the cage.

"Move," Pete ordered her.

She had to scoot on her butt to the opening of the door. She breathed in fresh air and climbed outside. The collar was heavy around her throat. She glanced around but only saw a white industrial-looking, two-story building. The parking lot was small and overhead lights glared down from above as though it were daylight. All she could spot were trees, assuring her the unfamiliar building was remote.

"Let's go, you stupid bitch." Pete pulled on her chain.

The metal double doors were locked with a keypad. Pete punched in five numbers, blocking her view with his body to make certain she couldn't see. The door beeped and both men led her inside the well-lit, large room that appeared to be an old reception room of some sort.

It didn't take a genius to figure out that the building had been abandoned when she spotted broken windows at the back of the room high on the walls or the layers of cobwebs and dust covering a few outdated desks that had been left behind. She tried to spot any clues to tell her what company used to own the place but no logos or names were painted on the walls. They led her down a dark hallway with a lot of pitch-black openings and the smell of mold assaulted her nose. They kept her between them, holding the chains that assured she couldn't run.

A scary snarl, though faint, came from somewhere ahead. She jerked to a halt and wanted to spin around to flee. The men holding the chains pulled them taut between them, trapping her in place.

Mike laughed. "She's a little spooked."

"Who the fuck wouldn't be if they had a brain? Pull on her and I'll follow. I'm sure the doctor is tired of waiting."

Tammy's gaze adjusted to the bright lights as they entered another large section of the warehouse. Concrete floors and walls with at least a fifty-foot ceiling greeted her. A wall had been constructed at some point to cut the room in half but it didn't reach the ceiling, which she could view beyond it. Long, fifteen-foot lights had been strung at intervals above her from one side of the room to the other. They'd all been turned on until their bright strength nearly hurt her eyes.

"You're finally here," the older man in glasses stated, walking around the wall that divided the room.

It was the man Tammy had seen when she'd been sprung from the trunk. She now had a face with the title. His icy-green eyes swept over Tammy, then back to the two thugs who worked for him.

"It's about time. He's awake, has been fed, and I tossed him in an extra five pounds of meat to make certain he wouldn't be hungry. He didn't finish it all but I assume he's full. I've made certain he's got nothing to feel cranky about. Now we'll get to see if he'll breed with her."

"Should we strip her down before throwing her in? It might motivate him to want to fuck her more."

"No." The doctor frowned at Mike. "She was living with one of them and I'll assume her clothes will hold his scent. We need to retain as much of that as possible in hopes he'll accept her. Just toss her inside the way we discussed. Immediately join me inside the monitoring room. I don't want him killing her just because he wants the satisfaction of having an audience to perform a grisly task for."

"Please," Tammy begged frantically. "Don't do this."

All three men ignored her.

"Here we go," Pete said, tugging on her chains to pull her toward the opening where the room had been separated. "You better hope he smells something on you he likes."

Mike chuckled. "We'll find out real soon."

They passed an archway and Tammy dug her heels into the floor, stopping. Someone had placed a large cage in front of the concrete walls in the back corner. The thick bars lined all four sides and the ceiling of the cage. A solid metal floor rested on the existing concrete.

A single twin bed, just a frame and mattress, adorned the cell and a toilet sat in a corner of it. That didn't hold her attention. The male inside sent terror straight to her heart. He was big, had wild black hair that fell midway down his naked back, and they had him wearing off-white pants that had thick seams down the sides of the legs. They hugged his waist low and fell loosely to just under his knees. Bare, muscular calves and big feet were planted a foot apart where he stood. He turned his entire body to snarl at them, revealing sharp teeth, a flattened nose, and those strong, wide cheekbones that New Species all seemed to have.

Pete yanked hard on the chain attached to her wrists to make her stumble forward. Tammy whimpered. Her gaze refused to look away as the large New Species furiously stormed closer to the bars. His hands gripped them, which made her glance at his muscular arms and chest before he made loud sniffing noises. Dark, nearly black eyes met hers.

"We brought you a friend," Mike laughed.

"Play nice," Pete taunted. "She's someone you might like. She enjoys spending time with beasts a hell of a lot. She's screwing one of your kind. We caught her just for you, 927."

They stopped by the cage door about seven feet from the enraged New Species who sniffed loudly again. The weight around her neck dropped away, the collar gone, and she barely took notice as the shackles were removed from her wrists. She remained terrified and focused on the New Species. They planned to push her into his cage.

He was almost as tall as Valiant. Maybe an inch or two shorter at about six-feet-four, if she were to guess. His shoulders, thick chest, and muscular arms were very similar in size to Valiant. It was his face that terrified her the most.

A vicious, low growl of warning rumbled deep from within his throat as sharp teeth flashed. Like Valiant, this one had more dominant animal features than most of the New Species. That probably accounted for how terrifying he looked as he snarled at her, flashing teeth that looked as if they could easily tear her apart without effort. Fear sizzled along Tammy's spine like lightning and ran down the length of her body.

Tammy realized something as a hand shoved her forward, past an opening into the cage. A thick glass wall partition stood between the man growling at her two captors and the door they'd just opened. The man behind the glass suddenly lunged and his body slammed into the clear barrier. A loud crack came from the action and parts of the glass spider-webbed.

"Son of a bitch," Mike hissed. "Hurry up. That isn't going to hold for long. He's really being aggressive today."

Pete pushed Tammy hard, knocked her off balance, and she stumbled farther into the cage but managed not to fall face first on the metal floor. The door slammed closed behind her and she turned, lunging for the bars that now locked her inside. She jerked hard but the door didn't move. She stared at Mike and Pete, pleading with them silently. They refused to even glance her way as they spun and disappeared into the other half of the warehouse at a hurried pace, seeming not to be able to flee fast enough. The hair at the back of her neck rose.

She knew why. Her breathing increased and her fingers clung so hard to the cold metal that she knew they were turning white. *You can't get out. You're going to have to face him. Maybe he can be reasoned with.* She drew in a deep breath and blew it out. *You have no choice. Just talk. You have nothing to lose.*

Tammy slowly released the bars and turned, dread making her stomach heave a little. The scariest eyes she'd ever seen watched her from the other side of the partition just feet from her. His seemingly black gaze narrowed and he growled at her again. She backed up, moved away from the door, and pressed against the bars as far away from him as she could get in the small space.

His hands lifted and he glanced at them. She followed where he looked, wishing instantly that she hadn't. His hands ended in thick fingernails similar to Valiant's but they hadn't been clipped. They resembled short but lethal claws that scratched over the damaged part of the glass. A piece of it fell away, letting her know he could get to her. A scream rose but became trapped inside her throat. He scratched the divider with his nails again. It was a hideous sound when more bits of the glass fell away to ping on the metal floor.

"Please," Tammy begged softly. "Don't hurt me. I was kidnapped and brought here against my will. I'm not your enemy. I don't work for Mercile Industries."

The New Species stopped watching his hands to peer at her instead. She only saw aloofness in his stare as their gazes met. His hands pulled away from the glass, he backed away, and she hoped her words had meant something to him.

He suddenly lunged forward, his body turning at the last second, and his shoulder slammed into the glass. More of it cracked. Tammy whimpered again and slid along the bars until she reached the corner a few feet away. She couldn't escape. He was going to break through and reach her.

Her knees seemed to turn to liquid and she slid down to the cold, unforgiving floor, on her butt. She drew her knees up in a protective manner and wrapped her arms around them tightly to hug her body. He moved with her to the edge of the cage. He growled again.

"Listen to me. Please? I know a lot about people like you. Do you know that a lot of them are free now? The testing facility they were imprisoned inside was raided by the government and they're no longer locked up. They live outside, no bars, and no cages." She sucked in air, knew she babbled, but was proud she could at least speak. She kept going. "They call themselves New Species. They are really free and if they knew where you were they would come to save you. Do you understand me?"

The man's eyes narrowed more and he stopped growling. He did continue to glare at her. She hoped that he wouldn't break through the glass and just kill her in the blink of an eye. Her talking seemed to have at least distracted him from battering through the glass.

"I live with one of your kind. He tells I belong to him all the time. It kind of annoyed me until he told me that he never owned anything, never was allowed to care about anything, because it was used against him. He named himself Valiant. He's part lion. He has the most amazing golden eyes. He loves me and I love him. We live at New Species Reservation. It's a large area of woods and open land. It's where your kind live and work together to have better lives. It belongs to them and they are in charge there."

The man growled at her, tensing. She saw his muscles bunch and he put his hands against the glass. He started to push. The glass groaned and she heard a cracking sound. He would break through. She only had about four feet between her and the barrier. She fought back tears.

"The first time I met Valiant he scared me. He growled the way you are right now. I'd never seen anything like him before. I thought he would kill me but he didn't. I'd accidentally gone to the wrong place and ended up at his house. He terrified me but he was also the most beautiful man I'd ever seen. His eyes are amazing and he has this mane of reddish-colored hair with blond streaks running through it." Her voice broke and she blinked back more tears. "He's a little bigger than you are. Taller. That's another reason he scared me. He picked me up, carried me into his house, and we started talking."

The glass cracked more while the New Species continued to push on it. Tammy darted her focus away from his eyes to the barrier between them. Large jagged splinters in it had spread upward toward the top of the room and down to the floor. She didn't have much more time before it gave way.

"Valiant told me I'm family to your kind now that I'm with him. They call each other that since none of them had parents or blood relatives. That means I'm family to you too. Valiant…" her voice broke from emotion and hot tears slid down her cheeks. "He loves me and he's got to be terrified for me right now. He doesn't know where I am. I was kidnapped from Reservation. He'll be looking for me and he'll never stop. Please don't kill me."

The man backed up to study the glass. Tammy stopped talking to watch him. She hugged her body harder, trying to appear as small as possible while she pushed back tighter into the corner. She knew he examined the glass, searching for the weakest parts. Her words didn't seem to matter and nothing she'd said made him want to stop attacking the partition to hurt her.

He moved suddenly, backed up about five feet, his attention fixed on one section of damaged glass. She held her breath when he paused but gasped as he lunged forward. He twisted his massive body at the last second before he threw his entire weight against the partition and to her horror, it gave way. He came barreling through it and slammed into the bars only feet from where she huddled. The wall section where he'd broken through crashed to the floor, barely missing her.

Tammy whimpered and lifted her head as he straightened to his full height. He rolled his shoulder that had taken most of the impact from the glass and the bars. A few scratches marred his skin but the wall had broken in chunks, obviously some kind of safety glass. He turned toward her, glaring, and growled. He took a step toward her and another until only inches separated her body from his legs.

"Please," she begged softly. "Don't do this. I'm telling you the truth."

He spread his thighs as he crouched, pinned her between them but didn't touch her as he sniffed. Tammy stared into his dark, terrifying eyes, hoping he'd have a harder time killing her if he were looking into them. She saw emotion flicker in those dark depths. His hands reached for her, fisted her shirt between her breasts, and yanked her hard from the floor when he quickly rose to his feet.

Tammy heard material tear when she was forced to stand. She whimpered again. He had her by her shirt and used it to slam her against the wall bars at her back. She stared up into his face and locked her knees together to keep from collapsing. She shook badly when he hunched down to get closer to her face with his own.

Black eyes narrowed into slits as he continued to sniff her. His mouth tightened into a grim, tight line when he stopped. A soft grumble came from his mouth, far too near her own. He pressed in closer until his hot skin touched her arms, which still hugged her waist, and his head lowered more. He smelled her hair, his nose brushed over it, and he bumped his chin against her cheek, pushing.

Tammy squeezed her eyes closed and turned her head away even though she could feel his warm breath fan across her neck as he continued to examine how she smelled. *Please don't tear out my throat with those sharp teeth.* She couldn't get the actual words out, too terrified to speak with his hands on her, and his body nearly crushed hers against the cold metal. His sharp teeth never touched her.

His body against hers turned rigid. Her heart hammered inside her chest so hard that it began to hurt. He moved, easing the pressure of his chest away from hers until she breathed easier. It took every bit of courage she had to look up at him again as she turned her head back. He glared into her frightened gaze.

He backed away and released her torn shirt. "Stay." He snarled the word.

Tammy didn't dare move. He watched her intently until his gaze lowered down her body to study her. It shocked her when he suddenly dropped to his knees before her, his hands gripped her hips, and his face pressed against her skin between her breasts where he'd torn open her shirt. She sucked in air but managed not to scream, too terrified it would set him off. A hot tongue suddenly licked the side of her breast and he snarled.

She stopped breathing but his tongue left her skin. She took a shallow breath as he sniffed her then pulled his head back. One hand released her hip to grab the bottom of her shirt, which he yanked up to expose her stomach. He shoved his nose against her belly but it didn't hurt. He inhaled deeply as he rubbed his face downward to the top of her pants. He paused at the waistband.

I'm not dead. He's not killing me. That's got to be good, right? She tried to think of something to say but decided now would be a time to keep her lips sealed. That was until the guy spread his thighs to lower his body and he suddenly pressed his face into the vee of her legs.

"Stop!"

Her hands reached for him without conscious thought, grabbed his broad shoulders, and she pushed at him. He didn't budge an inch, too strong and big to move.

His head snapped up, mouth parted to reveal sharp teeth, and he snarled at her. She jerked her hands away as if he'd burned her, terror jolted through her at that deadly glare he gave her, and he lowered his head again. He pressed his face back into the vee of her thighs and nudged against her sex, sniffing her there, as if he really were a dog. He jerked back, stared up at her, and released her shirt as he rose to his feet again.

Tammy fought back a scream when he spun her body around, pressed her face against the bars, and began sniffing from the top of her shoulder and down her back. He moved the shirt out of way by jerking it up. She stared at the concrete inches in front of her nose where the cage had been pushed against the warehouse wall. He growled a few times as he lowered, his hands holding her in place, and crouched behind her to even sniff the back of her thighs. He didn't bury his face against her ass at least. She tried to take comfort in being spared that.

He spun her back, staring at her in way that left his thoughts and feelings a mystery but he didn't appear enraged anymore. His dark gaze actually didn't seem as cold or frightening. He suddenly reached out and his hand encircled her upper arm but his hold didn't hurt. He actually seemed careful not to bruise her with his big hand.

"Come." His voice came out gruff, deep, but it wasn't a growl or a snarl.

He backed up, pulling on her to make her follow. She moved on wobbly legs, not sure what would happen next. He backed up more, pulling her another few feet, and turned his head to stare at the gap he'd created in the partition. He inched through it, careful not to touch his skin against any of the rough edges, and left her no choice but to step through it as well. She meekly followed him, too grateful he wasn't killing her, until she realized where he'd led her to.

Fear made her try to pull out of his grasp when she spotted the cot just feet away. "No."

His dark gaze narrowed in a threatening way. "Lie down now."

"I belong to Valiant." She couldn't help the rush of tears that blinded her until she blinked them back. "Please don't do this."

His mouth moved, twitched, but that was the only show of emotion on his face. "Rest. I won't mount you."

Chapter Thirteen

ဢ

Some of Tammy's panic and fear eased as she decided the New Species probably wouldn't lie to her. He was big enough to force the issue if he wanted to rape her. He could have killed her by now. The fact that she still drew breath had to be a great sign that he wasn't as vicious as her kidnappers believed or that he'd smelled Valiant on her and it meant something to him. She let him direct her to the bed where she carefully sat on the edge.

The New Species crouched in front of her, knees wide open, putting her legs between his thighs. He seemed to enjoying pinning her in by doing that, she noticed, and didn't like how he also had a preference for invading her personal space. He was too close for her comfort.

His gaze searched hers. "How many?"

"I don't understand."

"How many New Species freed?"

"I'm not sure of the exact numbers, but hundreds."

He took a few deep breaths but seemed to get angry again. "How many hundreds?"

Tammy hesitated. "I don't know. New Species don't really want that known to the general public, um, humans. I would guess at least three hundred of them live at Reservation. There's also Homeland, a big converted military base they were given, and it's another big piece of land where more New Species live. There have to have a few hundred there too. Probably more."

"Tell me some numbers you know."

"I don't understand. I just said I'm not sure of how many of them there are in total."

He lightly growled. He pointed to himself. "927. What are the numbers you know? What is Valiant's number from before?"

She understood. "I don't know any. They don't ever use their testing-facility numbers. They all picked names when they were freed. I never wanted to ask Valiant what his was when he was still imprisoned. I didn't want to make him sad by making him remember his life from before."

He blinked. "They chose their own names?"

She nodded. "Yes. Most of your kind have names like Justice and Breeze." She paused before listing off the other names she'd heard. "Tiger. Flame. Brass. Rider. Smiley." She paused. "I was told they picked names of things they loved or something that had some meaning to them." She stared into his gaze. "They would have come to break you out if they'd known about you." She whispered. "They don't know about the testing facility in Colorado. They thought they found them all and had set everyone free."

He suddenly lifted up and spun away from her. It made Tammy flinch as he snarled loudly and began to pace the cell. She scooted until her back rested against the bars of the cage wall. She hugged her chest and pulled her knees up, just watching him silently. He appeared agitated and really angry. She'd answered his questions but regretted saying that last part. Perhaps he was so angry that others had been found when he hadn't been.

"Valiant will never stop searching for me. That means he'll find us. Me *and* you. They'll free you." She said it softly, hoping her voice didn't carry to wherever the doctor and his two thugs had gone. "We really do love each other and he won't give up."

The New Species stopped pacing to regard her. He slowly approached and crouched next to the bed. "The technicians will take you away from me if I don't mount you soon." He whispered the words.

Tammy shook her head frantically, afraid, and knew exactly what that meant. Sex. "No."

"I will scent you and it will buy time."

"What does that mean?"

He suddenly reached out and grabbed Tammy by her calf, gave a hard jerk, and his other hand gripped her arm to turn her on the bed where she fell flat. She gasped but had a few hundred pounds of muscled New Species pin her down when his body dropped over hers.

Tammy stared up at him and whimpered, thinking she'd been safe, sure he wasn't going to hurt her after they'd talked. His face remained inches from hers and he looked grim. He lowered his face and buried it against her neck.

"Relax. I won't hurt you," he breathed very softly against her ear. "They listen always. This close and soft they cannot hear. I won't mount you but I need to make them believe I am interested. They will take you from my cell otherwise and they could kill you if they think the experiment is a failure. Do you understand?"

"Yes," she got out softly, struggled with her fear, but forced her tense muscles to relax. "They have microphones listening to what we say?" She kept her voice just as soft as he had.

"They watch with cameras too but do not search for them with your eyes. They will become suspicious."

He shifted over her, pinned her closer to him, completely covering her with his body. He was careful not to crush her. Tammy experienced raw fear at how tiny she felt, how helpless, and had no choice but to trust that he wouldn't hurt her. The man was big, smelled of a strong soap and sweat. It wasn't unpleasant, but foreign. She was used to the way Valiant smelled. She put her hands on his chest. His skin felt as hot as Valiant's, almost as if they ran a fever, but they just had a hotter temperature than humans. She resisted the urge to attempt to push him off, already knowing it would be a useless effort.

He buried his face against her neck again, sniffed really loudly, probably for the microphones, before he spoke softly to her again. "Will Valiant really come looking for you and not stop?"

"Yes." Tammy had no doubt. "They all will. The New Species, I mean."

A soft growl tore from his mouth. "I will do my best to keep you here. They will kill you if they believe I won't do as they wish by mounting you. You'll have no value to them otherwise. They'll take me from here, back to where I came from, and consider the test of breeding me to another human a failure."

Tammy closed her eyes and fought more tears. The man dropped his face against her neck and adjusted until he'd wiggled his hips until he'd wedged between her thighs. Fear and mental exhaustion finally caught up to her. She wanted to cry, admitted to a little self-pity that this had happened to her, and she gripped his skin just to find some comfort.

"Lie here with me and rest. You are safe from me, little one with pretty eyes."

"My name is Tammy."

He inhaled her skin at her neck. "It is good to smell another of my kind on you."

"They don't let you see others?"

"No."

He was alone. She shifted her arms and wrapped them around his neck. He didn't protest the hug-like hold she had on him. He had her totally trapped under his big body but she didn't feel threatened.

Deep down she understood one thing. He was alone and he needed to hold her too, probably longed for the comfort just as much as she did. She closed her eyes and relaxed. Her mind instantly drifted to Valiant. He'd find her somehow. He had to. A yawn surprised her and all the adrenaline started to drain from her body.

* * * * *

Tiger glared at Charlie Artzola. The man had been found tied up inside his car near Reservation. He'd pleaded innocent to willingly stealing Tammy but Tiger wasn't buying it. The human was ignorant of their sense of smell or he just thought they were really stupid.

"I told you. I was in my office and suddenly this man entered. He held a gun on me until Miss Shasta and her officer arrived. I didn't have time to even warn them before he killed her security officer. It horrified me. He forced me outside with her and explained if I didn't drive them out of the gates, he'd blow her brains out. I was trying to save her life when he shoved her into the trunk, climbed in with her, and told me to close the trunk. I knew he'd kill her if I tipped off the officers at the gate. I was terrified for her life so I did what he said."

Tiger growled and took two menacing steps toward the attorney. He didn't even glance at Justice for permission. He reached the human and backhanded the man's cheek hard.

"You lie," he snarled. "We scented your office and followed your trail to your car. We also scented your car. Only she was inside the trunk. There was no other human male. You took her and you are going to tell us where you are holding her. Where did you take her?"

The man groaned from the pain and he licked his bloodied lip where it had split near the corner. A red mark marred his pale skin. Charlie Artzola's wide gaze focused on Justice.

"You know I'd never lie to you. I've worked for you for almost a year. I'm trusted, and everything I've said is the truth. That is what happened. I had no choice. The guy with the gun told me where to drive and that's what I did. Maybe he wore something to hide his scent. He did have military-type clothes on and a cap over his hair. That's why you probably didn't smell him. Another man waited at the location where I was told to drive and he held another gun on me, ordered me to open the trunk, and his friend climbed out. They took Miss Shasta, tied me up, and drove away with her. I sat there helpless until your people found me. I swear, Justice. I'm a victim in this as much as that woman is."

Justice slowly reached up and loosened his tie. He kept a calm expression on his features. He yanked the tie off over his head and reached for his jacket buttons next, unfastening each one. He shed his jacket and unbuttoned his white shirt. He removed it and his chest was bare. He reached for his belt next as he kicked off his loafers.

"What are you doing?" The attorney's voice shook with fear. "Justice? Why are you getting undressed?"

Justice snapped his gaze up and glared at Charlie Artzola. "This is a two-thousand-dollar suit. I don't want to get your blood all over it. My people found you because we put trackers on all your vehicles but unfortunately we can't track your destinations until they are activated. We don't know where you took her because you'd already parked when we realized she'd been taken. You knew that though since you were the one who drafted the agreement that allows us to make all human employees agree to those devices and you knew your car would be found. You should have disappeared. Instead you counted on my trust and your ability to lie well to shield you from our rage."

"I'm sorry you lost one of your men but it wasn't me. It's that guy's fault who forced me to drive him and Miss Shasta out the gates. I didn't tie myself up. See? That's proof I'm not lying."

Justice folded his pants, now wearing only his black boxer briefs. He turned and handed all of his folded clothing to one of the New Species officers positioned at the door. "Please take these to another room. Blood splatters."

"Jesus Christ," Charlie Artzola moaned. "What are you doing? It's me, Justice. I'm your friend. You know I would never betray your people. Never. I know we are all upset that Miss Shasta has been taken but I just drove her out of here to prevent them from blowing her brains out."

Justice turned, growling. "Friends don't kidnap one of our women and hand her over to the enemy."

"She's not New Species. She's a human. I wouldn't do that to your kind and I sure as hell wouldn't do it to mine."

"She is one of ours regardless of her blood. Talk, Charlie. Talk now or I will make you. No one but New Species know we have you. There is a lot of ground on our Reservation to dispose of your body when we are done. You will tell us where to find the woman if you want to live." Justice prowled closer, growled and bared his teeth. "We learned torture from having it done to us. I'm an experimental prototype, Charlie. They really hurt me badly and there are thousands of ways to make you scream and bleed without killing you. You will suffer."

"Justice, I swear. There was another man and he ca —"

"You didn't kill my officer," Justice snarled. "He survived. Whoever you are working with, and we are aware since someone did tie you up that you have at least one partner, is either an idiot or set you up to die. Did he or she give you the drug you used on Flame? It was a very strong sedative but not enough to stop his heart. He's going to wake soon and when he does, he'll be able to tell us exactly what happened when he escorted Miss Shasta to your office."

* * * * *

Valiant jerked out of Brass' hold, had seen more than enough on the monitors, and wanted to tear the human apart to get answers. He'd told Justice he'd give him a chance, knew his rage was too great at that moment, but it was taking too long. He lunged toward the holding cell.

The door exploded open when he entered. Valiant snarled as he stormed into the room. His attention locked on the man tied to the chair in the corner of the room. Valiant threw his head back and roared at the human who'd taken Tammy.

"Jesus!" Charlie Artzola screamed, staring at Valiant.

"Do not kill him," Justice ordered softly. "He needs to tell us where he took her and who he delivered her to. He has a partner."

Valiant growled, showed teeth, and his body shook. His hands fisted. "I understand. I will contain my rage but it's difficult."

Justice cleared his throat. "I was just about to show him how much pain it will take to get him to tell us the information we need."

"Allow me that pleasure," Valiant snarled, opened his mouth wide, and his muscles strained while his body tensed in anticipation of beating the truth out of the human. He wanted his blood. "I'll make him tell us everything."

"Jesus Christ," the attorney moaned. He wet himself and piss pooled on the chair until and ran down its legs. His terrified gaze darted to Justice. "Don't let him near me. She said he'd tear out my guts and feed them to me."

Justice glanced at Valiant with raised eyebrows as their gazes met. Justice turned suddenly, putting his back to the attorney, to only reveal his grin to the Species. "So she told you what Valiant would do to you?" He growled the words. "She warned you what betrayal would cost you." Schooling his features, Justice faced the prisoner again. "Where is she? Where did you take her? To whom did you deliver her? I want answers or Valiant will do exactly what she threatened he would. We will watch him do it without lifting a finger to make it stop. You will suffer untold agony and it will take hours to die."

"It is very painful," Valiant growled. He licked his lips and showed his sharp teeth to prove the point. "Flesh is easy to tear apart."

The attorney nodded frantically. "Just swear he won't touch me. I want to live."

Justice paused. "You will live if you help us get her back and she is still alive."

"He doesn't plan on killing her but it's not my fault if the New Species he took her to kills her," Charlie Artzola stammered quickly. "He wanted her to give to one of your kind. The man I work for is Dr. Adam Zenlelt. He worked for Mercile Industries and approached me after I got the job at Homeland. He offered me a lot of money and I needed it. I've got an ex-wife and a ton of bil—"

Valiant roared again, edged closer, and his fingers curved into claws.

Justice glanced at him and then the attorney. "He doesn't give a shit why you did it. Stop excusing your betrayal and tell us where the woman is and more about this human who has her."

"I don't know all that much about him. He wanted Miss Shasta because I told him that one of yours planned to marry a human woman. He pays me to tell him that stuff. He has a New Species and he's been trying to run tests on him but it's an insane one who keeps killing any women shoved inside his cell. Zenlelt likes to be called "doctor". He realized that two New Species can't breed and he's planned on testing one of you against a human woman to see if she can get pregnant. Zenlelt thought that since one of you would fuck her, his guy would do her too. That's why he needed her so bad and bribed me to take her to him. He's going to lock her inside a cage with that thing to see if he'll fuck or kill her the way he did the others. That New Species he's got is really an animal, Justice. I saw him once and he doesn't have an ounce of humanity left inside him."

Valiant lunged. Justice moved, grabbed him, and tossed him back into the wall. Justice struggled but managed to pin him there. "We won't find her if you kill him," he snarled.

Valiant closed his eyes and nodded. Justice eased his hold and released the bigger male. He turned to glare at the human he'd mistakenly trusted.

"Tell us everything you know."

The attorney nodded frantically. "I will. They have a house they've rented and that's where I saw them a few days ago. They had the New Species locked up and drugged inside a cage at the time but he wasn't fully asleep. He scared the hell out of me because he's got these black stone-cold, dead eyes. Serial-killer type. I was ordered to take her to the house, which I did. Zenlelt has two guys working with him and they took her into the house. They have another location but I don't know where it is or the location of where they are keeping the New Species. I just know I heard them say they were going to wait until dark to get the New Species prepared for her before they took her to him. They call him 927 and sometimes they call him the beast." Charlie Artzola swallowed. "I heard Zenlelt say that out of all the males he had, that one tested with the highest sperm. I don't know where they brought him from or where Zenlelt's set up normally but he came here looking for a woman who had sex with a New Species."

"Where is this house?" Justice inched closer, his hands curled into fists.

Charlie Artzola paused. "You swear that you won't kill me or let him hurt me?" His gaze jerked to Valiant, who stood against the wall where Justice had pushed him, before staring at Justice again. "I want your vow on the lives of New Species I'll walk out of here alive and in one piece if I help you find her."

"I do not break my word," Justice growled. "I am a man of honor. I swear you will not be killed and I will not allow Valiant to have you if she's still alive. As for walking out of here, that I refuse to promise. You betrayed my people but I'm willing to hand you over to your justice system. It's far kinder than ours."

The attorney gave the address of the house but paused. "But they have moved her by now. The sun was going down when your men found me."

"What were they going to move her in? Did you see the other car?"

"It was a large white van without windows. It wasn't marked and I didn't look at the plates. These aren't guys you want to be nosy around. The back two doors had no windows either. It's all I can tell you."

"You do not know where they were taking her?"

The man hesitated for a second too long. "No. I don't."

Valiant growled. Justice glared. "You lie again. You stink of dishonor. Tell me where they took her or I will let him hand you your guts." He glanced at the officer by the door. "Tiger? Have you scoped out a good location to bury the human's remains if we have to kill him?"

Tiger smiled coldly. "Of course. It's smack dab inside the Wild Zone. He will never be found."

"I really don't know," the attorney nearly sobbed. "I just know it was close to where the house is. Yesterday I took Zenlelt information and one of his men left to go feed the beast. He was only gone about twenty minutes. I swear, God as my witness, that's all I know."

Justice relaxed. He turned and met Valiant's gaze. "Let's go."

Outside the door someone handed Justice a pair of jeans and a T-shirt. He'd asked for clothes to be brought to him before he'd entered the room. He nodded his thanks as he accepted the clothing and studied Valiant.

"Well, she was alive when he left her. She is strong, Valiant. She threatened that man to the point he felt terror the second you walked into the room." Justice smiled. "Where did she think up tearing out his guts?"

Valiant shrugged, too worried and angry to be amused. "I don't know but that's my Tammy. She's smart." His voice broke.

Justice reached out and gripped his arm. "We will find her."

Tiger nodded. "We'll get her back, Valiant. The SUVs are ready. Let's go."

Chapter Fourteen

 හ

Valiant buried his face against the mattress of the small bed. He inhaled deeply, growled, and fought the urge to roar. "My Tammy was here. They had her chained down and she was very frightened. I'm also picking up a strange smell mingled with her sweat. They drugged her with something. It's faint but there."

Tiger examined the handcuffs still attached to the metal frame of the headboard and foot rail. He didn't see or scent blood on either set. "We'll find her."

Justice nodded. "We hiked in from the woods so we wouldn't be spotted. The upstairs bedrooms are currently lived in. Someone will return. Their things are still here."

Tiger nodded at the five men inside. "We watch and wait."

Valiant moved, climbed up on the bed, and pressed his nose against the mattress again. Tammy's scent lingered there. The smell of her terror was strongest there. He didn't want to move for fear it would fade away. He had to find her. He sensed Justice and Tiger watching him.

Justice sighed. "Does it help?"

"A little," Valiant admitted softly. "I do not want to live anymore if we don't find her." He turned his head to stare at them.

Tiger cringed and Valiant understood why. They all knew it happened sometimes with New Species inside the testing facilities. They gave up hope and just stopped eating. They allowed their bodies to die. He never thought he'd be one to release life once they were freed. He refused to regret falling in love with his Tammy though.

"I hope I never fall in love if it means losing a woman makes me want to give up my hold on life," Tiger muttered.

"Hopefully the male she's been taken to won't hurt her," Justice said. "He will scent you on her unless she showered and changed her clothing after you left her."

He shook his head. "She did not. She'd already changed into her clothing when I left. I held her and my scent is all over her. He won't be able to miss it."

"Good." Justice turned his attention on Tiger. "There are more of Species still imprisoned by Mercile. We need to find them and we'll be able to if we find her."

Tiger lifted his cell phone. "I'll go upstairs and let the others know. We will try to find out who bought or rented this house. Maybe they are using the same name or funds to pay for wherever Tammy is being kept. I doubt that Zenlelt is a real name. They set Charlie Artzola up to die. They've been dealing with New Species who've never known freedom. I'm sure they assumed we'd behave the same and kill him instantly. They gave him the weapon that took Flame down and had to know he'd survive. I can't figure out why they didn't just shoot the attorney instead of sending him back to us alive."

Justice growled. "Mercile enjoys trying to make us appear dangerous and unstable to humans to justify what they did to us. They probably thought we'd murder the bastard with humans around to witness it. That or they just think we're stupid and it was worth the risk of leaving him alive on the chance of keeping an insider in place if we believed everything he tried to lie about. I dread trying to discover how much he's betrayed us and what information he's passed to them."

Tiger glanced at Valiant. "I'm sorry, man. We'll get her back."

Valiant couldn't speak. Emotion choked him. Justice turned away to whisper to Tiger but he still heard the words.

"He's so fierce. To see him this way breaks my heart. Let's give him some privacy with his mate's scent. Make those calls and order our men to stay hidden. Hopefully they will return here. I don't know what else to do."

* * * * *

"Wake up," a voice growled next to Tammy's ear. "They come to feed us. Stay on the bed and do not go near the bars."

Tammy's eyes snapped open. She met 927's gaze as he lifted off her. He stood, putting his body in the path of the cell door and her. Tammy sat up and noticed with some alarm that the broken glass wall had disappeared but the debris from it remained on the metal floor. *How did I sleep through that?*

Her attention lifted to the top of the room when a hum sounded and she saw a two inch gap in the cage roof. The length ran across the room where the glass wall had been. She heard a louder noise, a whine of an engine, and another glass wall was lifted by some kind of crane system from the other side of the warehouse.

She gaped, watching as it was positioned over the cage, lined up with the slot of the opening and lowered slowly from the ceiling. She stared in shock at it. Obviously the glass walls were removable from the top and the broken one had been lifted out. A new one slid in all the way to the floor to separate the cell from the door.

The New Species with his back to her tensed and growled deeply. Tammy realized he did it in an attempt to protect her. That seemed a vast improvement from being sure he'd kill her when she'd been tossed into the caged room with him. He'd held her instead while she slept and hadn't hurt her. Gratitude toward him and hope that Valiant and the New Species at Reservation would find them flooded her. She just needed to stay alive.

"You didn't mount her." Pete approached the cage. "Why not? Do you like men, 927? The doctor said to leave her in there and your nature will eventually make you fuck her. That smell thing must have worked since you are interested in her. I guess you guys don't mind sharing, huh?"

Mike snorted. "If you bend her over it's just the same as taking a man."

"One asshole is as good as another. Just close your eyes and pretend she's Mike."

"Hey, that isn't funny. Don't have him fantasize about bending me over. I don't want him looking at me that way."

Pete laughed. "Better he thinks about you that way than me and we're the only two he sees unless you want to count the doctor. Nobody would want to screw him."

"True." Mike laughed. He opened the cell door and set down a large platter and a container. "Come and get it." He slammed the cell door and both men left.

A minute later the loud noise sounded again. The glass partition started to slowly rise. 927 relaxed and turned to meet Tammy's gaze. "I will go over there. You can use the toilet without me watching you."

She nodded. "Thank you."

There was no privacy inside the room. She glanced at 927. He had walked to the cell door and stared out of it, keeping his back to her. The toilet was just that, a portable one that had been set on the metal with tubes shoved between the wall and the cage that led out of sight.

Toilet paper sat on the back of the lid. Tammy hurried and used it. There was a hose and a drain hole had been cut through metal next to the seat on the floor. She used it to wash her hands. It was similar to turning on a garden hose and just pointing the weak spray into the hole on the floor. This had to be his only way to get clean. It was barbaric.

"I'm done. Thank you."

927 turned and nodded. He picked up the silver container and carried it to the bed. 927 pointed to the floor when he took a seat there, indicating she should sit next to him. He used the

bed for a table. She cringed when he lifted the lid to reveal the food. It was "Valiant food" only. She could tell it wasn't cooked much. They'd brought steaks, sliced into strips, seared only, on a bloody plate.

She sat. "I can't eat that. It's too raw."

He frowned at her. "You will eat. You need strength. Close your eyes and think why you must survive. You must take down at least one."

She cringed but knew he had a point. She hadn't eaten in a long time and her belly ached from hunger. He picked up a chunk of seared meat and held it out. Her hands shook as her fingers gripped an end of it, careful not to let blood drip onto her clothes.

He lifted another and locked gazes with her. He showed her how to sink her teeth into it and yank to tear the meat. She tried but the meat was very tough and her teeth weren't sharp enough as his were. She had to fight the urge to be sick at the taste of blood. The meat had dripped it into her mouth when she'd bitten into it, trying to tear it unsuccessfully. She tried to bite into it but since it was so tough and thick that she just took it out.

"I can't eat this. I can't even get a piece. I can only gnaw on it."

He reached over and used his fingers to open her lips, his knuckle against her teeth to nudge them open too. Tammy opened her mouth for his inspection. He frowned. His fingertip ran across the edge of her teeth before he explored her back teeth. He pulled his finger away.

"They are too smooth. Why did your kind allow someone to grind your teeth down? They are useless."

"They just grow this way. We don't have a need to tear things with our teeth. We use forks and knives."

He pulled the meat from her fingers. He opened his mouth and tore a small piece of meat from the steak and handed it to her. She hesitated and took it. *Good thing I'm not a germ freak, huh?* She cringed as she ate the small piece of bloody meat. He tore another small piece off and placed it on the tray in front of hers. He used his teeth and kept tearing her small strips, making a pile.

"Thank you," she whispered.

Never in a million years would she think she'd eat raw meat and thank a man for using his sharp teeth to rip it apart to make the bites small enough for her to chew and swallow. She also never believed she'd be hungry enough not to gag at either reality.

Tammy couldn't eat it all. What she didn't eat, 927 did. He ate more than Valiant had. He removed the empty tray and walked to the cell door. He turned the tray and shoved it outside the cell. When it dropped it made a loud crash that Tammy winced over. He returned and twisted open the metal thermos. He sniffed it before handing it to Tammy.

"It is safe. Sometimes they put drugs in my drink but I'd smell it."

She smiled at him after enjoying the icy-cold water and handed it back. He drank while staring at her. Her smile slipped at the odd expression that darkened his eyes and made him study her a little too intensely for comfort.

"What?"

"You are attractive. You smell sweet."

An uneasy feeling made her nervous. "Valiant said when I'm scared I smell that way. I've been scared a lot since yesterday."

He hesitated. "You belong to this Valiant?"

She nodded. "We're getting married."

"Married? What is this?"

She considered her words. "It's a ceremony that binds us together until we die in my world. He wants to marry me to make sure human law acknowledges that I belong to him."

He nodded. "But you already belong to him?"

"Yes."

He softly growled. "That is too bad. I want you."

She inched back from him, feeling fear. "No."

He frowned. "I said it is too bad. Do you not understand this?"

"I belong to Valiant."

"Keep your voice down or they will hear us. I know. I agree."

Her heart rate returned to normal. "I was afraid you didn't care that I am his. The way you said that implied you were going to...touch me anyway."

He shrugged. "I would want him to protect you if you were mine and you were taken from me to be given to another. I would kill him if he mounted you. I will not force breed you, Tammy. I may want to but I can control it. My mind rules my body."

Good thing.

"I just hope that this Valiant comes for you soon." He stood. "You smell too good. It has been a long time since I allowed my body to give in to the urge to breed. Much too long to be this close to you."

That made Tammy uneasy again. It almost sounded as though it were a threat. As if he warned her that his control would only last so long. She bit her lip. "What do you do in here to keep busy?"

He shrugged. "I grow strong."

She glanced at the large room. There was the twin bed and the toilet. The small hose with the twist-turn to shut it on and off and the drain in the floor were the only other things. She had no idea what he meant.

"You must get so bored."

"Bored?"

She tried to think of a way to explain it to him. "You have nothing to do."

"I get strong." He moved to the floor beside her and did pushups. She watched as his muscles strained and tightened while he quickly lifted up and down. He eventually stopped and glanced at the wall. He ran at it, twisted, and slammed his body against it. He did that a few times, switching shoulders as he hit it. She stared at the bars and realized they'd bent slightly, just barely, and she wouldn't have noticed if she hadn't been searching for damage.

He stopped doing that and walked to the front of the cell where the bars were. He gripped them and did pushups while standing. He finally turned and strode to the center of the cage. He suddenly crouched down and leapt high into the air. His fingers caught the bars of the roof, his body hung feet from the floor and she watched in amazement as he did pull-ups. He seemed to do them forever until sweat dripped down his body. He released the bars and landed gracefully on his bare feet. He turned and looked at her.

"I get strong."

No wonder all the New Species men were huge and buff. It's not a mystery anymore how muscular and in shape they are if this is what they did all those years inside their cells.

She nodded. "I saw that."

"I bathe now. You may turn away."

She did. She put her back to the area with the hose. She heard water come on and she heard the odd sound of Velcro. She wanted to look to see what it was but she didn't. He wanted to bathe and even she knew their definitions of that couldn't be too different. The sound of water running lasted a while. It shut off. She heard that sound of Velcro again.

"I am covered."

Tammy turned, still sitting on the floor, and faced 927. He had washed his body and his hair was wet. She saw him return something behind the toilet as he bent.

"What did you put behind the..." She pointed.

He leaned back down. "Soap and deodorant." He lifted them and showed her. The soap hung from a tiny rope and he'd been given a travel-sized deodorant. "They give us these to keep clean and not to smell. We do not enjoy bad odors from our bodies. It makes us irritable."

"At least they give you toilets. I guess that is good."

"They do not clean our rooms. We would kill them if they got so close."

"I understand." The jerks who'd brought her there didn't want to have to clean up the cell if he didn't have the ability to go to the bathroom decently.

He moved closer and sat in front of her. "Tell me about New Species. Tell me everything."

Tammy took a deep breath. She started to tell him everything she knew from the time she'd started to follow the news. 927 watched her with interest. He smiled a lot. She continued to talk.

* * * * *

"Someone comes," a voice over the radio warned softly.

Valiant leapt from the bed and watched Justice and Tiger stand from where they had been resting on the floor. The men moved out of sight of the front door. Justice gave Valiant a hard look.

"Do not kill them or hurt their ability to speak. They know where Tammy is."

"I know that." Valiant growled softly. "No one wants her back more than I."

"I know but I see your rage, my friend. I understand. I would want to destroy them if someone took my woman...if I had a woman. I am just reminding you in case you are not thinking clearly. We need them to tell us where she is."

"She's not even my woman and I still want to kill them," Tiger sighed. "They work for Mercile, took one of our women, and they need to die for that."

"Quiet," Valiant suddenly whispered. "I hear a vehicle coming."

An engine died outside and a door slammed. A man walked up the front walkway, his shoe tread soft, and keys jingled. In seconds the deadbolt slid and the door swung open. The human who walked inside was a man in his twenties. He wore white clothing, similar to the technicians from the testing facilities, and Valiant bit back a snarl to remain silent.

The human hooked his keys on a nail in the wall and slammed the door closed behind him. His arms rose as he stretched his torso, yawned and turned. It took him five steps before he realized he wasn't alone. He froze.

Valiant, Tiger and Justice spread out around the man the second they walked out of hiding from the next room. Terror instantly shrouded the human's face and the stench of it rolled off him.

"Fuck me," he cursed.

Tiger growled. "Not even if you begged. You aren't our type."

The man blanched. "What do you want?"

Valiant growled. "You know what we want. Where is my woman?"

The man started to shake and sweat as he stared at Valiant. His gaze swept over the big New Species from head to foot. "Shit."

"Where is Tammy?" Justice growled from behind the human. "Talk quickly because my friend wants to make you scream and bleed. The bed smells strongly of his woman's fear. He is very angry."

The human's mouth moved but nothing came out. Valiant roared, the sound filled the room, and he advanced. The human spun quickly to flee, lost his balance and collapsed to the floor in terror. A high-pitched scream tore from his throat as Valiant crouched and grabbed him by his arms, making sure his nails dug into them painfully.

"Where is my Tammy?" Valiant snarled the words. He yanked the man's upper body closer to his sharp teeth.

"At the warehouse," he sobbed. "She's at the warehouse."

"Release him," Justice growled. "Do not break him. He is going to tell us where that is, aren't you, human?"

The man jerked his eyes to Justice. He nodded, terrified. "I will. Just get him off me."

Valiant released him and backed up. He shook with rage. The urge to kill nearly overwhelmed him. This was the human who had taken Tammy to a warehouse to be thrown in with an imprisoned Species for a breeding experiment. It took everything he had not to lunge and tear out his throat.

"Is she still alive?" Tiger inched closer to intimidate.

"She was when I left a little while ago. 927 won't fuck her and he didn't kill her."

Justice moved, blocking Valiant when he took a step toward the human on the floor. Justice shook his head. "Control."

"I am." Valiant growled.

Justice turned his furious glare on the human. "What is your name?"

"Pete."

Justice blinked. "You are going to take us to this warehouse. What is the security there? How many guards are protecting the site? Are they heavily armed?"

Pete stared at him. "You mean how many men are guarding it? None. It's just me, Mike and the doctor."

Tiger growled. "Lie. They would never guard a testing facility with just three men."

Pete turned his terrified eyes to the cat-eyed man glaring at him. "It's not one. We just brought the one from the testing facility in Colorado. The doctor wanted to bring more of them but we have to wait until more men are available to build more cells to hold them. Right now it's just the one we have and just the three of us can handle him."

"You are going to take us there but first you are going to tell us where this testing facility in Colorado is located." Justice demanded. "And you are going to do it now."

Valiant roared again. The man on the floor nodded frantically, his terrified gaze locked on Valiant.

"I will. Anything you want. Just stay away from me." He rattled off an address.

Justice shot Tiger a look. Tiger nodded, grabbed his back pocket and flipped out his cell phone. He gave the address to the person he spoke to. He paused.

"How many New Species are being kept there? What is the security like?"

The man closed his mouth. "They'll kill me."

Justice growled and clapped his hands once. The men from upstairs came down and surrounded the cowering human. Pete stared at the eight New Species closing in on him. The smell of his fear became so strong Valiant could almost taste it.

"You talk or we start at your toes and fingers. It is amazing how many bones can be broken before shock starts to kill a man." Justice growled, inching closer. "Answer my questions."

"Don't do it," Pete rasped. "Fuck. Just stay back. There should be eighty-two males and six females there unless some of them were moved over the last week when I left there. Security is tight." He paused.

"Keep talking," Valiant growled at him. "Where would they be moved to? Where are the other testing facilities?"

"It's not like that," the guy hissed. "When the first testing facilities were breached, people panicked. We found an abandoned building and it took us some months to prepare the new location to hold them. Everyone was scared shitless that our testing facility would be discovered, we wanted to get out of there as fast as possible, but it takes time to build sturdy enough holding cells to keep your kind locked up. We moved them to the address I gave you and sometimes we lend some of them out to a few of the other doctors who weren't arrested. I don't have nothing to do with that and I don't know anything except sometimes a handful of them disappear but are later returned. You're going to have to talk to the doctor about where they go and who has them. He's in charge. Nothing gets done without his approval. His name is Adam Zenlelt."

"How many guards are there? Where are our people?"

"They are being kept underground on the second level. It used to be a parking lot two floors down but they enclosed it to house those bastards. They usually have about twelve guards topside and maybe six downstairs. I don't know all the doctors and support staff but I'd guess maybe twenty in all onsite during a work shift."

"Is it rigged with explosives?" Tiger growled.

Pete shrugged. "Hell if I know. I'm not security. I'm just the doctor's assistant. Me and Mike are the muscle. That's all. We take care of 927 and whatever test subjects the doctor personally is working with."

"What about Tammy?" Valiant moved closer, glaring. "Tell me everything."

The man swallowed. "We threw her into the cell with 927. He killed the last two women we put in with him. He just fucking killed them. He's crazy. He won't kill your bitches but he kills regular ones like me." He slammed his mouth shut. "That came out wrong. You know what I mean. He broke through the partition we have in place to keep him back when we open the cell door. He sniffed her a lot and she was yakking up a storm to him trying to get him not to kill her. He just took her to his bed and lay down with her. When I left he was feeding her, and hell, he tore up the meat for her. It was freaky. If he will use his teeth to make bite-sized chucks she can eat, sleep with her, then you would assume he would fuck her. We think he's gay."

"He slept on her?" Valiant growled.

The man winced. "Well, it is kind of cold at night and we don't give him blankets."

"Calm," Justice ordered Valiant. "He did not breed her." His gaze fixed on Pete. "Right?"

The man shook his head. "I told you. We think he's gay."

"What does that mean?" Tiger frowned.

The man on the floor hesitated. "We think he likes men. She isn't a man. He won't do her."

Tiger laughed. "You think because he won't breed her that he is physically attracted to men?" He shook his head. "Did you ever think he might not be into forcing women?" His smile died and he growled. "That is your sickness to want to rape them, not ours."

"Well, I never grabbed a woman and snapped her neck but he did it," Pete ground out. "Two of them and trust me, they were smoking hot. I would have done them in a heartbeat if someone had tossed them at me. He didn't even talk before he killed them." Pete snapped his fingers. "Just like that."

Justice frowned, his gaze pausing on each man inside the room.

Tiger softly cursed. "He's either gone over the edge or he had a good reason for killing helpless females. We will find out."

Justice nodded grimly. He turned his full attention to the prisoner. "Pete? We are going on a road trip. You will lead us to where you took Tammy."

"I'll do it. I have no choice. Just back off."

Justice motioned his men back with a wave of his hand. Pete crawled to his feet on shaky legs. He glanced at Justice, who obviously was in charge.

"I want immunity against being prosecuted in a court of law for kidnapping and anything else the cops want to tack on. You promise me that and I will drive you there myself and take you right to 927."

Justice blinked a few times before a slow smile spread across his face. "I swear I will give you immunity from your law. It is a deal. Take us to the woman and the New Species now."

The man stared at Justice. "You can do that, right? Give me immunity?"

Justice's smile died and his eyes narrowed. "I am New Species law. I am Justice. I can give you anything I wish. This is a Species matter that does not involve your law unless I say it does. I give you my word as Justice North that your cops will not send you to prison if you help us. Now let's go."

The man nodded. "Sure. I don't want to go to prison. It's just a good-paying job. I'm going to need some money too, just to get me a started. I want a hundred grand."

Justice was grim. He jerked his head in a nod. "You got it. You will get the money after we get the woman back, verify that the testing facility in Colorado is where you say it is and our people are there."

Pete smiled, looking less frightened. "I understand. Let's go. It's not too far from here."

* * * * *

Tammy laughed. "No. I'm not defective. There are a lot of women my size."

927 nodded. "I did not mean to offend you if I implied you have physical imperfections."

"None taken. I've seen a few of your women and they are really tall. I understand how you could think that way. I am short for the average woman. I—"

927 suddenly moved, cutting off her words. He lifted to his feet in a heartbeat and reached for Tammy. She gasped as his hands gripped her arms and she was yanked to her feet. She ended up behind the large man. He tensed and growled toward the cell door.

The older man and Mike walked up to the cell door. Tammy got a glimpse of them before 927 shoved her back and used one hand to keep her in place behind him. He was too wide to see around and far too tall. Another deep and vicious growl tore from his throat.

"I see you like her." The older man chuckled. "You need to breed her, 927." The man's voice hardened. "I'm going to have Mike pull out his gun and kill her if you don't."

Fear tore through Tammy. *Why would they do that?*

"Yeah," Mike laughed. "See this gun? Boom! The doctor is tired of waiting while you court the bitch. Just bend her over and find the right hole. It shouldn't be too hard. I know you like men but just pretend."

"Enough!" The older man sighed. "I keep telling you boys that he's not a homosexual. He's bred with his females in the past. It is unaltered females he has issues with."

"Maybe he realized he's attracted to men. It happens. I had a cousin who came out of the closet in his thirties. He married someone and they had four kids before he told his wife."

The older man sighed louder. "927? Either breed her or step out of the way and allow Mike to put her down. It's that simple. You seem to like her and I'm sure you'll breed her. You are doing this just to piss me off. I understand that but my patience is at an end. I have wasted enough time."

"You will have to shoot through me," 927 warned, his voice dropping to a scary growl.

There was silence. The older man finally spoke. "I'll gas your cell and when you are out, we will get her. I'd hate to do that because I'd have to order the gas but I can get it by the end of the day. Breed her or move out of the way."

"Gas us," 927 growled.

Tammy's terror was instant. "Gas us?" She gasped.

927 turned his head and stared at her. "Do you want to breed with me? They will take you from me afterward and you will be alive until he decides he has learned what he wants. They will strap you down and hurt you. They did this to our females. They cried and screamed. Sometimes they would take our females to other males to breed with and it would start again. Is this the life you wish?"

She shook her head. Definitely not.

He nodded. "Do you want me to move to allow him to shoot you? Is all of your hope gone now?"

She shook her head again. "I'm not ready to die."

"They will have to gas us. It will take time," he whispered.

Tammy stared into his eyes and nodded. "Gas us."

927 flashed her a smile and turned. His smile gone, he said, "Order your gas. It is the only way you will get her from me."

"Fuck," Mike growled. "Let me shoot through him, Doc. I'm pretty sure I can miss all the vital organs. He'll recover."

"It was just a ruse to get him to breed with her. We'll drug his food. He'll have to eat or drink at some point. Turn off the water to his cell. Once he takes the drugs he'll be forced to breed her. I didn't want to cloud this experiment but he's too stubborn. We'll have to use the breeding drugs. Perhaps if it doesn't take the first time we can get him to breed her without the drugs after he's had her once."

"Why don't we just gas their asses, force him to give up his goodies, and inject them into the bitch if you want to see if she can get a doggy in her oven?"

"I tried to explain this to you already." The older man sighed. "We've been testing them for years. Their sperm is different than ours. We discovered that during intercourse their sperm load is high but only if they are aroused. When it is manipulated manually, if we force their sperm, their count is substantially lower. It also has a very short lifespan. It dies quickly, almost within a minute, and until we can figure out if it's because of being exposed to oxygen or if it's a temperature issue, we can't effectively resolve the problem. We lost a lot of our equipment when we abandoned our facility. I need him to breed her naturally for there to even be a chance of success."

"Why didn't it work with the animal bitches?"

"The females aren't producing any viable eggs. It is only the males who have the ability to reproduce. I need to make a few calls to order the drugs I need and see where we are on the transfers. The men are coming tomorrow to enclose more space and add in four more cells. If this one won't breed her, maybe the other males will."

Mike laughed. "Wow, you are going to have her doing five of them? Think she'll survive that?"

"I don't know. It depends on if the other four kill her or not. This is important work."

"Who gives a shit if they can breed?"

The older man hesitated. "We lost the ability to make more of them a long time ago. We haven't been able to replicate what the doctor who created them did. Every attempt has failed. It is faster to deal with their reproductive issues than to start from scratch to try to replicate how they were created. We tried that for years and couldn't do it. If you enjoy getting paid we have to figure this out. When Mercile got busted, all their assets were frozen. We've nearly run out of the money we transferred out before that happened. We've had to turn to more creative ways to make money off them and figuring this out is a priority."

"Wouldn't they be weaker if you breed them with regular bitches?"

"No. They have very aggressive and dominant, engineered genes. They will come out fully engineered just the way we made them to be if we can breed them with humans."

"Cool."

"Cool is if we can work out the problem and get this one to impregnate her. We'll be able to breed our remaining males to regular women and have hundreds of products within the first year. Think of the profit margin and how quickly we can replace the ones lost. We've learned a lot over the years and won't make the same mistakes with the younger ones. The newborns will be trained from birth to take orders."

"Way cool."

"It's more about survival. We're probably all wanted by the police and unless you want to flee to some third-world country to sell trinkets to tourists, you better get on board fast to make this work. This is going to keep a paycheck coming your way."

"Damn." Mike looked grim. "I didn't know things were that desperate."

"Let's leave them while I make those phone calls. Maybe he'll breed her soon. He hasn't had use of a female in a long time. It was another reason I wanted him. His resistance has to be down."

Tammy listened but she didn't hear them anymore. She watched 927 carefully. His body finally relaxed and he released her arm, turning to look down at her.

"You are frightened." He inhaled. "I would not allow them to take you."

"It is because of what they were saying." She stared up at him in horror. "They want us to have children they can train to obey them? And what does product mean?" She knew the answer, but it was so horrible to contemplate, she just needed it confirmed.

"We are products. I have heard this before. First we were to help them create drugs that they tested on our bodies. Now they always talk about needing money and wanted to force us to fight for them and I've even overheard them say they want to sell us. I listen often and heard their plot to create more of us, younger ones, who do not know of their cruel ways. The think they can fool the young ones into becoming what we refused to be."

"That's horrible." *And evil. Vile. Sick. Heartless.* She stopped before she started cussing.

"That's why I had no choice in what I did to the women. I saw what they did to our women for years, trying to force their bodies to breed. You could not survive inside your mind and your weaker body would break. Our females are stronger."

"That part was true? That you killed the other women they brought? I thought they were trying to scare me."

He hesitated. "They were screaming when they saw me and terrified. They were crying and weeping. They fell apart at the sight of me. I knew they would not last through breeding or be strong enough to face the testing. They would be passed from cell to cell the way our women have been during their breeding tests. It got worse recently and they focused on breeding tests. They would make our females breed with eight or nine of us. We refused, if they refused. Most of our women grew very sad but we tried to keep them strong. It was at least contact, and we treated each other well. Our females have very difficult lives. It was a mercy I killed the humans painlessly. Their suffering would have been greater by far, every moment they lived. Our women have shared what was done to them during the testing the doctors did to their bodies away from us." He shivered. "They would have killed the women anyway, if they had managed to survive the breeding and tests. I would prefer to die. It was fast and painless. It was kinder to kill them before they were tortured to the point of insanity."

"That's what is in store for me?"

He nodded grimly. "You are stronger. You didn't scream and cry loudly when they brought you. You put yourself into a corner and talked to me. You said things that made me know you might be strong enough to survive and I realized you were honest. You must survive and give your Valiant time to find you. I will not harm you and will treat you as well as my own females if they make us breed. You must survive the testing when they torture you. You must do what you have done with me if they take you to other males. You need to talk to them and do not scream. They will scent me on you. You must keep your mind strong. Our females survive it because we comfort them. I will comfort you, Tammy."

Tammy wanted to cry but fought tears. The man was so calm about telling her what kind of hell she might have to endure. 927 slowly moved closer. Tammy didn't protest when he lifted her into his arms, walked to the bed, and sat with her on his lap. His arms hugged her tightly to his warm body.

"I will protect you in weakness. You cry, little one with pretty eyes. You have been very brave. I will hold you and you know I am here."

"Thank you." Tammy let go of the small bit of control she had left. She clung to the man holding her and cried softly against his chest.

They were going to make him breed her and planned to bring more New Species and toss her at them too. They'd take her baby away as if it were a puppy or a kitten if they succeeded. They would probably keep breeding her until she wasn't of any use anymore before they killed her. *How many babies will they steal from my arms before it ends?*

Tammy made a decision while she cried. She'd be strong, she'd do whatever it took, but she'd fight to live. Valiant would find her. Maybe not soon but eventually. She just needed to pray she didn't get pregnant if the worst happened. She didn't want to give those assholes a helpless baby to torment.

Chapter Fifteen

❧

The building was an old warehouse. There was one car in the parking area, no other businesses or homes nearby, and two metal doors seemed to be the only way in unless they climbed high to windows near the roof. On the back side of the building an old docking ramp sat against a thick metal garage door. Their team had parked a mile back and made the human walk with them. Pete had complained every step of the way. Valiant was ready to kill him but Justice wouldn't allow him the pleasure.

"There are only two ways in or out and they have alarms," the human explained softly. "There aren't any outside cameras. I told you that. I don't know why you sneaked up on the place."

Justice shot him a glare. "Be quiet unless we tell you to open your mouth."

"Fine," the human said. "Be that way. I'm helping you."

Tiger motioned to the team and they surged forward to the front of the warehouse while a few broke off to approach from the back. They didn't want to be seen until they breached the building. Valiant feared the two men inside would kill Tammy and the Species male they held captive if given the chance.

Justice glanced at the human. "We will move quickly. You are in front. You get those doors open fast and stay silent. If you try anything, I will kill you or allow him to do it." He pointed to Valiant. "I'd be kinder."

A soft growl instantly tore from Valiant's throat. He wanted to hurt the human badly for touching Tammy and helping to bring her to this place in the woods. Not even

Justice or the entire team of males would save Pete if she was dead. He'd go through them to kill him.

"I understand." Pete reeked of fear. "I want that money you promised and you don't have to keep threatening me. I'm doing what you want. Immunity, right? And I get the hundred grand?"

"Yes," Justice nodded. "Get us inside. Let's go."

They moved as one. The team crept up to the front doors. Pete punched in the code, the alarm beeped, and he swung open one of the metal doors. Eight heavily armed New Species and the human inched inside. He'd given Justice, Valiant, and Tiger the inside layout and they knew what to expect. One of the New Species grabbed Pete the second they entered the building and put a knife to his throat.

"Do not move or make a sound," the man growled softly at him.

Pete blinked and froze. He kept his mouth firmly closed.

Valiant had to refrain from rushing forward to a dividing wall that blocked his view of where Tammy should be. He sniffed the air and Justice suddenly grabbed his arm, flashing him a warning look. He nodded, understood they needed to proceed cautiously.

Tiger waved his fingers in the air, dividing the men to spread out to find the humans. Valiant could pick up two scents, both of which seemed to be coming from a room near them. As soon as the team with Tiger closed in, Valiant moved. *Tammy!*

Valiant's heart rate increased when he inhaled a faint trace of her scent. The sweet smell of her fear nearly drove him insane. It tore at him that he hadn't been there to protect her. As he and Justice silently moved through the warehouse the scent grew stronger. They passed the dividing wall and Valiant got his first glimpse of the bars and the front of the cell. Justice suddenly reached out and grabbed him.

"Do not spook him. Go slow and remain calm. We do not know what condition he is in. We do not want him to harm her."

Valiant forced his instincts back, knew how unstable a captured Species could be, and had to keep it together for Tammy's sake. "I know."

The body against Tammy tensed. 927's hand froze on her back and suddenly he lifted her up. The man was strong. He went from sitting position to standing with her held inside his arms in an instant. She sniffed and wiped at her tears. Her gaze flew to his.

"What is it?"

He inhaled. She saw shock in his eyes. He looked at her. "I smell them."

"Who?"

His gaze jerked to the cell doors. "Valiant and another of my kind."

Tammy's head twisted to stare through the bars toward the divider where they'd have to enter. Her heart pounded and she wiggled inside his arms.

"Put me down! You smell Valiant? Are you sure?"

He nodded as he bent, placing her on her feet. Tammy saw movement and Valiant stepped into her sight. Justice was to his immediate right, gripping his arm, and both men were dressed in all black outfits. Their hair had been pulled back from their faces. Justice held a gun in his hand while Valiant gripped a deadly-looking knife in his. Tammy lunged toward the wall of the cage.

"Valiant!"

She hit the bars and reached her arms out through them. Valiant rushed forward to grasp her hands in his. The knife clattered to the floor and he reached for her. He leaned against the cage, lowered his head, pressed his face to the bars until their skin touched forehead to forehead in the small space. His golden eyes looked suspiciously wet as their gazes held.

"I found you." His voice came out raspy, choked with emotion.

Tears flowed down her cheeks but she didn't try to rein them in. "I knew you would."

He released her hands and reached through the bars to cup her face. His thumb brushed away her tears. His other hand reached in and gripped her hip. She wished the bars didn't separate them. She wanted him to hold her but he couldn't.

"Are you hurt?"

"I'm fine. I was just scared." She suddenly remembered they weren't alone. She turned her head enough to glance back into the cell but not enough to break contact with Valiant.

927 remained standing where she'd left him. He stared at Valiant and Justice with open curiosity and wonder. He remained utterly quiet and motionless. Tammy glanced at Valiant and then Justice, who stood nearby in a relaxed stance, staring back at 927.

"This is 927," Tammy said softly. "927, this is Valiant and that is Justice North. He's the one I told you about who leads your people. I told you they would find us if there was a chance."

Justice finally spoke. "I am Justice, formerly known as 152. We will get you both out of the cage as soon as our men secure the two humans who've kept you captive and bring the keys." Justice straightened. His gaze never left 927. "You are free now. We are here to take you home to our people. You will be a part of a loving and caring family we've established and you will never know imprisonment again. You are a man now and no longer to be known just as a number. You'll have a real name once you decide on one."

Tammy glanced at 927 to see his reaction. He blinked rapidly when his eyes seemed to grow watery and lowered his head until his dark hair hid his features. A few deep breaths later he seemed to get his emotions under control. His head lifted and he stared at Justice.

"I would be very happy to have a home and a name."

Justice smiled. "Having a home is a wonderful thing. You'll be happy with us and I'm sure you'll pick a perfect name."

Tammy fought back tears while watching a miracle take place—for 927, after a lifetime of being a prisoner. He would finally know freedom. Tammy smiled and stared at Valiant. She reached up and touched his face.

"I love you so much."

"I love you too, sexy." Valiant darted a look at the man behind Tammy. His eyes lowered to hers and his features tensed. "Did he harm you in any way?"

"No."

Valiant relaxed but he kept touching Tammy and she understood why. They were both grateful to be back together. Tiger rushed into the back of the warehouse, jingling as he ran.

"Both of the assholes are alive and secure. I have keys to his cage." He pulled a ring of them out from a pocket in his vest. He peered at 927 before glancing at Justice. "Is he stable? Should I call for backup with a package?"

"No need." Justice accepted the keys. "He's fine." He moved to the door. "I'm going to let you out now."

The second the door swung open, Valiant entered the cell and grabbed Tammy. He scooped her off her feet and almost squeezed her to death in a bear hug while he backed them out of her prison. She didn't mind at all, just hugging him tightly back, and rested her head against his shoulder to watch what would happen next.

Tiger chuckled. "He's happy to see her."

Justice smiled. "Yes." He turned his attention on 927. The man stood motionless inside his cell. Justice slowly entered the room, an expression of dread on his features. "I hate entering these cages. They bring back so many bad memories." He paused just inside the door.

"Are you ready to leave here and start your new life?"

927 hesitated. "I'm really free from this, from all of it?"

"Yes. There are more of us outside waiting to greet you. We will help you learn how to live beyond these bars. We all had to do it and it is frightening at first. Humans had to help us adjust to our new way of life but it will be easier for you now that we're in charge. We will take you home now."

927 took one step and then another until he walked out of his cage. He stopped next to Tammy. Valiant swung her down to stand on her feet at her silent urging. She stared up at the New Species who could have hurt her but hadn't. She smiled when he spoke softly.

"You did tell me the truth."

"I did. You're free," Tammy said softly.

Valiant studied him intently and held out his hand. "Thank you for not harming her. She is everything to me. My heart and soul. The reason I breathe."

927 glanced at the offered hand with confusion.

"Shaking hands is a custom we picked up from humans," Justice explained. He moved forward and shook Valiant's hand. "We shake the hands of males as a sign of respect."

927 shook Valiant's hand. "You are welcome. I treated her as I wished another would treat a female I cared for. You must be very happy to be loved so greatly by her."

Valiant pulled Tammy closer against his body. "I have never been happier in my life."

"I'm Tiger." He stepped closer. "I'm head of security at Reservation. It's where your home will be while you adjust to freedom. You're going to love it there. There are miles to run and all the deer you can take down." Tiger grinned. "No more bars and there are trees as far as your eyes can see. The sky is beautiful. We'll have some disgusting-tasting beers and watch the sun rise and set. You will hate the taste of the human drink but you'll do it because it's an experience." He grinned. "You'll see."

927 blinked hard. Tammy saw his tears though before he could get control of his emotions. She fought the urge to cry too. Had the guy ever seen the sun rise or set? Ever seen no walls surrounding him or trees as far as the eye could see? She knew the answer and it just about broke her heart.

Two more New Species slowly entered the room, almost seeming fearful of spooking 927. They each said their name and introduced themselves to him. He seemed a little overwhelmed at seeing so many New Species males or it could have just still been the shock of being freed. Tammy understood. She squeezed Valiant's hand and eased out of his hold.

"This is a lot to take in, huh?" Her gaze met 927's as she looked up at him.

"Yes."

"It's normal if you're feeling a little afraid but it's going to be great. We're all going to be here for you. I know it's a lot to take in but just take it one step at a time. Everyone here is your friend and cares about you." She held out her hand. "I'll walk with you. Take my hand. You're not alone."

Valiant growled. Tammy turned her head to frown at him. She knew he was possessive but she owed 927 enough to help him through a rough spot. He'd done that for her. She didn't want to upset Valiant but she wanted him to understand.

"Do you remember your first day of freedom? Well, I remember my first day at school. That was kind of a whole new world. I'm his friend. I'm going to hold his hand the way my mom held mine and I'm going to walk him outside. I love you so don't feel jealous. I totally belong to you and I am so happy about that."

Valiant relaxed. A smile split his lips. "School? You compare being set free to school?"

She shrugged. "Well, you guys were set free from a living hell. I got imprisoned in the school system for thirteen years of my life. It was a form of mild hell. You're missing the point. It was all new and scary to me. My mom held my hand and walked me to my first class. She stayed around until I got settled. It made me feel better. It's my only fond memory of her. He doesn't know any of you but he's spent some time with me."

Justice suddenly laughed. "She's taking his mother role."

Tiger winked at 927. "Lucky you. You have a mommy."

927 looked confused. "A what?"

"She is protective of you as though you are her child," Valiant sighed. "Welcome to the family, son."

The New Species laughed. Tammy frowned at them. She dropped her offered hand. "Fine."

927 reached out and gripped it suddenly. He grinned down at her. "Thank you. I'd love for you to walk with me outside."

Tammy smiled at him and squeezed his hand. She shot Valiant a smirk and started to leave the room. 927 stayed close to her side. Tiger and Justice led the way. Valiant came up behind Tammy and took her other hand. She looked up at him, grateful he understood. They walked outside together.

Two New Species jogged off to drive the SUVs to their location. Tammy glanced at the three assholes who stood in handcuffs with two New Species guarding them. Pete, Mike, and the doctor appeared pretty scared now that they were the ones under the control of others.

Valiant growled when Tammy faced the three, released his and 927's hands, and took a few steps closer to the prisoners. Valiant's hand halted her by gripping her upper arm.

"Where are you going?"

Tammy gazed at him. "I just wanted to talk to them for a second. They are all shackled up and those men gripping them aren't going to let them go, right?"

Valiant frowned. "You should have nothing to say to them."

Anger gripped her. "I don't plan to talk to them." She pulled out of his hold. She walked up to Mike and Pete. She glared up at both men. She hesitated for a second before kicking Pete hard in the shin. He cursed, hopping on one leg. Tammy turned to Mike and kicked him in the balls. He doubled over with a loud gasp, groaning in pain.

Tammy reached up to the doctor, took his glasses, and just tossed them away. She didn't bother kicking him. When she backed away and turned, it was to find Valiant gaping at her, his shock apparent. She met his eyes, shrugged, and returned to his side.

"I owed them."

"You bitch," Mike groaned, doubled over.

Valiant lunged and punched him in the side of the face. Mike hit the ground hard and groaned. A snarl tore from Valiant. "Don't talk to her. You're lucky I'm not allowed to kill you or I would." He spun and marched to Tammy.

"Thank you, Valiant. He made a remark about holes that I didn't particularly like." She rubbed his arm. "My hero."

Valiant hesitated. "Any time, Tammy. Do you feel better now that you kicked them and took the property of one away?"

Tammy hesitated. "In one second I'll feel great." She turned and stormed over to the older man. "I hope you rot in hell, you miserable bastard. I hope they give you ten years for every day you tormented them and those poor women. You're a vile monster."

The older man glared at her, his eyes squinted since she'd taken his glasses. "I'll never see prison."

"You think not?" She snorted. "If it's not prison, you'll be facing the death penalty."

"I know I won't. I'll cut a deal. I know too much."

Justice was there suddenly. "You think so?"

"I'm too valuable not to be given a deal. I know where two smaller testing facilities are located where more of your kind are being held."

Justice paused. "Do you want total immunity for your information from your law? I can give you that. I have the authority."

Outrage blasted through Tammy. "You can't give them that."

Justice shot her a look. "Quiet, Tammy. I know what I am doing. Saving New Species is paramount."

She closed her mouth and stewed silently. Valiant squeezed her shoulder. She studied his relaxed features, it dawning on her that he'd be really mad if there were a real possibility of any of those men being released to harm anyone else. It made her understand that something was going on that she wasn't aware of and she should trust Justice.

"Yes," the older man said. "I demand total immunity for any crimes."

"Fine. We'll take you to Reservation, you will tell us whatever it is that we need or want to know and you shall have total immunity from prosecution on all charges, from your people."

"I want that too," Mike groaned from the ground.

"I will give it happily if the information you share saves the lives of more of my people." Justice glanced at him with a frown. "You better know something useful."

Valiant gripped Tammy and turned her. He took her for a walk far from the men. Tammy was steaming mad but she held her tongue until they'd moved out of earshot of Justice and the captured men.

"He's going to give them immunity? Are those jerks just going to get away with everything they've done?" She hissed the words to make sure they didn't carry.

Valiant leaned down, his face inches from hers. "Justice is giving them exactly what they are asking for. Immunity from the human prison system." His eyes sparkled. "Justice will learn everything they know before he introduces them to New Species law."

It took her a few seconds to grasp that meaning. Her anger drained quickly. "What is the punishment for kidnapping and being evil bastards who enjoy torturing people under your laws?"

Valiant pulled Tammy into his arms, holding her. His lips brushed her ear. "They will be locked up and eventually they'll die. We have the right to defend ourselves and the right to punish those who put themselves under our law. By asking for immunity from their own justice, they now belong to ours." He turned his head, his gaze purposely fixing on Justice North. "He'll show them the same amount of mercy they showed you and our people."

Tammy was glad he held her when she glanced at Justice North. As she studied the handsome New Species leader, she detected his anger and nearly felt sorry for those jerks. That was until she replayed everything she'd overheard them say since she'd met them.

That old doctor had been doing horrendous things to Valiant's people for a long time. The two thugs who had helped him had made a twenty-dollar bet on whether she'd get raped or murdered. Her sympathy fled instantly.

"I'm glad," she admitted. "They deserve it."

Valiant suddenly growled. "His scent is on you."

"Whose?"

"927." He pulled back, frowning. "Did he touch you? I smell him all over you. I was told he slept on you. Why?" His voice dropped deeper.

"It was cold. He didn't touch me in any sexual way, Valiant. I swear."

He forced his temper back. "I need my scent back on you."

She paused, knowing he was weird about how she smelled and it probably was rough on him to smell another man, to know someone else had touched her. "How far are we from Reservation?"

"About half an hour."

"It will be all right. We'll go home, I'll shower, and you can hold me. I'll smell like you again before you know it."

Valiant shook his head. He growled and turned to Justice, calling out, "We are taking a walk. I hear water."

"The SUVs should be here any moment." Justice frowned.

"I must share my scent with her now," Valiant demanded. "It's driving me crazy smelling another male all over her."

Justice stared at him for a few heartbeats and gave a sharp nod. "I understand. I'll send one SUV on and another will wait for you. Just hurry."

"Thank you."

Valiant suddenly grabbed Tammy and scooped her into his arms. He strode quickly for the tree line. She wrapped her arms around him and didn't struggle in his hold.

"What does sharing your scent with me entail? Valiant, why are we storming into the woods?"

Valiant didn't answer. They reached a small creek not far from where they'd been. He set her on her feet and held out his hand. "Give me your clothes."

Her mouth dropped open. "You want to have sex right now? Here? Seriously? I'm not exactly in the mood for that."

He sighed. "I want your clothes. I'm throwing them away."

"What would I wear?"

Valiant started stripping out of his clothes. "Mine."

"Is this really necessary?"

"Do you want me to kill your 927 because his scent on you is driving me insane? I was relieved at first that you were fine but I can't be locked inside a small space with you for a long period of time without it making me angry, Tammy. You are mine but you smell of another male. The drive to Reservation will take too long for me to keep fighting my urges to mark you again."

"Shit. Really?"

He nodded. He pulled his shirt over his head and bent to remove his shoes. "I can't take the scent of another male on you. It's agitating me."

Tammy glanced around the area, seeing nothing but trees and water. "Fine but if anyone sees me naked, I'm going to be mad and really embarrassed."

Valiant grinned, stepping out his pants. "I would beat them bloody and remove their eyes for looking at you."

"Funny."

Tammy stripped out of her clothes until she stood there naked. Valiant didn't stop removing his clothes until she could view every inch of his body. She stared at him. The man turned her on every time he was naked, the sight was that appealing. Her gaze lingered on his chest and muscular arms.

"Tammy," Valiant growled. "Do not look at me that way unless you want me to fuck you on the ground right here."

She forced her gaze away from his. "That wouldn't be a good idea since they are waiting for us."

"Wash your skin in the water. I would do it for you but if I touch you I will want to do more. Much more," he growled.

Tammy moved. The water was icy. She washed her body as best as she could. Valiant waited for her on the bank. She shivered hard as she left the water. Valiant smiled at her, staring at her taut nipples.

276

"Beautiful."

She wrapped her arms over her breasts, hiding them from his view. "I'm not excited. I'm freezing."

"Sorry." He chuckled.

He handed her his shirt and boxer briefs for her to put on. They were still warm from his body. She felt like a small kid in his large, baggy clothes. Valiant just wore his pants and footwear. His arms opened as he walked to her, hugged her tightly, and began rubbing against her, nuzzling her with his face. She laughed, wrapping her arms around him.

"What are you doing now? That tickles."

"Returning my scent to you. When we're safely home I'm going to remove those clothes and mark every inch of you."

"Mark me, huh? What does that mean?"

"Lots of rubbing and touching," he growled. He shifted her in his hold, one arm hooking behind her legs as he swung her up, the other one clutching her tightly to his chest. "Let's get back. Justice is waiting."

Tammy glanced at her discarded pile of clothing as they walked away. She sighed. *I loved that top. Oh well.* She had to admit they'd probably only bring back bad memories if she insisted he didn't abandon them in the woods. He carried her back to the warehouse.

One of the SUVs waited. Justice, 927, and Tiger had remained behind. The three prisoners and the five other New Species officers were gone. Justice smiled at the couple when they walked out of the woods.

"Is it better now, Valiant?"

"Much." Valiant grinned at him. "She smells more of me than him."

"It's a weird thing," Tiger sighed. "Mated men get obsessive about their women having their scent and no one else's."

927 nodded. "Do we all have mates now? Will I get one?"

Justice laughed. "We would be lucky to find one but only a few of us have found women to claim. I do not have one."

"I don't want one." Tiger looked horrified. "They are cute as hell and the regular sex would be nice but I want to keep my freedom."

"I am free," Valiant growled.

Tiger arched his eyebrow. "Really? Do you want to go hunting with me for a solid week? I know you love chasing deer."

"I won't leave Tammy for that long but I would go if she comes with me."

Tiger nodded. "My point is made. You would have said yes in a heartbeat before. Now you always have to think of her before you make a choice. I like it just being me."

"The sex is not regular," Valiant growled. "It's amazing, addicting, and worth every second I won't be chasing deer with you. I'll have a better time with my Tammy."

Justice laughed. "I can believe that. Nicely said, Valiant." He grinned at 927. "Don't listen to Tiger. A mate would be a wonderful thing. I am sure you will find one when the time is right."

"But you have not found one? Do you want a mate?" 927 cocked his head to study Justice curiously.

Justice hesitated. "I would love to have a mate but I haven't had the time to look for one yet."

"You are very busy," 927 agreed. "Tammy explained your job to me and everything you do for us." He paused. "Will you find where I came from and set them free?"

"Yes," Justice swore. "We are already working on it. We'll do whatever it takes to bring them home."

"I would like to be there when you do."

Justice hesitated. "We'll see. First we need to get back to Reservation. We don't like to be away too long and we usually have a human security detail with us. It's a task team that I control. We didn't want them to be part of this mission though because we weren't sure what we'd have to do to retrieve her or you. I didn't want to make the task team uncomfortable or feel torn between their loyalty to their own kind and ours. Some of the humans who don't work with us feel hatred and fear toward Species. Most don't but the ones who do have a tendency to try to kill us when given the chance. We're vulnerable to attack without more backup. We're safe on Reservation but not always in the outside world yet."

927 nodded. "I think I understand."

Valiant took a seat in the SUV with Tammy on his lap. He wouldn't let her go but she didn't mind having his arms wrapped around her. She clung to him. Tiger drove with 927 in the front passenger seat. On their drive they wanted him to have the best view of the world he'd missed out on seeing.

Justice took up the back bench seat. He'd brought his computer and cell phone. He removed his shoes and his shirt to get comfortable before he started talking softly on his phone while viewing something on the laptop screen. Tammy realized he never stopped working. She turned her head to glance forward. 927 grinned widely as he peered, with sheer amazement, out the windows at the world. She smiled, finally turning her attention to Valiant.

"I'm kind of glad this happened."

Valiant growled, a look of horror crossing his handsome features. "I'm not."

"I was a little afraid to get married. You were so set on it and I felt as if we were rushing into it too fast. I learned something from all of this. I want to marry you and spend every day of the rest of my life at your side. I even want to have a baby. I hope we have at least three."

He laughed. "Only three? I was thinking of trying to get eight."

"Come on," she gasped. "Eight? Are you kidding me?"

He laughed. "Yes. I am kidding you."

"Thank you." She chuckled. "As I was saying, I'm not afraid anymore. This whole thinking I would die and afraid I'd never see you again really slammed home how much I love you and how I want my future to be with you."

"Good. Now your heart, your body, and your law will know you belong to me forever."

"Yes." She ran her fingers through his hair. "And we'll get married the first chance we get."

"Tomorrow," Justice spoke up.

Valiant and Tammy turned to stare at him and he grinned. "I just heard from my staff. The license came through. We can schedule your wedding for tomorrow if you want. I'll still be here. I postponed everything on my schedule for a few days to be on hand for this crisis. I want to be present while we plan the assault for Colorado."

Valiant grinned. "Tomorrow is perfect."

"Tomorrow is perfect," Tammy agreed, hugged him hard, buried her nose against his neck and just clung to him. She'd been so terrified she'd never see him again and now she knew exactly what she wanted. *Him.*

Valiant closed his eyes, breathing in Tammy, and his arms refused to release her. She sat on his lap, safe, and once again he realized what a phenomenon she was to him. All the things that could have gone wrong began to filter through his thoughts.

She could have died, the newly freed male in the front seat could have forced bred her and killed her. When they breached the building the human males could have rigged the cell with explosives they might have set off. She would have died before he reached her and that would have torn his heart—

"Valiant?"

Tammy halted his grim thoughts and his eyes opened to stare deeply into her beautiful ones. Her small fingers slid into his hair and she caressed his scalp.

"It's okay. You look so angry but I'm fine. I'm right here with you."

"Don't ever leave me."

She smiled. "Never."

He pulled her tighter against his chest, brushing a kiss on her forehead, and knew he'd never survive if he lost her.

Chapter Sixteen

∽

Tammy frowned at Valiant. "No."

He stared back at her. "I told Justice I would go."

"But we're going to get married today, remember?"

He frowned. "We will when I get back. Justice personally asked me to go with them, Tammy. Please understand. We all owe Justice so much. He asks little of me. When you were taken, he did everything to get you back to me. He asked and I couldn't say no."

She nodded. "I'm being kind of petty when you put it that way, aren't I?"

He moved forward, pulling her into his arms. "It is not petty to feel disappointed that we won't get married today. Nothing will stop us tomorrow. We are leaving on helicopters to go to Colorado within the hour and I should be back by morning."

Tammy nodded. "Be very careful and come back to me."

"I will always come for you."

"Is this going to be dangerous?"

Valiant hesitated. "It is a heavily armed place. They are holding over ninety of our people, Tammy. Species just like 927."

"I understand. Is he going too?"

"Justice decided not to bring him. He is too fresh from the experience. We need control and the skills we have learned since we were freed. 927 is angry but he understood. The important part is getting our people free."

"Did that crazy doctor jerk tell Justice where the other places are too?"

"Yes. They are working on that. We will find them and get our people freed."

"We? You would go too?"

He hesitated. "No. This will be my one and only mission. I've calmed since I met you and Justice is worried that this place might be rigged with explosives. My senses are stronger than most Species and he needs me as an asset on this one. The doctor we captured isn't sure if they rigged the cells or not. I plan to take care of you and this is the last time I'll risk my life. I just need to do this one thing and I feel I owe them that much for all that was done to get you back to me. I'll work with some of the others in the Wild Zone who are like me, have the same keen sense of smell, and make them more stable. That way Justice can take them if he needs help in the future."

"Explosives?" Fear gripped her, imagining him being blown up.

"That's why I must go. I can smell them. I'll be safe."

She nodded. "Good. Spending one night away from you was horrible and I don't want to do it again."

"But another man held you." His jealousy showed.

"It was cold and I didn't really have a choice. There was one bed and he scared me. I wasn't going to fight with him, Valiant. I was too happy he hadn't broken my neck or tried to touch me in a bad way."

"I am angry still. I hate that anyone held you besides me."

"I love you. Don't be jealous."

"I know that. I will be gone for a short time. We'll fly there and at dark we attack."

"Are you guys going in alone?"

He shook his head. "No. They are sending in a special task force with us. They do this regularly. Justice says he knows the two teams who will work with us. He said they are all good men who were assigned to assist us. They are under Justice's orders at all times. I will be back by morning."

"Will you call me after it's over and let me know you are all right? I will be worried sick about you."

"I will call. Justice always has a phone with him. I've been ordered to stay by his side."

Tammy smiled. "Yes. He does always carry his phone and a laptop."

"I must go." Valiant leaned down and brushed his lips across Tammy's.

Tammy gripped his shirt and yanked him closer, opening his mouth with hers to deepen the kiss. Tongue met tongue. Valiant growled, pulling her closer. Tammy inwardly smiled. It was one of the things she loved about Valiant. One kiss and he was ready to take her to bed.

Valiant broke the kiss. His narrowed eyes sparkled. "You did that on purpose."

"I did what on purpose?" Tammy tried to sound innocent.

Valiant took her hand and pressed it to the front of his black cargo pants. "This."

Tammy rubbed the hard length of his rigid cock. He groaned, pressing his hips closer to her hand. Tammy gripped the outline of his erection through his pants and reached for his zipper with her free hand. She eased it down and unfastened the top button.

"Tammy," he growled.

"You have a few minutes." Tammy shoved down his pants and underwear. She lifted her skirt, yanked down her panties, and kicked them away. "Pick me up."

Valiant grabbed her hips, lifting her higher into his arms. Tammy wrapped her legs around his bare hips. Her body was primed already when Valiant quickly entered her. His hands cupped her ass tightly and he thrust into her pussy hard and fast. Tammy pressed her face against his chest, moaning loudly against his shirt, wishing it were his skin.

She used her arms on his shoulders for leverage to grind her hips, making sure his shaft pounded into her the way that brought her the most pleasure. In minutes Tammy screamed his name as the climax tore through her. Valiant roared when he came. He held her limp, sated body against his.

Tammy chuckled. "That's how we should always say goodbye."

Valiant laughed. "I agree."

Tammy lifted her face, smiling at him. "Just come back to me safe."

Valiant brushed his mouth over hers again. He put his nose against hers when their lips parted. They gazed into each other's eyes. "I have everything to live for. I have you. I will be very careful."

The doorbell chimed. Valiant sighed. She unlocked her ankles from around his hips. Valiant eased out of her body and placed her on her feet. Tammy laughed as Valiant righted his clothes and walked to open the door. She didn't have to worry about fixing her clothes. Her skirt fell past her knees to hide the loss of her panties. Tiger stood in the hallway.

"I take it from the loud noise I heard on the elevator that you both have said goodbye?" He grinned.

Tammy blushed. "You heard that?"

"Everyone inside the building heard that. We are all looking forward to when Justice allows you both to live at Valiant's when this is over. It's remote out there and far enough away that we might miss knowing when you two have sex." Tiger stared at Valiant. "Are you ready now that you've properly said goodbye to your mate?"

Valiant leaned down and picked up something off the floor. He grinned. "I am now." He walked to Tammy and handed her the pair of panties she'd kicked away. "Keep these on while I'm gone so I can think about tearing them off when I return. I love you."

Tiger laughed.

Tammy ignored Tiger and the embarrassment she suffered. Her hand brushed over Valiant's chest where his heart beat as she accepted them. "I love you too. Hurry home to me."

She watched the men walk away. There was no longer an officer posted outside her door. They had caught their mole who had been feeding information about Justice and what was going on at Reservation. Everyone knew she belonged to Valiant, no one would bother her, and they trusted her not to leave the hotel without an escort because some of the Wild Zone occupants could pose a danger to her since some of them weren't mentally stable.

Charlie Artzola would never to be a problem again. That's what she'd been told. She closed the door and locked it, wondering for a split second if the attorney was dead. She mentally shrugged. She really didn't care about his fate as long as he'd never cause trouble again. Justice had assured her that he wouldn't.

* * * * *

It was past midnight when the phone rang. Tammy lunged for it. "Valiant?"

"How did you know it was me?" His deep voice sounded amused.

"Because no one else would call this late and you promised me you would. Are you all right? How did things go? Did you get them? Is everyone all right?"

"Slow down," Valiant chuckled. "I am fine. We had a few injured but all will survive. We rescued all of them. They were not expecting us and since it was at night, they were lightly guarded. The humans ran instead of trying to kill our people before we could get to them. It was pretty easy to take them."

Tammy blew out a relieved breath. "I was worried."

"I know. Thank you for caring about me that much. We are transporting them to Reservation within the next twelve hours. We only have the two helicopters and have to fly them a few at a time. Justice does not want to traumatize them more with a long drive and we do not want to expose them to the outside world by trying to charter a larger plane. Too many questions and too much red tape. I'm staying here until the last group has been evacuated. You go to bed and rest, sexy. I should be home tomorrow by lunch."

"Okay. I miss you."

"I miss and love you."

"I love you too."

Tammy hung up, sad, missing him badly. She'd give anything if he were stretched out next to her on the bed. She couldn't believe how addicted she'd become to him. She climbed out of bed to use the bathroom.

The doorbell chimed. Tammy frowned after glancing at the clock, seeing it was just past midnight. She donned a robe and padded through the hallway to the living room. She felt a little uneasy since she knew she no longer had an officer posted in the hallway. She walked to the door and bit her lip.

"Who is there?"

"It is Breeze. I brought ice cream. I know Valiant is gone and I thought you wouldn't sleep well. May I come in?"

Tammy unlocked the door and threw it open. She smiled at the tall brunette. "Come in. It's so good to see you. Did you say ice cream?"

Breeze walked inside holding a covered tray. "Not any ice cream. I brought double-dipped chocolate sundaes. Ellie taught me how to make them. They have chunks of brownie inside them too." She smiled down at Tammy from her much-taller height. "Are you sure you don't mind me visiting so late?"

"No. I'm really glad you are here. I doubt I'll sleep. Valiant just called."

"How did it go?" Breeze set the tray on the coffee table and lifted the lid. She sat on the couch and handed Tammy a spoon that had been rolled inside a napkin. "I haven't heard anything yet."

"Valiant said they got them all and everyone is fine. A few injures but nothing life threatening."

"I am so happy to hear that. I must make arrangements for the half-dozen women we were told were being held there."

Tammy hesitated, not sure if it was her place or not but really wanted to do something. "Do you need help?"

"I would love that."

Tammy lifted her sundae and examined it. Her eyes widened. "Thank you so much. Wow. This is just…wow! Look at all that chocolate. Are those walnuts?"

"Yes."

"I love walnuts and brownies. Chocolate hard-shell syrup." She took a bite. "And small chocolate chips. This is so good. You have to thank Ellie too." She paused. "You can eat chocolate? Valiant says it makes him sick."

"Some Species get ill from it and some don't." She grinned, took a big bite, the enjoyment showing on her face. "I love it."

* * * * *

Valiant watched silently as six women were led past him by one short human female. His gaze followed the woman. Her hair was eye catching. It was flaming red and in a ponytail that fell to her ass. The human female led the Species women to the waiting helicopter and they climbed inside. Valiant frowned. He turned, looking at Tiger.

"Who was the small human woman with the bright hair?"

Tiger glanced at the helicopter. The woman was clearly visible since the doors were still open. She checked each seat belt of the six Species before taking a seat last. The pilot closed the side door and climbed in the cockpit.

"That's Jessie Dupree. She's the human female who usually is on hand when our Gift Females are found. She is part of the human task force assigned to us by the government. She comforts our women when they are found. I am surprised she is here. She usually only deals with our women who were sold."

"You would think she would be afraid of our females. She is small compared to them."

Tiger shrugged. "I don't know what her deal is but she's the one the humans send in when they locate one of our females. I don't know why she's here since these women weren't sold but instead were still contained for testing. We did invite the humans in on this one and it was their call to bring her with them."

Valiant nodded. "She is flying with them to Reservation? Are the rest of the humans on her team coming as well?"

"No. Just her. She demanded to personally deliver them and get them settled. I got tired of arguing with her so I agreed she could go. She is small but her mouth is loud."

"Justice doesn't mind?"

Tiger shrugged. "I do not know. He is still inside with the human task teams, thanking them for their help and smoothing niceties. He didn't get to meet her and he's lucky for it. She's fierce with her mouth. He'll take the last flight with us." Tiger glanced at his watch. "Do you want food? The humans had pizzas delivered to feed everyone. They taste amazing."

Valiant nodded. "I could eat. I need to learn more about human food. I don't think Tammy enjoys watching me eat. I've noticed she avoids looking at me during meals."

Tiger chuckled. "Let me guess. Seared meat? Yeah, most humans get grossed out by that. You'll enjoy pizza. It's really good. She'll love it too. I think all humans eat it the way we do meat. It must be a nutritional requirement or something for them." He shrugged. "Everything on it is cut up into bit-sized slices to help them because of the flat teeth they have."

Valiant followed him. "If we have a baby this must be good to feed them."

"Yeah. They probably just cut the slices smaller for their little mouths."

"I must try this food. Tammy will be pleased I am preparing for fatherhood."

Tiger patted his back. "You're a good mate, my man."

"I will try to be." Valiant missed Tammy. He couldn't wait to return home to marry her and remove her underwear. Not in that order though.

* * * * *

At 5:10 in the morning Breeze's pocket chirped. Both women jumped. They had been watching a scary movie on the television. Tammy laughed. Breeze grinned, reaching inside her pocket. She fished out her cell phone.

"This is Breeze." She listened. "I am on my way now. Thank you." She stood and smiled at Tammy as she hung up. "I must go. The helicopter is about twenty minutes out. It is the one delivering our freed women. We have made arrangements for them to live here inside the hotel. It is going to be a long morning for me. I do not know how bad they will be. I got elected to do this job and I am not really good at dealing with women in shock. I know I suffered from it when I was freed. We aren't equipped to deal with newly freed women. We usually send them elsewhere but it happened too fast and Justice decided they would be happier here. He is probably right. I just wish I had some experience in this. All I have is my memories of the humans who took care of me."

Tammy stood. "Do you still want help? I wasn't just offering to be polite."

"You helped make a list to order clothing for them. You want to help greet them and get them adjusted too?"

"I'd love to. I'm not going to sleep. It's already morning." Tammy grinned. "Can I go with you? It beats sitting around here waiting for Valiant to return. I won't sleep until he's back."

"Yes. I would appreciate that."

"Give me two minutes to toss on some clothes and run a brush through my hair and brush my teeth."

"May I use your bathroom?"

"Make yourself at home. There's a second bathroom down this hall. Follow me."

Tammy hurried. She put on one of Valiant's discarded sweaters from the floor. It smelled clean enough. She wanted to carry his scent and hopefully the women would accept her a little easier. She put on a pair of black cotton pants. Once she used the bathroom, brushed her teeth and her hair, she met Breeze in the living room.

Breeze inhaled and grinned. "You are smart."

"The sweater? It came to me the second I saw it draped on the back of a chair. I think Valiant wore it two days ago. I take it you can still smell him on it?"

"It's faint but enough. You smell of Valiant. They will know you are human of course, your features show what you are, but they will see you as less of a threat."

"Good. So where are we going?" Tammy put on her slip-on flats and grabbed the key to the room. She shoved it down the front of her bra since she didn't have pockets and wasn't taking a purse.

"We are meeting them at the helicopter pad. We have a van ready to drive them here."

"Have the clothes we ordered been put in their rooms yet?"

Breeze chuckled. "Yes. It was done immediately. Clothes and food will be waiting for them. I had each room fully stocked and they have cleaning products for their bodies."

"Sounds good. Let's go."

A bunch of New Species males Tammy had never seen before were milling around inside the old hotel lobby. Breeze and Tammy stepped out of the elevator and all conversation stopped. Tammy took a few steps and then paused when Breeze did.

Tammy glanced at the taller woman. "What's wrong?"

Breeze suddenly growled and turned. Tammy saw a man quickly approach. Two more men followed him. All three New Species appeared angry. Breeze stepped between the oncoming men and Tammy.

"What do you want?" Breeze sounded pissed.

The man growled back. "Move."

"Back off," Breeze growled deeper. "She's with me."

Tammy nervously stared at the three men. She realized that the room had gone deadly silent. There had to be at least thirty New Species but none of them spoke. She didn't recognize a single face as she glanced around. Tammy's gaze slid back to the man who'd been the most aggressive.

"Is there a problem?" Tammy frowned at him.

"She's human." He flashed sharp teeth at Tammy, taking another step closer.

Breeze kept in his path, putting her hands out. "She's a human who lives here with one of our males. She belongs to him and he will beat you to a pulp if you so much as breathe wrong at her. Justice North invited her to live with us. She's one of us despite being human. I realize, as a Primate, your sense of smell isn't that strong but she belongs to him."

The man growled again and so did the two men behind him. Tammy sensed danger. She took a deep breath, trying to calm her fear. Valiant always told her his kind could smell it. She lifted her chin.

"Calm down. I'm not the enemy." She was proud her voice came out strong and didn't shake as badly as her hands started to.

"What is going on?" 927 suddenly spoke. He had silently strode up behind both women.

Tammy started, glanced at him, and smiled, feeling a little relief at seeing him there. "My guess is they don't like me."

927 snarled, glaring at the males. He stomped forward to stand next to Breeze. She looked uneasy when she glanced at the new male and her body tensed more. 927 didn't spare her a glance. He continued to defiantly stare at the three men.

"She's the reason you are free. Dr. Zenlelt kidnapped her and her mate tracked her to me. She isn't like the humans we have known, 861. Back off. She is family to us." 927 glanced around the room, meeting every man's curious gaze, and his voice rose. "She is family and a friend."

"Humans will never be family," 861 growled. "It offends me to look at her."

"Get over it," Breeze snarled. "She isn't going anywhere. She lives here too. So does another human woman who is a mate to one of us. Smell her. She belongs to one of our own."

861 moved closer to Breeze and inhaled. He frowned and moved closer. She backed up to keep him from touching Tammy. The man inhaled again and stepped back. "I do not like this."

"You do not have to. She is here and no harm will come to her. Where is your gratitude? We would still be locked up inside our cells if not for her mate's love for her and our people helping him find her. Show respect," 927 demanded in a harsh tone.

861 snarled back. "Never for humans."

Breeze softly cursed and reached back. Her fingers fisted the front of the sweater Tammy wore and pushed, moving Tammy toward the elevator. The pounding of booted feet drew everyone's attention as more New Species wearing the NSO black uniforms rushed into the lobby. They quickly assessed the two men circling each other and Tammy saw what they saw—the men were going to fight. 927 would protect and defend her.

"It's the primate in the red," Breeze called out loudly. "He came after Valiant's mate."

The man in the red, 861, lunged for 927, and the fight was on. The New Species officers rushed forward, pushing everyone out of the way. In seconds they had grabbed 861 and restrained him flat on the floor.

Tammy relaxed. Breeze's hold on the sweater eased and she turned her head, studying Tammy.

"Are you all right?"

"I'm fine. What was that about?"

927 approached. His hand was gashed from where he'd hit the other man in the face. A sharp tooth had cut his skin. He stopped a few feet back. "I apologize. These men are from the same place where I was locked up. They do not trust or like humans. When he calms I will speak to him rationally."

"It's all right." Tammy sighed. "I guess I can understand that." Her gaze dropped to his hand. "Do you want me to clean that up and bandage it?"

One of the New Species officers approached. "We'll let him calm down and have a talk with him." He glanced at Tammy. "Are you unharmed?"

"I'm fine."

He inhaled. "Just frightened." He turned and met 927's gaze. "Thank you for defending her until we were able to take him down. Let me take you to medical and they will care for your injury."

927 agreed. "Of course." He flashed Tammy a smile. "I apologize. I will talk to all of them. You will be safe from harm. It would not hurt if Valiant spoke to them as well. He will intimidate them if I don't."

Breeze laughed. "He's good at that. I'm Breeze. Thank you for the backup there."

927 studied her carefully and smiled. "I'm 927. It is a pleasure to meet you."

Breeze's smile widened. "You are a charmer. You're also new. Come look for me if you need any help settling in."

"I will."

The officer smiled. "Let's go to medical, hero."

Breeze gripped Tammy's hand and led her out of the lobby to where a white van waited. One of the New Species officers sat behind the wheel to drive them. Breeze turned to Tammy the second they were inside and the door closed.

"You know that male? He's gorgeous and did you see those dark eyes?" Breeze fanned her face. "I need to change my pants. I'm that wet. When he picks a name it should be something as sexy hot as he is."

Tammy grinned. "You like him, I take it?"

"I think I'm definitely in lust. Do you think he is attracted to tall women?"

"He looked interested in you to me."

"He did? I will make a point of finding him later after I get some sleep. I wish to be well rested when I seek him out."

In minutes they reached the helicopter pad. The helicopter had just landed and was already being refueled. The side door opened when the van pulled up and women began to climb out. Tammy stayed with the van at Breeze's side to welcome the new women. She hoped none of them would attack her. Tammy had never considered that anyone would hate her on sight or want to hurt her. 861 sure had.

"Wow," Tammy whispered, spotting the flaming-red hair of the woman who climbed out of the helicopter first. "She's the smallest New Species I've ever seen and what do you think she was mixed with to get that hair color? It looks as if someone set her hair on fire with something really bright. It's gorgeous."

Breeze laughed. "She's one of yours. I would say she's mixed with a hair dye. That can't be natural."

"Maybe the black pants and black shirt just makes her hair more striking." Tammy shrugged.

Breeze smiled and shrugged too. "We could ask her."

"No!" Tammy laughed. "Never ask a woman if her hair color is real or her age. Human women get all pissy about it."

"Really?" Breeze let it sink in. "I'll try to remember that."

The redhead approached. She nodded and stopped by Breeze. She lowered her gaze and her head. She waited a few seconds before glancing up.

"I am Jessie Dupree. I wanted to personally escort your females here. I'm the human representative for the United States Government, a part of your human task force that handles search and retrievals of your lost females. I ask your permission to escort them to their new homes and stay to help with their integration into your society. They trust me." Her gaze flickered to Tammy and took her in at a sweeping glance. The woman frowned slightly. "I don't know you. Who brought you in?"

Tammy blinked at her. "Valiant did."

Breeze chuckled. "You think she's New Species, do you not, Jessie Dupree? She is not a recovered Gift Species. She is a human mate to one of our males. Her name is Tammy Shasta."

The redhead with bright blue eyes blinked and her eyes widened. "Oh. I apologize. I was under the impression that no humans lived on Reservation. Because of your size and your lack of facial markings I assumed you were one of the rare Gift

Females. Some have been recovered, and until you see their teeth or ears, you can't really tell they aren't fully human."

"Valiant told me what was done to them. It is so horrible it makes me sick. But I'm human. Sorry for the confusion."

The woman nodded. Her attention returned to Breeze. "May I have permission to help get them settled? I'd really appreciate it. I know they are not Gift Females but I have the time and I am very experienced in helping your females handle the sudden change in lifestyle."

Breeze glanced at Tammy, who shrugged. "She's got experience."

A grin split Breeze's face. "Sure. They put me in charge of this task and to tell you the truth, I have no idea what I'm doing. We don't handle this kind of thing. They are usually sent somewhere else but Justice wanted them brought here. We would appreciate the help."

"Thank you." Jessie smiled. She was a really pretty woman in her late twenties or early thirties. "I'd love to do everything I can."

Tammy studied the New Species women who exited the helicopter. They were all tall, sturdy women. They were muscled and in excellent physical shape. Their clothes were off-white and their pants were exactly like the ones 927 had worn. She even spotted the same thick side seams of their clothing as one of the woman walked past. The woman glanced at her and Breeze but no one objected to her being there.

"What is up with the clothes? Why are they all dressed that way?" Tammy kept her voice low, her gaze on Breeze.

The taller woman showed signs of anger when her nostrils flared. "We were restrained with chains on all our limbs. It was easier for our captors to strip us and change our clothing with seams that pull apart. They have Velcro that sticks when pressed back together. It kept them from having to pull the pants down our legs or shirts over our heads."

The answer sickened Tammy and she felt a whole new appreciation for the kind of hell the survivors had endured. The ugly clothing had a purpose and it wasn't a good one, in her mind. She pushed those grim observations back and tried to appear friendly to the freed women.

Everyone fit in the van. Tammy smiled at the women but none of them returned the friendly gesture. Five out of the six New Species women openly stared at her though. A few of them looked baffled while one of them appeared frightened. Two of them completely hid their emotions. Tammy focused on the frightened woman sitting on the seat behind hers.

"I'm Tammy. It's safe here. Everything is going to be fine."

"They are in shock," Jessie explained softly. "It will take a few days for everything to sink in. Their entire lives have drastically changed forever in a matter of hours."

Tammy smiled sadly at the woman still staring at her with fear on her face. "It really will be okay. This is a great place to live. I live here now and I love it."

The woman licked her lips. "What are you?"

Tammy blinked. "Human."

The woman shook her head. "You're more."

"Oh." Tammy moved slowly and extended her arm. "You smell Valiant. I'm wearing his sweater. He's New Species and we live together."

The woman gave her a blank stare.

Jessie spoke. "New Species is what you all are called. It is the name your kind came up with since you are all different mixes of different species."

The woman behind Tammy nodded. She hesitated. "You live with one of our kind?"

Tammy nodded. "We are..." She faulted on how to explain.

"Mates. They exclusively breed together," Breeze explained, coming to the rescue. "They have decided to stay with each other until death."

The woman appeared shocked. "But she's human."

Breeze smiled. "She's a good one who would never hurt our kind. She loves Valiant and he loves her."

The women kept staring at Tammy as if she were something they couldn't figure out. She tried not to allow it to bother her. She was something they didn't expect.

"Do you feel as if you are an occupant of a zoo?" Breeze asked and chuckled.

Tammy grinned. "Just a little."

The rest of the ride to the hotel was silent.

* * * * *

The lobby of the hotel had been cleared. Tammy was relieved that the males were gone, not wanting to risk another confrontation. Jessie and Breeze talked softly about the accommodations the newly arriving women were given. Tammy noticed the six women were still watching her. In the elevator they all pressed together and they sniffed at her. She tried not to let it bother her. She was a little more than relieved though when the elevator doors opened on the fourth floor.

Tammy, Breeze and Jessie showed the women to their separate rooms and demonstrated how to use everything inside. They had no idea how to turn on the shower or run a bath. They didn't know how to use a phone, how to open the windows or how to lock a door. Hours later Tammy, Breeze and Jessie left the fourth floor, tired but satisfied that everyone was settled.

"Wow," Breeze sighed. "I didn't realize how little I knew when I was first released."

Jessie nodded. "At least they all can read and write. Some of the Gift Females were never taught. I'd say only about half of them were. It depended on how old they were when they were given away."

"That's so horrible," Tammy sighed, remembering what she'd learned about those poor women.

"Yes," Jessie agreed. "It is. I'm the one who goes in every time. There are two Special Forces teams that make up the task force that was put together solely to work with the New Species Organization. They are all men. At first they didn't realize they really needed a woman to go in with them when they recover New Species females. The first two times they went in without a woman they highly traumatized the recovered females more than necessary. Think about it. It was just stupid. They just didn't think about how that would affect a female who has been abused, locked up for years, and suddenly she's surrounded by two-dozen men dressed in full assault uniforms who are armed to the teeth." Jessie clenched her teeth and shook her head. "They brought me in finally. The guys kick ass and I handle the females."

"How did you get the job?" Tammy glanced around the cafeteria as they walked into it.

Jessie laughed. "My father, actually. He's a senator who was appointed to represent the New Species issues in Washington. He volunteered me when they realized it might be smart to have a woman present who was nonthreatening to the females they found. The first woman they hired was a shrink. That didn't go over well. After that, my father got his way and I ended up with the job. I was a little pissed at first since he didn't ask me but I love what I do. Unfortunately, there's a lot of downtime. I wish more of them could be found. I wouldn't mind working eighty hours a week if it meant we were rescuing more of them."

"Do you find them often?"

Tammy grabbed a plate and started to fill it with food from the buffet. She grabbed some donuts and a muffin. Not much was out in the early-morning hours. The cook hadn't started preparing breakfast and wouldn't until six, according to the wall schedule. The other two women filled their plates as well.

"They are hard to find. In all, we've recovered twenty-three. We were able to track some of the Gift Species who were unaccounted for, but most hadn't survived."

Tammy cringed. "That's so sad."

"They are not like us," Breeze stated softly. She met Tammy's curious gaze. "They are small and unable to defend themselves. They were severely abused, comparable to kicked puppies."

"Oh."

Jessie sighed. "It's hard for the New Species to accept some of them because they are so traumatized that they can't be around men at first. Several churches with secluded women's retreats were nice enough to take some of them in. We send them there when we find an especially fragile female."

"They cry and shriek around men. They jump and shake." Breeze's voice sounded upset. "And it makes us very angry to see that."

Jessie clenched her teeth. "It's not their fault they are that way."

Breeze frowned. "We are not angry at them. We get angry that this happened to them and that they were made weaker and taken from our men who treated our females well. We feel rage that they were completely alone. It was rare that we saw other Species unless they were breeding us but we could scent them on the humans who came into our cells. It was comforting. They didn't have that. It angers all of us." Breeze stared at Jessie. "Our anger is never directed at them. Never."

"I'm sorry." Jessie sighed. "I have seen the reactions of your kind when I take the women in. I just assumed the rage was directed at the Gift Females because they are crying and very frightened when they see others of their kind. I know you really respect strength and courage."

"We do but we want to protect the weaker. We understand they need our compassion most."

Tammy finished her breakfast. "Wow. The sun is out." Her gaze drifted away from the window at the back of the cafeteria.

"You should get some rest before Valiant returns." Breeze chuckled. "He will want to take you to bed but he will not allow you sleep. You need all the sleep you are able to get while you can."

Tammy nodded. "We're getting married today."

Jessie choked on her coffee. "What?"

Tammy grinned. "We're getting married. He asked and I accepted. He wants it all legal-like and I'm happy about that."

"Another one." Jessie smiled. "So you're going to be the second married, mixed couple. That's great. I didn't mean to blow coffee. It just surprised me."

Breeze chuckled. "Wait until you see them together. That will surprise you even more. Where she is short, he is tall. He's a big male—six-foot-six and weighs well over two-hundred-fifty pounds."

Jessie winked at Tammy, grinning. "Brave woman."

"He's a sweetheart."

Breeze laughed. "To her, he is a sweetheart. We shake in fear when he is angry. She laughs at him. Just do not be afraid when you hear really loud noises today, Jessie. I will have to put you on the third floor by their suite. You will need a room for a few days while you stay to help with the woman. Valiant is lion mixed. Just remember that."

Jessie appeared confused. "What am I missing?"

Tammy knew her cheeks warmed with embarrassment. "He roars after sex. On that note, I'm leaving." She waved. "I hope to see both of you at the wedding. Come if you can."

"She was kidding, right?" Jessie sounded stunned.

Breeze laughed. "No. She was not. She is what your kind call a 'screamer' too. We all know when they breed. We look forward to when they will go to Valiant's home just so we can get some undisturbed sleep."

Tammy groaned as she walked away, grateful to move out of earshot after that. She quickly reached the elevator, happy there were no lingering males in the reception area, and made a beeline for her suite.

Chapter Seventeen

ഌ

Tammy might have been a little nervous but Valiant didn't seem to suffer from it. He held her hands while he grinned at her. The New Species had brought in Pastor Thomas to perform the ceremony. The elderly pastor appeared a little uneasy, being surrounded by a few hundred New Species but the fact that he'd agreed to marry them touched her deeply. There was only one other human present besides Tammy and the pastor. Jessie Dupree had shown up to witness their marriage.

Her best friend had refused to come when Tammy had called to invite Tim. She was a little sad but staring into Valiant's exotic golden eyes made it not matter after all. Tim would either get over his prejudice or he wouldn't. It was his problem, not hers.

She'd never thought so many New Species would show up to witness their joining but they had. It warmed her heart that they cared. The lobby was the largest room besides the cafeteria that the hotel had to offer and it was packed—standing room only. There weren't enough chairs to seat so many people. Justice stood at the front of the group, grinning widely. He had stayed to witness the ceremony.

"Do you, Tammy Ann Shasta, take Valiant North to be your husband?"

They had changed the vows to make it easier for everyone to understand. "I do, happily."

Valiant grinned wider.

"Do you, Valiant North, take Tammy Ann Shasta to be your wife?"

"I do, with honor and happiness." He winked at her.

Tammy laughed. She'd have to talk to him again about how wrong and weird that looked. They listened as the pastor spoke, telling them what marriage meant before he pronounced them legally married.

"You may kiss your wife, Valiant. She's all yours now."

Valiant released Tammy's hands and gripped her hips. He slowly raised her off the floor. Tammy laughed and grasped his broad shoulders to keep her balance. He lifted her until they were the same height. Her hands slid around his neck and she closed her eyes as he drew her tighter against his body. His arms slid around her waist, hugging her.

She hoped he would just brush his lips over hers. After all, there were hundreds of people watching them. Valiant didn't do that. He really kissed her. His mouth opened over hers and he invaded her mouth with his tongue.

Tammy kissed him back, unable to resist the sensual touch of the man she loved and her body instantly responded. Valiant always had that effect on her. He purred and she moaned as the passion ignited between them.

"Uh…" Pastor Thomas coughed. "I think that will do."

Valiant growled but he broke the kiss. When he pulled away, they looked at each other and their gazes held. Tammy couldn't wait to get him alone and with the blatant desire on his features, she knew the feeling was mutual. The room remained totally silent. Valiant slowly set her back on her feet.

"Mine."

Tammy laughed. "Yours."

Breeze laughed. "We have a car outside to take you to Valiant's house as a wedding gift to everyone staying at the hotel. We would like to be able to sleep and we know how you both are. We thought it would be worse since you are celebrating marriage. We think Valiant won't allow you out of bed for days."

A few of the New Species laughed. Tammy blushed. Valiant smiled and nodded at Breeze. "That is my plan."

"Thank God," Jessie whispered softly. "I thought the roof would collapse when I heard them. Congrats! I'm going to go eat before a long line forms." She grinned and spun away, walking through a mass of people.

Tammy blushed more. Valiant threw back his head and laughed.

Pastor Thomas frowned. "I don't understand."

Breeze stepped forward. "We want Valiant and Tammy to enjoy their alone time together and we'll all sleep better when they are far away."

The pastor still looked confused. "What am I missing?"

Justice chuckled, walking forward. "It's a New Species thing if I just walked into the conversation topic I believe I did. Don't worry about it."

Valiant turned to Tammy and suddenly grabbed her. He scooped her into his arms with a grin. "Let's go home."

Tammy wrapped her arms around his neck. "Are you actually going to give me a tour this time? I've yet to see anything inside your house but the entryway, the stairs, and your bedroom."

He laughed, carrying her through the crowd that parted for them on their way outside. "Maybe in a few days."

"You have to let me eat." Tammy teased.

"I thought of that already. I will have food delivered from the hotel."

A Jeep waited outside and Tiger jumped into the driver's seat. He just laughed when Valiant took the passenger seat with Tammy curled on his lap.

"I'm on it," Tiger smiled. "Food delivered...what? Four times a day?"

"Make it six." Valiant chuckled. "She is going to be very hungry."

Tiger started the engine. "Six it is. And just so you know, do not be alarmed if you smell some of us nearby. We have set a security detail around your home. Not too close though. Just near enough to keep an eye on the house while you and Tammy are there."

Valiant sighed. "I understand."

Tammy glanced at each man. "I don't."

"You're human," Valiant said softly. "The men will be there to help protect you since we are not at the hotel. We have enemies, sexy. You're a target now that we're married. The Wild Zone should be safe but it will make Justice feel better if he knows there's extra security around to help safeguard us."

Tammy dropped her head on Valiant's chest. She snuggled into him. "Okay, but make sure they aren't too close."

Tiger laughed. "Not a problem."

Valiant nuzzled her cheek. "Mine."

She laughed. "Are you ever going to stop saying that?"

"I like to remind myself and you that you really belong to me. I might say it more if we have children."

Tammy grinned. "I'm definitely not having eight kids though. Every other word out of your mouth to us would be 'mine'."

"I love you, Tammy."

"I love you too."

Tiger laughed. "I love that you two are going to be miles and miles away from me when I go to bed tonight. I haven't slept a solid eight hours since you moved into the hotel. She's small, Valiant. You should ease up some on the sex."

Tammy and Valiant both shot him a glare. "Never," they said in unison.

Also by Laurann Dohner

∾

eBooks:

Zorn Warriors 4: Berrr's Vow

Print Books:
Cyborg Seduction 1: Burning Up Flint
Cyborg Seduction 2: Kissing Steel
Cyborg Seduction 3: Melting Iron
Cyborg Seduction 4: Touching Ice
Cyborg Seduction 5: Stealing Coal
Cyborg Seduction 6: Redeeming Zorus
Cyborg Seduction 7: Taunting Krell
New Species 1: Fury
New Species 2: Slade
Riding the Raines 1: Propositioning Mr. Raine
Something Wicked This Way Comes Volume 1 *(anthology)*
Something Wicked This Way Comes Volume 2 *(anthology)*
Zorn Warriors 1 & 2: Loving Zorn
Zorn Warriors 3: Tempting Rever
Zorn Warriors 4: Berrr's Vow

About the Author

න

I'm a full-time "in-house supervisor" (sounds *much* better than plain ol' housewife), mother and writer. I'm addicted to caramel iced coffee, the occasional candy bar (or two) and trying to get at least five hours of sleep at night.

I love to write all kinds of stories. I think the best part about writing is the fact that real life is always uncertain, always tossing things at us that we have no control over, but when you write, you can make sure there's always a happy ending. I *love* that about writing. I love to sit down at my computer desk, put on my headphones and listen to loud music to block out the world around me, so I can create worlds in front of me.

න

The author welcomes comments from readers. You can find her website and email address on her author bio page at www.ellorascave.com.

Tell Us What You Think

We appreciate hearing reader opinions about our books. You can email us at Comments@EllorasCave.com.

Why an electronic book?

We live in the Information Age—an exciting time in the history of human civilization, in which technology rules supreme and continues to progress in leaps and bounds every minute of every day. For a multitude of reasons, more and more avid literary fans are opting to purchase e-books instead of paper books. The question from those not yet initiated into the world of electronic reading is simply: *Why?*

1. *Price.* An electronic title at Ellora's Cave Publishing runs anywhere from 40% to 75% less than the cover price of the exact same title in paperback format. Why? Basic mathematics and cost. It is less expensive to publish an e-book (no paper and printing, no warehousing and shipping) than it is to publish a paperback, so the savings are passed along to the consumer.

2. *Space.* Running out of room in your house for your books? That is one worry you will never have with electronic books. For a low one-time cost, you can purchase a handheld device specifically designed for e-reading. Many e-readers have large, convenient screens for viewing. Better yet, hundreds of titles can be stored within your new library—on a single microchip. There are a variety of e-readers from different manufacturers. You can also read e-books on your PC or laptop computer. (Please note that Ellora's Cave does not endorse any specific brands.

You can check our website at www.ellorascave.com for information we make available to new consumers.)

3. *Mobility.* Because your new e-library consists of only a microchip within a small, easily transportable e-reader, your entire cache of books can be taken with you wherever you go.

4. *Personal Viewing Preferences.* Are the words you are currently reading too small? Too large? Too... ANNOYING? Paperback books cannot be modified according to personal preferences, but e-books can.

5. *Instant Gratification.* Is it the middle of the night and all the bookstores near you are closed? Are you tired of waiting days, sometimes weeks, for bookstores to ship the novels you bought? Ellora's Cave Publishing sells instantaneous downloads twenty-four hours a day, seven days a week, every day of the year. Our webstore is never closed. Our e-book delivery system is 100% automated, meaning your order is filled as soon as you pay for it.

Those are a few of the top reasons why electronic books are replacing paperbacks for many avid readers.

As always, Ellora's Cave welcomes your questions and comments. We invite you to email us at Comments@ellorascave.com or write to us directly at Ellora's Cave Publishing Inc., 1056 Home Avenue, Akron, OH 44310-3502.

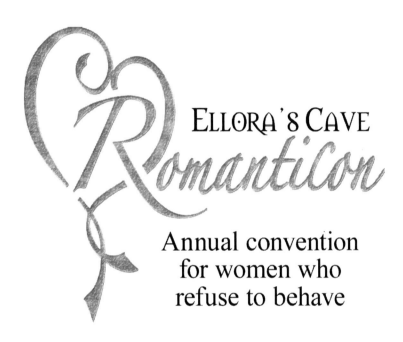

ELLORA'S CAVE
Romanticon

Annual convention
for women who
refuse to behave

www.JasmineJade.com/Romanticon
For additional info contact: conventions@ellorascave.com

Discover for yourself why readers can't get enough
of the multiple award-winning publisher

Ellora's Cave.

Whether you prefer e-books or paperbacks,

be sure to visit EC on the web at
www.ellorascave.com

for an erotic reading experience that will leave you
breathless.